JANE, DIVIDED

PRAISE FOR CRAIG LANCASTER'S BOOKS

THE ART OF DEPARTURE

"Have you ever felt in your pocket and found a twenty you didn't know you had; how 'bout a hundred dollar bill, or a Montecristo cigar or a twenty-four-karat diamond? That's what reading Craig Lancaster is like—close and discovered treasures."—*Craig Johnson, author of the Walt Longmire series of books*

THE FALLOW SEASON OF HUGO HUNTER

"Craig Lancaster may very well be the best writer I know when it comes to telling the stories of broken misfits struggling toward the light."—*Tyler Dilts, author of* Mercy Dogs

THIS IS WHAT I WANT

"Who we are, even in our darkest moments—our dreams, our what-ifs, and our final reckonings—can all be found in this masterfully told story."—*LynDee Walker, Thriller Award nominee and bestselling author of* No Love Lost

EDWARD UNSPOOLED

"Simply put, the Edward books invite Lancaster to deploy all his talents, to make use of all his quirks and inclinations, all the wit that rolls out of him unceasingly."—*Last Best News*

JULEP STREET

"Like only the finest novels, it manages to be both heartbreaking and hilarious, and often within the same paragraph."—*Allen Morris Jones, author of* Sweeney on the Rocks *and* A Bloom of Bones

JANE, DIVIDED

a novel

Craig Lancaster

MISSOURI BREAKS PRESS

Missouri Breaks Press
missouribreakspress@gmail.com

Missouri Breaks Press paperback ISBN-13: 979-8-9903324-4-7

Visit the author's website at www.craig-lancaster.com

Printed in the United States of America

0 9 8 7 6 5 4 3 2 1

*For Jane Estelle and Jim Jensen, together in the cosmos.
I miss you both, but for different reasons.*

Dear Claire

December 15, 2015

The apartment is half packed and you're asleep, and I'm soon to follow, but first this. You haven't had a lot of questions, which surprises me, but maybe you're doing me the favor of spreading them out so I'm not overwhelmed. If that's so, I thank you, because I am overwhelmed. I'm also ready. I think you are, too. I hope you are. Either way, it's happening.

I've wondered when you might come around to where we're going and why. It's a fair question, if you ever do ask it, and not knowing when you'll see this, maybe I'll just rehearse whatever my answer is going to be, hoping I can replicate it when the questions come.

I've decided that you leave Texas the same way you leave any other place—little by little, then all at once. You talk yourself into leaving early on, convince yourself that Texas doesn't serve you, it's never really served you, that you're free to go and should do so as soon as possible. And you hold this to yourself for a while, because it's still audacious, even if you're entitled. Long ago, I didn't dare share with my friends that I was thinking of leaving—that I'd about decided on it—because I knew they would never think of leaving, and thus what made me think I should? A thousand things, really. More than I can explain right here, right now.

What I needed was a crutch, some reason for going that I could lean on, and some way of making the leaving inevitable.

A job is a crutch. There's not a Texan alive who doesn't grasp the value of a place to work and the ability to put food on the table. I can remember your grandfather talking years ago about some East Texas politician defending an asbestos plant, for crying out loud, saying that a little crud in the lungs was worth the tradeoff for economic security. The guy died of lung cancer, too, so that's nothing if not loyalty to a premise.

I didn't have a job offer, though. I needed something else.

A man filled that need. I'm sorry, Claire, because whenever you read this, it'll be obvious to you that the man was your father, and here I am, dispelling any idea you might have that ours was a romance for the ages. Maybe, if I'm honest enough, you'll know it wasn't before these words ever pass your eyes.

It rubbed me wrong, the feminist stance I'd always been proud of juxtaposed against the reality of leaving under the guise of a man's opportunities, but it played with your grandmother and her sisters. It went over well at a Sunday picnic as the potato salad was passed around. "There's this fella I'm seeing, and well, he's just got a peach of an opportunity, and, well, we've talked about it, and it just seems like the thing to do." I actually talked like that. And that got them all to nodding and clucking and saying, well, we love you and we'll miss you, but it must be done.

First, though, I had to talk to your grandma and grandpa. Grandpa, he just took it in, considering, smoldering, pretty much silent except to say, "Well, it's your life," and perhaps he didn't recognize what a breakthrough that was, a man of his age and station conceding something like that.

I thought it was damn near profound. Seems pathetic now.

Grandma, on the other hand, picked at a few things. "You're so close to your degree." And, yeah, I was, but there were colleges where we were headed, and so I told her not to worry, that I'd get it done. She came back and said she didn't know I was serious about Paul, whom she called "this boy." They'd all been boys to her, every last one of them, even though I was twenty-two and had been lying down with men since I was seventeen. (Jesus, that was hard to write, but I promised myself I would be honest, if nothing else, and there it is. Whenever you read this, let me know if we need to talk.)

I couldn't bring myself to tell them what the score really was, that he was a way out, not my soulmate. So I told them things got serious when I wasn't looking. And finally came this from your grandma: "I just never pictured you anywhere but here." You can't even engage with that, because what might she have thought if she ever bothered to look at the picture I saw?

So one fine spring day, we headed out, and there I was, waving from the passenger seat of the Mustang your father still complains about not having anymore. We had dabbed your grandma's tears and hugged your grandpa. We were gone. It was nearly eight hours before the immensity of Texas let go and released us into New Mexico, and I thought, well, that's it, I'm finally free. And your father, long before he was your father, reached over and squeezed my knee, and I never liked that, but it was almost comforting that day.

Texas was gone, falling behind us a mile a minute, and I was relieved and scared all at the same time. You leave Texas little by little and then all at once, yes, but Texas is also a magnet—a big, southerly magnet pulling at everyone else in the country with myths and manufactured romance and jobs and cheap living and low taxes. You can get away, but can you ever really leave? Expats from Delaware or Maryland probably don't confront such questions.

"Denver tonight," your father said. "Montana tomorrow."

And I said, "Texas, never again."

Well, Claire, that was a lie. Here we go.

DECEMBER

One

On the second day of the trip, a storm blew hard across Kansas with an onslaught of snow and ice that started at the western line with Colorado, as if the vagaries of nature could somehow hew to a mapmaker's dotted boundaries. The car crossed over as daylight broke through, and Jane gave silent thanks for the cold clarity of the sun as she picked her way east, her eyes darting at intervals from the newly frozen interstate to the rearview mirror and its assurances that her daughter lay still.

Jane battened down a smile. *That's the gift of youth, sleep amid chaos and as much of it as you want.* She had been surprised at her strength in carrying the girl from the bed to the backseat, done in the wee hours after it became obvious that her own slumber wasn't going to come and that the hundreds of miles in front of them weren't going to roll up for her. First, she had left Claire dozing in that pillowy bed at Aunt Glenda and Uncle Jon's house, and she had showered and dressed sensibly for the day ahead, a pair of sweatpants and the Montana State University Billings pullover that had gone from disappointing Christmas gift to steadfast garment in the four years since Paul had given it to her. It was the only manmade thing touched by his hand that she still owned, the sole survivor of the dissolution and purge of their marriage. After she had showered and pulled her hair into a tight ponytail, it had been a simple matter of gathering her things and her girl and carrying them in silent footfalls to the car in two loads, the last with Claire dangling from Jane's arms and her neck, murmuring into the curve of her jaw.

She checked the rearview, then her eyes turned vigilant again to the hardpacked snow on the interstate. This was all an adventure to Claire, every bit of it, and Jane envied and felt fiercely protective of the girl's naivete, that marvelous ability of hers to bounce up to the world and open to it as if only possibility might be offered. When she thought of a coming day when Claire would not be so untouched and so available to any experience, she could feel the hostility rise inside her like a monster.

"You'll be changing schools," she had said to her daughter just two weeks earlier, when the contents of their lives were still strewn about their apartment in Billings and not on a Freightliner bound for them sometime after Christmas.

"That's OK."

"You won't know anyone."

"I won't know anyone yet, you mean."

"Texas," Jane had started, then she had stopped, having no idea what to say about a place that was now every bit as foreign to her as it was to Claire.

"Mom," Claire had said, "the stars at night are big and bright," and they had tumbled into hysterical laughter at that, and for an evening, at least, Jane had packed her gnawing concerns away. The kid would be OK. For now. Later would have to be worried about...later.

Her attention found the road again, and she took in a sign noting the mileage to Colby and to Hays and to Russell, the litany of flatland towns that slowly punched skyward, one by one, on the endless horizon. She figured Colby, a few miles ahead, for a good place to get fuel and breakfast, the promise of strawberry pancakes a sure countermeasure for Claire's perpetual sleep.

It occurred to Jane now, as it did that final night in Billings, that the one caveat she hadn't given Claire was the scarcity of her father in Texas. That would have opened a line of discussion Claire seemed content to keep closed, and one Jane wasn't sure she could address with the equanimity the subject required. That Claire seemed to accept Paul's inconsistent visitation and vacillating interest left Jane relieved and, as was often the case with her emotions toward him, a little angry. There was less damage Jane had to undo, yes, but that couldn't stave off her bafflement at what kind of father could be so coolly detached from his own child. When she had broached the possibility of their move to Texas—*possibility* had been her word, but certainty her intent—Paul had accepted it the way he might greet the news of a change in dinner plans. "It's cool," he had said. "Gonna be a lot of out-of-town work anyway. We'll figure something out when you get settled." Just like that, he let them go. *How fortunate he is to be so unaffected*, Jane thought now.

From the backseat came sounds of emergence. Claire kicked a foot into the door molding and growled a greeting.

Jane found her daughter's face in the mirror. "Hello, sleepyhead."

The girl rocketed into a seated position, crossing her legs, then leaning into the opening between the front bucket seats. Once Claire had shaken off the baby fat and begun transforming into the girl she was, she had been all arms and legs—perfectly slender, perfectly proportionate, the high cheekbones of her father and the smaller nose, thank God, of her mother. But ever since the corner had been turned on eleven years old, Jane had begun to see in her daughter what was to come, the breathless beauty that was within and without. It would, Jane figured, be the source of some difficult days ahead. For now, the kid was mostly gaping wonder and an open heart, and Jane wished she could envelop those qualities in bubble wrap and save them from a world that would not be kind.

Claire scrunched her nose. "Where are we?"

"Kansas."

"It looks like the arctic."

"And you'd know this how?" Jane checked the rearview, and Claire's grin told her that the jibe had been taken in the good-natured manner intended. She couldn't always be sure of that anymore, another manifestation of the changes at work on the girl and her shifting moods and sensibilities. Wonder and open-heartedness went a long way. So did the occasional snit or foul burst of temper.

"Books, Mom. You've heard of them."

"I have, indeed." She gave Claire a mirrored grin. "I thought your generation didn't need books anymore."

Claire bounced forward, her shoulders all the way through to the front compartment. "Whatever. What time is it?"

"Just after seven."

"What time did we leave?"

"Just after four."

She felt Claire's head settle into her shoulder. "I didn't get to tell Aunt Glenda and Uncle Jon that I love them."

"They know." *This kid*, she thought. *This amazing kid.*

Now, the kinetic force that was Claire dropped fully into the backseat again. "I'm hungry."

"As it happens," Jane said, pointing ahead to the clustered assemblage of buildings that constituted Colby, a rise on the unending plain.

"Pancakes!" Claire said.

"Of course."

And a recharge, Jane ticked off in her head. *And a cup of coffee. And a chance to tell myself, again, that this is all for the best.*

As Jane wheeled the car into the parking lot of the Village Inn—she had seen the billboard miles earlier and fixated on the manufactured hospitality of the advertisement—a rear tire caught a patch of ice and sent them fishtailing into a parking space.

"Wheeeee!" Claire said.

While they waited for the food to arrive, Jane used her phone to show Claire the route they would be following, how Interstate 70 stretched all the way across Kansas and kept on going, but they would turn south at Salina, nearly dead center in the state, and make tracks for Wichita and a chance to rest their heads at Teryn's place.

"You remember her," Jane said. "She used to bring you gum."

"Oh, yeah!"

What Jane didn't say, because it was moot and because there was no need to chance a quarrel, is Claire would be staying with Teryn's daughter, Sabrina, for a few hours, that she and Teryn needed nothing so much as time together and a few beers and maybe some appetizers, so she could unload all this stuff she had been carrying alone. For that opportunity, Jane was willing to entrust Claire to a fifteen-year-old, an unprecedented concession in her tenure of motherhood.

It wouldn't be right to say Teryn was an old friend. They had known each other only briefly, both working temp office jobs and building and filling spreadsheets in those days after Jane had left Paul and the house and was rubbing pennies together to make the rent. Their employer, in the process of closing up shop in Billings, had offered them jobs in Wichita. Teryn had accepted, blowing out of town like her life depended on it. But what they had lacked in time invested had been covered by unshakeable fealty—the occasional Skype chat, handwritten letters from Teryn that were all breadth and no depth but welcome just the same, text messages that would launch Jane into peals of laughter. She looked forward to seeing that face and the irrepressible spirit it beheld.

"When do we get to Texas?" Claire asked, driving a stake back into now.

"Tomorrow."

"Will I like it?"

"I think so." *I hope so.*

The food arrived, airy pancakes for Claire, eggs and bacon and toast for Jane.

"The stars at night..." Claire began.

Jane took the girl's hand and squeezed. "Save it for the car," she said. "Eat now."

Belly full, Claire found sleep again on the road after a few robust bars of a song to which she knew only one stanza. Jane had shushed the girl and felt bad for it, but Wichita remained hours away and the car's interior couldn't contain Claire's high spirits and Jane's need to concentrate. The girl had made one last stand against going under, fighting another losing battle about having to sit in the back seat, a standoff Jane always ended with "sorry, it's the law, kid." Finally, Claire offered another lament about not saying goodbye back in Denver, and Jane assured her that they would write a letter once they made it to Texas.

What Claire didn't know is that her mother had already left a note behind, an explainer of sorts for the way she had parried the queries about why she was headed home after all these years, what had happened with Paul, as if that could be covered over a serving of meatloaf, and what her larger plans were. For one thing, she hadn't wanted to get into it while Claire was bouncing happily in her chair, chasing kernels of corn into her mashed potatoes. For another, she hadn't wanted to get into it at all. Such questions pre-supposed a linearity, as if any single decision could be traced to any single stimulus. For Jane, the answers carried no such order, and decisions were made by necessity first and expediency second. She could not account for them and frankly was not inclined to try.

In Salina, where Interstate 70 funneled them off to Interstate 35 and the southerly shot to where they were headed, Jane stopped for gas, and she made mental calculations of what that $35.52 would do to the dwindling resources at her disposal. She had enough to get where they were going, anyway, assuming there were no surprises. She peered through the window at Claire, who was coming out of groggy slumber in the backseat. She rapped a gloved hand against the glass, and the girl turned her way.

"Need anything? Bathroom?"

Claire shook her head and nestled in again.

Jane blew frosted rings on her way into the convenience store. Inside, she chose strawberry licorice for Claire and a cup of coffee for herself. Her phone's GPS program told her she had ninety-two icy miles left. Then, tomorrow, another five and a half hours and it would be done. An ending to launch a new beginning.

Back at the car, she tossed the candy to Claire, who tore into the packaging.

"The stars at night..." Claire began again.

"Honey, please."

"You don't like my voice." The girl effected a pout.

"It's beautiful. You know this."

"You don't like my song?" More pouting, betrayed by an impish grin, one Jane returned almost as an involuntary reaction in the rearview mirror.

Jane made a right turn out of the gas station and joined the access road, building careful speed toward the interstate.

"I love everything about you," she said.

Two

The ambience at the bar and grill pulled them in like a hug, and Teryn wanted to know everything about everything, a request so sprawling it couldn't be scaled. Nonetheless, a glass of the house port gave Jane the gumption to try.

She saw in her friend something different from what she had known back in Billings, perhaps a confidence that had been lacking when they had been a couple of temp employees stringing together a few paychecks. Now, Teryn looked hale and in her element, quick with a gentle joke, eyes alight, well familiar with this restaurant they had come to in a town Jane had never seen before. Teryn, born and reared in Billings, looked as though she had known no other home.

"You have to get the carrots," Teryn said when the server ("Geoff," she'd giggled, repeating his name back to him upon introduction) came by for their orders.

"That good, huh?"

"The best," Geoff said.

"See?" Teryn said.

"OK, the roasted chicken and the carrots."

"The same," Teryn said, and when Geoff was gone, she turned back, clinked her beer against Jane's wine glass, and set in again.

"Seriously, doll, tell me everything."

Jane careened her head and offered a shrug. "There's not so much to tell."

"But Texas. It's so random."

Jane tipped her glass and let the wine linger on her tongue before swallowing it. "It's where I grew up. Not random at all. Now, Wichita. Wichita is random."

"Wichita has been a good thing," Teryn said.

"I can tell. You give me hope."

Teryn reached across and clasped her hand, and Jane gave a squeeze back and a smile, bottom lip pulled snugly over the top.

"But seriously, doll," Teryn said, "this guy you knew in college just calls—"

"High school," Jane interrupted. "I knew him in high school, and, well, on Facebook now, of course. But yeah, he knew I'd kept my certification, and he said he was losing an English teacher at Christmas break, so he invited me—"

"It's a Christmas miracle!" Teryn giggled. She was already on her second beer and seemed intent on stretching her lead.

"I don't know about that," Jane said. "I'm scared to death."

That dropping of the guard brought momentary sobriety from her friend. "Why?"

"It's been years since I've been in a classroom," Jane said. "You know, I kind of thought they'd look at my application and say, 'No thanks,' but they didn't."

"Maybe this guy—what's his name?"

"Tim."

"Maybe Tim put in a good word."

"Yeah, more than that. He made it happen. I think he knows I needed something. He's been a good friend through this."

"Maybe more than a friend?" Teryn goosed the innuendo along with an arched eyebrow.

Jane, heaven help her, could only laugh. Two beers, a third soon to come, and her long-distance friend was lit. Her own glass of port sat only half-drained.

"Yeah, that's all I need," Jane said. "An affair with the boss. Sorry, but I've seen that movie, and I know what happens."

"Do tell." Teryn giggled.

"Literal movies, Teryn. And books and, Jesus, life. One, there's never been the slightest hint with Tim. Two, it's a complication that would only end badly for me."

"I could use a little complication," Teryn said. "Do you think Geoff is available?" She giggled again.

"Maybe."

"Good," Teryn said. "I need another drink."

Jane drove back to the apartment, and with Teryn too far gone to provide reliable direction, she leaned on the mechanical voice in her phone's GPS app to handle the chore.

Low-slung, pulled-cotton clouds hovered over the city, casting the night in a diffused brightness. Effluent steam rose from the gutters, and in the cold stillness she found it reminiscent of the place she had just left—at least on the surface, if she didn't look too far afield for what she would have seen in Billings, with the house lights on the Rimrocks and a red glow from the microwave towers atop Sacrifice Cliff. But from the sturdy little homes that hugged the curbs to the patchwork business districts that mingled the high-end and the ordinary, she could see, at least in this low light, how Teryn might have found something familiar and welcoming here. Jane sat up straight and adjusted her hands on the wheel, finding ten and two, as she had learned from her father all those years ago. There it was, another infusion of hope into this journey spent so much in quiet questioning. The idea that maybe it would all start to turn in her favor now.

Beside her, Teryn spun out of inebriation for a moment of clarity. "Doll, what about Paul?"

"What about him?"

"What's he think of this?"

Jane released a chuckle, fortifying it with a bit of ruefulness. Paul hadn't come up at dinner, which had surprised her, given that the friendship with Teryn had been built, in large part, on unloading shared acrimony about exes during lunch breaks. But once the circumstances of the job offer had been unpacked and set aside, and once Teryn had exhausted her supply of ridiculous innuendo about new-boss nookie, they had settled into old, shared topics at dinner. How to guide daughters through this world. The perilous journey of finding well-fitting clothes in middle age. Aches and pains. Seemingly out-of-reach fantasies like home ownership with their divorce-blitzed credit ratings.

"He didn't have enough thought to form a complete sentence," Jane said at last, and a bit too acidly even for her own taste. "Honestly, I think he's happy any time his responsibilities are reduced, which they are now."

"Have you decided on visitation?"

"Nothing formal, no."

Teryn shifted in the seat, then let loose a hoppy belch, which ignited a string of laughs that popped off like firecrackers. "Oh, I think I'm gonna pee," she said.

Jane, hands clenched around the wheel, said, "Please don't," and Teryn, chastised, stifled her laughter.

"Sabrina's dad rarely comes to see her," Teryn said, her voice now grave, and that abrupt turn from joy to seriousness gave Jane emotional whiplash. "He works overseas, so it's hard to bring her to where he is. He's prompt and attentive, mostly, though. I get the support checks on time, and he remembers to call her on her big days, but she misses his presence. That part sucks."

Jane cast a quick glance over at her friend. Teryn's head hung, and she clasped her hands in her lap.

"Pretty much the same from Paul. He's been good about the support money, too," Jane said at last. "It's like he thinks that's enough, half of what it takes to keep her going—"

"You should have gotten more," Teryn said, old ground. Jane should have—her lawyer said as much, and was just as correct as Teryn—but she'd been bound and determined to uphold fifty percent of the burden. She remembered what her lawyer had said: "You're being proud, not sensible." Yeah, well, whatever.

"Anyway," Jane said now, "Claire seems to know the score. I tell myself sometimes that it's good feminist training. You know, the whole idea that she needs a man. Good to dispense with that nice and early. But he's her dad. He disappoints me."

Teryn lurched forward, her head up now. "Shitheels, the lot of them. Right, doll?" She looked over for affirmation, and Jane gave it to her.

"Absolutely."

At the apartment, they found that the girls had filled the time amply if not productively. Claire's face peered out from under slathered makeup, her first experience with that sort of thing, and she had made all the predictable, regrettable choices—the most strident shades for every surface, leaving the delicate-featured young woman with pink cheeks and electric-blue eyelids and lips the color of fake movie blood. When Jane told her to wash her face before bed, Claire pitched a desperate argument, complete with road-weary tears, and at last Jane relented. In the morning, she would see the horror, and like so many things before, it would serve as both a chastening and a lesson.

She and Claire folded themselves in together on the futon in Teryn's spare bedroom. An angry wind scratched at the window, and Jane drew up covers to swaddle them.

"I like Sabrina, Mom."

"That's good."

"She knows about a lot of stuff. Boys, especially."

The skin tightened across Jane's face. She had hoped for another year, at least, before this became part of the motherly deal. Bras and boys, the two coming topics of intense interest. One Jane could handle, and the other, she knew, was devoid of simple answers.

"Do you want to talk about it?"

"Not really."

Jane exhaled. "So you had a good time?" she asked.

"I loved it."

"I'm glad."

Claire turned onto her left side, away from Jane and toward the wall, but she burrowed her backside until it was against her mother. The girl's frame was angular and harsh as her body's growth outpaced the filling-in that would come later. Jane turned the same way and draped her right arm across Claire's stomach.

"I love you, Mom."

It wasn't the sing-songy declaration she usually got from Claire, the one with the rising notes and the attendant request. *"I love you, Mom. Can I have some chocolate?"* It was plaintive and sincere, and in the calm between one long day on the road and another, it caught Jane square in the most tender part of her. An echo was all she could muster lest more tumble forth.

"I love you, too."

Claire squirmed closer, and Jane held her tighter.

"I get to see Texas tomorrow?" Claire asked.

"Yes, you do."

"Will I love it?"

Such questions, such observations from this girl. Jane thought it odd, this pairing of the words "love" and "Texas," as she hadn't considered the possibility. This was about escape and re-establishment, about control and finding something that could belong to them. And yet, her memories now flooded with pictures from her own turn as a pre-teen, where it had happened, what she had seen, and those blooming feelings she'd had to manage, and damned if love wasn't just about the most elusive thing she could think of, then and now. And now she—they—were headed back there. To chase security. Love could go pound sand.

"I hope so," Jane said. "Now go to sleep."

Three

Ten minutes into Texas, the car dumped its right front tire in a shredded mass of rubber and cabling, leaving Claire shaken in the back seat and her words frantic—"Mom, what's wrong?"—and Jane fighting the insolent machinery across two lanes of traffic to get it onto the shoulder. It was only after the car was safely parked and Claire was calmed and Jane's own heart had slowed its rhythms that she laughed, ever softly, and said, "Welcome home. Now, go to hell."

"Mom," Claire chided her.

"I know, I know. Just a joke."

"Cussing isn't funny."

"You're right, honey." *Fucking-ay, kid.*

The crueler jokes came in succession, as Jane remembered that she had no spare tire and that nobody would be quick to answer a service call on Christmas Eve. She fished into her purse for her cellphone and the only lamentable option left to her.

"Dad," she said as he picked up, "I need some help."

Jane and Claire sat in the car, biding their time with an old game, *Blue Car Red Car.* As the passing motorists hurried by, Claire cheerfully counted the blue ones in falsetto escalations, while Jane made her own, more laidback tally of the reds. What years earlier had been a fun diversion for a little girl—complete with hybrids like *Orange Car Green Car*—was now a time-filler that kept Claire engaged and Jane from diving too deeply into her apprehensions before she had a chance to properly face them.

"Twenty-eight!" the girl chirped. "Twenty-eight to nineteen."

"Twenty," Jane corrected as a Jetta chugged past.

Jane had tried to blunt her father's queries—*where are you and why didn't you have a spare tire, for chrissakes?*—so as not to appear weak in front of her daughter. Now, having gently guided Eric Driskell from his outrage to the pragmatic idea that the sooner he arrived the sooner they could get on with it, she bristled anew at the interrogation and her role in inviting it. She had known about the absence of a spare, of course, and had made a calculated gamble that the ninety or so dollars that stayed in her bank account were more valuable than the insurance of an extra tire. She had been wrong about that, of course, and he had let her know.

"Mom, you missed that one."

"I'm sorry."

"I'll give it to you."

"Thank you."

"Thirty-three to twenty-one."

"OK."

A Ford pickup blew by, shaking the car with its draft.

"Thirty-four!" Claire said.

Jane checked the dashboard clock. They had made such good time, not rushing out on Teryn too terribly quickly but also not overstaying. The bottom half of Kansas and then the bisection of Oklahoma had fallen away in due time, and Jane had allowed herself to hope for a smooth arrival at her long-ago home, an early dinner, then off to bed for Claire while she cobbled together some sort of Christmas for them.

Now, the hours grew longer and the day shorter. They would be lucky to eat by eight, she thought.

"Forty," Claire said. "I win."

"Yay you!"

The girl did a seated dance, with jutted jaw and duck lips. Jane adored her.

"How much longer will Grandpa be?"

Jane had the same question and no good answer. When Texas had been home to her, this stretch of interstate had been bordered by pastureland, traffic a gentle trickle north and south at most hours. Now, progress crowded in from all directions and the highways clogged like age-burdened arteries. Jane had figured on an hour, maybe ninety minutes. They had cleared the latter threshold ten minutes back.

"Soon," she said. "Be still."

"Can I listen to the radio?" Claire asked.

"Sure. Softly, please."

While Claire scanned up and down, at last settling on something syncopated that Jane would have no chance of naming, her mother watched the orb of the sun settling on the western horizon, casting orange and pink against a fast-darkening sky.

"Come on, Dad," she murmured. Claire, head bobbing and eyes closed and mouth pinched in song, didn't hear her.

After Eric Driskell kissed his daughter on the forehead and wrapped his granddaughter in a bear hug, he crawled around the car with a flashlight and confirmed the obvious and the obscure.

"Sure as shit it's blown," he said, drawing a rebuke from Claire.

"Grandpa, no."

"Sorry."

"Gonna be tough on you with this one around," Jane said. "You'll have to clean it up."

Her dad chuckled. "I can take it," he said. He pointed to a thin strip of rubber down the middle of the good front tire. "Tread's good, except for here. Means they're overinflated. That's where it came apart."

"I had no idea," Jane said.

"Neither did they, probably," he said of whoever had pushed the air into the tires. "It's why I do my own tire work."

"I bet you don't stop there," Jane said, pointing toward the tow truck he had shown up in, bounding across the median between the northbound lanes and the southbound as if it weren't there. "I thought you were retired."

"I am." He patted his barrel chest proudly. "Kept the one truck, though. Never know when you're gonna need it. Like today."

They rode three-across on the truck's bench seat, Jane's car hooked up behind them. "Probably got the right size tire at the house," her father said. "If not, there's always the day after tomorrow."

Claire bounced between them, happy as ever. Jane leaned into the door, face pressed against the window. She had wanted a different introduction for this uncomfortable arrangement.

"Why in God's name were you coming from Kansas?" he asked.

"Saw a friend there."

"But, jeez, girl, that's like a hundred more miles."

"I know."

"You have that hundred miles back, you'd have made it on that tire."

"Only to blow it out somewhere else," she said. "Believe me, Dad, I've considered the various implications. I don't need a refresher."

"OK, OK."

"I tried on makeup in Kansas," Claire tossed in.

"I bet you were as pretty as a flower," her grandfather said.

Jane chortled, thinking back to that morning at the bathroom mirror and Claire's predictable reaction to her made-up face in harsh daylight.

"I looked like a deranged clown," Claire said. "That's what Mom said."

He shot Jane a look. "That's not very nice."

"Accurate, though," Jane said. "I guess you had to be there."

The house came on like a scattershot of random memories, sending Jane sideways through all the time she had spent in it and all the subsequent years when she had managed to stay away. It hadn't been out of malice, she had assured herself at times as the calendar pages had flown by. Obligations pile up. Free time dwindles or gets squandered. Time off and money to burn are precious. And the truth of the matter is that her father had been all too happy, especially after her mom died, to make the drive north to Montana and spend drunken fishing weekends with Paul.

"Here it is," Eric said, as if recognizing that introductions would have to be renewed. "Home."

If it wasn't quite so cozy as the word, it was, at least, familiar. Jane found old family photographs hanging where they had always resided, furniture arranged in timeworn ways. A new flat-screen TV big enough to contain his beloved Dallas teams was her father's only visible concession to advancing time. Most of all, she was taken with the scent, straight out of childhood, as if she might look up and see a pre-teen version of herself come running through the door they had just entered.

"It's nice," Claire said.

Jane's father had suggested a swing through McDonald's as they closed in on the house, and considering the hour, she hadn't objected. But she also knew that there had been entirely too much fast food in those frantic last days before leaving Montana, and she wanted to get back to some scintilla of normalcy sooner rather than later.

"Let's eat," Jane said. "Getting late."

Her father passed out napkins at the dining room table, and they ate in mostly separate silence, the weight of things landing on them in different ways. *So here it is, then,* Jane thought, *back home at forty-three. Not what I'd imagined.*

Before the move, she had done the math every way she could, trying to figure out how quickly she and Claire could disengage from here and get their own place, even a small one-bedroom apartment. First and last, deposits all around, some thrift-store furniture—she figured she would need two paychecks, maybe three, before they could pull it off.

"Mom," Claire said. "There's no Christmas tree."

It hadn't even registered with Jane. She looked to her father.

"Not really my thing anymore," he said.

"Aren't we going to have Christmas?" Claire asked.

"Of course," Jane said, reaching for her hand. "Don't worry. Come on, Claire, finish eating."

Jane looked again to her father. He chewed on his dinner.

"Probably some stuff in the attic," he said.

She patted Claire's hand again and gestured at the girl's fries, and her mind spiraled with all the ways time was crushing her.

Four

The late-night harvest from the attic yielded thirty-year-old tinsel, a sad plastic tree, and stockings that hadn't been hung from the chimney (there was no chimney) with care or otherwise since the Reagan years.

"Oh, this," Jane said, showing her father an ornament made of yarn with body fashioned from an ancient roll of Lifesavers. "I think I made this in the third grade. Want to clear your palate?"

Eric shook his head. "I dropped the ball," he said. "I didn't get her anything."

"Cash will do just fine."

"No."

"Yes," Jane said. "Seriously. It's game over when she finds out about the mall in this town. She likes being able to buy her own stuff."

"Didn't get you anything, either."

"Right back atcha," she said, then she instantly regretted it, not because she meant it or that it would hurt her father, but because a sharp riposte always seemed to come easier to her than anything else where he was concerned.

"Seriously, Dad, you're doing enough," she said. "Hero stuff. We're not going to be easy, I'm afraid."

"I'm glad you came, anyway." He gripped her shoulder. She leaned in.

Her father set up the tree and plugged it in, and they both delighted when the long-dormant built-in lights flickered on. She dangled the scant tinsel from various branches, trying to spread it thinly. He tacked the stockings to the mantelpiece, turning his wife's around so the name didn't show. She found a Sharpie and penned Claire's name onto the backside felt. He slipped a hundred-dollar bill into an envelope for the girl. She went outside and fetched the various gift cards she had hidden in the car, for just this occasion.

Together, they made it a Christmas.

After they checked on Claire, now deep into her dreams, Jane's father asked if she would like a beer, and despite the miles and the worries and the blowout and the work, she said she couldn't think of a better way to close out the night.

"What's this job?"

Jane's father popped the top on his own beer, then on hers. He handed the bottle across the distance and gave it a clink.

"Like I told you, English teacher, Smithfield Middle," she said. "Seventh grade."

"Where you went."

"Yeah. Last century."

"That's good," he said. "Close. Familiar."

She nearly gagged on her beer, the way the chortle burbled up in her. "I don't know about familiar," she said. "It's been a long time. But I'm glad to have it."

"Also been a long time since you've been around here," he said. "Too long."

"I'm here now."

He finished his beer. Her bottle sat half-full. He slipped a fingernail under the labeling and began lifting it around the perimeter.

"Your mother would be glad you're teaching again," he said. "Never could figure out why you quit. Neither of us could."

It was a topic too convoluted for the hour. How could she explain to a man who overhauled carburetors for nearly fifty years that she was burning out at thirty-one, holding together ill-fitting pieces of a marriage, soon to be with child, and she didn't want it anymore? How could she expect him to understand that, or to find empathy for it?

"Got pregnant," she said. "Paul traveled a lot for work. Somebody had to stay home."

"How is Paulie?"

She laughed again and took a swig to smother it. "You probably talk to him more than I do. I should ask you."

"I do not talk to him." Her father's words came hard and indignant, and he all but pouted there in his chair. She moved to placate him.

"Paul's fine," she said, a sigh heavy in her words. "Reliable in all the ways he thinks he ought to be. And, Dad, it's fine if you do talk to him. He's important to you."

He waved that line of discussion away. "I assume he's going to come and see Claire."

"Probably," she said. "We haven't really gotten to all that yet. This came up quick."

"You done?" Her father gestured toward her bottle, and she nodded. He scooped it up, along with his, and went to the kitchen to dispose of them.

"Maybe would have been easier to stick it out than starting over now," he called to her.

Easier—now there's a word loaded with projection. She wondered, not for the first time, what it was about looking in from the outside that allowed people to be so damned cocksure about the proper path for someone else. She remembered the phone call, months earlier, to her father to let him know the marriage had cratered, and how blithe he had been with expressions of concern and how rigidly he had attempted to diagnose the real trouble between them. As if he knew. As if he could possibly know. He had never talked about marriage trouble—his own or his daughter's—with her, and if he had heard anything from Paul it was only half the story.

"No," she said. "It's best to let a dead thing die. It's late. Time for bed. Claire'll be bouncing off the walls before sunrise."

Her father came back into the dining room, but only just. He smiled at her from a distance. "Good night, honey."

She stood up. "Good night, Dad."

Five

In the morning, after the gifts had been showered on Claire and the breakfast had been eaten and everyone had laughed at Eric's face, dotted with cotton balls as a makeshift Santa beard, Jane and her girl bundled up and went for a walk. The storm that had chased them into Kansas two days earlier had stumbled south, meekly giving north Texas a dusting.

"A real white Christmas," Jane said, taking Claire's hand.

"Big deal."

Jane bristled, just for a moment, as she tried to suss out Claire's attitude. She decided the girl hadn't said it with defiance so much as a pre-teen's world-weariness, a suggestion to Jane that she would have to try harder if she wanted to impress her daughter. There would be more of this coming. Jane was certain of that.

"Maybe not to you, coming from Montana, but a rarity here."

"I guess."

"Listen," Jane said. "Do you want to see where I played when I was your age?"

"I want to go to the mall."

"Oh, Claire, not today, OK? Grandpa's working on the car, and it's Christmas. Let's just stay around here. Tomorrow, I promise."

"Promise?"

"Absolutely."

"OK."

Jane reached out a hand for the girl again. "I want to show you around." Claire, in turn, looked past her mother's bid and set out in tall-girl strides, making Jane jog to catch up.

The more they walked, the more Jane realized that she really had nothing to show Claire aside from the fixed locations of houses pinned with long-ago memories. The once-open field at the bottom of the block, where Jane and the passel of kids right around her age had whiled away childhood summers, now held nested housing tracts, as far as she could see and with an upper-middle-class sameness that was trance-inducing. The stories she could have told about that vast place, about BB guns and hide-and-seek and stolen kisses and pre-sexual tomfoolery and catching toads, but she opted out, unsure that she could describe things vividly enough to charm Claire.

They ended up walking the streets of her older, more blue-collar neighborhood. Jane stopped occasionally for an anecdote—"my best friend, Marcia Collier, lived there" or "Jimmy Ray Eagleton drove his Camaro into that lamppost on New Year's Eve in 1989"—but mostly she just enjoyed the sun on her face and Claire's high-twitch energy beside her.

On the last turn toward home, a man emerged from the old Brooks house, pushing a bicycle with training wheels as a little blonde girl toddled along behind.

Jane waved. "Now that's a Christmas present."

"We'll see," he said with cheer. The little girl now beside him beamed. "My bike," she declared.

They continued up the hill now. Beneath their feet, the leavings of snow melted fast.

"Mom," Claire said, "are you nervous?"

"About what?"

"You know. School."

Jane smiled to buy herself some time. Here, again, was a potential life lesson disguised as an innocuous inquiry. Should she fend it off with a simple, understated "a little"? Should she hijack Claire's simple question with a complex and overwhelming acknowledgment of just how nervous—no, no, how fucking *petrified*—she was? She pondered where the sweet spot was between helping Claire face up to the world without fear while also accepting the intruding terrors as natural byproducts of living. Try as she might to bring equanimity to bear in all things with Claire, she wondered sometimes just how successful she was.

"I guess I wouldn't be human if I didn't feel nervous," Jane said. "Excited, too, though. It's going to be different for both of us. What about you? Nervous?"

"A little."

The house loomed now. Jane's father had the car disengaged from the tow truck, upright and strong on four full tires. He stood in the driveway, awaiting them.

"I'm back in business," Jane said.

"No sweat," he said. "You need to get a spare pronto."

"I know. I will."

"Shouldn't have come to this."

"I know."

"OK, then." He bent down to face Claire, a needless consideration as her eyes were near level with his chin. "What about you, girly? What do you want to do?"

The girl turned up her nose. "My name is Claire."

"What do you want to do, Claire?"

"I don't know. Netflix, I guess."

Eric looked to his daughter. "I'm not made for these times."

"Different world, for sure," Jane said. "Come on. I'll play you some gin rummy."

The freezer in the garage held chicken breast tenders that weren't too far gone, and Jane cobbled together rice and stewed tomatoes and spices from the pantry, giving them all a hot meal they had been needing along with some time together around the table. She didn't want to stay long at her father's, but while here she aimed to make it a comfortable home for Claire. Dinner together, three generations, went a long way.

Her father nursed a beer, his third, in the living room while watching college football on TV. Claire, in the love seat, fell deeper into her tablet. The doorbell disrupted the gentle ennui.

"I've got it," Jane said, dashing through living room.

She opened the door on a man she recognized, after a beat, as the bicycle-pushing father from earlier.

"Jane Driskell?" he asked.

"Sperling. But, yeah."

"Who is it?" Eric bellowed.

"I didn't put it all together until I saw you go in the house here," the man now said. "And then I was all, 'That's Jane Driskell.'"

"I'm sorry, I—"

"Let him in," Eric said. "Close the door."

Jane smiled thinly and waved the visitor in, leading him to the living room.

"Hey, Chuck, sit down," Eric said. "Tech's playing."

It all spiraled in on Jane now. Chuck Brooks. She would have never recognized him, not if she passed him on the street a million times. Facebook had taken some of the mystery out of how long-ago friends had aged, but she had never seen Chuck there. Nor had she wondered much about him. The way it goes.

"Chuck Brooks," she said.

Sitting next to her father on the couch, he held an index finger aloft and shook it happily at her. "It's all coming back to you."

"Is it ever."

"I didn't mean to disturb you folks. Just wanted to say hi again. You're visiting for the holiday, I guess?"

"Well, no," Jane began, then she switched direction. "Gosh, I'm sorry, Chuck, this is my daughter, Claire. Claire, this is Chuck Brooks. An old friend from when I was a kid."

"Hi," Claire said, a hand up and back down again just as quickly, her eyes never leaving the tablet screen.

"She's the diplomat of the family," Jane said.

"So you're not visiting?"

Eric sat forward in a grumbling sigh, holding his beer bottle toward Jane. "Honey, can you get me another?"

She took the bottle from him, brusquely enough to deliver a message, and headed for the kitchen.

"She's moved back," Eric said to Chuck. "Gonna teach at that middle school."

"What he said," she called as she came back in with the beer. She handed it off with a similar show of force.

"Oh." Chuck stood. "That's great, really great. Listen, I gotta get back—"

"Stay," Eric said. "Good game."

"No, I can't. I've got Eli watching Annabelle, but his attention wanders."

"Your kids?" Jane asked.

"Yeah. But listen, I'd love to catch up. Maybe we could get together some night and talk."

"Sure," Jane said. "That'd be nice."

"Maybe Friday?"

"OK."

"OK, then. Looking forward to it. I'll see myself out. Y'all take care. Bye, Claire. Nice meeting you."

Another quick up-and-down salute. "Bye."

Jane followed him out and locked the deadbolt after he was gone.

"Nice guy," her father said when she returned.

"Always was."

"Might be someone worth getting to know again."

At this, Claire looked up. "Who?"

"That's enough, Dad," Jane said.

Claire persisted. "Who?"

"Who? Who? Who?" Jane teased. "Are you an owl or something?"

"You're so immature," Claire said, and she dropped back into her game.

"I know you are but what am I?"

No use. Claire was gone again. Across from her, on the couch, her grandfather took pulls from his beer and disappeared under the spell of college football.

Jane retired to the dining room and cleared away the last of the dishes.

Six

After more of a struggle than Jane anticipated, she cajoled her father into taking Claire shopping while she went to the school and got a first look at her classroom. Tim Meyers had called early to make sure she had arrived safely and to extend the invitation.

"It's a damn zoo down by that mall," Eric bellyached.

"You've only lived in this town, what, fifty years?" Jane said. "You can handle it."

"There wasn't going to be no damn babysitting," he said.

Jane felt her blood go up. "No *excessive* babysitting," she said. "Anyway—"

"I'm not a baby," Claire said.

"What she said," Jane finished. "You were always caterwauling about not getting to see enough of us. Well, here you go. Don't think of it as babysitting. It's being a grandfather."

He wasn't done with his pout. "Nothing to do over there."

"Oh, good god," Jane said, wrapping her words in a laugh so she wouldn't betray just how frustrated she was. "Spend some time with her. You might learn something. You might have fun."

"Yeah," Claire said. "Come on, Grandpa."

"Fine," he said.

"Thank you." Jane exhaled with enough force that her father turned an angry stare on her, one she tried to blunt with a nod. "We appreciate your sacrifice, don't we, Claire?"

"Whatever," the girl said. "Let's go."

"*Don't we*, Claire?"

"Thank you, Grandpa."

The sun had come out again, and with it a late-December day like those Jane carried in her heart. She decided to walk to the middle school, a little over a mile away, a distance that seemed more daunting in middle age than it ever did when she was a schoolgirl and covered that span without a thought twice daily except in the worst of weather.

Her father's subdivision sat at a wide bent elbow of Davis Boulevard, a thoroughfare that had once been pockmarked with homes and odd warehouses but now was pinched on both sides by newer housing tracts, fast-food restaurants, and gas stations. Rather than crossing Davis as she emerged from the neighborhood, as Jane would have done without trouble thirty years earlier, she thought it best to stay on her side until she reached the stoplight at Main. She walked far to the shoulder, as close as she could get to the mud and the muck beyond the asphalt without stomping into it. As a girl, she had kicked horse apples down this road, delighting at how they would thump and roll and split in two. Now she held herself against the bluster of the cars racing up behind and whipsawing her as they passed.

"Bad idea," she mumbled.

At Main, she crossed over with the light, past the shell of an abandoned convenience store where the boys in her classes had played video games before the first bell, over the train tracks, and into the neighborhood hugging the school. Here, familiarity bloomed in the older houses and chain link fences she well remembered. Gone was one of the last farmhouses in the town proper, long since razed and memorialized only by an abandoned foundation riddled with interceding weeds. She remembered how Troy Taylor had sidearmed a rock into a flock of chickens ranging in the yard all those years ago. His aim was true, taking down a hen and prompting the old farmer to barrel out of his house with a shotgun, a skyward blast of which had scattered the kids who had witnessed the act. Back in the now, Jane marveled anew at the randomness of what the mind held, and what it let go.

She crested the slight hill and the school came into view, more imposing than she remembered, a new façade, a parking lot remade for the realities of twenty-first-century child drop-off and retrieval. And, leaning against the back of an SUV, head down and fixated on a screen, Tim Meyers—*Principal Meyers*, she would have to get used to saying—awaited her.

She quickened her stride, and he looked up and found her and unfurled a smile, and adrenaline flooded her system, because ready or not, it was time to do this.

Jane walked among the desks of her room and considered what had been left to her, the artwork and the posters and the markers and the books and the A/V equipment, and despite the years away she found in it all a familiarity she'd begun to feel desperate to experience. She had done this once. Maybe she could do it again. Right here.

"Kathy—your predecessor—was nice enough to leave her materials," Tim said. He stood with his back to the wall, giving her distance that she greatly appreciated.

"Why'd she leave?"

"Husband got a big job overseas, and he had to start immediately. The kind of thing that doesn't respect a school's clockwork calendar."

"I see."

He opened a desk drawer and pulled a few items to the tabletop. "Left the gradebook and a couple of weeks' worth of lesson plans, too," he said. "Nice."

"Can I take them with me?"

"Of course."

She crossed the room and gathered up the folders. She hadn't known what to expect going in and now flushed with gratitude for the consideration. She could try to cozy up to names and grades and give herself at least a chance of not being stampeded by the fast-coming week.

"That'll give you an idea of where she was headed," Tim said. "Don't get me wrong, it's your classroom now. But Kathy was one of our best, so it'll come in handy."

"I'm sure."

"And we've got a grade-level PLC here, so—"

"PLC?"

"Professional learning community," he said. "There's support here. Not every school is like that, even within this district. We've got a good thing going. You'll be among some really top-notch colleagues."

"I'm glad to hear it."

He shifted his weight from foot to foot. *Corpulent.* There was a vocabulary word, and Tim Meyers embodied it. He was far from the middle-distance runner he had been in high school. But then, she too was a far distance from whatever she had been in those years.

"So, listen, it's like I said on the phone, it's for the next five months," he said. "I can't promise—"

"I know. Tim—Mr. Meyers—really, I'm just so appreciative. However it works out."

He smiled at her. "What I was going to say was, I can't promise anything, but I can be pretty sure we're going to need a seventh-grade English teacher next fall. You do well, and there's no reason you won't be in line for the job."

She adjusted the folders in her arms, rolling her shoulders to hike up her purse strap. "Like the Zen master says," she said. "'We'll see.'"

Seven

Eric inched his pickup forward, then stopped again. Ahead of him, six cars up, the light went from fleeting amber to strident red, the fourth time he had seen the change without getting through.

"I told your mother it would be a zoo down here," he said. "I told her."

He turned to side-eye Claire, who slumped a bit as if sensing the fast turn of his mood. She pointed out the window.

"We're really close," she said.

Yeah, he thought, *but it's one of those so-close, so-far deals. Like being on the wrong side of a rushing stream when the bank you want to fish from is in sight but you don't dare put a foot in the water.* Left to his druthers, he would swing this thing around and go back to the house, if even that could be managed.

"The damn mall," he said.

"Thank you for taking me, Grandpa."

The light flipped to green, and Eric mashed the horn in the center of the steering wheel with the heel of his right hand, and the idling vehicles ahead of him lurched forward like a set of railcars jolted by the tug of a locomotive, slowly at first, then not nearly fast enough, then, finally, with fluidity. Green ceded again to yellow, and Eric goosed the accelerator and rode through on red, nearly up the tailpipe of the car directly ahead.

"Fuck it."

"Grandpa!"

He looked to the girl and back again at the lineup, now queuing at the next—and last—light before the turn-in.

"What?" he said. "Did I offend you?"

"You're not supposed to say that."

"Who says?"

"Mom."

This, Eric supposed, was neither the place nor the occasion to fill Claire in on the many creative ways her mother, his daughter, had foregone her own advice on profanity, most recently several weeks ago, when she had come to him with the request of a favor. There had been some back and forth, sure, but had he denied her anything? He had not. He had just wanted to know the terrain of what he was getting into here, and he had wanted to make his own boundaries clear, and here Jane had come with "I mean, fuck, Dad, do you really think I want to make this request of you?"

"I'm sorry," he said now to Claire. "What should I say?"

"You can say *eff it*," she offered. "Or *farts*. Dad sometimes says *farts*."

"He does, does he?" That didn't jibe with Eric's recollected evenings of unrestrained jawboning with Paul, especially not after a couple of beers had loosened their tongues and added grandiosity to their memories of past exploits, but good on him for reining it in a bit around the girl.

A long, angry blast from behind them jolted Eric's attention, and Claire pointed and said, "Grandpa, go," and he released the brake, but not before the light flickered from green to yellow to red, and he jammed it to a halt again.

"Fuck," he said.

"Grandpa!"

Northeast Mall was a damn monstrosity, a beast grown far beyond its humble beginnings when a trip down here had been easy enough, no mixmasters, no extreme congestion, no resultant indigestion. He couldn't precisely remember the last time he'd been to the place, and that was neither hyperbole nor a nod to the things that were increasingly slipping away from his mind's reach. It had just been a damned long time ago. There had been an occasion or two when Jane had been in that swale between having a bit of early teenage money and when she could drive herself, and Margery had begged off the chore for some reason or another, and he'd piled his daughter and some other girls into his work truck and dropped them off here. He didn't much care for it then and didn't expect his attitude was going to change now.

"Where do you want to go?" he asked Claire.

"I dunno."

"Well, you got to pick something."

"Ooh." She pointed out the window as he circled on the access road. "There's movies. Can we go?"

"Not today."

"Aw."

"Here," he said. "JCPenney."

"I don't want to go there."

Eric swung into one of the large parking lots fronting the structure. "You don't have to go *there*, girly," he said. "You can walk *through* there and go where you want."

"My name's Claire."

"I know." He angled the pickup into an open space and brought it between the lines, then shut it off. "Come on," he said. "Let's get this over with."

Once they were in the anchor department store, Claire's sense of direction and her fixation on all the specialty shops that lay beyond it kicked in, and she was off with geometric precision, the shortest distance between two points being the angle of her stride. Eric, stubby-legged in the best of times and now arteriosclerosing around the far pole of life, struggled to match her gait and her preternatural swerves around mannequins and other shoppers.

"Claire, hold up," he said.

"Let's get this over with," she tossed over her shoulder.

"Smartass."

At the other end of the store, the mall widened out to its cavernous belly, still teeming with shoppers but now in a space less constricted and carrying the jingle of holiday music and the melding scents of the unseen food court. Eric caught up to the girl and grasped her hand, squeezing a "grandpa!" out of her, and he said, "Dammit, hold up."

"I want to go there," she said, pointing at a clothing store.

"You're not going anywhere until I've got a handle on things," he said, and he tugged her forward, toward the intersection of the shop-filled walkways that radiated outward. "We've got to find a place to meet up, and then you can go where you want."

"Mom always comes with me."

"Yeah? Well, I'm not tromping all over this godforsaken place."

"But it's right there," she said, pointing again.

"And it'll still be there. Come on, girly."

He tugged her again, harder. She said, "You don't have to hold my hand," and he said, "Oh, yes, I do," and they made their way forward as a knot of human friction.

"I want to go there," she said, repeatedly, and he grew tired of telling her that she could come back because why did he have to keep repeating himself, and he wondered why he had to come here to find out this kid was such an unrelenting brat sometimes.

At the fountain in the middle of mall, he laid it out for her. "It's 12:31 now," he said. "Back here at 1:30. Not a minute later. Got it?"

"That's just an hour."

"It's fifty-nine minutes."

"Aw, Grandpa."

"About to be fifty-eight."

She huffed, which was her right, and she left, which was the better idea, and she stamped back the way they had come.

Eric watched her until she slipped into the stream of shoppers and became one with it, then he looked about and tried to formulate his own idea for how to blow almost an hour in such a joint. What had seemed to Claire a stint of cruel shortness struck him the opposite way. What in the world would anyone want with all this bullroar?

He looked at his feet. Inside a sneaker, his right toe was disengaging from and crashing into the tile floor at a frantic rate.

"Well," he said under his breath, "new shoes, maybe."

Eight

Tim offered Jane a ride home, after the quick tour of the campus was over and she had brokered a peace between her memories and all the changes brought on by nearly thirty years away from the place. On the way to the car, he was incredulous that she had actually walked to the meetup. "I thought you lived nearby or something," he said, and she braved a white lie in response: "It was a nice walk. Besides, the living is just temporary."

On the drive, he inquired generally about Claire and more specifically, if also respectfully, about what had brought Jane home after so long.

"I remember seeing your Facebook post," he said. "That was the thing that got my wheels turning."

Jane didn't need the reminder, nor did she want it. When leaving Paul and struggling to find work and raiding a small retirement account had conspired to take her hope away one afternoon, Jane had put some blunt truths into the social realm. Later, she had regretted it, but not enough to take down the post. It was perhaps the most truthful thing she could say about the marriage, certainly more pointed than what she had been willing to offer directly, and it was a damn fine piece of rhetoric to boot. Killing it off would have been wrong.

"I found someone to talk to," she said now. "Facebook is better for cat memes than personal distress."

"So that's where the Zen master comes from?"

"Sure," she said. "You been divorced?"

He showed her his wedding band. "Twenty-one years married."

"Congratulations," she said, and she meant it. She bore no animus toward the institution or toward anyone else's achievement of domestic harmony. She simply found the concepts incongruent with her own experience. "Anyway, there comes a point in that process—and it's so much more polite to call it a process than what it really is—where you have a lot of questions and no good answers. 'We'll see' takes some of the pressure off."

"I see." She looked at him, and he grinned at his slight wordplay, and she rewarded it with the smile he seemed to expect.

He drove on. Jane tried to smother a flash of panic that she had offered too much, that however Tim might position himself as a friend would always be in some conflict with his status as her chief administrator. She couldn't allow a blurring of that line.

"I'm impressed," he said at last. She turned to him with a tight smile she hoped would say what she could not.

"Why?"

"You seem to have made your peace with it."

"Maybe," she said. "I suspect it's more that I just didn't want to go to war with it anymore."

"Surrender, surrender," he said, and he chuckled.

"Huh?"

"Cheap Trick. Sorry," he said. "Bad joke. Lame, as my daughter says."

"Turn here," she said. "Up the hill on the left side. Seventy-twenty-five."

Once the SUV was at rest in her father's inclined driveway, he set the parking brake and let it idle.

She offered a handshake, and he accepted. "I really do appreciate this," she said.

"You're welcome."

She opened the door, climbed out, and closed it behind her. He lowered the window.

"Jane," he said.

She turned.

"Ms. Sperling," he corrected. "Sorry, gonna have to get used to that." She waited. "I think this is going to work out just fine."

He closed the window and backed out to the street. Jane headed to the front door, warm with gratitude for his gesture of saying so, and she allowed herself the thought that maybe this hope thing might at last be worth the effort.

Nine

Eric rocked forward onto his tippy toes, watching himself in the reflection of the floor-to-ceiling glass of an empty storefront. A lot of those, he had noticed, enough to be surprising even as he had read about the slow, choking death of America's shopping malls. He was no defender of this particular slice of Americana, not by a long shot, but if this place were indeed on borrowed time, he naturally wondered what someday might take root in its place. The one-time competitor a town over, North Hills Mall, had long since been consigned to bulldozers and made into the new site of city hall. This place, a much bigger assemblage of stores, would leave a much bigger crater.

The new shoes looked robust, though, brown leather uppers, with laces and a substantial rubber sole, the kind that would give him a better chance of staying steady and upright. He admired them again as he fell back to flat-footed. They felt good, too, so much so that he had asked the clerk to box up his old sneakers. He would give them an extended afterlife of walking behind the lawnmower. It was probably a dead heat as far as what would give out first, the well-worn shoes or his energy for such a task.

"Eric?" The word, breaching his ears from behind, turned him around.

He very nearly did a double-take before peering closer at the owner of the voice. "Jocelyn?"

"Yes. Hi!" That brought from him a grin inspired by seeing through the years to recognize an old friend and by her obvious joy at having picked him out of a crowd.

"I can't believe it," he said. "What's it been, twenty years?"

"Twenty-five if a day."

She moved up on him and brought him into a hug, and he felt the delicate bones of her back through the sweater she wore. *Twenty-five years.* It simply wasn't possible, and yet he wouldn't have to do any complicated ciphering to figure she was probably right. Time stacks up. When you start compressing the years in your memory, the stacks seem to grow ever higher, ever faster.

He disengaged from her and held her by the shoulders. The scent of the transfer lingered on his nose, a smattering of apple and bergamot and autumn spices that instantly evoked memory. Swimming pool parties in the Blankenship backyard, her boys, two and three years older than Jane, and his daughter, and her husband and his wife, and boating outings on Grapevine Lake and picnics at Chisholm Park and, then, eventually, nothing, because time pulls away and your kids pull away, from you and from each other, and...what's that Jane used to say when she turned insolent in her teenage years? *Shit happens.*

He let her go. "How's Ed?"

A wan smile now from her. "Ed died," she said. "August." The words at once were mournful and matter-of-fact, and Eric knew the drill, having heard similar dirges too many times these past several years from too many other friends, and having had to offer them to others when Margery had shuffled off. The dull, monotone delivery that masks the hurt inside and gets you through the moment, only for another moment to arrive in the churn of life that goes on in the aftermath.

"I'm sorry," he said. "I didn't know. I quit taking the damn *Star-Telegram* because the obituaries became too damn depressing. And besides, they hadn't caught up to me yet." An uninspired joke. He hoped she wouldn't take offense.

"It's OK," she said. "He went quietly, no hubbub. Just as he preferred."

"Margery will be gone six years come April," he said.

"I know. I'm sorry, too."

"The bargain of life, I guess," he said.

"I guess."

Eric looked at his watch, getting the context of the encroaching time.

"I'm sorry," she said. "I'm keeping you from something."

"Not at all. It's just...well, I'm here with my granddaughter."

"And you're not with her?"

"What's the big deal?" he asked.

Jocelyn laughed. "Never mind. I wasn't sure it was you. I figured I'm more apt to find a hippo in my pantry than Eric Driskell in a shopping mall."

"Tell me about it."

"What's her name? How old?"

"Claire."

"Beautiful," she said.

"She's eleven. And is living full out every one of those years, if you get my drift."

Another laugh. "Jane's daughter?"

"Yeah."

"How's she?"

"Jane is Jane. Listen, I'm really sorry, Joc, but I've got to get going. Do you want to come with me, meet Claire?"

"No, I better not," she said. "I have to get home, too."

"Still live on Lowery?"

"Still," she said. "Fifty-one years."

"I'm still on Payte."

"I know. It's good to see you, Eric."

"You, too."

He watched her turn, and she merged into the slipstream of post-holiday shoppers, and it wasn't long before she was gone in the wake. Not long at all. And then he tried to find his own bearings again, and they had scattered, and every turn he took about the place gave him a view that looked like the one he'd focused on previously, until finally he chose a direction and started walking, the soles of his new shoes squeaking on the polished floor.

Ten

The fissures Jane had spent the preceding weeks worrying over and hoping to somehow stave off split open in the afternoon, when Eric and Claire came back and the girl stormed into the house, long arms peeling off shopping bags and casting them in all directions on her way to the back bedroom. Jane jumped as Claire barricaded herself in with a slammed door. Up the front hallway, Jane's father exercised his own frustration by kicking the rug.

"What happened?"

"That daughter of yours has a tart mouth," Eric said, advancing on her. "I wonder where she got that."

"What happened?"

Claire's muffled rejoinder shot out at them. "Shut up, Grandpa!"

Eric pushed past Jane and toddled down the hallway on old-man legs, shouting at the door. "You don't talk to me like that. You don't ever say something like that to me."

Jane found her own bearing and lit out after her father.

"Everybody just stop. Dad, what happened?"

Eric U-turned in the hallway, clipping her again. "I'm leaving. Next time that ungrateful little girl wants anything, you do it."

Claire again, her voice scream-strained into thinness: "I'm not a little girl!"

"Dad—"

Eric wheeled on her again. His face puckered. "I told you I didn't want to go. I told you. Goddammit."

He left now, keys in a jumble, another door slammed, the gunning of a motor and a rubber squeal of tires down the street.

Jane, gut-punched by the swiftness of the undoing, as if radiation had flashed amid them, gathered herself and tried turning the handle to the bedroom door. It rattled, locked.

"Claire, let me in."

The girl's muffled crying leaked out, and Jane held fast to the door, and she waited and tried again. "Claire, come on."

Getting a straight story out of Claire proved more arduous than coaxing her to open the door. After Jane worked her way through Claire's preamble of "he's mean" and "all I wanted to do was shop a little bit" and "I don't know why we even came to this stupid place," she eventually pieced together the bare bones of what had gone down, how some miscommunication over where and when to meet had set her daughter and her father at odds. Jane tamped down her own internal explosion at her father's recklessness in just turning Claire loose in such a place. *In calmer times*, she thought, *we'll be talking about that.*

"He told me the water fountain at one-thirty," Claire said. "That's where I was."

"And he wasn't there?"

"No." Claire whimpered, on the verge of another cry. Jane sought to short-circuit it, to keep the words coming so she could divine the truth of them, or at least get near enough to the truth that she could stumble the rest of the way there.

"So what happened?"

"I left and went looking for him."

"What time was this?"

"I don't know."

The softness of the time element, Jane figured, threw some considerable doubt into things. Her father could drive his truck into the holes in any story. She grasped for more clarity.

"Where did you go? Come on."

"I just...I just went." Exasperation now from Claire. "He set the rules. I was just trying to do what I was told."

"I know."

"He's awful."

Jane nodded. *He certainly can be.*

Enough nudging and Claire eventually brought out the bottom line: Each had crisscrossed the mall looking for the other, Claire becoming ever more nervous and, Jane surmised, Eric's gut steadily filling with bile. When they finally intersected, Claire said, her grandfather had seized her by the wrist and pulled her along toward an exit. Jane grimaced at the image. She also found it entirely believable.

"He didn't know where he parked," Claire said. "He kept dragging me around, but he didn't know where to go." She teared up.

"Oh, honey." Jane stroked her daughter's hair and tucked a strand behind her ear.

"I laughed at him. That made him really mad."

"Oh, honey." This, too, conveyed truth. She and Claire would have to talk another time about fear and frustration, about trigger and response. As the picture clarified, Jane set most of the responsibility for what had happened on her father—the adult, after all, and the one who made the critical, incorrect decision to part ways—but she also cringed at how he must have felt, belittled by this eleven-year-old girl.

"Did you know where to go?" Jane asked her.

"Yes. JCPenney."

"Did you tell him that?"

"Yes."

"You did?"

"Eventually."

"Ah."

"Well, he made me mad."

"And you sure got him back for that, didn't you?"

"Well, yeah."

"That's not nice, Claire."

"I know." She dropped her head. "It's his stupid mall in his stupid town. Why didn't he know?"

"He probably got confused. He was probably scared."

"He didn't seem scared," Claire said. "He was mad."

"There's not much difference, sometimes."

"He hates me," Claire said. "He was awful."

"He doesn't hate you."

"Well, I hate him."

"No, you don't."

"I know. I don't like him, though."

"We can work on that."

"I don't like it here."

"We can work on that, too."

When the hysterics had, at last, subsided, Jane left Claire to her tablet, relieved that the girl had walked to the precipice of a bottoming-out, then had clawed back. Some time alone, for both of them, and for her father, wherever he had stormed off to, would have some restorative value, she was sure. She hoped, anyway.

She moved to the kitchen. She was with Claire on the whole not-liking-it-here thing, as far as it went. Three full days in, she was still waking up in the morning astonished that she was back in this house, back with this man, back in so many ways to the first square when she had spent the preponderance of her life trying to hop away from it. In other, unexpected ways, she found moments of grace and ease. Cooking for three, even if she didn't particularly relish the duty, could be scaled with better food usage and economics than cooking for two. She enjoyed tipping a beer with her father later in the evenings, after Claire had turned in, and she even appreciated the conversations they had. They were little tender moments she had never taken in before. She liked the early-morning walk she granted herself after she'd gotten up from the couch in the den and ventured into the break of day, her breath frosty, the sky a swirl. It wasn't home yet, not after she had been gone so long, but somewhere here, perhaps she could find one.

Jane sliced chicken breasts into ribbons and talked to her father as she talked to herself.

"Come on home, Dad."

Eleven

Eric came home eventually, maybe gone an hour, a stretch Claire spent in her room and Jane spent in the kitchen and on the couch, silently waiting him out, hoping for the mending that often came with time and distance from injury.

He came into the house, grim and tightlipped, and Jane rose and went to him and hugged him briskly, then pulled away.

"Are you hungry?" she asked.

"I could eat."

Breaking out her mother's chicken-and-dumplings recipe proved to be a good unifier. Having found herself alone at the house earlier, Jane had driven to Kroger and gathered up the fixings, envisioning an evening meal of comfort rather than reconciliation. Now, she cast herself in the role Margery Driskell so often played, keeper of home and hearth and provider of nourishment and nurturing.

She ladled up the bowls and passed them out. Her father

received his with silence and deference, and Jane reached for an understanding of where his attitude lay. He could go either way, in her experience—hard toward the anger that had driven him away in the first place or toward shame over having lost control. She had seen both and knew her way around both, though the strategies of coping were far different, a matter of riding it out or waiting for him to reel himself in.

Claire, predictably, was downcast. She had emerged from the room tearfully before his return, insistent that she didn't hate her grandfather at all, that she really did love him, and that she regretted the harshness of her words toward him and about him. Jane had held her and promised that he knew and loved her right back. It was Claire's most glaring immaturity and one of her best qualities, all in one, this tendency to oversell an emotion and, in time, a seamless ability to atone when she hurt someone else.

Jane sat now and regarded them both. "Claire, honey, you wanted to say something."

The girl's face rose and she turned to her grim-faced elder. "Grandpa, I'm sorry. I shouldn't have wandered off."

Jane started to prompt her again, and Claire tacked on, "And I shouldn't have told you to shut up."

"Thank you," he said after an uncomfortable moment. "I'm sorry, too."

"Now," Jane said, the table's load lightened, "let's eat. And let's also all remember we've got cellphones. I'll make sure we've all got each other's number, OK?"

Claire giggled. Eric happily loaded his spoon.

Jane exhaled and started in on her dinner. She gave herself credit for a reasonable approximation of her mother's skill, in the kitchen and at the front lines of family life. And she knew, much as Margery always seemed to, that she couldn't linger long on this victory because another coming crisis could catch her unaware. You take the win, you maybe allow yourself some interior satisfaction, then you gird up.

Paul called a few minutes after Jane had nudged Claire off to bed by countering the girl's objections with a reminder that they would both be back in school in a week and thus needed to curtail the late nights to which they had become unduly accustomed.

"Merry Christmas," he said when Jane answered.

"That was yesterday."

"I know," he said, chastened, and Jane again found herself regretting that she possessed no change of pace with her ex-husband, no ability to strike a tone more nuanced than exasperated bluntness. "Yesterday, I was in the middle of East Bumfuck, Alberta. I'm sorry I didn't call. How's Claire Bear?"

"Asleep."

"Already?"

"It's an hour later here, Paul."

"Oh, right."

Jane held her silence. She couldn't say these occasional dealings by phone were disagreeable; the fact was, after that first horrible evening when they had agreed on nothing except that divorce was the only option left to them, matters where she and Paul were concerned were never less than cordial despite the injuries they had inflicted on each other, but Jane had begun to despise cordiality just the same. It required politeness and aloofness in equal parts when all she really wanted to do sometimes was get in his face and ask him why he never tried to fight for anything.

"Should I call back tomorrow?" he asked.

"No, I'll get her."

"I don't want to wake her up."

"She's up. I just—"

"Yeah?"

"She's up. Hold on a sec."

She carried the phone into Claire's room and gave it to the girl—"It's your dad"—and retreated to the living room. She wished the instant, excited chatter from Claire upon taking the phone didn't bother her so.

"Paul?" her father asked as she settled into the couch.

"Yeah."

"Wondered why he didn't call yesterday."

"He was only a day off. That's not bad, for him."

"Sweetie."

"I'm just saying."

Eric adjusted his newspaper, folding it over and then in half. "It's not good to be bitter."

An urge to respond, to call out hypocrisy where it lay, surged through her, reaching the base of her tongue before she swallowed it back down her gullet. "Not bitter," she said as the indignant flood receded. "Just experienced."

"I'm just saying."

"I know you are. So am I."

In time, Claire padded out and brought Jane the phone. "Dad wants to talk to you again."

Jane took it from her and said, "OK, good night, sweetie." Claire kissed her on the cheek, then dropped into her grandfather's waiting arms. "Sleep tight, girly," he said.

"When is spring break?" Paul asked when Jane was back on.

"I'll have to check," she lied. Jane had memorized the district calendar by now, every staff development day and student half-day and the one extended break before summertime. It's just that she was still working herself around to January and had no capacity yet for late March.

"Well, let me know. Maybe I could come down, or Claire could come up."

"It's just a week. Better if you come here, if you can."

"We'll work something out."

"Sure," Jane said. "Whatever it needs to be."

After they said their goodbyes, and after Jane's father had given up on his newspaper and headed off to bed, she sat in the living room and considered the wall, and she cast her own doubts upon it, the better to see them in congregation. When she, too, at last closed out the night, she hoped Paul had been circumspect about spring while he was talking with Claire. In Jane's experience, any hard promises he had made would only heighten the odds that she would have to step in with a kit for mending once the blossoms appeared and Claire's heart had been broken.

Twelve

Chuck Brooks drove the distance of five houses Friday night and picked Jane up for dinner. It had been an exhausting exchange all the way around for her. She had started by offering to meet him at the restaurant, relented when he had said, "That's silly, we're both right here," to which she had replied that she could at least walk down to his house when it was time to go. He'd had none of that. He arrived on her doorstep with two red roses, one for her and one for Claire, who blushed in accepting it.

"You're spoiling us unnecessarily," Jane said.

"Just being nice."

He took her to a Cajun place, a distance that would have been a ten-minute drive, tops, in her day but now stretched into a twenty-five-minute ordeal, traffic a weekend-night snarl, the stacked mixmaster a teeming colony of internal combustion engines. Jane peered out her window at the ghosted avenues of her past, where unrecognized buildings and businesses crowded into spaces only partially resonant in her memories, and she wondered how so many people could have found purchase here. For the first time since leaving Montana, she missed it. She missed space. She missed altitude. She missed latitude.

"Come on, come on," Chuck said, drumming the bottom of the steering wheel with his fingers.

Ahead of them, in the other lane, the dam broke, and he swung wide and sharp, cutting off a semi and eliciting a blast from its horn. Chuck waved meekly at his rearview mirror and goosed his sedan along until he found his pace in the flow. Two exits up, the car left the freeway and Chuck negotiated a smooth arrival into a parking lot and an empty space.

"See?" he said. "It would have been pointless to take two cars."

"Yes," she said. "Much more efficient for us both to die in one."

"Huh?"

"Just a weak joke," she said. "Forgive me."

As they waited on their food, the most robust conversation centered on shared remembrances and the curation of times past. Jane sent across multiple inquiries about people she no longer knew, just to keep things from spilling too heavily into the now, a time and place where she was much less sure of her willingness to engage.

She couldn't hold that line indefinitely, she was certain. As she picked at an appetizer of fried dill pickles, she discovered that Chuck knew the shape of things, if not the substance. He knew about her divorce, knew her ex-husband's name, knew the timeline. "I have a beer with your dad every once in a while," he said by way of explanation. She smiled from the other side of the table. It bothered her, this recitation of events. Chuck, with all good intentions, reduced her life to a tracing, when she could see nothing but the colors and textures between those lines. "Divorce, that must have been hard on you," he said, a perfectly reasonable if also banal intuition, but she sensed nothing from him beyond that—no interest in *how* it must have been difficult, not that she would have told him.

"Tell me about your kids," she parried. "Annabelle and—"

"Eli."

"That's right. Thank you."

"Annabelle's four," he said. "Eli's fifteen. We didn't plan for Annabelle. I mean, you know, that explains the gap. Anyway, Jolene—that's my wife—she didn't, I mean, Annabelle was born, but—"

Jane set down her water glass, sunk by the unfinished sentence. "Oh, God."

"Yeah," he said.

"I'm so sorry."

"Thank you."

Jane knew women who'd had difficult pregnancies. She had endured her own forty-one weeks of carrying Claire, knowing the risks, having read entirely too much information about entirely too many possible complications, and she had released no small measure of relief when both pregnancy and delivery had turned out to be textbook. In all her friendships with other adults, she had never known someone who had faced the worst outcome with such intimacy. Without any other evidence of the woman's existence, Jane found herself wishing she had known Jolene Brooks.

"Eighteen out of every hundred thousand births," Chuck said, as if sensing her bewilderment and being compelled to calcify it with statistics. "The odds seem remote, until they land on you."

"I'm so sorry, Chuck."

He brightened as if prompted. "But we're fine, we're good. Eli's getting to be a man, Annabelle's a delight. We're hanging in there."

The server dropped by and set down their meals. Cayenne filled Jane's senses. "It smells great," she said. "I can't wait to taste it."

"It's good stuff," Chuck said. "I'm glad you could come."

She wrenched open her coming challenge as Chuck drove them back to their neighborhood. In the classroom after a twelve-year absence. Going from a small private school to a large public campus in the suburbs. The chat with Tim Meyers had settled her nerves, she said, but her first dive into the gradebook—all those names, all those teaching sessions—had frazzled them anew.

"I remember Tim," Chuck said. "I liked him."

"He's a good man," she said.

"We do exist."

While Jane considered what, if anything, to say to that, Chuck bore in on a different front. "How old is Claire again?"

"She'll be twelve in May."

"Do you think she'd like to do some babysitting?" he asked. "Eli usually watches his sister when I need him to, but his after-school schedule is a little nuts."

"She hasn't done it before," Jane said. "But she's a mature girl." She looked sideways at Chuck, who looked sideways at her. "Mostly," she said, sputtering, then she gathered herself again. "But, yeah, I think she might like that."

"Good deal. Be nice to have somebody that close."

Jane tensed her hands, rubbing her index fingers with the adjacent thumbs. "We're not staying with my dad," she said. "I mean, we are, but it's not permanent or anything."

"Oh?"

"I'm not raising my daughter in the house where I grew up." Her regret was instant, burning, shameful. It was too much to say in one sentence, especially with no willingness to spell things out further.

"It's worked out all right for me," Chuck said.

"I'm sorry. That came out all wrong. What I mean is, well, Claire and I have been on our own for a while now. That's all. We're used to it."

"I see."

Jane scrambled some more, making a quarter-turn in her seat. "Anyway, that doesn't have anything to do with whether she can babysit. She'd love to, I'm sure. And I'm thankful you thought of her."

Chuck looked at her and nodded, then turned his attention back to the road. He turned left into the subdivision, then right onto their street. Jane faced the window and wished for a swift exit.

"If you want to just let me out at your place—" she started.

"It's no trouble."

"OK."

In the Driskell driveway, she faced him again. "Thank you for a lovely evening."

"It was good to catch up, wasn't it?" he asked.

"It was."

"If you'd like to," he started, and then the words faltered. "What I mean is, I haven't really gone out in a while. If you'd like to again, it would be nice."

Jane had one hand on the door handle and one clutching her pants leg. "It's just that, with school starting up again and everything, Claire, my dad—"

"I understand."

"—the thing is, I'm not really looking to date."

"It doesn't have to be a date," he said. "We're a couple of old friends."

"I know. It's just a really crazy time right now."

"OK. Just think about it, OK? No pressure. I had fun tonight."

"I'm glad," she said.

"So maybe we could do it again sometime."

"We'll see."

She let herself out into the cold dark. Her father hadn't turned on the houselights. She picked her way up the slope of the driveway, breath turning to frost. She turned and waved as Chuck backed out, then she let herself in the front door. She slipped into the warmth of the house, shut the door behind her, leaned into it with her weight, and closed her eyes.

"There you are," came Claire's sing-song voice from the shadowed hallway. "He was nice, wasn't he?"

Dear Claire

April 8, 2014

I saw a man today. I had to. It's so big and encompassing, this thing, that I'm not sure I'll be able to explain it in full. I just had to. That's what you need to know.

I decided, first thing, that what I like about this guy, a counselor, is the mandala table in his waiting room. It's round, as mandalas often are, an aluminum underpinning topped by thick glass. The design is one of concentric circles, flowing inward and outward, and I figured if this guy I hadn't even met is into the whole Buddhist thing, if he buys the idea of a time-microcosm of the universe, perhaps we'd at least have that to talk about if nothing else. (Then again, maybe he was just filling space while at the furniture store. That's what your father would have done. "Hey, cool, it's round. Let's get it." I'm sorry, honey. That honesty thing again.)

In any case, I had certainly found nothing to talk about with this guy's wife. It was she who at last, exasperated, sent me to him, the only grace note between us in two weeks of butting heads. "I don't think we're communicating," she had said. No shit (sorry, Claire). The only true thing I ever heard her say. She told me I need somebody who can help me with my masculine, whatever that means. The way I figure it, access to the masculine is the whole problem in the first place. But whatever. Today, I went to see him.

I wish you could see this guy. He's tall and thin and neat, except for the hair, which whips out from his head like frenzied cotton, giving him a look vaguely reminiscent of a scientist clutched by madness. Only his manner—quiet without being meek, and a gentle touch in the handshake, which had a little tremor to it—dispensed with the suggestion of wildness.

I sat down, and I noticed another mandala framed on the wall, just a few inches to the right of his head. This, I decided, cannot be a coincidence.

He asked where we should start.

I said it was his show. He'd seen my file.

He said he had a referral, not notes. He told me to start where I wanted. I'll piece together the conversation as best I remember it, so you can imagine how it must have been there in his office.

"No notes?" I asked.

No, he said.

"Well, that's good. We didn't exactly get along, your wife and me."

He said that was of no consequence. Blank slate.

So I asked: "Should I start with why I'm here?"

"If you wish. Or you can start somewhere else. We'll get there in due time, in any case."

"You're not like her."

"As it should be," he said. "She is who she is. I am who I am."

"What an enlightened point of view."

"I have my moments."

"Rare in a man."

"Oh, I don't know."

"Rare in the men I've known."

"Let's talk about that," he said.

"OK."

"But let's adjust the lens."

"What do you mean?"

"Let's look at it this way: What has attracted you to men you consider unenlightened?"

I told him maybe nothing.

"But maybe something?"

"Maybe."

"After all," he said. "You are the common denominator."

"Why is this on me?"

"Who else should it be on?"

I glared at him. This is about the spot where Delilah, his wife, would start heading for the stratosphere in her frustration with me, but he showed no such escalation.

So I sucked in my breath and I started in. I'm here, I told him, because I don't want to mess up anything else as much as I've messed up my marriage. Good or bad, enlightened or not, it was something I had and something I've lost, and I told him that you have lost it, too, and I'm going to do what I can to never lose like that again. More than that, I said, I never want it again. That's where loss comes from. Having.

He smiled and said "OK." Asked how long I was married, so I told him: "I'm still married, technically, but it's dead. Over."

"How long?"

"Seventeen years."

He asked how old you are, too. I told him that. And then he said a curious thing: "And you messed it all up yourself, did you? The blame is one hundred percent yours?"

That landed on me with blunt force, I have to say, not least of all because I'd never taken the time to parse it out in percentages. So I told him, well, a lot of it. Definitely not all. But a lot.

"No," he said. "Not all. Probably less than you think, not that it matters. How about let's start by dispensing with blame? Blame and guilt, let's not have either one. Guilt is emotion wasted on the pointless idea that you should have been perfect in everything. Blame is a way of finding fault. Let us be not interested in that." For real. He really talks that way.

So I asked him what we're interested in.

"You tell me."

I told him he confounded me. He said it would make sense eventually. I told him I believed him, because I do.

"So," he said. "Why are you attracted to men you consider to be unenlightened? What is it in you that makes them attractive to you?"

So I told him the deal, plainest I've ever said it.

"I understand them," I said.

No idea why I'm writing this, except that it all seemed so profound in the moment and so hard to capture, that I just want to put it down, pen to paper, so I'll have it if I ever want to remember it. You're a good girl, Claire, perceptive beyond your years, so maybe one day you'll see these lines and perception will give you the words in between them.

But you're not ready for this. I hope you never are, but I don't have much hope that I can keep that door closed on you forever. I'm sure going to try.

Thirteen

Three days before the end of the calendar year, five days before the start of the second half of the school year and whatever else this life was going to be, Jane received two invitations for the pleasure of her company on New Year's Eve, the arrival of which landed in such an order that she could be grateful and effectively apologetic.

Tim—*Principal Meyers*—emailed in the morning and invited her to a faculty get-together at his place. "We'll have heavy hors d'oeuvres and some soft drinks, but if you want to bring alcohol for you, hey, everybody's an adult. It won't be a full crew— people have their own parties, imagine that—but you'll get to meet some of your coworkers before, you know, you meet your coworkers. I'm so sorry I didn't say anything earlier. Totally slipped my mind."

She fired off her reply, accepting, as she puzzled anew over how to handle Claire and her father. They were friends again after the boondoggle at the mall, but Jane had attenuated sensitivity to how much she asked of him as well as to his own pre-emptive protestations about having to tend to Claire too often.

The solution, and a whole new problem, trudged up Payte Lane in the early afternoon and rapped knuckles on the door.

"Is anyone getting that?" Jane called from the kitchen and the entirely-too-frequent unloading of the dishwasher.

"Not for me," Eric said.

"Claire?"

"I am busy," the girl huffed.

Jane crossed the room. "Never mind. I'll get it."

On the other side of the door stood Chuck Brooks. He was ready with a smile and clenched hands in front of his blue jeans.

"Hi, Jane."

"Hiya, Chuck."

"You look nice."

"Yeah? This is my hamburgers-for-lunch look. I can do better."

"Could have fooled me."

"Let him in," Eric bleated from the living room. "I'm not paying to heat the neighborhood."

Jane stepped aside and let him into the hallway, then led him into the main house. "Have a seat," she said. "Claire, please move over for Mr. Brooks."

The girl harrumphed and slid right.

"I won't stay long," Chuck said, sitting.

Eric: "Have a beer."

"No, I really can't." He fumbled between Eric and Jane, apparently wanting to be appreciative of the offer while not straying from whatever reason had brought him by.

"It's just...I was thinking about the babysitting we talked about, and—"

Claire's attentions surfaced. "For *me*?" she asked, her look at Jane at once accusatory and shattered.

"Honey, please."

"I am *too old* for a babysitter."

"No, no, no, I'm sorry, I'm not being clear," Chuck sputtered. "I'm sorry, Claire."

"Mom?"

"Honey, shush. It's not about you."

"It better not be."

"Oh, Jesus," Eric said.

"Well, it is, in a manner of speaking," Chuck said. He had turned in his seat and was now talking only to Claire, who despite her fast-rising pout was probably his easiest audience in the room. "I'd like you to do the babysitting for my daughter."

"The little girl?"

"Annabelle," Chuck said. "She's four."

"What's this?" Eric scoffed.

"Chuck, negotiate with me, OK?" Jane said.

"Wow, babysitting?" And there it was. Claire headed for the clouds.

"Go talk somewhere else," Eric said. "Game's on."

Jane beckoned Chuck into the kitchen, after first telling Claire, who had gone all bouncy, to sit still and wait and that they would talk about this thing after Mr. Brooks left.

"We could have talked about this last night," she said now, voice low. In her sight, beyond the back of Chuck's head, her daughter clenched hands in *faux* prayer and mouthed "please, please, please." Jane averted her eyes into his.

"We did talk about this last night."

"We talked about the *prospect* of this," Jane corrected. "We didn't have a specific date on the calendar."

"I didn't know last night."

"Uh-huh."

"I didn't, Jane. Some old friends—your old friends, too—messaged me today and said they were getting together for New Year's Eve. Sounded fun. Eli's going to the Mavericks game with a buddy and his family, so—"

"Who?"

"I don't think you know them."

"No," she said, "the old friends. Just curious."

"Paige Clarke. Billy Looper. Remember?"

"Vaguely."

"Well," he said, "you haven't stuck around. We all have."

"Sure."

"Anyway, I was hoping you might want to go."

"I can't."

"Really?" He looked let down. Jane wondered if perhaps she should have larded up her declination with sweet words meaning nothing to spare his feelings, but what difference would it have made? The answer was what it was. "Cool nightclub in downtown Fort Worth, all '80s everything," Chuck said. "Paige is going as Madonna. I'm thinking Rick Astley."

"You could pull that off," she said.

"You think so?" That drew him back into a smile. "You sure you can't come?"

"It's just that I have plans. Tim Meyers is hosting this faculty thing, and—"

"Of course," he said. "Tim again. I understand." He went from hopeful to crestfallen, an emotional flop that seemed entirely outsized to the situation, and furthermore, he surely didn't understand a thing. Jane felt the walls pushing in on her.

"I know you mean well, Chuck, but this is the bind I'm in. I don't mind Claire doing a little babysitting when it's just down the street and I'm here. It will be good for her, as I've already told you. But I *won't* be here. And you've dangled this thing in front of her, so now I have to deal with both the offer and her. Do you appreciate my frustration here?"

His head drooped. "Yeah. I'm sorry. Just forget it, OK? Sorry."

"No," Jane said. "That's not going to work, either. I can forget it, but you don't know my daughter if you think she will. Then I'm just the bad guy who took it from her, or you're the bad guy who offered and rescinded. I'll try to figure something out."

"OK."

"When do you need to know?"

"Whenever is fine."

"OK," she said, her teeming exasperation now out in the open. "I'll get back to you soon."

"I'm sorry," he said.

"I know. Shit happens."

Later, it was just Jane and her father, Claire having piled into her appointed bedroom for a video chat with a friend back in Montana, still agitating about the babysitting offer, and Jane unloaded her idea and stood behind it as Eric had his say.

"Absolutely not, no. I'm gonna end up having to tend to the both of them. I told you, I'm not going to be a nanny. No."

"Dad..."

"No."

"I need to be gone that night. OK? And Claire—Jesus, you saw her. You want to disappoint her like that? Whatever grief you think you're in for on this one night, it's going to be way worse if we deny her this."

"I'm not denying her nothing. This is your deal, not mine."

"Wait," Jane said. She got in front of him. "Look at me. There is no deal, OK? There's an idea. This will be good for her."

"She's too young to babysit anyway," he said. "Bad idea."

"Maybe. But she'll learn. All I'm asking is that she do the babysitting here, where there's a responsible adult."

"You mean me."

"Obviously," she said.

"So you get to do what you want to do and she gets to do what she wants to do, and frigging Chuck Brooks gets to do what he wants to do, and I gotta do this thing that I don't want to do?"

"What do you want," Jane asked, her patience cut to paper-thin, "except to drink a beer and watch some dumb ballgame? You can still do that."

Eric burned silently. A good sign, on the whole. Relentlessly logical arguing—with a dollop of sarcasm, yes, which Jane hoped hadn't undermined her effort—tended to wear him down into silence, a trick she had learned in her own prepubescence. Acceptance, however reluctant, tended to follow.

"I'll be home by ten," she said.

"You better."

"I will."

"That frigging Brooks kid," Eric said. "He's making my life difficult. Gonna have a talk with him."

"Yeah, well, stick to the subject," Jane said. "I'd say you two have been talking enough."

Her father looked punctured. "What'd I do?"

"How'd you know it was Chuck at the door?"

"I didn't."

"Right. You said 'it's not for me.' What are you, psychic?"

"It wasn't for me," he protested. "I didn't recognize the knock."

"You sure invited him in quick."

"Better that than all the heat ending up on the street."

"I don't want him, Dad. Just...just don't encourage him."

"What?"

"You heard me."

"Hey, it's your life."

"Yeah. Heard that before," she said.

Sitting cross-legged on her bed, Claire, having been made to wait longer than usual for a yes or no, pleaded her case again before Jane could get the verdict out.

"I would be so good at this," the girl said, her voice stretched in persuasion. "I am so mature for my age. You say it all the time."

"You are."

"Please, Mom. Please let me do it."

"Claire, nobody told you no."

"Nobody told me yes, either."

"Fair enough: yes."

"Really?"

"Yes."

Claire went wide-eyed, on the brink of one of her manic fits, a mixture of gratitude and I-have-to-make-extensive-plans-right-now and frenetic pinging around the room. Jane had always assumed such displays were more a manifestation of Paul's DNA in the girl than of her own, but she sometimes wondered if it was just a kid thing that was natural enough in the wider world but foreign to her. Claire's grandfather would have never countenanced such histrionics in his own daughter, and thus Jane had tacked more toward her mother's bearing: calm, understated in all things, determined to move through the vicissitudes of a given moment.

"But here's the thing, Claire Bear: It'll have to be here, so grandpa can keep an eye on you."

"Where will you be?"

"At a small party."

"Why?"

"Because I was invited."

"Was I invited?"

Jane smiled at her, reached out, tugged her chin. "You will be busy babysitting."

"Yay!"

And then, at once, Claire's mood turned sober. "I wish I had my dolls."

Right. They were on the truck. Along with about near everything else. Jane had heard from the driver the day before, a promise to deliver on the 30th, just two days out. He'd been delayed in suburban Denver by a lack of local labor, and there was a blown gasket in Oklahoma, and a guy's gotta have a day off once in a while, right? Jane had bitten her lip and said "fine," because what else can you say except that, and now she worried over the calendar. If not the 30th, then probably not the 31st, and if not then, surely not the 1st. If the load got delivered on the 2nd, she and Claire would be in school and Eric would be receiving their goods and cursing the day he said yes to their moving in, however temporary the situation might be. Not good.

Jane pointed now across the room, to the closet behind the cheap, hollow-core folding doors. Her old closet in her old room, a space into which they had carved enough of a clearing for a twin bed that could hold Claire's resting frame. The rest of it held the castoffs of fifty years of living and dying, the things her father didn't use anymore but couldn't bear to part with, the things her mother left behind when she spun off the coil, random memories at a glance, like Jane's teenage albums and cassettes and books she had deposited onto a shelf in 1992 or thereabouts, and those things had remained there, inert unless they were somehow plucked into prominence again. It all called out for a thorough going-through and a culling down to the essentials, something she aimed to do before she moved out, a task that would surely hold built-in debates with Eric, who would insist that he wouldn't have kept that—an all-purpose demonstrative pronoun—if he wasn't going to need it someday.

"Let's see what's in there," Jane said.

Claire rose and crossed the room, kicking aside a couple of boxes to clear the path. The right-side folding door receded nicely; the left went halfway and stuck, resistant to Claire's leaned-in weight.

"Jiggle it just a bit," Jane said, and the girl complied, and the door finished moving along its path. What greeted them were more boxes still, more detritus piled, a passel of clothes hanging from the rack—*my letterman's jacket*, Jane noticed, bringing forth memories of senior-year choir—and a closet shelf that moaned under the weight of the past.

"A bunch of junk," Claire said.

"Maybe," Jane said. She went over and joined Claire, and she started digging into the stacks. Soon enough, she unearthed what she was seeking, two plastic bins that got extracted with no small amount of upset to the rest of the collection. Claire played center field, catching a sheaf of tumbling magazines. ("*Playboy*, what's that?" "Never mind and put it back.")

Next, Jane set the bins on the bed and removed the lids, and it was a jackpot of memory and present-day usefulness. Barbie dolls in their many iterations of professional glory, the kind that lived lives of independent fabulousness and the kind that were steeped in Ken codependence. A baby doll whose eyes flew open when she was tilted forward. Other babies whose plastic heads had calcified in age and neglect, turning brittle and yellow.

Jane handed a Strawberry Shortcake doll to her daughter. "This one's hair smelled of strawberries," she said, and Claire took it and held the doll's head to her nose and said, "Not anymore." Oh, well. Thirty-five years don't go by without a toll.

"What's with this one?" Claire asked, holding up a larger doll with a floppy fabric body and a delicately curved plastic head that had been tattooed with a black-Sharpie star over the left eye.

"That is a Cabbage Patch Kid," Jane said, taking it from her, and Claire's face knotted up in immediate judgment of the moniker. "I wanted this as bad as you want..." She searched for a comparable, but none rose to meet her tongue.

"My own room again?"

"Yes."

Claire took the doll back. "Why did you draw all over it?"

"You should ask Bobby Drury that, because he did it. He turned my beloved Petunia into Paul Stanley."

"Who's Bobby Drury?"

"He used to live across the street."

"Who's Paul Stanley?"

"He's the lead singer of KISS."

"Who's KISS?"

"The kind of rock band a guy like Bobby Drury listens to."

"Who's Petunia?"

"My doll." Jane took it back again.

"That's a silly name."

"I was a silly girl sometimes. Like you."

"I'm not silly."

"No?"

"I'm a big girl."

"Yes, you are. And do you know what big girls do?" (In her head, Jane heard *they don't cry-yi-yi.*)

"What?" Claire asked.

"They put these dolls back in the bins and set them aside until Annabelle comes over. And they start getting ready for dinner, OK?"

Jane left her to it, back into the rest of the house, down the hall, across the living room in front of her father's TV, into the kitchen for a tossed-off meal of ham steak and boxed mac 'n' cheese. Against the standard of her mother—which no one was holding Jane to except herself—she was failing at mealtime mastery. Margery Driskell would have spent the afternoon on something scrumptious and filling, something around which the family could rally. Jane was cutting corners to allow herself a bit of time elsewhere. Alone, preferably, just for a few minutes. A walk, maybe. That would be nice.

"All squared away with Claire?" Eric called to her.

Jane peeked from under the vent hood. "Yes. Thanks again."

Dear Claire

June 6, 2014

I told Jim about Bobby Drury today. I'm near certain I'll never tell you about him, but with Jim, I had to, and I further had to write it down. It's Jim's idea, these continuing letters to you. He asked me once if I might have benefitted from someone—my mother, your grandmother, I guess—writing to me in this way, and I had to concede that I probably would have. So he suggested that I write to you. Even if you never see these notes. Accountability, he called it. I guess it makes sense.

Anyway, on those rarest of occasions when I would entertain the subject of my first time, a conversation that I hope is far in the distance for you and me, I would say that Bobby Drury's intentions that night had been made plain, that I had reached the end of my interest in the abstracts of sex and was ready to have some direct experience in it, and better with Bobby Drury than with some boy for whom I had genuine feelings, when those feelings would surely get crushed by some future disregard. Bobby Drury, on the other hand, could never speak to me again and all would be well.

Besides, there was some history there, some playing doctor in the woods at the end of the street, some summertime spin the bottle, some stolen kisses during games of freeze tag. Once, even, Bobby had taken my pants down in your grandfather's garden shed and tried to get a look at me, and I'd let him, and I'd gone about my life afterward and he'd gone about his, and there had been nothing else said, aside from the fact that I never forgot about it and thus did all the talking, to myself. It's been thirty-two years now, and not a week goes by that the memory doesn't come for me, sometimes directly, sometimes glancing, always there.

This is what people do, of course. They talk about the first time. Someday, you'll have a first time, and you'll talk about it, too. Maybe you'll be getting to know a guy, and you'll be talking to each other about who you are and where you came from and what informed the way you are, and in those delicate negotiations that lead either to bed or to let's-just-call-it-off, you'll talk about your first time. Or you'll have a girlfriend, a neighbor, someone you really like, and you'll talk about surface things and you'll talk about deep things and you'll talk about formative things, and it will come out naturally in the talking. The first time.

When that's happened with me, every time—every single time— I've said, eh, Bobby Drury wasn't that great. Sure, yeah, in retrospect, I should have waited for someone else, but it was Bobby Drury. No biggie. Literally, no biggie, and then we can laugh together, because if I can't reconcile the fullness of the Bobby Drury situation, at least I can make fun of his dick size.

Today, though, it was different, when Jim asked me if I think I've ever been in romantic love, and I said no, and that furthermore, I considered love storybook stuff, and I was beyond storybooks. He expressed surprise first and sorrow immediately after, because love, real love, is such a beautiful human experience, he said.

He wondered how I could have read all the fiction I had to read to get through college and not have seen the blooming possibilities of it.

To which I said, yeah, well, you said it yourself: fiction. I guess, for some people, love comes and stays, and he asks what I meant by that, and I realized I was going to have to go to the beginning if we were ever going to reach the end.

So I told him about Bobby Drury. I told him about a cold February day in my senior year. I told him about Bobby Drury, my neighbor since I was a kid, grown-ass Bobby Drury and his Jeep Wrangler and his six-pack of beer. I told him about the hell of it, that the entire reason I said "sure, let's go" was a big, fat fuck-you to your grandpa, who had been saying for years that Bobby Drury was no good and I should stay away from him, and by then I'd had quite enough of what your grandfather thought or did. I told Jim that nothing made me angrier in those years than knowing your grandfather was right, because he was so wrong so much of the time. I told him I knew the score with Bobby Drury when he was eleven years old and baiting traps for squirrels and setting them on fire. Why did I get in the Jeep and go, knowing what I knew, he asked me, and I said, "I guess I wanted to fuck my dad over so much that I was willing to fuck Bobby Drury to do it." (Gosh, that was hard to write.)

So I told him the rest. How Bobby took the tangle of backroads between the Mid-Cities and Arlington, into a place called Mosier Valley, and how he pulled the Jeep off the road and popped open beers for me and for him, and how it was—you know, it wasn't nice, which would have been giving Bobby Drury far too much credit, but it was calm enough and fun enough, drinking beer and talking about old times and hearing how he was pulling together some money to start a business and telling him that I was figuring on Colby College, or maybe Bates way up in Maine, and that I just had to get through this last semester and I'd be gone. Bobby Drury, against it all, had become, for that moment at least, someone to talk to.

So then I told him the last of it. How Bobby Drury leaned in and kissed me, sloppy and awkward, and I kissed him back because I'd kissed boys before and wasn't averse and it would be another little twist when I got home, that yeah, I went and drank beer with Bobby Drury and I even kissed him, and what do you want to make of it? Because how much fun would it be to make my dad's head come flying off his shoulders, right?

And then I told him how it went from awkward and stupid to threatening and inescapable without any transition in between, how Bobby Drury took what he wanted and how I ended up in the back of the Jeep, tossed there as if I was made of nothing, and of how it hurt and how Bobby Drury rubbed me there with his raw hand, frenzied, and how I closed my eyes and I waited and he finished and he told me how good I was and he took me home and I didn't say anything on the whole, interminable drive and he let me out on the street in front of my house and he said, hey, I'll see you later, Jane.

I told Jim all of this, and he pushed across a box of tissues to me, and I grabbed them and blew my nose and dabbed my eyes and I finally said, well, that's pretty much it.

Jim said he was sorry that had happened to me.

I told him it's a common story. I'm not special.

"But you are," he said. "And it's your story."

I don't know what to make of that.

And here's the hardest part, Claire: I told him how that was the first time with Bobby but not the last, how I went to him—WENT to him—other times and thought, well, since he didn't attack me, we were on more of an even footing, and I asked him how fucked up that was, and Jim's answer was typical of him.

"Pretty fucked up," he said. "Also pretty common. Our feelings and motivations and compulsions are inscrutable, contradictory things. If they weren't, I suppose you and I wouldn't have work to do."

I told him the truth of the matter: Bobby just wasn't very smart, and I preferred him that way. Further, I thought I could manage him, could get the better of him, could keep him from having dominion over me, if I somehow called the shots.

I'm guessing I think much more about him than he ever does about me. But, then, I'm not really thinking of him. I'm thinking of how stupid I've been.

Fourteen

Tim Meyers' house stood as a testament to the value of choosing a career path, getting in good with an employer, and riding through the seasons to a place of prominence and prosperity. It dominated a corner lot in a new subdivision north of where he and Jane had grown up, one that bore a fanciful, ahistoric name (Belvedere Estates) and couldn't be penetrated by anyone with less than a half-million dollars in buying power. It was a monster house—three stories, brick, three-car garage, and not at all unusual in its context. Jane's dad had told her on the drive in, after the tire blowout, that the northern part of the county had filled in like sodden squares of grass in her absence, mostly with mini-mansions, paradise if you could afford it and almost obscene if you could not. Jane could imagine a circumstance where, had she made different choices and not been so in need of rubbing dollars together like kindling, she might have been able to swing such a thing financially. What she wondered now is who in the world would want to clean a house like that.

Of course, she didn't begrudge Tim for the finer things he and his family had been able to accumulate. She had been following him long enough on social media to know that he had hustled and earned his promotions along the way, from third-grade math teacher to teaching high school classes and coaching tennis and paying his dues as an assistant principal at three district schools before getting his own shop at Smithfield Middle. She knew he had taught summer school and driver's ed and had tended to his own ongoing education and raised two kids who were now in college. And certainly, his wife, an administrator at UT Arlington, had put her own shoulder into the plow. Envy, sure, Jane had some of that. But not animus.

What sometimes got to her, when her guard dropped just a bit and she found herself looking back in regret rather than forward with resolution, were the poor choices that had been tangled up with outcomes good and bad, a knotted mess of a life that couldn't be separated out and redirected toward paths not taken. She couldn't bypass Paul without also bypassing Claire, an unthinkable what-if. She couldn't have passed on running off to Montana if it had meant staying in Texas. She couldn't have come back, momentarily beaten but necessarily hopeful, if she weren't intent on something more.

Twenty-five years ago, when she and Tim were seniors at Richland High, they had been on equal footings, with her toes maybe even slightly ahead of his. She was carrying a full-ride offer to Texas Wesleyan, her second choice, and a promise from Bates that if she just got herself there in the fall, some more work-study could be found for her. He was a TCU legacy with grades only just good enough to get him in so he could extend the line of Meyerses passing through its doors and emerging with a mortarboard. Jane had often found it ironic that teaching math had been his way into his career, because he would have never cleared the bar of Algebra II had she not carried him over it back in Mrs. Thompson's class. The retrospective view wasn't a gripe;

it was, simply, a fact. There was nothing owed, and even if there were, Tim had repaid it with the chance he was putting in front of her now.

Jane watched from her car, across the street from the house, as a couple walked hand in hand down the sidewalk, up the walkway gilded with solar lights casting seasonal splashes of color, into the portico, and here came a ringing of the doorbell and an ushering into the New Year's party.

Jane squeezed the steering wheel with both hands, closed her eyes, and opened them again, and she reached for the bottle of wine that had been riding shotgun, then she let herself out and closed the door and locked it. The wine bottle under an arm, she opened her coat and she smoothed her dress and she closed the coat again and drew it up tight. She took the bottle now by the neck and she headed toward the door, and here went nothing.

The names came at Jane in such a rush that she had to concentrate on employing what her father had taught her when she was just a girl, that upon meeting new folks, you slow down and shake their hand deliberately and firmly and you look them in the eye and you repeat their name. "You won't forget them, and they won't forget you," he had said, wisdom he had fortified in all his years of doing a job that ran on the strength of repeat business, underpinned by loyalty and goodwill.

So it was that she repeated Rosalie Lacy—one she had best remember, as Mrs. Lacy was her department head—and Debra Sain and Melinda Brogan and David Bourque and Tina Bingham. Tim, to his great credit, took the initiative in ushering her around and making the introductions first to her English department colleagues and later to the wider sprinkling of teachers and staffers. With each new meeting, Jane tried to tuck away some distinctive memory so she could pull it up again in a couple of days when the interactions would be more formal. Rosalie Lacy had a skin tag on her left eyelid, *L is for lid, L is for Lacy, L is for*

RosaLie. Got it. Debra Sain had a wide-eyed look about her, as if she were permanently astonished, and *insane is the inverse of sane or Sain. Got that, too.* And on it went.

"We're not pinning the tail on the donkey or anything," Tim leaned in and said to Jane as he released her into the group, a hint of Shiner beer on his breath. "Just eating and talking and letting loose a little bit before it all starts again. Have fun."

"Thanks so much," she said.

"It's a good group."

"I can tell."

"Glad you could come."

He swam back toward the kitchen and took a tray from his wife, Gennifer, *Gennifer with a G, that stands for Great, spelling on your own unconventional terms*, and Jane turned for the area where everyone else had found purchase, a massive, step-down bowl of a room subdivided by a two-way fireplace and graced with fine modern furniture. She envied the appointments, not for their tastefulness or price tag but for a more practical reason. Probably not a bit of it required the kind of manual effort she looked forward to once she and Claire had their own four walls and enough clearance in the pocketbook for assemble-it-yourself bookcases from Target.

On the other side of fireplace, Jane got her first good look at the centerpiece visual, attached as it was to the white-brick column shooting up through the middle of the room. She couldn't have missed it coming in—no one blessed with vision could have overlooked it—but Tim had swept her away into the waves of new colleagues and she hadn't had time to really ponder it. It was a massive portrait of the Meyers family, five feet wide, at least, by maybe four feet deep. They were all dressed in white, late summer but not yet Labor Day (oh, *faux pas*), and water shimmered behind them (the Gulf, perhaps?), and they were... perfect. A girl and a boy, fraternal twins, Jane remembered now even as she couldn't dredge up their names, and a husband and a wife, and perfect rows of perfect teeth and perfect smiles that stretched from here to a perfect tomorrow. Jane knew this was a trick of the light or of the photographer's software, that no one venturing outside on some given day for a photo shoot comes to such pleated perfection without a technological assist, and still she mourned for what she didn't have.

Before Claire came along, she and Paul almost never took photos of themselves, even in those first years that were enjoyable, at least relative to the ones that followed. There were no doubt some Polaroids and Kodak prints of them taken by friends at backyard parties and barbecues and on camping trips when those were still an extant occurrence, but they weren't at the ready and certainly had never been turned into murals. Starting from the year 2004 A.C.—*After Claire*—the documentary process picked up, if only because their girl was so photogenic and each new breakthrough in her development was so very precious that it had to be captured. Even those were Jane and the girl or Paul and the girl but only rarely the three of them together, and never had they sat for anything like *this*. Moreover, since she and Paul had detonated a marriage and any common cause that existed outside their daughter, Jane would have little sense of her day-to-day appearance or moments of frustration or whimsy if not for Claire and the ceaseless selfies into which she drew her mother and posted to the Instagram account that Jane continually monitored and kept locked down from the eyes of a world that might sense vulnerability there.

Jane stood, the party swirling around her, and she took it in, and at once came the tidal onrush of what she was into of her own volition and what she would have to do to push it back out to sea, and for the first time since she and Claire had pointed the car south, she wondered if she could even start, let alone finish.

She slipped sideways against the stream, full-effort smiles for the people she was now to call colleagues, and she let herself into the backyard, and the air of the winter evening swept into her nose and mouth and lungs and kept Jane on her feet.

Fifteen

Two little girls and a bunch of toys could make an awful clamor, something Eric had forgotten during the years-long accumulation of silence. It had started well enough, the Brooks kid coming again to the door, dropping off the little one, turning down Eric's offer of a beer, and his kid coming in, bright and bouncy and smiley. She was an awfully cute little girl, Eric had to acknowledge without even having a grudge about it, and Claire had done as she promised, taking control and keeping her full attention on their little visitor.

But the damn noise, those girls scootching around on the living-room floor, the damn doll in the business suit telling the one in the swimsuit this or that or some other thing, that little girl laughing all the time and hitting those high notes that creased his damn eardrums. He couldn't concentrate on the Mavericks game, couldn't hear the resonant voice of the play-by-play guy, couldn't properly appreciate those two kids from overseas who might make this team relevant again.

"Claire, you've gotta move this into the bedroom."

Claire went to a full-on pout. "There's no room."

"Make some room."

"Aw, grandpa, I—"

"This isn't a request. Do it."

"Come on, Annabelle, let's go." They picked up the scattering of toys, two armloads, and they scooted down the hall, but not before Claire hit Eric with a focused glare that got his attention and unnerved him just a little bit, if he were to tell the truth of it. He didn't realize facial expressions could be inherited, but there it was, Jane's staredown from a similar age, pressed into service again by the next generation.

"Thank you," he said.

When Eric heard the slam of the door—that shit was not going to continue, if he had anything to say about it, and he was increasingly doubtful he did—he turned up the sound and lay back in his recliner. He tilted his beer to his mouth and drank deep, then he set the bottle in the chair's cupholder and he wiped the condensation from his hand onto the thigh of his jeans.

He hadn't asked for this, not one bit of it, and he resented the intrusion. Look, when your kid—even if that kid's probably past the halfway point of her own life—calls you up and says, *hey, Dad, I need a place to live for a while*, you must come through. Jane had put it in the form of a request, but the idea that he could have said anything but yes was just damn foolish. And, yeah, OK, there was a part of him that was happy to be needed, but no matter how Eric sliced it up and looked at it, he felt like he was being maneuvered here. She had sure as shit gone away from him and her mother without many lookbacks when it had suited her. *So sue me if I moved on, too*, he now thought. And then, years later, here she is, back, just like that, and she's carrying the leftovers from the mess she's made of her own life *and* a sack full of obligations for him? That's just not right.

Now he heard voices, loud voices, strong enough to penetrate the walls between the girls and him. Loud, high, sing-song voices, louder than before, louder than his game, louder than his head could smother.

"Goddammit."

He folded the recliner up, scrambled out of it all haphazard and awkward, like a turtle on its shell trying to get right-side up. A splash of beer hit the floor in all the jostling. "Goddammit!"

He rambled down the hall, angry, chopping half-steps that he took just to keep him upright, and he grasped the door handle and threw it open to the inside. Astonished, the girls, who stood there in a cleared-out space, clammed up and looked at him, fearful.

"What the hell are you doing?"

The frustration that morphed into anger in his pitched voice, that did it. The little one burst into tears and jammed herself into Claire's side.

"We were singing," Claire said. "We weren't hurting anyone." She looped an arm around Annabelle's head and clutched her. "It's OK," she said.

"You were hurting me. You were hurting my ears. I sent you back here to be goddamn quiet."

Annabelle wailed.

"Shut that girl up," he said.

Annabelle found another, higher key.

"You're an a-hole, Grandpa."

Eric stepped to Claire and grabbed her by the shoulders. He gripped her tight, and she grimaced and then, upon reconciling the force and the anger behind him, she began to cry, and he let her go. Only twice could he recollect giving into the anger that swept him up when Claire sassed him, both targets of his past violence being men, both deserving of it, and now comes this. Claire's mother had stood before him and said some foul things and he had restrained himself. This? This was failure. Everything inside of him sank toward the soles of his feet.

Claire fell back, seated, on the bed, hugging herself and rubbing her shoulders and looking at him, terror-stricken. The moment shut up even Annabelle, who stood there staring at him, her face drawn gaunt by the horror.

It wasn't until he had backed out of the room, closed the door again, found his bearings, gone back into the living room, lightheaded and nauseated, that the wailing started. The two of them, in stereo but out of rhythm. Eric stood in his living room, and it was as if the whole world had splintered without warning.

Sixteen

"Nice, isn't it?"

Jane glanced right, seeing the face of the person she had heard come through the door to the backyard. She had kept facing forward upon being aware she was no longer alone. Her gaze went long, across the covered swimming pool, to the curvature of the poured sidewalks and the photinia hedges that would be a weekly chore for whoever drew the duty come spring and summer. Now, she connected the face and the name from earlier—*David Bourque, nice hair, like David Bowie, D.B., David Bourque, got it*—and she smiled and appreciated that he had taken his time in approaching. As ever was the case, casting eyes beyond herself had settled Jane.

"I was just thinking the same," she said.

"I'm David," he said, extending a hand. She shook it.

"I know. We met in there." She nodded toward the door.

"Yeah, but you met *everybody* in there. It's a lot to take in all at once."

"Sure. But I remember."

"OK, good."

He drew a deep breath and let it go, the expulsion turning into a light mist as it hit the air on the last night of December. She could see that he was attempting to follow her gaze, to perhaps alight upon whatever had drawn her attention. *Good luck with that, buddy. It's far beyond this subdivision.*

"It's cold," he said, rubbing his hands together. "Aren't you cold?"

She gave him a side-eyed, amused smirk. "It's not so bad."

"Oh, that's right. You're from, like, the snowy plains or something, aren't you?"

"Montana."

"Ah."

"But I'm from here," she said.

That turned him a full ninety degrees. "You don't say."

"Yep. Went to our school." It sounded strange to invoke the possessive personal pronoun in that way. "It was called Smithfield Junior then."

"It's a homecoming," he said, tossing his hands skyward, and the playful lilt of his words juxtaposed themselves against the anxiety she had only just settled down. Jane felt exposed, then felt silly for feeling that way.

"I guess."

"Well," he said, "I'm cold, anyway." He turned back toward the door and pointed. "But there's a heat lamp over there and, of all the luck, an outlet we could plug it into. Would you like to sit down?"

Jane regarded him, taken with his vocal flourishes. "Sure. That would be fine."

He fairly pranced toward the house, scooping up the power cord to the lamp and plugging it in, then looking to the energized tower and saying, "Let there be heat," and Jane failed to stifle a giggle as he bounded next to a wicker chair and drew it back from a round glass table and invited her to sit. She did.

"Now," he said, "do you need a drink? I shall fetch it."

"OK," she said. "I brought a bottle of red wine, if you can find that."

"Find it, I shall," he said. "May I imbibe with you?"

"Of course."

And he was jauntily off, back into the house, and Jane was alone and a bit bewildered by the frenzy. Such an odd fellow. She was hesitant to guess at his age, which could be a perilous and pointless exercise. She had often been told, by new friends and by colleagues, that her appearance tacked younger than her years, but she wondered whether that was true now even if it had been then. Certainly, she felt every one of the forty-three years that had been stacked upon her. Anyway, those assessments were external, not internal, and whatever advantages she had over time in the latter were unable to offset the former. Extended mirror time was a luxury she didn't often have, and even so, how she regarded her own face was entirely transient, defined by the vagaries of a given moment more than by her base complexion. These past couple of years had carried more than their share of sunken days and cried-out nights, and the image of her that stared back had often reflected them.

Whether this David was twenty-five (maybe) or forty-five (highly unlikely), she didn't need a number to assign a motive to him. He was flirting with her, which she could endure so long as it stayed in bounds. Or he was showing off. Or, maybe, he really was just one of those delightfully off-kilter people whom she envied but didn't quite understand.

He returned to her, a goblet of wine in his left hand, and he set it down for her. His other hand gripped a mug with two dogged fingers. His nails were unbitten, a mild surprise.

"These jackals have consumed your vino," he said. "I got the last splashes of it."

"That's fine."

"You'll get them back," he said. "Tim will have another party next year, and you'll steal a bottle then."

"I will *not.*" *God, he is funny.*

"*I* will steal a bottle then, and I will deliver it to you in a place to be named later, under the cover of night, and I shall say, 'We must never speak of this,' and then we will rejoice at the plunder."

She simply looked at him, her face a wonderment, her mind silently racing. *Who is this?*

And now a more moderated tone came from him, along with a slightly embarrassed grin, and he sat down and said, "A little over the top, huh?"

"Just a bit."

"Sorry," he said, and he leaned back and patted his abdomen. "I've had a bit much." He leaned forward again and grasped the coffee cup. "The java will do me good. Sorry if I overwhelmed."

"You didn't," she said. "It's OK."

"So...Montana to Texas. That must be a story, huh?"

"It's several stories."

"I'll bet," he said. "But don't tell them all at once. A lot of year left. A lot of hot-plate lunches in the lounge."

That drew a smile from her.

"So you were teaching up there?" he asked.

Here we go. "A while ago," she said. "I took some a break from it when my daughter was born."

"How old is she?"

"Eleven."

He whistled. "Long break."

Jane felt her jaw clench, and she curled angry fingers around her glass. "I did what I had to do."

"I've no doubt," he said. "Glad you're here. We need you. Kathy—your predecessor—she was the glue of the English department. Not to put any pressure on you or anything."

"None inferred." Jane felt herself slowly release.

"Well, if you need anything, I'm happy to help," he said.

"I appreciate that. I'm sure I'll take you up on it."

"Good. My classroom is right next door to yours."

"Well," she said, "here's to the spring semester, neighbor." She clinked her glass against his mug.

"May the weeks peel off quickly, may the tests all be aced, may every parent-teacher conference be rosy, and may summer vacation never end," he said. "I'll drink to that." The mug rose to his lips, and he took in a mouthful, then spat part of it back into the rest. "I'll drink to that *slowly*. Good god, that's hot."

Jane, amused again, sipped her wine.

"So, tell me, Miss Montana—"

"Please," she said. "Don't call me that."

"I meant no offense."

"I'm sure."

He shook it off and tried again. "So, tell me: What's your jam in teaching English?"

"My?"

"Jam. Bag. What lights your fuse, what gets your toes to tapping, what do you dig about teaching these little hooligans?"

"Wow."

"I mean that only in the finest way," he corrected. "Hooligans, of the stately north Texas hooligans, of course. These fine children. The future of our world. The kids."

"I follow."

"So, what is it?"

"Literature. Reading."

"Victorian? Modern? British?"

"Whatever is on the curriculum," she said.

"Ah, very diplomatic. Tim will *love* that you said that."

"No, I'm serious," she said. "Certainly, it's easier and more enjoyable to read what we like, but lifelong reading and learning is built on not just enjoyment but also challenging ideas and challenging books, right? So the point, to my mind, is to help light that habit. When I see a kid tumble into books and want to stay there, best feeling in the world."

He nodded and smiled. "A wonderful answer," he said.

"Seriously. Please forgive my rampant silliness and cynicism."

"Nothing to forgive." She shrugged. "We all have our moments. What about you, Mr. Bourque? Yours is dramatics, I assume."

"Call me David."

"I won't be calling you that the day after tomorrow."

"Touché."

"What about yours?" she pressed.

"Grammar," he said.

"Seriously?"

"Oh, yes," he said. "Sentence structure, the road signs of punctuation, the clarity and precision of careful language. Give me a passel of sentences to diagram and I'm in heaven."

"Wow," she said. "I mean...just, wow. I don't believe I've ever heard anyone say that."

"It's true. Of course, fat lot of good it does me when we don't teach it anymore, much to our—"

She set down her glass. "We don't teach grammar?"

"Not like we used to," he said. "Used to be, the eighth-grade year was full-on grammar, start to finish. Which, when you think about it, is all most people need to get through the world, right? Subject, verb, object, preposition, maybe enough knowledge to avoid a dangling participle when they write something formal, if they ever do anymore. The building blocks, that's what I'm saying. It's not like we need to churn out a bunch of people who know what a cognate object is."

"Right," she said. She had no idea what a cognate object was, but she was determined, later, to look it up.

"I mean," he said, "those people are *really* boring at parties."

She snorted. "You talk about it like it's some woebegone artifact of your long-ago career," she said. "I mean, I don't know how old you are, but—"

"Twenty-eight."

God, she thought. *God, what am I doing here?* "Sorry," she picked up. "I wasn't fishing."

"How old are you?"

"Older than twenty-eight."

"Right," he said. "Say no more. No, you're right, I'm playing the old fuddy-duddy, for sure. The truth is, I didn't get that eighth-grade year of nonstop grammar, either. I had sort of what I'd call an intuitive sense of language, and I back-constructed my education on my own time, then took a deeper dive in college. Rosalie Lacy showed me some of her old lesson plans from back in the day, because she knew how nutty I was for grammar, and I was astounded. It almost made me want to be alive in 1985."

What am *I doing here*, Jane thought again.

"What's your degree in, if you don't mind my asking?" he asked.

"English education and applied mathematics. I was a double major."

"Oooh," he said. "Ambitious. How the hell do those two things go together?"

"Badly."

"Huh?"

"Never mind," she said.

"Well," he said, "you're more ambitious than I am, anyway. Mine's in linguistics. Linguistics! I can teach kids language arts or I can be the hamburger jockey with the most fulsome vocabulary. How about that? I chose summers off."

Jane hadn't quite formulated a response to that, one that could nestle into the unthreatening in-between of *this has been a lovely chat* and *gosh, I hope we become great friends*, when he stood up and said, "We should go back inside, yes? This shouldn't become a great scandal, where Rosalie is sitting in there and watching us and wondering if I'm drawing you into my grand plan for departmental sabotage."

"You have a plan?"

"No," he said. "But things are livelier around the ol' schoolhouse if she thinks I do."

Seventeen

The surreptitious pathway, not trod by Eric since he was a younger man, had remained true even as the years had multiplied. After slipping into his own backyard by way of the side gate, he picked his way down his north fenceline, between his own row of mature hedges and the matching one Scottie Roberson had planted on the other side of the chain link. The dueling foliage had been the two men's mutual raised middle finger, one to the other, and had, in quite the unplanned way, become something for which Eric was thankful. In another time, he would walk the fence between the houses unseen both to Scottie and to his own family, and he would reach the corner post, clamber up and over, and cut behind the Mitchells' long garden shed, still shrouded on the other side by Scottie's hedgerow, until he reached the opposite corner. Up and over again, and he was in the alleyway. And in the clear.

So that's what he did now, with the deepening darkness offering even more cover, and the only variables he hadn't accounted for were the intrusions of old age. Scaling the corner post was a much more fraught proposition at seventy-five than it had been at fifty, and as he went over, the tongue of one of Eric's new shoes snagged the loop of the chain link at the top, and he busted ass down the other side, arresting his fall with calloused hands while the bottom half of him flopped onto the hardened dirt.

"Son of a bitch."

He drew himself up to one knee and then, slowly, onto his two feet. As he pushed up, the little finger on his right hand screamed with pain, and he put his lips around the end of the digit and he sucked on it, and the copper taste swam through his mouth.

He knelt now and made sure his shoes were still tied, and he fingered the torn tongue on the left shoe. "Shit. You're so stupid." He rose again.

Now, he threw a hand skyward, at the end of it his actual middle finger, upwind of the Roberson place, the required salute on past traverses. Scottie Roberson, of course, was no longer there to receive it, having gone to heaven or, more likely, the other place three years back after a one-sided tussle with ass cancer. Eric didn't much believe in what some folks called karma, but cancer of the ass—the very personification of Scottie Roberson—seemed poetic, at the least. Evaline was still there, though, and Eric had no quarrel with her. He brought the hand down and sheathed it in a pocket, sheepish that he'd done such a thing, and he headed for the opposite corner post and, he hoped, a graceful crossing of that boundary line.

Once the alleyway brought Eric two blocks east, past Crabtree Lane and onto Lowery, one last bit of skulking was in order. The house sat in the middle of the row, enclosed not by chain link but by eight-foot knotty pine, an unusual extravagance for the neighborhood. Eric jiggled the black handle, same as he'd done so many times, and the latch released and the gate swung outward toward him. He looked the alleyway up and down, satisfied he was alone, and he slipped inside, closing the gate behind him. Now, at last, he could walk upright and unguarded, along the stepstones to the crushed-gravel walkway ringing the swimming pool. He skirted right, around the diving board and the launching pad for infinite Ed Blankenship cannonballs, then went under the roof of the veranda, running a finger along the barbecue grill. The light beams from the house flared out through the windows, and he stepped softly as he neared them. She used to know he would be coming, but that was then.

Jocelyn sat in an overstuffed chair, facing the big window but unaware of who lurked outside it. She cradled a book, and reading glasses rested at the end of her nose. The house, from what he could see, looked as it had when last he had been there, at least in physical dimension. Other things had changed, though. New splashes of paint on the walls. Different furniture. A bookcase moved from here to there. Time, it doesn't stand still for anybody.

Eric sucked deep of the night air and expelled it, and he waggled his fingers and steeled himself for what all at once loomed as some task requiring great courage rather than just the momentary impulse that had sent him out of the house and down here.

He set his knuckles against the glass and held them there for a beat, and then, in a burst of nerve, he drew them back and rapped the window.

Startled, she dropped the book to her lap and looked in his direction, and he raised a meek hand and waved.

"What in the world?" she said, and he could hear the words and wished he could give an answer that would suffice. She came up out of the chair and walked toward him, and he stood up to his full height. "Eric?" she asked, and he nodded, and she motioned that he should meet her at the door.

"What in the world?" she said again once she had opened up and they were face to face, and no good answer had come to him in the interim.

"I did something stupid," he said, and he brought both hands to his face in the astonishment of the moment.

"And you've bloodied yourself in the doing," she said. "Hold tight."

Now in the light, Eric inspected the wound while Jocelyn dashed off into the kitchen for something to stanch the flow. It wasn't horrific, a cut at the cuticle that had nicked him just so and unleashed side channels of blood down his forearm and, no doubt, along the pathway, the alley, the Mitchells' backyard, and so on—the point being that Eric would have never gotten away with anything a forensics department could pin on him.

She returned with a wad of paper towels. "Here, wrap these around it and come in."

She led him through the living room and down the hallway, into a half-bath.

"I'm awfully sorry about this," he said.

"Just sit down there on the pot and let me look at it," she said.

He did as he was told, stretching the finger toward her.

"It's not too deep," she said.

"No. Just looks like a horror show."

"Band-Aid ought to do it," she said.

"I think so."

"Here, put it under the faucet." He leaned toward her, and she turned on the spigot and dangled her fingers under the current until it was warm, then she ran the flow on the wound, the blood going to pink as the water diluted it. "Now," she said, "hold it up and squeeze the paper towel around it." Eric followed her instructions.

She reached into the medicine cabinet and pulled down a box, then extracted the right bandage for the job. With precise fingers, she peeled back the waxy paper and exposed the adhesive, then she readied for application.

"OK, let me have it."

"OK, after this."

"Eric, behave."

He stretched the finger across to her, and she had the bandage in place before the blood could well up and spill again.

"Thank you," he said.

Eric sat opposite her on a two-seater couch, squeezing the injured finger inside a fist made from the other hand. She regarded him, and he her, and he took note now of just how the years had played on her, putting crinkles where once there had been none, washing the last of the dirty blonde from her hair on its journey to full gray, turning her stature a bit more slight, something he had noticed a few days earlier as he held her in remembrance. She was older, frailer, and still alight in the eyes, looking as intently at him as he must have been at her. *God only knows the differences she sees in me.*

"So what'd you do?" she asked him, and given time to clear his head and mend his wounds, Eric realized his answer would sound no better delivered with equanimity than it would have had he spilled it frantically upon his arrival.

"I'm a bad grandpa," he said.

"I doubt that."

"I grabbed her. I was going to shake the sass right out of her. I was so mad."

Jocelyn looked stricken—on behalf of Claire or for him, Eric couldn't be sure. "Oh, no."

"She mouthed off, and I lost control."

"Oh, no."

"I never, ever raised a hand to her mother. Wanted to. Almost got there a few times, truthfully. Never did."

"Jane could push some buttons, as I recollect," Jocelyn said.

"Point is, she never got to me. This one did. Faster than I could think it through and stop myself."

"What'd Jane say when it happened?"

It was then that Eric realized he had walked into a patch of weeds much more tangled than just the split-second decision to come to Jocelyn, to lean on her as if he hadn't spent a quarter-century strenuously keeping his distance. There were family dynamics as charged as they ever were, if also entirely recast. There was the inexplicability of current circumstances, the way Eric was calcifying in retirement and struggling with the basic stuff: what to get up and do, what to be interested in, whether any of it made much difference anymore, simple things like steps and sentences and grocery lists now tentative, unreliable, sometimes entirely botched. And there was also the plainest fact of all, that he had been thinking of her for days and wondering if he could, or should, act on those thoughts. Now, with the chance to spring them loose, he took a pass.

"She doesn't know," he said. "Yet."

"Ah."

"I better get back."

"I understand."

He showed her his bandaged finger. "Thank you for this."

"Any time," she said, then she laughed. "Just don't take me up on that, please. Let's limit the injuries."

"I wouldn't."

"I know."

He pushed himself up and headed for the back door, and she said, "Eric?"

"Yeah?"

"You can go out the front."

"OK," he said.

"Nobody who'd care is still around to see it."

That brought a laugh from him, one a bit on the rueful side, and laughter felt a damn sight better than what had been churning through his guts.

"Come on," she said, and she led him to the front door and opened it. The porch light sprayed onto the lawn, illuminating a path to the street.

"Thanks for patching me up," he said. "Sorry to be a bother."

"You weren't."

"I'm glad."

She reached for him, straightening his collar. "Come by for coffee sometime?"

"You know," he said, "I might."

"Good night, Eric."

"Good night. Happy year new, I guess."

"Year new?"

He shook his head, as if to clear cobwebs. "New year."

"Happy new year to you."

He left even as he preferred to linger, finding his footing on the asphalt and listening to the gravel crunch under the soles of his shoes. Cars jammed the street, filling the spaces between driveways on both sides, and Christmas lights twinkled, and front windows lit up. Parties were in swing behind those closed doors, and Eric tried to remember the last time he had been to one. He came up empty on that pondering. The turn of a new year—any new year—didn't hold much interest for him anymore aside from the relief, and occasional horror, of continuing to find himself on the fresh side of the dirt. Better to plow those feelings at home, with a beer and in a comfortable chair, so he didn't have far to travel when he roused himself and headed off to sleep.

At the end of the street, he turned right, the overhead streetlamp casting him in a long, monstrous shadow, and he sucked in a lungful of sustaining air. The night smelled of memory, not just on this corner but also with every step. Here, though, is where the past often caught him unaware, if he didn't take the time to gird himself for its intrusion. He walked straight into it now, last Tuesday of July, 1977, and he's coming home this way after turning off Davis Boulevard, and he's behind Matty Roberson, who's on that Honda motorcycle that was always kicking up a fuss outside and waking little Jane in her bassinet, and he's drumming his fingers on the steering wheel, *come on, come on, let's go, Matt,* and here comes the city garbage truck on its rounds, making that looping turn toward them, and off comes the front tire, the lugnuts popping outward, and the truck tumps into an uncontrolled swerve, right at Matty, right at Eric, and it's all done in a sickening second, unavoidable. Matty, rended and gone, no chance at all. Eric, thrown against his own door in a sideways skid, his shoulder shredded by glass, an injury that ends up being the least of anyone's worries given the pieces of Matty Roberson scattered in the street.

What does anyone do with that? Eric Driskell swallowed it and kept living—what else is there?—and kept remembering, because how could he forget? Scottie and Evaline Roberson buried their firstborn boy and kept grimly to themselves, same as they had before, and quietly collected the casseroles that were left on their front porch and grinded through the grief, and eventually got back to the ceaseless task of pulling themselves and their other two boys through their days. For all these years, Eric wondered what he could have said, what gesture he might have made to ease the Robersons' suffering, and there was none. He couldn't even tell them anything illuminating about Matty's last moment of being gloriously alive, his feathered hair thrown back by the breeze, then all of him gone in a blink. The only truth of the matter is that Eric had resented the boy's presence in front of him, in no small part because he found the father to be such a relentless bastard, as if that were a reason for such inextinguishable heartache to be visited upon a family. The rest of it was just the cruel vagaries of circumstance. Thank God for Margery, who had both the delicate touch and the unerring manner to let the Robersons know they were in the Driskells' prayers.

Eric breathed in again through his nose, the crispness of night filling him, the smell of burning oil and blood and sweat coming back to him, and he lit out now, as if shot through with youth, his ponderous legs carrying him as far from the past as he could get and back into the treacherous present.

Eighteen

Back inside, Jane and David parted ways upon his declaration that he would stand sentry at the *hors d'oeuvres*—"bacon-wrapped jalapeños, I love those bad boys"—until it was time to go home. Others among the gathering had already taken a notion for the door and had cleared out, leaving the party well diminished by a quarter after nine.

"Not a midnight crew, I guess," Jane said to Melinda Brogan, who laughed and replied, "Not on our circadian rhythms."

"I should be getting home, too," Jane said. "My daughter's first night as a babysitter. I don't want to push my luck, or hers."

"How old is she?"

"Claire is eleven."

"Sixth-grader?"

"She is, yes."

"Well," Melinda said, "I will be on the lookout for Miss Claire."

Jane smiled tightly and said her goodbyes, then went to the kitchen to thank the hosts.

"Home already?" Tim asked.

"Restless father," she said. "Daughter who's had a bit too much latitude on bedtime this month."

"We'll walk you out."

Outside, down the lighted pathway and to the car, Jane had a perspective on the neighborhood she hadn't grasped coming in, fixated as she was on finding the right street number and calming her restless nerves. Every house on the block, all in equal grandeur to Tim's home, twinkled with seasonal lights that cast the night air in a dreamy hue. The effect was to bring forth, quite unexpectedly, sentimentality from Jane, who didn't often allow herself the indulgence. She thought of the street full of luminarias in Billings, the endless orange lights such a delight to Claire, and she thought of the season they were now turning from and how she had foregone the usual holiday trappings and had just tried to keep each day of packing and travel and settling from running off into a ditch. She thought of her daughter and how she had borne it without too much complaint, and she thought of how much she wished she could promise Claire something better was coming. She thought of how she dared not do it, in case she turned out to be wrong about that, too.

"You made friends with one of your colleagues, I see," Tim said. Coatless, he leaned into his wife for warmth.

"Who's that?"

"David Bourque."

"Ah, yeah. Interesting guy."

"He is, at that," Tim said.

"We just struck up a conversation. I meant to mingle a bit more."

"Well," he said, "you'll have plenty of time. Starting in about..." He held his watch aloft and engaged the interior light of it. "... Gosh, thirty-three hours. It does come up fast, doesn't it?"

"It does. Thank you again. For tonight and for the opportunity."

"You're welcome, Jane. Glad you're here."

"Good night, Jane," Gennifer said. "So happy to have met you."

"Good night."

Jane folded herself into the car and started it, and she waved as she drove away. Once free of the housing development, back on a road she knew well even amid all the transformations of time and tide, headed for her old neighborhood where at least she had the tracks of memory if not the attendant comfort, she breathed fully again and her mind lit up with possibility rather than dread. It had been a big step, the whole evening of meeting strangers who were supposed to become close-knit colleagues. Bigger leaps yet to come if this was all going to flow her way. It might. It might not. We'll see, said the Zen master.

Jane's phone pinged. She retrieved it from the cupholder.

Come home. Annabelle got hurt.

Jane mashed the accelerator.

The phone pinged again. She looked at it. *And grandpa is an a-hole.*

Nineteen

Jane dabbed the little girl's head with a cloth, soaking up less blood than before, and she got her first good look at the weeping wound.

"Is she OK?" Claire asked.

"It doesn't look deep," Jane said. She looked into Annabelle's sorrowful eyes. "Scared you, though, I bet."

"Hurt," the girl said. "Blood."

"I know, sweetheart."

"I'm sorry, Mom," Claire said.

"I know you are."

Claire's mournful regrets were the least of Jane's concerns. *Where the hell is he*, she wondered. Getting the straight story from the girls had been easy enough, after she had run breathless into the house, after she had called her father and he hadn't answered, after she had assumed the worst, after the girls had gathered around her, crying, Claire holding one of the good hand towels, now blanched with blood. They had turned on the light in the garage and tumbled into it for a game of hide-and-seek, the long-awaited delivery of their household goods having created an ideal venue for their shenanigans. Claire, upon finding where Annabelle had tucked herself away, had given chase, Annabelle had run and tripped, and her head had met with the marbled corner of their living-room table, and there you go. Pain. Blood. Frantic texting.

"I didn't mean for it to happen," Claire said.

"I know you didn't."

Jane uncapped a bottle of hydrogen peroxide and flooded a gauze square with it.

"You're going to be good as new in a few days," she told Annabelle. "Now, I need you to be a brave girl, OK?"

"OK."

"It's going to sting just a little."

Annabelle shut her eyes. "OK."

Jane touched the wound with the gauze, and Annabelle said "owwwwee," and she clung to Jane's free arm, and she cried, and Claire began to cry, and Jane wanted to cry. Along the fault line of broken and jagged skin, the medicine bubbled angrily, then dissipated. Jane dropped the gauze into the trash can and embraced the little girl sitting on the closed lid of the commode.

"Still hurt?" she whispered.

"A little," Annabelle said.

"It'll pass. Just keep being brave."

"I will."

When it was done, when Annabelle's tears had been cleared, Jane sent the girls off to Claire's room—"no rough-housing, please, and don't let her fall asleep"—while she commandeered Eric's recliner and rocked it steadily in controlled fury and waited on men, a position to which she had become accustomed and hostile. Claire hadn't been entirely forthcoming about the whereabouts of her grandfather—"He just left," she had said— but there had been intimations of more to say after Annabelle's pressing needs were met. The clue hadn't just been the *grandpa's an a-hole* text but also Claire's renewal of "I hate it here" upon Jane's arrival. She knew the score because Jane had made it clear, that they would be staying only as long as they needed and not one day longer than that. It wasn't like Claire to keep landing on this negative declaration when there was nothing to say to it except "I know, but just be patient."

So who would it be first, her father or Annabelle's father, he of the *what the hell happened?* text when Jane had pinged him and said, *hey, you better get home because Annabelle hurt herself.*

She'll be fine. She banged her head. I'm sorry.

How'd she do that?

She's a kid. Kids get rambunctious sometimes.

Shit. K. I'll be right there.

Sorry.

A whole batch of lessons were coming Claire's way tonight. How things can go from simple to screwed up without any in-between. Potentially, the implacable anger of a parent whose kid was hurt—which is why Chuck Brooks would meet Jane, not his babysitter, first off. The opportunity cost of work that goes sideways. Claire's first job would be a freebie.

Jane kept rocking in short, furious sweeps.

Who wants to go first?

Dear Claire

July 3, 2014

Today, Jim said he wants to talk about infidelity. This is a hard one. And I was all smartass about it, because it's so hard, and I said that's just a dandy idea, so long as the two of us will eventually get to the other consumptive sins, because I have some profound thoughts on gluttony now that I'm using SNAP benefits at the grocery store and trying to stand there and get through it with my dignity intact as the fellow shoppers in the queue stare me down.

So he pushed on: "What are your thoughts on infidelity?"

"On the actual act—or, in my experience, the ongoing acts? Or on the infidels themselves."

"Wherever you care to go."

So I told him: Assholes. Liars. Cheats. Cowards. And other words I could come up with, but you get the drift.

"Harsh, isn't it?" he asked.

No, I said. Justified.

He leaned back and regarded me with bemusement, which he often does, and that's a tendency that irritates me to no end.

I won't get it exactly, but he said something like this: "I tend to frame human frailty in less strident language. You've heard of black-and-white, right? I see a lot of gray in those areas. But what I think is of little importance here. I want to know what you think."

I told him my framing is informed by experience, not philosophy.

So he said "let's go deeper," and I've learned that this is a prelude not only to whatever direction this conversation will go but also to the reading and writing assignments he'll send me home to ponder until I see him again next week. He'll have me reading poems or dense sociological texts, he'll have me keeping a journal of my thoughts, and he'll load me up with this work along with a disclaimer: "I can't make you do this, Jane. You're not earning a grade here. You don't pass or fail. But I know it works if you work it."

So I've been going home and putting forth an earnest effort, because I'm certain of what I said about never screwing up like this again, even if I'm uncertain of everything else. I read the poems. I write. I pour it out. I cry at night after you're asleep and again in the morning before you awake, and then I get on with it in between the two.

It breaks trust, I told him today. And it's broken forever.

So he says: "What if I told you that I know literally dozens of people who've repaired that broken trust?"

Simple, I said. He knows better people than I do.

"But I don't."

"Agree to disagree."

But here's the thing, Claire: My mind settled on a memory, the high-def kind, the kind that could have happened yesterday, so vivid and crisp are the edges of it. The day I figured it out. The day I told my dad what I knew. The day I said I'd never forget this awfulness but that I wasn't going to make anyone else carry it, that I would bear the load alone and wordlessly. Just one condition, I told him: "It ends today."

A lot ended that day, as it turns out.

And Jim said, you've left me again, Jane. Where did you go? What are you thinking?

I told him I was trying to remember if I left my purse at work.

Twenty

"Well, shit," Eric said aloud as the driveway, and Jane's car occupying it, came into view. The short-burst run had carried him to the bottom of the hill, his energy spent, leaving him to make the slow climb up to the house with the idea that he could come back home, make his apologies, send across some sort of entreaty to Claire that would keep private what had happened between them, catch his breath, and settle in. Damn, maybe even see if the Mavericks could sew this thing up. Happy New Year.

Well, it'll have to be another plan. On the porch, he leaned against the brick of the entryway and formulated a defense of the indefensible, on several fronts: what he'd done to Claire, being gone, his overall handling of something he specifically, explicitly did not want to do. What he was left with, he decided, was less a solid defense than a spackling job to haphazardly cover his mistakes.

He opened the door and stepped through, right into the perimeter of his daughter.

"Where the hell have you been?"

"I—"

"*Where?*"

She was into his physical space now, as close as a baseball manager gone stratospheric over balls and strikes gets to an umpire, and with a grievance infinitely heavier. Twin impulses fired through his synapses, each entirely inadvisable. He could push her off and deal with the escalation that was sure to follow that bit of physicality, or he could turn and run and deal with the almost immediate dead end of that. He backed up a step.

"Jane, I was just—"

"You were just where?"

"I was just—"

"He left," came Claire's voice, turning them both toward her. "After he hit me."

"I didn't hit you," Eric said.

"You grabbed me. You bruised me."

"Claire, go sit with Annabelle. Her daddy will be here soon." The girl lingered, darting looks toward both of them. "Go, Claire," Jane said. "Please."

She left. Jane turned to her father again.

"You *hit* her?"

"I grabbed her arms. I'm not proud of it. But that kid's got a mouth on her."

"*Grabbed* her? What the fuck is that?"

"You know," Eric said, and he mimicked how he'd taken the girl by the arms. "I didn't hit her."

"I can't believe it," Jane said.

"It didn't hurt."

"She said she's bruised."

"Her feelings, maybe. It didn't hurt."

He backed up again, nearly to the door, as Jane closed the distance. The entirety of her twitched in fury.

"You are in *no position* to say what hurts or doesn't hurt."

"Jane—"

She slapped him. Right hand, left cheek, quicker than the lights go out after the switch is thrown. His own hand came to his jaw after hers. His ears rang. The tingle radiated out from his face, hot.

"Did that hurt?" she asked.

He opened his mouth as if to speak, expelling only silence. She slapped him again. Left hand, right cheek. Same effect, with a multiplier.

"How about that?"

Eric grabbed his daughter by the wrists, and he found nothing substantial there anymore, the rage she let loose having expended her. He held her tight and pushed toward the living room.

"Let go," she said.

"I will. Just shut up for a second."

Through the living room, into the dining room, he planted her into a chair and took the one opposite her. "We're going to talk."

"There's nothing to say," she said.

"Maybe not. We're going to do it anyway."

He tried to pull the notions scurrying away from him into a singular line of thought. The steady, even tone he had somehow conjured at least had the effect of keeping her there, seated in front of him, boiling. She looked like she would just as soon kill him as listen, and he wasn't inclined to say she was wrong for feeling that way.

"What?" she asked.

"I messed up. Tonight, I really messed up."

"You sure as hell did."

"But I told you," he said. "I told you I didn't want to do this, and you pushed it, and I lost my temper, and I messed up. Big-time, I messed up."

Jane shook her head, incredulous and mournful. "Don't put this on me. You *hurt* her."

"I messed up."

"You *left* her."

"Jane, I messed up."

"Annabelle fell and hit her head, and you were gone."

"What?" Eric didn't think his stomach could plunge deeper, but there it went.

"Claire texts me and is all *Annabelle's hurt* and I'm trying to get you on the phone and you're not picking up and—"

Eric launched into the self-recriminations. *Because the phone was here and you were off tiptoeing through the past, you moron.*

"Is she OK?"

"She'll live," Jane said.

"Jesus, Jane, don't be flip."

"She has a small cut on her head. Chuck's coming to get her. I hope he wasn't a good friend, because that's probably over."

"I'm sorry."

"You should be."

"I am."

Silence moved in. Eric sat and regarded his daughter, who seemed to be strapping on the weight of what she had done in her own loss of control. She sat slumped and alone with it. He knew the feeling. If he could haggle out some trade that got him the past ninety minutes or so back and let him make some different decisions, he would pony up and give it a go. What an awful night it had turned out to be, all the way around, and he couldn't tap into any hope that a better tomorrow might be coming, though a long life had taught him that those polar opposites had a way of peeling off consecutively.

"I will make it up to Claire," he said. "I promise."

"Your promises are for shit."

"I will try," he said.

"What if you can't? Her decision, you know. You blew it."

"Then I can't. And, yeah, I did. You want to keep arguing about it? You're right."

She looked at him, nodded, then dropped her head and considered her clenched hands.

"Can I make it up to you?" he asked, and that brought her attentions again, her eyes wide and glassy.

"Can we make it up to each other?" she asked. "Did I hurt you?"

"Not where it's going to show. Can we?"

"I don't know," she said.

"Jane—"

"Dad," she said, cutting him off, "I'm stuck. This has to work, because there's nothing else."

"I know."

"And it kills me to say that, to acknowledge it, to be vulnerable to you, because I can't trust you with it."

"I know."

He reached for her hands, and she pulled them away, and he retracted his venture.

The sound of knuckles against the door came to them.

"That'll be Chuck," Jane said, and she rose, and she set a hand on his fallen shoulder, and he brought his own up to cover hers, and she pulled away from him.

"Claire," she called out, leaving him. "Annabelle's dad is here."

JANUARY

Hey, gurrrrrrrrrrl...

January 1, 2016

Happy New Year to you and Claire. I meant to write on Christmas, but you know, I'd just seen you and, besides, I figured you'd need some time to get yourself settled and stuff. I hope that's all done, because tomorrow's the big day, right? BACK TO SCHOOL, baby!

It was a Christmas miracle here in Kansas, let me tell you. Sabrina's dad—god, Jane, have I ever told you his name? Bert. For real. Like Bert and Ernie, only his name is actually Norbert, which I was dying to call him at the end just to piss him off but didn't because I am a kind person, sometimes. Anyway. Yeah. Norbert. Bert. Because if you're named Norbert, I have two questions:

1. How much do your parents hate you?

2. What else are you gonna go by but Bert?

Anyway, BERT called me on Christmas Eve, a few hours after you left, and he had just cleared customs in New York—he's in the

the U.S. government (USDA is the agency) working in Africa; I mean, surely I've told you that, only I don't remember because the Long Island iced teas at that place we used to go to downtown were SO GOOD and I want them again—and he was, like, hey, I'd like to fly down to Wichita and see Sabrina, and I was all, hey, you should before she forgets what you look like, you know? So he flew down, got a room at the Holiday Inn, and he spent Christmas here. And, news flash, it was nice. He brought some gifts, told some stories, talked with his daughter. It was just a nice, nice surprise.

Of course, he left the next morning. Had to go back to Billings to check on his house, then back to Africa. So who knows when she'll see him again.

So...how are you? How is Claire? What's it like there? Give me the 411, lady. Have you met anybody yet? Don't give me that Jane I-don't-need-to-meet-anyone thing. Everybody needs to have some fun once in a while. Even you. And especially me.

Slim pickings here. I went to a party thrown by some work friends last night. Sabrina spent the night with a friend, so I was FREE. Got shitfaced. Came home alone. Paying for it now. WORTH IT. So fun. Just not fun enough, you hear me?

Good luck tomorrow. I'll be back in Data Aggregation Land, which shares a border with Not This Shit Again Land and is as far away as it can possibly be from Teryn Gets Pampered and Laid on the Regular Land. God, I so want to believe that's a real place.

Love you bunches.

Teryn

Twenty-one

Jane considered the flourish of the "g" in *Ms. Sperling* on her dry-erase board and found it pleasing, certainly a far better hand script than she had ever been able to manage during those long-ago days with chalk on a blackboard. There had been a fleeting moment in the main office, as she checked in, when she wished she had fallen back to *Miss Driskell*, a surname she hadn't used in so long that it honestly didn't feel like anything that had ever been a part of her. The sensation of imagining herself as Jane Driskell was rather like seeing herself in some old photo and not having any recollection of the shirt she wore in it or where she'd been when it was snapped. She had shaken off that notion. Everything was tacking toward the past enough on its own, with no need of reinforcement from her inclination toward backtracking.

She turned now to the rows of desks, slowly filling with restless and recalcitrant children whose two-week furlough had played out and deposited them back here. What came back at her was the full range of youthful expression—downcast eyes intent on not engaging, nervous smiles, looks of preemptive defiance from a couple of boys at the back, and Jane made a mental note about the possibility that she would have to separate them for the good of class harmony.

It was the first of eight periods, homeroom, a clearinghouse of sorts for attendance reports, aptitude benchmarking when those infernal tests came around, and general management of the student populace. The next several hours would pump these kids into the hallways and other classrooms while drawing other children into Jane's room for specialized seventh-grade English instruction. The interior of the building—utterly unrecognizable to her now even though she had spent three intimate years in it half a lifetime earlier—was like a big circulatory system of juvenile learning, pulling the kids in, pushing them through the veins of the school, sending them into the great pumping heart of public education and, it was hoped, moving them along to other destinations without too much plaque buildup.

Jane breathed deep of the uncharged, odorless air, sweeping it into her lungs to partake of its steadying qualities, and as she expelled it, the second bell came and the rest of the group tumbled into the room.

"Everybody, just take whatever seat has been yours," she said, and the rumbling din of humanity abated only slightly. "People, come on. Let's get settled and be quiet, please."

That turned the sentiment of the room against her a tick more. Nobody could do sullen and inexplicably offended quite like an adolescent. Jane knew. She had one at home—and, somewhere, in this building.

"Who're you?" came a voice from the back. It was one of the kids she had eyeballed upon arrival, one who walked with an air of preemptive defensiveness and rehearsed insouciance, the clash of the two qualities unnoticed by him even as the incongruence sparked from his manner.

Jane pointed to the board, to her written handiwork. "We're going to get to that. Come on, folks, settle down."

When the rumble was quelled and then, at last, gone, Jane started in on the short speech she had been rehearsing in front of bathroom mirrors for three weeks.

"Welcome back," she said. "Did everyone have a good holiday?"

A generally affirmative murmur came back to her. Good enough.

"My name is Ms. Sperling," she went on, "and this is homeroom. I'm the replacement teacher for Mrs. Andersen and—"

"Where'd she go?" a girl up front interjected.

"OK, look," Jane said. "We're not going to have a ton of rules here, but this is one: If you wish to speak, raise your hand and I'll recognize you. It'll keep things orderly, OK?"

The girl, mortally inconvenienced, raised her hand. Jane nodded at her. "Yes?"

"Where'd Mrs. Andersen go?"

"She moved away with her husband."

"That sucks."

The gathered kids tittered. "Well, let's all try to survive it, OK?" Jane moved on. "Now, I know all your names, but I don't have the faces that go with them, and more important, I don't yet know you, nor do you know me. Let's start working on that today, OK? We'll start by livening up roll call."

Twenty-four sets of eyes—two fewer than were on the student manifest, evidenced by the two empty desks—blinked back at her as if to say, *yeah, OK, you first, lady.*

Jane ran her hands down the hips of her slacks, straightening the fabric. "I'll start, OK? As I said, I'm Ms. Sperling. I went to school here many years ago, and I grew up in North Richl—"

"And you came *back*?" Again, the kid in the back.

"Raise your hand, please."

"Forget I said anything."

"Anyway," Jane said, trying to beat back the rise of the funny portmanteau her father had inadvertently coined years ago, *flustration*, "I grew up here, but I lived for many years in Billings, Montana. My daughter and I moved here last month."

"How old is your daughter?" Same kid.

"What's your name?" Jane asked him.

"Roderick."

"Nice to meet you, Roderick. Will you please do me the courtesy of raising your hand? Let's not start off this way."

He raised his hand, cupping the right elbow with his left hand. "Yes, Roderick?" Jane said.

"How old is your daughter?"

"She's eleven."

"Is she cute?"

The quick-strike anger—it went from nothing to venomous in a single heartbeat—might well have spilled from Jane had the line not also offended some of the other kids, who turned and shouted the boy down. "Shut up, Roderick," one girl said, rising from her seat. Given the vagaries of child development, whereby adolescent girls often outpaced their boy counterparts at this stage, she looked big enough to reinforce her point physically.

"Everybody, please, let's just sit down. This is an easy assignment, OK? We're going to talk for the rest of the class. Let's just settle down and be polite, OK?"

"OK," several kids said.

"Roderick?"

"OK, ma'am."

"Thank you." Jane went to the dry-erase board and drew a thick line underneath her name, then put bullet points below that:

- Name
- Favorite school subject
- Something interesting about you

"OK, everybody, we're going to go around the room. You all might know each other, but I don't know you, and you don't know me. So this is what we're going to share. Who knows? You might learn something about your friends you didn't realize until today, OK?"

She got nods all around. "So I'll finish up," she said. "My favorite subject in school was reading and—" A chorus of good-natured jeers interrupted her. "Hey now," she said. "Reading is fun. And—" More jeers. "—*And* something interesting about me is I can sing the alphabet song backward."

"Do it."

Jane looked at Roderick, who wilted. He then raised his hand. "Yes, Roderick?"

"Will you do it, please?"

Jane sucked in a fresh mouthful of air. This most assuredly was not part of how she had scripted first period, but it's where things had taken them, so she aimed to see it through. "Real quick," she said, "and then we have to move on." Another deep gulp, and she was off.

"ZYXWVUT," she sang, the upward lilt of her voice out of step with the letters arranged in reverse. "SRQPONMLK," came the next bit, complete with the downbeat on the final letter. "JIH," she sang, an upward sweep again, and then "GFE." And now, the finish: "DC," she sang. "B and A. Now I know my ZYXs," and at that she and the rest of the class fell into shared laughter. At last.

"Now," Jane said, pointing to the big girl in the front row who had threatened Roderick. "Your turn."

"Do you want me to stand up?" the girl asked.

"If you wish."

The girl pushed back her seat and rose, her knees clipping the underside of the desk. Jane felt a brush of sympathy for her. She was so much larger than her classmates, the rest of her having not yet caught up with what her growth plates had in mind. And then Jane banished sympathy, because the girl seemed utterly unfazed by whatever was going on, with a seeming confidence unburdened by awkwardness.

"Rowanda Jerkins," she said. "But people just call me Ro. I like history. And I'm going to be the first woman to play in the NFL."

"Whatever, Ro," came a voice from behind her, and that wheeled her around.

"I *am*," she said.

"Hey," Jane said, pointing in the general direction of the naysayer. She had been so engrossed in the girl's answers that she hadn't picked up on who had said it. "We don't trample people's dreams in this class. You hear me? We support each other. That's what friends do."

"I *am*," Ro said again.

"We're rooting for you. Thank you, Ro." Jane pointed now to the boy, next in line along the front row. "OK, go."

Together, they went through all of the names and the faces, Jane doing her little mnemonic trick as best she could at the pace—*Cassie Akins, C is for curly hair, C is for Cassie, got it* and *Tyler Scoggins, Tyler is sitting along the east wall, Tyler is a city in East Texas, got it*—as the class exercise filled in the remainder of the period. Right along, she marked off the names on the attendance list for filing with the office after the bell. It was a bit like a scholastic *Hotel California*—once you were checked in, you could never leave. Until the end of the day, at least.

Down to the last kid and the final couple of minutes, Jane said, "OK, Roderick, play us over."

"Huh?"

"Go."

The boy stood. "Roderick. That's it."

"Last name, please."

"Roderick A. Watson. The 'A' stands for awesome."

"I'm sure," Jane said.

"Favorite subject: me."

"Come on, Roderick."

"Something interesting about me: everything."

"Humor us and name one," Jane said. "Please?"

The kid had the entire class enraptured. Jane had to give him that. Maybe he was telling the truth about his awesomeness and the ceaseless fascination of his own existence. She had arrived having made a compact with herself that she would take these children as she found them, that however they might have been defined by others in times when she wasn't present would not be carried over into her dealings with them. She wondered now how she could maintain that ethos and ask someone trustworthy—*David, nice hair like Bowie*, for example—what gives with this one.

"Well," Roderick said. "I've made every teacher I have cry."

"And you think that's interesting?" The words were flying out before Jane was even aware, and she regretted them.

"Burn," Ro said.

"I'm gonna make *you* cry," Roderick said. His jaw jutted a bit. She had pierced him.

"Thank you for the warning." The bell rang. The students piled out en masse. Jane went to her desk and pressed her hands atop it, leaning into them. She closed her eyes. One down, seven to go, with lunch and a prep period thrown in there. The end of May had never seemed so distant. Her belief that she could get there was being tested in a whole new way.

"Did I hear singing?"

Jane looked up. "Oh. Mr. Bourque. Hi."

He pursed his lips and gave her a sidelong, teasing stare. "Did I?"

"Yes," she said. "Just a little."

"Mellifluous, it was."

"You're too kind," she said. He took a deep bow. "Or insane. I haven't decided."

"So," he said, "you've taken the plunge. How does it feel?"

"Terrifying."

"It'll get better, I'm sure."

"I hope so," Jane said. "I've had my first direct challenge."

"Who?"

"Name's Roderick."

"Ah. Roderick A. Watson." He nodded.

"His reputation precedes him, I guess," she said.

"Smartest kid in this school," David said. "I wish I thought that would make a difference."

"Huh?"

He gestured to the desks in front of them, slowly filling in with a fresh round of students.

"We'll talk later," he said. He pointed a finger upward, and as if on cue, the second bell came. "Time to teach."

Twenty-two

After Eric parked his truck in the upper lot, they walked down into the expanse, past cherry trees and Japanese maples and magnolias and bamboo, over short, arching wooden bridges that traversed koi ponds, the morning air cold but not punishingly so. Pleasant, even. He tugged at the scarf coiled around his neck, loosening it. She put on sunglasses. The silence owned the initial moment, breached only by their crunching steps on the frosted grass.

"It seems like we came in springtime," he said, and Jocelyn nodded and said, "Yes, I think so."

"I remember the blooms," he said. "Not so much of that now."

"*Mono no aware*," she said.

"What's that?"

"Transient, bittersweet beauty."

"Huh?"

She pointed across the way to a small oasis with long, white bench. "Let's go over there and sit down."

Eric, not for the first time, felt a flush of wonder at being in her company. He hadn't expected it—not in the long lens of time nor in the shorter glimpse of these past few days, when she had been at the front of his thoughts after being so long below the surface of them. He had called after the girls had shuffled off, and he had suggested that they get together for the coffee she had offered, and she had said yes, that would be nice, and he had said, "Or we could take a drive," and she, bless her, had said yes to that as well, and here they were.

The day, the second of the year, was bright and cold and clear, the sky cloudless. Perfect for a walk and some chatter, and lord, did they have ground to cover. Eric wondered how they could possibly get to it all, or remember it all for the getting.

Jocelyn settled herself onto the bench and patted a place for him next to her. He dropped into it, his brittle hamstrings no longer suited to the job of a more leisurely sit.

"It's peaceful," she said.

"It is."

"And right here, in the bustle of Fort Worth," she said, delight infusing her voice. "University Boulevard there. The freeway there."

"Us here," he said.

"The biggest surprise of all."

She leaned into him a bit. He let her.

"Now, nomo..." he started.

"*Mono no aware.*" She giggled. He liked that.

"Which means?"

"I told you. Transient, bittersweet beauty."

"Which means?"

"Blooms are for springtime," she said. "We are in winter. If there are blooms all year, nothing will ever be special. That's the way the Japanese see it, anyway."

Eric looked at her, astonished. "You're smart," he said. "How did I never notice this?"

She nudged him. "Maybe you just weren't looking hard enough."

"I guess."

She laughed, enough to lurch her forward and to her feet. She reached for him, and he took her hand, and she helped him to get up far less gracefully than she.

"Come on, goofball," she said. "You owe me a coffee."

On the drive back, they found their way to the weightier subjects that had been intentionally skirted, things that had been walked up to and turned away from in favor of easier lines of conversation. It wasn't as if Eric hadn't expected that they would end up in such tangled briars—only so much could be said about now without going deep on then.

"I feel like a damn fool," he said.

"Why?"

"I should have known about Ed. I should have said something."

"I knew about Margery and didn't say anything."

"Yeah, well, that was different."

"How?" she asked.

"I'd pretty well shut it down. It would have been awkward, you saying something then."

"I would have been a friend expressing condolences to another friend for his loss. Perfectly reasonable."

"It still would have been awkward."

"Maybe. Maybe that's why I didn't."

He pressed on. They were now part of the swift current of late-morning traffic, a never-ending blight. Not that he had tried in a good number of years, but he had heard tell that a drive southward to Austin, two hundred miles, was bumper to bumper anymore, clogged up and unpleasant no matter when you cared to go, and he thought that was a shame. Time was, he would go halfway there just on a whim, stopping in at the Czech bakery outside Waco and dragging home some kolaches, just because. Oh, and Margery would needle him every time, saying, "You drove a hundred and eighty-some miles to indulge your sweet tooth?" Damn right he did. Until he didn't. These last several years without her had been shot through with *didn't*.

"I don't regret it," he said now.

He glanced at her, and she held the gaze, as if understanding all that wasn't being said. "Neither do I. We said we wouldn't."

"I just wanted to be clear."

"I understand," she said.

"I thought you might've been angry."

"Nope. We said we wouldn't be, and I wasn't."

Eric wasn't altogether sure he grokked this conversation from way back when that she kept referencing, but it didn't matter. There had been promises, explicit or implicit, made to each other even as they were broken to others. There had been understanding that circumstances might shift in a way that put more than just their desires in jeopardy, and they would have to be willing to leave what was between them to save those things that should override the rest.

In those first years after he had cut things off, he'd just put his head down and stuck to trying to keep the faith, with himself and with Margery, the rest be damned. The things he missed, well... they were just the things he missed, common burdens borne by anyone who has wanted more than he can reasonably have. Later, after Margery was gone, on those occasions when it all crossed his mind, he had sometimes pondered whether he could have followed a different path through the same crossing. Could he have told Margery of his home-and-hearth love for her and of his yearnings that lay beyond their common bed? Could she have understood that or lived with it? Could he have let her go to her own extracurriculars, had it come to that, not that he had any evidence such things existed? Ponderable questions, all of them. Unanswerable questions, too. A good number of those tangents looked like copouts no matter how generously he gazed upon them. It was probably better that he never gave them air.

"How are things with Claire?" Jocelyn asked.

God, the things she didn't know that had been piled upon the things she did. "We're sort of..." he flailed, not getting a grip on the words he wanted. "What's the word? Stalemate?"

"I'm sorry."

"Yeah, Jane's pissed, too."

She answered with pursed lips. Good enough. What was there to say?

"You need to get over," she said, leaning her head toward the highway lane to their right. "Unless we're going to Oklahoma."

"Christ." He tugged the wheel hard, cutting off a Mazda, a cacophony of angry honks in response, a raised, regretful hand from Eric to the rearview mirror. He merged into the new flow of cars shooting toward the Mid-Cities. His hands agitated on the wheel. He didn't much care for being in these vehicular gaggles anymore.

"I don't know where my mind is," he said.

"In the past, I imagine," she said. "Given the topic."

"Yeah, probably."

"There's nothing back there," she said.

"No, probably not." A go-along-to-get-along response, that. Everything was back there, and lately, it all seemed to be coming out sideways here and now.

"Tell me," she said. "What has your attention?"

"Nothing, really," he said. "You got me to thinking about Claire. Need to set things right with her."

"Anything in mind?"

"I'm still giving it a think."

She let it ride, which was good, because he wasn't sure what more he could say about where those thoughts were taking him. *Family dynamic*, there was a phrase that had been slow to penetrate his consciousness, if indeed he even understood it now. There had been nothing to parse or reconcile within his own family, in a different set of years. Margery had the day-to-day control of the agenda and the pocketbook, he was brought in for punishments or tough talks or muscle, and Jane had been a good enough kid, mostly, if a little willful and mouthy in her adolescent years, which didn't make her terribly special.

"How're your kids?" he asked her.

"Off in their own lives, as it should be," she said. "Brent's in Orlando. Has a landscaping business. Rob's down in San Antonio, teaching philosophy at Trinity."

"I wouldn't even recognize them, I bet."

"Nor I Jane. It's been a long time."

"It has."

She sighed heavily and clasped her hands in her lap. He waited on her.

"I don't see much of them," she said now. "There's been some suggestion, mostly by Brent, that I ought to sell the house and come live closer, but..."

"A lot of people doing that," he said. The houses on his own block that had been cleared out by old age and infirmity would stand out like missing teeth if he were to take to his front porch and count them. He felt something tugging at him, almost minor panic, at the thought that she might join the outflow.

"Not me," she said. "One, it's a trap."

"What is?"

"Florida," she huffed. "I'm not moving there. Two, I'm just stubborn enough to think I've still got some say over what I'll be, where I'll be, and how I'll be."

He looked at her, a glance he was happy to see she had caught. "I'm glad you came."

"Me, too," she said.

"I'd like to see you again."

"Me, too."

He grinned, impish. "When are you free?"

"Whenever."

"Really?" He looked to her again. "I figured you'd have a full dance card."

"Figure again."

"Well, I'll be."

He eased through a mixmaster, a full task even without subdivided attentions, and got spit out onto Davis Boulevard, leaving him just the straight shot to their old neighborhood on the west side of it. The years had overseen the teardown and rebuild of much of what he had committed to memory, but there was no chance of driving off errantly now. The timing and the rhythm were old hat, and like the bass notes of an old Hank Williams tune, he could hit them without thinking.

"What about you?" she asked.

"Me what?"

"What about your dance card?"

He chuckled. "Torn up. Shredded. In the trash."

"No!"

"Well, maybe I've got space for one name."

"Thank you, sir."

Eric was tickled by the exchange. The truth was, it had been six years, as opposed to just a few months for Jocelyn, and no one had even made an inquiry in that direction. He couldn't lie: It had left him a bit disappointed, and time was that he'd even contemplated going next door and calling on Evaline Roberson under the guise of offering to trim back her crabapple trees or some other such domestic function. He had just as quickly disabused himself of such a notion. Those were lives, his and Evaline's, that weren't made of compatible puzzle pieces. Better to sit alone, missing everything, than to press for something nobody should have.

He turned left off Davis onto Cross, an immediate right on Cox, all of it deep muscle memory, a zigzag that would carry her home. He hated to see her go.

In her driveway, truck idling, he said, "How about tomorrow? I never did get you that coffee."

"How about?" she said. "That'll be fine."

"Great."

"This time," she said, "I'll make it."

"Sounds fine."

"Come through the front door," she said. "It'll be unlocked."

He smiled at her. "I will."

She leaned in, quick but deliberate, and she kissed him on the lips, just a peck, really, and she disengaged before he could lend full participation.

"I wondered what it'd be like," she said.

"So did I."

"Not half bad."

"No."

"I'll see you tomorrow," she said.

She opened the door and was out and on her way to the porch before he got his mind going.

"Tomorrow," he said to the stolid air. He put the truck in gear, backed out, went up the street and over toward his own, away from the toughest collisions with his memory and into the brighter intersections. He checked his watch. Just after eleven, a long time to go until the girls would be home. Any other day, he would be coming up hard on beer hour, when he could drop away, take in some suds, let go of whatever might be on his head. But this wasn't any other day, now, was it? He didn't fancy a beer or his recliner or the afternoon ennui. He didn't know what he wanted, and wasn't that just putting the spurs to him? He balled up a fist, rapped it twice on the roof of the truck, and he goosed it along to some fanciful somewhere.

Twenty-three

Come lunchtime, David showed Jane the ropes of how that trio of half-hours worked, that over the course of the semester they would have X number of weeks of playing monitor to the first-lunch group, X number of weeks of second-lunch duty, X number of weeks on third lunch, and X number of weeks of no mealtime responsibilities, a free-and-clear hour and a half.

"No lunch is the best," he said. "I make myself disappear for a while. Like magic."

"You can do that?" she asked.

"They're the kids, Jane, not us."

"*Ms. Sperling*," she said.

"Yes, of course. I'm sorry."

"It's OK, David."

At once, he looked chastened and delighted. "Was that...was that a joke?" he asked, one eyebrow headed for his crown.

"Just this once."

"I'll cherish it," he said. "Anyway, yeah, I mean, I don't think there's much point in letting Rosemary know how often or for how long—thankfully, she isn't super-engaged in watching us—but I damn sure get out. It's my lifeline to sanity."

They had drawn third lunch now, for which Jane was thankful when Claire approached the teachers' table, trailed a few feet behind by another girl. Jane had seen her in the line and had held back, waiting for Claire to recognize her and initiate the wave, which, thankfully, she did. It was all part of a process that was at once deliberate and counter-emotive. Claire was a little girl moving swiftly toward being a big girl and then onward to a woman, and Jane's daily fight with herself involved letting go enough so her daughter could find her own way into how things were changing while sticking close enough to step in and keep danger at bay. Only that morning, Jane had locked herself into the hall bathroom she shared with Claire and, quite unexpectedly, had thought of a time when Margery was a young mom. Her mother's gingham skirts and Dorothy Hamill wedge and light misting of Enjoli perfume had filled her senses and her memories, and she had wept at the memory. At Claire's age, Jane would have been mortified had her mother made any overt signal to her at *school*, in front of her *friends*, how utterly *embarrassing*, and by the time she had accumulated enough life to see things from the other perspective, Margery was gone. Jane had cried into a towel for the loss—the ever-present loss that, six years on, would move to the forefront of things and kneecap Jane when she least expected it—but also for the uncertainty of whether she might live long enough to someday have that talk with her own grown daughter. God, she hoped so.

"Hi, Mom."

Jane spun in her seat, opening up. "Hey there. How are classes?"

"Fine." Claire grabbed her friend by the hand. "This is Ashlin."

"Hi, Ashlin."

"Hi," the girl said, clipped and distant, then she fell back again.

"She's new, too," Claire said.

"Ah. That's good, then."

Jane motioned to David, seated next to her, who had made a curious turn toward the visitors. "This is Mr. Bourque. He's in the classroom next to mine. This is my daughter, Claire."

David offered a handshake, and Claire accepted it. "Nice to meet you, Claire."

"Hi." Claire flushed crimson.

"How are classes?" Jane asked her again.

"Fine." Same answer. Frustrating. Claire looked back for her friend, who had begun to wander. "I'm going back," she said now. "I'll see you after school."

"Just come to my room after last class, OK?"

"OK."

"Nice kid," David said after Claire was gone. "Seventh grade?"

"Sixth. And, yeah. Claire is a good kid." She trailed off and turned to watch the girl go. Claire and Ashlin fell into the gaggle of students leaving the lunchroom and returning to the classrooms. When they were out of sight, into one of the two massive north-south hallways bridging the wings of the building, she returned to her lunch, gone cold. "Trying not to let anything spoil that."

That drew a confused look from him. "You say that as if you're expecting something."

Jane put up the initial blocker of a sophisticated, time-honed shield system. "Oh, am I that obvious?" She laughed, but it came out half-hearted. Poor deflection.

"You turned out OK," he said.

"As far as you know, yeah."

He set down his fork and turned toward her, earnest. She pulled the armor tighter around herself. She preferred the flighty, *joie de vivre* version of this new...she couldn't even call him a friend. Acquaintance. Colleague. Whatever. What she sensed now was attenuation, and that, she was certain, would lead to more questions, unsolicited advice, an attempt at an intimacy of old friends—which they most assuredly were not—that she would have to try to parry lightly at first, then probably with aggressively heightened firmness. She wished they could just skip all that.

"What's going on?" he asked.

"Nothing," she said, then she tried a smile that seemingly weighed a thousand pounds but she hoped would convey reassurance. "Really, nothing. It's a stressful day for us, that's all. First day, you know? It's nerve-racking."

"You're gonna do great," he said, and he lifted the fork again, eating a bite of what the cafeteria staff charitably called cutlet, and Jane let go the breath she had sucked in, and the lunch period spun on. The moment that had troubled her soon passed.

"You think so?" she asked.

"Of course. Claire, too. I have a sense about these things."

The remainder of the school day unwound without incident, a victory to Jane's way of thinking. It had set up to her advantage, of course, with each of the periods bringing a new assemblage of kids, new names to hear spoken to her and new faces with which to pair them. By necessity and by numbers, those repeated mutual introductions had eaten away the bulk of each period's clock, a one-time-only reprieve from the onward march of regimented public education. Tomorrow—the one directly in front of her and the collective many that would follow on its heels—would bring assignments and homework and late-night grading and discipline problems and implacable parents and loggerheads with colleagues and...Jane shook her head, clearing the thought. She knew the *ands* could form a critical mass if she weren't careful to mete them out.

Jane filled her tote bag—gradebook and calendar and assignment sheets—and she thought again of the last class that had passed through, how it was eerily and uniformly quiet, and she remembered parallels with her past incarnation as a schoolteacher, how she would sometimes have to fight against a natural tendency to see the groups in front of her as monoliths rather than the collections of individuals they were. It was undeniable, at least anecdotally, that classes tended to develop personalities that transcended their disparate personas. Home room, particularly with Roderick and Ro, had been willful. Second period, rowdy. Third period, clever. Onward to eighth and its preternatural quietness. Jane shrugged. It could be a lot worse as each day faded to the outro.

"Ready?" Claire, as if teleported there, stood in the doorway.

"Ready," Jane said.

Jane brought down the lights and locked the door behind them. The hallways were empty of kids, silent, just like that after hours of intermittent rambunctiousness. Pavlov was right; you can condition behavior through a bell system. Loose paper, candy wrappers, and other detritus skimmed the floor, to be picked up in the evening, clearing the way for tomorrow's repeat.

As they passed David's door, Jane looked in. He was cleared out, gone. She still didn't know what to make of him. There had been little, in their chitchat, about the work. There had been much about all the ways he granted himself release from the premises. He was young yet. Maybe this wasn't for him. Maybe it wasn't for her, either. Having no options in reserve, she shuddered.

"That's Mr. Bourque's class?" Claire asked, as if catching Jane in the unlit corridors of her thoughts.

"Mmm hmmm."

"I like him."

"You barely even met him," Jane said.

"I liked him based on that."

"I see." Jane slipped an arm across her shoulders, over the backpack straps. It was a bid, an entreaty, something Claire could accept or shrug off, either answer as likely as the other. She didn't balk, and for that Jane was thankful.

"The other kids say he's the best teacher in the school," Claire said.

"They do, huh?"

"Yeah. They say he's fun and funny."

"I can see why they'd think so," Jane said.

"He's cute."

"Never mind that." The words were out before Jane could moderate her tone. She looked to Claire in attempt to assess how they had landed. She seemed unaffected.

"I'm just saying. Don't you think so?"

"I didn't think to rate him," Jane said.

Ahead, sunlight poured into the hallway from a large bank of windows, splashing on the carpet like spilled orange juice. Beyond the window, kids cavorted, waiting for the carousel of the pickup line to cue up their rides home. Beyond them, the faculty parking lot and Jane's car and the way back to the house on Payte. Freedom, then a different kind of holding cell. One day down, so many to go that they weren't worth counting.

"Ms. Sperling?" Rosalie Lacy emerged from the intersecting hallway. "Can I have just a minute?"

"Sure." Jane retrieved the ring of keys from her purse and handed them to Claire. "Go get in the car. I'll be there in a second."

Claire bounded out, with a wave to them both, and into the gaggle of kids on the sidewalk outside.

"Good first day?" Rosalie asked.

"Yes. Fine."

"Good. There's just one thing," she said, and Jane felt her body go tense. "It's essential that the attendance get taken immediately and forwarded on to the office, so—"

"Oh," Jane said. "I'm sorry. I had this idea that I could pair attendance with introductions, so—"

"The thing is, the system is set up so we can assess who's present and who's absent throughout the day, and when your report came in at the end of the period rather than the start, well, I'm sure you can see—"

"No, totally. I get it."

"It created a bit of a problem, all day," Rosalie said. "The office functions have a rhythm, you see."

"I understand. It won't happen again."

"I'm sure it won't. Is there anything else I can clarify?"

"No," Jane said. "I think I'm good."

"Have a good evening, then."

"Thank you. You, too."

Jane walked out, emerging from the stuffiness and into the sun. She nodded at the waves from three kids, two girls and a boy, obviously some of hers but not yet committed to memory. She focused on the faces so she would remember them the next day, when she could pair the eyes and noses and mouths with their given names and unify them, the way she had with *Rosalie, R is for rigid, R is for rankled, Rosalie is for Day One hadn't ended rosily, got it.*

Once there, Jane opened the car door and settled in behind the wheel.

"What did she want?" Claire asked.

"Just job stuff. Wanted to know how my first day went."

"What did you say?"

"Fine."

"Yeah," Claire said. "Mine, too."

"Just fine?"

"Yeah."

Jane started the car, then looked at her girl. "We can do this, can't we?"

"Yeah," Claire said.

"Good."

"We have to," Claire said.

"Yes." A mouthful, that, but yes, just the same.

Twenty-four

After dinner was through, Eric went to the bedroom and crawled to the floor, belly down, and pushed his head and arms under the bedframe and started pulling out the boxes he had put there all those years ago, wanting never to see them again and simultaneously unable to let them go. In that regard, it was an unpleasant unearthing of the past, coming as it did with a flow of memory that couldn't be stanched once it was cut loose.

He thought of those first few days after they found out about the cancer, Margery sleeping all the time, the palliatives sending her into more of what she had already been doing for a while as they, together, kept pretending that nothing was wrong when something so clearly was. Finally, confirmation and an uncertain timeline—maybe a month, maybe six weeks, maybe longer. Maybe not. Maybe eight days. Maybe she gets a diagnosis on a Tuesday and she sees one more Tuesday—not that *she* sees it, because she's done, out there at the edge of the cosmos, waiting to be let in as the heartbeat lingers and lingers and, finally, goes out, and that's it, she's released. He thought of how it was four in the morning on the second Wednesday since they had found out and the hospice nurse came to him on the couch and shook him awake and told him she had flown. He thought of how he went bleary-eyed down the hall and into the bedroom across the way—the one Claire occupied now—to tell his daughter, who had arrived too late to ever hear her mother's voice again. How he held Jane and he tried not to think about the raw deal this all was for her, let alone for him, that Margery was gone and he was still there.

He thought of the days that trailed that one, the flurry of sympathy cards, the casseroles on the porch, the phone calls, the drive out to D/FW International with Jane, putting her back on a plane bound for Montana by way of Denver, to the life she had going up there that could stand only a brief pause before its own machinery needed to move again. He thought of driving home, alone, finally, irretrievably, inconsolably alone, and how he'd ripped their room apart once he got there, the bed they had shared for all those years east-west in alignment, the morning sun moving across their bodies, and now, without her, in his ragged grief he maneuvered it north-south. He thought of how he had carried some of her things—those he might someday part with but couldn't imagine losing in the moment—into their daughter's old bedroom, out of sight as Margery remained forever on his mind. Back in their room, he pushed her clothes to the outer markers of their shared closet, and for several months that followed, he could close his eyes and walk himself in there and smell her, comfort and heartbreak renewed in equal measures. Other things, those items Margery loved best, he had packed delicately, carefully, lingering, touching them, then putting them away beneath that bed that had carried the two of them for so long.

That's what Eric was after now, extracting those boxes one by one and looking for the one precise thing, hoping it was there, fearing that it might not be, that in his grievous mania he had separated it from the rest and buried it deep within the artifacts of a long, stationary life—or, worse, that it had somehow ended up in the garbage heaps that had eventually been migrated to the curb and carried away. At this thought, he shut his eyes tight and made a wish that he hadn't been so reckless, and after a beat, he opened his eyes again and he drew out another box from beneath the bed railing.

This was the jackpot box, the one he had been seeking, and Eric opened it as if it were a sacred thing, turning back the tissue paper with delicate fingers, his breath catching and releasing as the bauble showed itself to the light after so long in the darkness. He slipped his index finger beneath the clasp and drew the jewel up, and he cupped it in his hand, and he closed it within a fist, and he backed out, and he turned off the light, and he closed the door and went to her, to show her what had been found again.

Jane stood on the patio with Chuck Brooks. She was surprised by the drop-in visit and relieved to see him under the circumstances, even more relieved when his tone had made clear that he came peaceably. Now, she considered the backyard, her own memories of it a thin haze over the top of the ways her father had claimed it for his own—a newer, bigger garden shed than the old tin one they'd once had that could be toppled by a high wind, a deluxe grill, a lightly used horseshoe pit that was being steadily reclaimed by the grass. Not much here for her anymore, and yet the bend of every tree trunk and every section of chain link holding everything in also harbored some crinkled memory. She pushed those off and clinked her beer bottle against his.

"Thanks for the drink, Chuck."

"Thanks for accepting."

He grinned at her, a little more sheepish than confident by her reckoning, and her conciliatory words and his collided in the air between them.

"I'm—"

"—sorry," he finished.

"No," she said. "I am. What a mess we left you with. How's Annabelle?"

"She's fine."

"Really?"

"Really." He nodded, lips pursed.

"It was quite a gash," she said.

"Looked worse than it was."

"I just—" she said, the trailing words a tangle. "I just—I didn't imagine anything would—"

"It's OK. I'm sorry I stormed out."

"Oh, you were entitled to storm."

"Still, I shouldn't have. It wasn't anybody's fault."

"I'm just glad she's OK," Jane said.

"There's a reason they're made out of rubber," he said. "Kids, I mean."

"I suppose so."

"Listen, if Claire's willing to try again," he ventured.

She looked at him. "Really?"

"Sure."

"I'll talk to her," Jane said.

"Sounds good. But, you know, maybe the plan we talked about before. My place, rather than up here."

"Ah," she said. "My dad."

"Yeah. Sorry."

She raised a hand to stifle the unnecessary apology. "No need. I get it."

"It's just—"

"I get it, Chuck. No need to put words to it."

"You know," he said, despite the stop sign, "he threw a pretty good scare into her."

"Oh, I know."

She'd had no trouble imagining the circumstance that had taken her father's fuse that night from lit to explosive without much in between. She had seen it before, and for that matter, so had Chuck. A flash of memory came to her now, an autumn night when they couldn't have been older than eight or nine, some minor offense given by Chuck to an older kid—one too young to drive and too old to be in the mix with the younger kids on this end of the block. The older kid—she thought it funny, and a bit alarming, that she now couldn't conjure his name, bound up as he otherwise was in her memory banks—had Chuck knocked to his hands and knees, a kidney punch coming, Eric and Chuck's father pouring out of the house, beer on their breath, pinning the older boy to the brick of the house, Jay Brooks bear-hugging the kid's lower extremities to hold him still, Eric's right hand at the kid's throat, his nose to the kid's nose, the drunken invective spilling from Eric's mouth and diffusing in the night air around them.

Jane shook her head. "I'm sorry," she said again.

"It's OK."

"Claire will be thrilled."

"Good. I'm glad," Chuck said. He laughed now, and she looked to him again. "Of course, I can't say when that'll be. I'm not exactly Mr. Social over here."

"She'll be thrilled whenever."

"Maybe you and I could try dinner again."

Jane tugged on the bottle's label, beginning the unraveling. "Maybe," she said. "But maybe that wouldn't fit with the plan, you know?"

"I don't follow."

"Me, staying nearby so I can swoop in if needed." She gave the words a lilt, as if guiding him to the sensible answer and away from whatever else he might have in mind.

"Ah, right."

"You see?"

"Yeah, of course."

She kept at the label, holding together the one-piece peel, feeling the leavings of the glue on her fingers, wet from the condensation on the bottle. She pinched thumb and forefinger together, feeling the stickiness. When she had the label fully disengaged, she used the same fingers to roll it into a ball, then drop it through the mouth of the bottle, into the shallow pool at the bottom.

"How was school?" Chuck asked, shaking her attention loose. "First day, right?"

She smiled and covered up. "First day. Still standing."

"Must be weird. Memory lane and stuff all over that school, right?"

"Not really."

"No?" he asked.

"Thirty-odd years," she said. "Feels like it happened to a different kid."

"I can see that, I guess. Claire like it?"

"You done?" Jane asked. She pointed to his bottle.

"Yeah, sure."

"Let's go in," she said. "You can ask her yourself. Maybe you'll get more of an answer than I did."

A knock on the door brought an invitation for Eric to come in, followed immediately by Claire's searing disappointment at seeing him, and a chill moved into the room with them. Eric stood there in his regular uniform, chambray shirt and jeans, and he shifted his weight from foot to foot as he searched for words not immediately forthcoming. He fingered the bauble behind his back and hoped she might speak first. Hope be damned, because she wouldn't.

"Did you have a good dinner?" he asked, banality at last something he could manage to put out there.

Claire shrugged. "It was OK."

"I wanted to cook steaks," he said. "I must have left them at the store." The errant late afternoon crowded his thoughts again, how he had met them both at the door upon their arrival home, a flourish and a couple of kisses on the cheek that Jane had taken delightedly and Claire had endured with a squenched face. "Welcome home, ladies," he'd said, and he had announced his intent to cook for them both, and that intent had been carried right up until the time that he went to fetch the porterhouses and had found them absent from the fridge and the freezer, a puzzler with the receipt still on the kitchen counter, verifying the purchase. About the time he was set to go stratospheric, Jane had stepped in and said they'd order something.

"I like pizza," Claire said now.

"Sure," he said. "Every kid does."

A heavy sigh from Claire. "Not every kid."

"No?"

"Lea Kendrick doesn't."

"Who's she?"

"My friend in Billings."

"Ah," Eric said. "The exception to the rule."

"Wendy Connerly doesn't," she said.

"Another Billings friend?"

"Yes."

"Maybe," he said, "Billings just doesn't have good pizza."

"It does," she said, resolute. "Better than here, anyway."

Eric sent his left hand toward the ceiling. Surrender. He could feel the room spiraling away from him, what with Claire's getting snottier and his getting closer to another unwanted detonation.

He lowered his hand. Claire glared at him, waiting.

"I didn't come to talk about dinner," he said.

"OK."

"I came to show you something."

"What?" she asked.

He drew his right hand out from behind his back and let gravity take the jewel, and it pulled tight against the thin leather strip laced through his fingers. It twirled there at the end of its tether, the dents of the stone catching the light. Claire's eyes widened.

"What is that?" she asked.

"Can I come show it to you?"

She nodded and set her tablet aside, and she scooted over and made room for him on the twin bed. He settled himself in at the foot of it, and he set the jewel across the creased blanket in front of her. Claire set a halting finger against the rock and pulled it back quickly after contact.

"What is that?" she asked.

"It's turquoise."

"Turquoise," she repeated. "It looks like a tiny ocean."

"It does, doesn't it?"

"Where did you get it?" She stayed back from it, awed. He scooped it up, the leather piece dangling from his hand, and he offered it to her. She took it into her own hands like some discovered treasure.

"New Mexico," he said. "A long time ago. I bought it for your grandmother."

"It's hers?" Claire asked.

"Was hers. Yeah." And wasn't this forever the way it was with memory and missing Margery? By now, Eric had long since felt the sharpest edges of his grief sheared off, where he could be mostly matter of fact about his wife's one-time presence and forevermore absence. Now, the moments that did damage were more glancing and less predictable, a head-on memory here, a juxtaposition there, an off-the-cuff comment to Claire that cast Margery in the past tense. He felt emotionally flipped onto his back by his own slippery words.

"We'd taken a trip," he said now, Claire's attention rapt, her fingers holding the jewel. "Albuquerque. All-day drive from here, hundreds of miles. It sounded like an exotic place. Your grandmother and me, we didn't have much money back then—weren't even married yet—and it was a big deal, the chance for us to go somewhere together." He drew up into himself, then emerged again. "Real big deal," he finished, quietly.

"When?" Claire asked.

"Nineteen sixty-six, I want to say." He thought about it, tried to do the math backward, but the years jumbled in the rearview. "Sixty-seven, maybe."

"Mom—"

"Yeah, your mom was a long way off still." He bore down now. Halfway into the story, he wanted to hear the windup as much as he wanted to tell it. "We stopped in this little roadside place—you know, gifts and postcards and candy and stuff, and—"

"I saw those places when we were driving here," Claire said.

"So you know what I mean. Anyway, we're just looking around, and your grandmother, she spots this. And she's looking at it just like you're looking at it right now. And I'm looking at her looking at it, and I'm hoping the price is right, because we don't have much, and I don't want to hitchhike back to Fort Worth because we can't buy the gas to get us home, you know."

"How much?"

"I don't even remember," he said. "Didn't matter. I was getting it. Had to."

"Smart move, Grandpa."

"I have my moments."

He held out his hand. "Can I have it for a sec?"

Claire looked saddened to give it up, but she did so. He turned the jewel over, revealing the back of its silver setting.

"When we got home, I had a buddy engrave it for me. Can you see it?" He handed it back to her, and she held it up near her face and squinted in.

"Your love is my light."

"That's right," he said.

"It's beautiful, Grandpa."

"It's how I felt. Feel."

Claire set the necklace on her leg, with the leather strip draping the curve of her knee and touching the bedspread. "I wish she was here."

"Me, too, kid. So much."

"I don't remember her very well."

"You were so little," he said. "But you aren't that anymore." He nodded at the jewel. "But you keep that. It'll keep her close."

Claire's eyes went wide. "Really?"

"Really," he said. "It was her favorite thing, and she loved you so much. She'd want you to have it."

"Can I wear it?" she asked.

"Absolutely, you can."

She pressed the jewel against her breastbone and tossed the loose ends of the leather piece over her shoulders and into the thicket of her long hair. Eric stood and went to her, corralling the ends and knotting them with practiced hands. He let them go and placed one hand on her back.

"That good, or should I cinch it up?"

"No," she said. "That's perfect."

"Let me look at you," he said.

She stood, and he turned her toward him. The turquoise peeked halfway up from her collar. He nodded toward it, and she looked down, frowned, slipped a finger under the jewel and brought it out in full.

"Good?" she asked.

"Beautiful," he said. "She'd be proud. I *am* proud."

Eric held his arms wide, a bid, and she stepped into them, and he closed them around her and kissed the top of her head.

"I'm glad you're here," he said.

"Thanks, Grandpa."

Dear Claire

July 10, 2014

This will be a tough one.
I walked in today, and Jim says, "Let's talk about your mother."
OK, I'm thinking, let's.
I asked what he wanted to know.
"Anything you care to tell me."
Well, Jim, I said, that's not terribly focused, is it? And he didn't know what I meant, so I pitched forward in my chair. I'd been feeling hostile all day. I have my reasons. Rent is two days late, and I have no idea where the rest of it is coming from. I've been barking at everyone—at you as you went off for your weekend with your dad, at Teryn at work, at the girl at the convenience store. In a way, it was just Jim's turn in the barrel. It's not really his fault. Just bad timing.

So I bullshitted him. Told him her full maiden name was Margery Magill Rodgers, that Magill is a family name that would have been better affixed to a boy, only she didn't come out that way, much as her father, your great-grandfather, a horrible old bastard, would have preferred. I asked him if knowing that would really allow him to know her. I was a smartass. No doubt. I was.

This is what he said: "I'd know quite a lot."

How, I wondered.

"I'd know more than I did before you said anything."

So I got mouthy. I said, hey, Jim, you're the one asking questions. If you want to know something, ask. Don't act like I'm holding out.

"But you are."

I told him I wasn't.

"For weeks now, you've glanced off the topic every time she's come up."

So I said, hey, she's gone. What does it matter?

"See?" he said.

This is how he does it, every time. He walks you down into it, prodding, gentle, not taking no for an answer, not taking bluster for substance, until you're left with either engaging or butting your head against the wall you've reached.

So he says, "Tell me about Margery Magill Rodgers."

And I told him: "Margery Beth Rodgers."

"Beth?"

And here's my reveal, right? That's also a family name, the one she actually had. Suited for a girl, which is all my grandfather, your great-grandfather, who wasn't a shriveled old bastard at all, really wanted.

He got mad, Claire. Sputtering mad. "Is that the truth?"

I told him he knows it is. I think that made him angrier.

"I know only what you tell me truthfully. Is that the truth?"

Yes, I said.

"Then why the Magill bit?"

I said it was because he pisses me off sometimes.

"It's not intentional," he said.

And I said maybe, but that's what it is.

I was glad I pissed him off. Real glad. Gladder than I should have been. But it didn't last. He looked at me, no expression. Just looked. I can't take it. He seems not to be swayed by the social nicety that most people have, the knowledge that it's rude to stare at someone else and not leaven the moment with words or glances elsewhere. He stares and he sort of smiles, then he waits on me to break, because he certainly won't. So, of course, I did.

I said I miss her.

I said she was brilliant. I didn't mean it the way you say someone is brilliant when all you really mean is that she can walk and talk at the same time. I meant it in the honest-to-goodness way. She read widely. She could have done anything she wanted to do. And I told him she squandered it, and that's what he seized on, asking how.

I told him if she'd had any ambition, any dreams for herself, she subjugated them to being a wife and a mother. And then she died relatively young, and that all feels like a squander to me.

And I knew he was going to push back on that. I knew it. He says, "Worked out pretty well for you, though, didn't it? Her being your mother?"

I said she could have done both. He said maybe she didn't want to, and that made me angry, because he didn't know her and I did.

"Are you sure you knew her?" he asks.

I told him to fuck off.

There's another thing Jim does, one that no doubt serves him well in his practice: He does not meet anger with anger. His wife, Delilah, certainly did, and for that reason as much as any other, I no longer drive to her office on Central on Wednesdays. This was the second time in four weeks I'd told him to fuck off, and while I can't be sure, I cannot believe I've told anyone in my life to fuck off twice in an entire lifetime of being intermittently pissed off at people and the stupid things they do. And today, just as he did the first time, he settled back and said, "Anger often flares when you're close to the truth. If it helps in that, go with it." The only giveaway that he was even a little addled was in his right hand, which tremored more than usual. I did notice that.

So I took a deep breath, and I said I knew her. Said I didn't understand her. I tried. I tried to get next to her thinking, to her choices, but I couldn't get there. And it never seemed like the right time to ask her point-blank, and then, without much warning, we were out of time. And that's what it is.

Jim leaned in, still one hand quelling the other, and asked me what choices.

I told him my father. They didn't match. They never did.

He wanted to know how.

That's a hard question to quantify. But it's basic, fundamental stuff. He was boisterous. She was not. She was supremely self-controlled. His appetites—for risk, for drink, carnal—were bigger than he was. She read. He never, ever did, not that I've ever seen.

"Have you ever heard the saying 'it's the differences that make it work'?" he asked me, and I said, yeah, I heard it. Even believed it once. I papered over a lot of stuff with your dad by telling myself the same thing.

"So you don't believe it now?" he says.

No. I don't. Now, those differences all seem like miniature, assured heartbreaks to me. Aggressions. Things that inevitably drove us apart. If I were to meet someone now—and I don't want to—and I found myself on the other shore from him in those regards, I would walk away and I'd never look back. More than that, I'd run. I'd be like Teryn and what she said about her ex: 'When I felt like I had to run, I laced up my shoes and I started running.'

Jim asked me if I thought my mother should have run.

I used to dream about it. Not when I was a little girl. When I was little, I adored my daddy. When I got old enough to realize who and what he was, the adoration was gone. I used to think about what it would be like if it was just me and her. What we would have done, how we would have been, where we might have gone. But we never did, and the leaving was up to me when I was able to do it. She never would. Even though I know she knew what she was in. She had to. I knew it. And that's what I thought of when it came to me and you and your dad. I know he loves you. But I also know I can't be there with him anymore. We'll have to do this separately, he and I, and we'll have to figure out how that all works. That's what I'm doing at Jim's every week. I'm figuring it out.

So Jim, at last, says this: "I want to ask you something. And I want you to consider it deeply. And if you need some time to think about it, I'd rather you took that time and we talked about it next week, rather than your giving a hasty answer now. OK?"

I told him to say it.

And he goes, "How do you reconcile giving your mother so much credit—she was brilliant, she was considered and self-controlled, she was deliberate—while also withholding so much regard for the life she chose to live?"

I started to interrupt him, but he kept going, said he wasn't finished. Said she wasn't career-oriented, that she didn't leave her marriage, that she seemed content to raise me, that she wanted to be a wife. Said I see all of that as failure and missed opportunities. So he asked me: How could she be both a brilliant person and a colossal failure?

Claire, the question landed on me with force, square and true. And my mind started moving everything around like chess pieces: my mom there, my dad next to her, me across the board, your dad lurking, you were in there, too, or maybe you were me and I was moving across the board to protect you, and your dad, like he's magnetized, is moving with me, and I'm glancing at my mother and trying to move her, and my dad is pulled along as she goes, and dammit, there's no winning move in any of this.

I told him I'd see him next week, and I got the hell out of there.

Twenty-five

Three days is what Jane got—three days of putting names to faces, of slowly integrating herself into cogent lesson plans and her classrooms full of kids into how she wanted their time together to unfold, of finding a rhythm with Claire that allowed her to keep tabs on the girl without being overbearing about it, of slowly satisfying Rosalie's standards for order and eliminating the after-school hallway chats, of anticipating David's drive-bys from the classroom next door and his obvious interest in her as some sort of exotic creature who had interrupted his suburban ennui. A *milf*, she believed the term to be.

Three days of grappling with how, exactly, she felt about that. Oddly flattered, which she hadn't thought possible. Eternally guarded, as it had to be.

On the fourth day, all bets were off when Roderick—Roderick A. Watson, "'A' stands for *asshole*, asshole," as he later said to Tim, to quite predictable results—took down the larger eighth-grader in the hallway before final period, pinned the kid's shoulders under his knees and struck the boy in the nose once, twice, three times before Jane was on the tile floor with them, her hands under Roderick's armpits, pulling him off, the larger kid spraying blood, the other kids moving in like a violent storm. "Fight, fight, fight!" the chant went up as Jane fell back with Roderick, her arms still clasped around his shoulders, the other kid now on his stomach, finished and humiliated. Claire pressed in from the edge of the crowd opposite Jane, looking at the scene in horror, finding her mother's eyes, pleading with her to—*what?* What could Jane do about this? Whatever it was she thought she should do, she was losing to the chaos.

As quickly as the gathering had formed, it dissipated. Other teachers, including David, and an assistant principal moved in and cleared the kids out. David uncoupled Jane from Roderick, who was now on his feet and in the grasp of a teacher she hadn't yet met, one of the coaches from the looks of him. "Are you OK?" David asked, and Jane, not really hearing him, nodded and tried to catch the breath that had run away from her.

"What happened?" David asked.

Jane leaned into the wall opposite her classroom door. Air had returned to her, but her heartbeat was still pumping it through her blood at time and a half. She glanced to her right at the boy who'd gotten the worse of it. She didn't know him, not that she expected she would.

"I don't know," she said. "Roderick was punching that kid." She nodded again toward the boy. "I tried to stop it."

"You should have waited for help."

"Oh," she said. "For a big man to come and do it for me?"

"Jane."

"I tried to stop it," she said, breathless again.

He nodded, conceding the point. She'd done it, hadn't she? It might have been hallway-fight triage, and perhaps there was some rule of engagement she had fractured unwittingly and would find out later from Rosalie, but where once there had been a fight, now there was only the outing of a boy's blood and the murmurs of over-stimulated students.

"Y'all get to class," David said, shooing the lurkers with their whispers and their camera phones. "Go on. Get to class."

The last of them cleared out. The beaten boy was escorted off to an appointment with the school nurse. Roderick A. Watson, the "A" is for *almost certainly expelled*, headed the opposite way to meet his fate, and Jane crossed the hallway to teach the last class of the day how to write a three-paragraph persuasive essay. David's last period was for prep, lucky him. Three days in, she'd noticed he often bailed on that responsibility.

"Are you going to be OK?" he asked.

"Sure, yeah," she said. "Just a little rattled. Didn't expect that."

"Who could? That was my first fight."

"Really?"

"Yep," he said. "Place was mellow before you came along."

"Don't tease."

"Sorry. Talk later?" he asked.

"Sure."

The hallway fisticuffs brought disorder to the last of the day, with Jane pulled out of her final class for a consultation with Tim about what she saw and what she did and what should become of the instigator. On the first two points, her answers were "not much" and "just tried to end it," and Tim's assessment fell roughly in the same range as David's: "I can't be too critical because you probably kept it from being a lot worse, but next time—and, God, I hope there's not a next time—maybe don't put yourself in that much peril. There are so many ways that could have ended up really, really bad for you. You understand?" And, of course, she did, even if ten replays would result in ten identical decisions from her.

On the last of the questions, Tim held the only vote that counted. Roderick was out, had to be out. There was no other way. "We're educators, not caseworkers," he said, and when Jane raised a quibble with that, pointing out that job titles said one thing and community expectations another, he said, "Well, yes, but the point remains. Too disruptive. He can go somewhere else. Or he can apply for reinstatement later. But that's the deal."

She could only accept the decision in the main and reject it on its premise. She didn't envy Tim this part of his job, the one where he had to dispense justice swiftly for the good of the order, even if the circumstances might demand a deeper, more nuanced consideration. At once, a memory tumbled into her, of her own time at this very school, when one of her classmates called a teacher "a shriveled-up bitch" upwind of one of the volleyball coaches, who proceeded to pull all the girls into the auxiliary gym during PE, line them up, then go through the line one by one and separate the kids into two groups, "good kids" and "bad kids." It hadn't been right. It hadn't been fair. It had been a miscarriage of justice in a pique of anger.

"Listen," Tim said at the door, as she prepared to leave. "You want to fight for this kid. I get it. I wouldn't want you here if you didn't. Just understand that I have to advocate for all of them."

"I know."

"You like him," he said. "I can tell."

"I don't know him. I don't know anybody yet, really. But, yeah, I'm concerned for him. Mr. Bourque says he's the smartest kid here—"

"I've heard that."

"So I'm just thinking there's more to it."

"Probably there is," Tim conceded. "But does that mitigate what happened today? I doubt it."

"OK," she said. "But let me ask you something."

"Sure."

"Can I dig into this on my own? Roderick? Can I help him?"

"You owe seven classes and one prep period your full attention from first bell to last, Monday through Friday," he said, a smile tugging at the corners.

"Right."

"That's a pretty full plate."

"I understand," she said.

"Whatever you do the rest of the time, within the boundaries of legality and good judgment, are none of my concern."

"Got it. Thank you."

Rowanda Jerkins came to see Jane after the bell ended the final period, lingering at the door shyly, as if she required an invitation.

"Need something, Ro?"

The big girl edged into the room but stayed on the periphery. It was a different stance from the one Jane had observed in their first few days together. Ro always had her armor up. Now, she appeared out of place and uncertain.

"Ro?"

"What's going to happen to Roderick?" she asked.

Jane dropped her eyes back to the stack of papers on her desk, her own homework bound for her satchel. "I don't know," she lied.

"He going to be expelled?"

"Maybe." Jane hated this. Ro clearly knew the score and was looking for confirmation, and Jane couldn't provide it because, honestly, she didn't know how much she could say and when and to whom. So she cracked the door open just a hair so she wouldn't feel like she was lying and obfuscating when the full truth inevitably emerged.

"It's not fair," Ro said.

"What isn't?"

"Expelling Roderick. That kid has been picking on him all year. I'd have whupped his ass a long time ago." Her face went flush. "Sorry. I shouldn't say 'ass.'"

Jane sat, and she waved Ro in and invited her to take a chair. The girl moved upon the bid, but still she led with tentativeness. In the doorway opening, Claire appeared, and Jane gave her a little wave, a stay-put-and-wait signal.

"Picking on him how?" Jane asked.

"You know, making fun of him, pushing him down, ganging up. Him and his friends. But mostly, it's been Noah."

"I see."

"I guess he finally had enough," Ro said.

"You say this kid's name is—"

"Noah Nelson."

"And he's just gotten away with it?"

Ro fidgeted. "Noah Nelson is the kind of kid who always gets away with it. Please don't let them expel Roderick."

"Ro," Jane started, "listen, I'm not sure—"

"Please."

"I'll try," Jane said. "I'm surprised. Surprised you're defending Roderick. You two go at it pretty good, don't you?" Jane had seen enough in the homeroom period, with Ro's guarded sense of her own, non-gender-specific destiny often at odds with Roderick's inflated view of himself. There had been collisions—minor ones, yes, nothing that set the world on tilt, but also ones that left a dent.

"Roderick's a jackass," she said, then she clapped a hand over his mouth. "Sorry, I shouldn't say 'jackass.'"

Jane waved her off.

"But he didn't do anything wrong," Ro finished. "He was sticking up for himself. A kid shouldn't get expelled for that, should he?"

"No," Jane said, neutrality be damned.

"That's all I'm saying."

"I'll see what I can do, Ro."

"Thank you." The girl finally made eye contact.

"No promises, though," Jane said.

"I understand."

Jane and Claire rode home in silence. It wasn't the stony, stilted kind, the kind they had certainly experienced in any number of other ways. It was deferential, somber. The hallway fight—Jane's involvement and Claire's witnessing the scene—hung in the air between them as something that would surely have to be talked about and put away, but not now. It was all too fresh, too visceral. Jane appreciated Claire's inherent sense of when to speak and when to stay silent, and she wondered where the girl had picked it up. Not from Paul, surely. And probably not from Jane, for that matter. No questions about Ro, either, for which Jane was thankful. The way she figured it, there had to be a church-and-state separation between what she and her daughter spoke about with regard to school in general and the specifics of Jane's—and Claire's, to some extent—involvements there. No way she could give Claire a little flavor of what Ro had said without a full taste, and Claire was no more entitled to that than any other kid was.

Jane pulled into the driveway, opposite the empty space usually occupied by Eric's truck.

"Grandpa's gone," Claire said.

"I see that."

"Guess you're making dinner."

"Guess so," Jane said. "What do you want?"

"Chicken and dumplings!"

"Oh, Claire, not tonight. So much chopping."

Claire pulled herself into a small pout. "You asked. I answered."

"OK," Jane said. "You're right. You have homework?"

"A little."

"You get on it. No online time until you're done."

"Aw."

"That's the deal. And chicken and dumplings it is. OK?"

The two of them got out and headed for the house, each carrying her own take-home pile from school. Inside, Claire veered left, down the hall and into her room, a reminder of Jane's no-online-time admonition trailing her. Jane went on into the living room, propping her satchel on the side of the couch. The day's mail sat waiting on the table, put there, as per usual, by her father. She thumbed through it. So far, the forwarding she had put in from the Montana apartment had yielded only flyers from the library and such, a minor relief. Surely, a few final bills from their old place—lights and water—would be coming, and Jane would have to find a way to stretch their dollars to cover them and whatever expenses flared up before her first paycheck at the end of the month. She had gotten adept at pulling on both ends of Abe Lincoln till he screamed, but the continual demands of frugality wore on her.

In the kitchen, she went to the fridge and pulled out carrots, a couple of yellow potatoes, celery, and onion, and she set them on the counter for chopping and dicing. She went past the washer and dryer in the adjoining utility room, out the door to the garage. She stepped onto the cold concrete and took in the scent of mustiness and oil and grease and the tailings of a full, boisterous life of a house and its inhabitants, past and present and renewed. She added to her mental list of the things she would try to get done before she and Claire would at last be able to leave this place for their own apartment. A thorough cleaning in here was decades overdue, it seemed.

From the deep freeze, she extracted a package of frozen chicken tenderloins. When she turned to re-enter the house, that's when it caught her eye, just a flutter in her cornea that somehow stopped her and compelled a deeper look.

There, on a shelf over Eric's workbench, the dripping of purplish liquid left streaks against the plywood, on its way down to the wooden bench tabletop, where it pooled in a sickly maroon.

Jane moved up for a closer look, seeking the source, and there it was. A Styrofoam bottom piece, wrapped in cellophane, with the blood of two prime porterhouses having found its way out and gravity taking things from there.

"Jesus, Dad." With her free hand, Jane gathered up the rotten package, and animal blood filled her palm. She set a foot into the door, springing it open, and she went into the house. On her way to the kitchen, she dropped ruined the steaks in the garbage.

Twenty-six

Eric jutted his face toward the backgammon board, bifocals low on his nose, and examined the scant opportunities available to him. Jocelyn had him in one hell of a pickle, one of his pieces on the bar after being knocked out on her last roll, five sets of her own pieces blocking his spaces to come out, leaving only the two-spot available to him.

He put the dice in the cup, covered it with his hand, gave the cup two shakes and tumbled them out.

"Acey deucey!"

"Luckiest roll ever," Jocelyn said.

Eric brought his stranded piece out with the two. With the one, he consolidated a position on her side of the board. And by moving his single stranded piece five spaces four times, by the rules of the game, he stranded another of her pieces and consolidated another spot on her side.

Jocelyn looked it over. She held the dice cup to her mouth and spoke to it. "Three and five, baby. You can do it."

She rolled. The dice came up one and four.

"My roll," Eric said, and he gave his own cup a maracas-style shake and shimmied his upper body and winked at her, and Jocelyn laughed.

"Double sixes!" he announced the tumble.

"You have got to be kidding me."

Eric moved two pieces into position No. 5 on her board, reducing her escape route to the No. 3 spot. On his bonus roll, his final two pieces came in safely, adding to the stacks at spots 2 and 4.

"You can still do it," he said.

"I doubt it."

"One way to find out."

She rolled, half-hearted, and got neither of her two stranded pieces back into play. Eric rolled again, double threes, and he moved two pieces up from the No. 6 spot to No. 3. Every escape route was now behind him. A bonus roll—a three and a two— brought one piece home and moved the other safely up to the No. 1 spot.

"It's over," she said.

"Not yet. Roll."

She did, again without much enthusiasm, and the tumbling dice validated that. A five and a six brought her fully into play but with no way of stopping him.

"It's over," she said again, and she began pulling her pieces back and arranging them in the tray. "Three games are enough for me. I know when it's not my day."

"I'm the champeen," Eric crowed, and he flapped his arms happily.

"Never should have taught you how to play it."

"Come here, you," Eric said, and he rose and went to her, and still sitting she leaned into him, and he stroked her hair and gave her a kiss atop the head.

"Better?" he asked.

"A little bit," she said. "Maybe one more."

He dipped his head again and smooched. He lingered on it, smelling her hair. He had wanted to do this the first time he saw her, the second time, the third time. He had been thinking of it, imagining it, since that day she pecked him on the lips while in his truck and he had been left wanting nothing more than for her to do it again and again. Now, he wanted nothing more than to progress from head kisses to face kisses to lip kisses to neck kisses and all that might lie beyond those. He wanted nothing more and he feared nothing more.

"A little dizzy," he said, bringing himself upright again. "Sorry." He slow-footed to the ottoman.

"Are you all right?" She stood and followed him, concern flooding in where bliss had just lived. She sat opposite him and reached for his hand.

"I'm fine. A reminder, I guess."

"A reminder?"

"I'm not as studly as I used to be."

"Who is?"

"Fair," he said. "Still, you know, the head remembers things, but the body sometimes is all, 'Hold on there, cowboy.' I wanted to sweep you up in my arms." He gave words to the thought as it came to him, allowing himself no room to back away from it.

"I would have liked that, cowboy."

"Well," he said softly, "maybe at some other rodeo."

They leaned toward each other, hands clasped, the fullness of the moment a buffer between them. He thought again of the past and how it informed the now, how audacious and ill-advised and beautiful and unprecedented and tender and unsustainable and heart-wrenching it all had been, their mutual plunge into infidelity. It had been a snap decision, underpinned by a lengthy and scarcely concealed longing one for the other, something that rallied from concept to reality in a time when the conditions were right. Her husband, detached and distant and gone too often, out on the road with the Texas Rangers, covering the team for the *Star-Telegram*. His Margery, tangled up in the final stretch of rearing their daughter, which he'd left her to, and the two of them in a particular era of a long marriage when they were traveling together but in separate compartments. Their grown and nearly grown kids—two for her, one for him—and their time-honored pulling away from the families. All of that, and their own rising desire, had given them an opening. It didn't excuse anything, they told each other then, but they weren't in it to hurt anyone, either. Surely there was some loftiness in intent, they tried to convince themselves. And when that notion hadn't taken root, they'd simply stopped talking about it and followed their passions where they led. Like most things, everything had a beginning and an end.

And now, he thought, *it has this.*

"Eric?"

"Mmhm."

"What are your intentions?"

The question caught him sideways, and he looked to her, and she stared back with earnestness that compelled an answer.

"I haven't thought about it," he said.

"Yes, you have."

"I don't have any expectations," he tried again.

"I asked about intentions."

"I haven't thought about it," he said.

"Yes, you have."

Her matter-of-fact tenacity disarmed and disconcerted him. He knew now that she would have to get a truthful answer from him, even if she had to foul off a dozen of his weak pitches, and that threw a scare into him.

"I want to see you," he said at last. "Whenever I can. Whenever it's OK."

"Good," she said. "I want that, too."

He exhaled, long and relieved, and he clutched her hands

tighter. "I'm so happy to hear you say that." He leaned toward her and kissed her lips, and she kissed back, then pulled away.

"I want something else," she said.

"What?"

"I want to be courted."

He dropped back into the chair, still holding her hands, his arms gone rigid. "What, like—"

"Silly," she said, a slight laugh in her words. "I don't want you to take me to the cotillion. I don't want you to ask my daddy for my hand—though, I must say, Albert Adkins would have liked you, I think," and at this, Eric brought himself back into a full sit, and he massaged one of her knuckles between his thumb and forefinger.

"I want to go out sometimes. I don't want to sneak. I'm too old—we're too old—and if I have to do that to have the things I want, well, I just won't want them."

"We had to."

"Sure," she said. "Then. Not now."

"I know," he said.

"I just want to be honest about what it is, if it's anything."

"It is."

"Honest not just with you and me. Honest with everyone."

"Jane," he said.

"And Rob and Brent. And anyone else."

"You've told your sons?"

"No," she said. "But I will. I mean, I'm not going to call them up and say, 'Hey, boys, big news: I'm dating Eric Driskell.' But—"

"Dating," he said, dreamily.

"*But*," she reasserted. "But when they ask what I've been doing, I might mention you. Maybe. If you behave." She nuzzled him.

"I understand."

She pulled away, just a bit. "You sound nervous."

"No."

"No?"

"Just thinking," he said. "It's going to be a hell of a shock to her, on top of the hell of a shock of being back home and working a new job and living with her old man."

"Sure. She's grown up. She can handle it."

"I'll tell her," Eric said. "Absolutely."

She came to him again now, and he held her shoulders, and he felt gratitude and reluctance filling him in equal measures.

"Invite me to dinner," she said. "Introduce me."

"I could do that," he said, even as a torrent of reasons he couldn't came bursting in. "I'll talk to her. See when we might have a good night for that."

She disengaged from him now and sat back on the couch, his right hand and her left still keeping the faith, entwined, their arms stretching to cover the distance.

"I need to say something," she said.

"OK."

"I've been rehearsing it, a little. But it might not all come together exactly right, so just bear with me."

"OK."

"I need to talk about what happened after it ended." When Eric began to break in on her, she hurried up her words. "I know we said we wouldn't, but I need to tell you this, OK?"

"Yes," he said.

"I know we talked about how if it ever threatened someone else, we'd just walk away, no questions, no hurt feelings, we'd just do it. And I was fine with that when we said it, and I abided by it when it happened. And I never, not once, held a grudge when you told me it was over. I didn't."

"I know you didn't."

"But I was hurt," she said. "I drew myself up into what I had with Ed—a house, a community, two boys we adored, a structure if not a substance—and I rode things out, because I'd been a part of choosing them and setting those things into motion, and I couldn't come up with a good enough reason to release myself from them. Right or wrong, that's where I came out on it."

Eric rubbed the skin of her hand, paper-thin, and he looked away, beating back what was welling up. He tried to make sense of the feeling he had—not guilt, exactly, because he, too, had simply abided by their stated ground rules. He thought of how they had stood under the willow in her backyard that April day, the rain hanging off their noses and chins and eyelashes, and he had said, "We can't anymore," and he had turned away from her and left, smothering any chance of reconsideration, how he had gone through her gate and away from her, and that had been that. It was the letter of the law they had written together, the spirit of it be damned. He had gone home to Margery, whom he still loved, whom he had always loved—and for that, he did feel and always had felt guilt, that he should think himself worthy of the love of two good women. He had gone home and gotten on with it, and he had made his intentions stick until Margery died. From that day to the one when Jocelyn had said hello in a crowded mall, inertia had held sway.

"I'm sorry," he said.

"You owe me no sorrow."

"And yet."

She squeezed his fingers. "I know. I'm just saying, I'm released from that life. I learned some things. I could be OK keeping my heart an empty chamber. I could go on sleeping in a loveless bed. I thought I would, and I was OK with that. And now I don't want to. But the agreement where you and I are concerned, if you and I are going to be concerned, must change."

Eric went from the chair to his knees, and he scooted himself until he was against her legs, and he took her face in his hands and slipped fingers into her hair, and he pulled her to him and he kissed her on the mouth the way he'd been wanting to. He placed his head on her shoulder, and she held it there, and she spoke softly to him.

"What a gift this has turned out to be."

Twenty-seven

Jane figured she hadn't been on Odell Street in twenty-five years, maybe longer. Whatever the length of the absence, she found it difficult to reconcile what she saw now with what unreliable memory served up. Here, on one of the oldest streets in one of the oldest parts of the county, what still endured and what was becoming held an uneasy, divergent coexistence. For every boxy, clapboard, working-poor, dirt-driveway house that still stood, two more had been leveled and filled in with a tidy, modern suburban kingdom, brick walls that pushed out to the boundary lines and an automatic garage door and four bedrooms and a toilet for every occupant.

Her house, then and now, sat not a ten-minute walk straight north, and it might as well have been a hundred miles for all life on Odell Street had ever figured into her own. It once surely teemed with kids, same as her own neighborhood had, but she couldn't remember a single name of anyone who had lived here, she didn't have any friends who piled into sleepovers here like all those long-ago kids did on Payte Lane, didn't recall a single time that her childhood play—when she and the neighborhood kids would bang out of the door after breakfast and range far afield until lunchtime—took her or her friends this scant distance from their homes. And school, then as now, simply tended to reinforce the stratifications that were already long set by where you had grown up and with whom.

Jane eased the right-side wheels of the car against the curb, hearing the groan of rubber against concrete, and set the brake. She looked to the passenger seat and verified the forlorn house number against the scrap of paper, jotted by her hand. They matched.

The house was short and squat and neglected if not unloved, a homely assemblage of deferred maintenance obvious to anyone who might give it more than a glance. Jane went around to the passenger side, the backseat, and opened the door and collected what she had been able to extract from her colleagues. Quizzes gone light from multiple copies and chapters and lesson plans scratched out in hurried handwriting. She left behind the rest of what she'd been given in those between-bells conferences, the expressed grave doubts about Roderick A. Watson's future and the dismissal of Jane's own quixotic compulsion and, quietly, the murmured encouragement from those teachers who saw something in him beyond another kid to be sent down the assembly line.

At the door, Jane's knock was met by a dour woman, who was wearing a bathrobe in the middle of the afternoon, her what-do-you-want stare ensuring that she didn't need words to push across her message. She pulled the door back in full but left the screen latched.

"You're Roderick's mother?"

"I am," the woman said. "Who're you?"

"I'm Jane Sperling. I'm his homeroom teacher."

The introduction drew the slightest of shifts in the woman's dead-set blank stare, nearly imperceptible, had Jane not been searching her face for some way into the larger conversation she wished to have.

"Well," the woman said, "this is new."

"New?"

"I get letters from you people," she said. "*Got* a letter. Got it yesterday, not that it didn't tell me anything I hadn't already heard. This is my first visit. And on a Saturday, no less." She lifted the latch from the hook and pushed the screen door out, and Jane stepped by to make room for the clearance. "Well, come on in, then."

Jane caught the screen door when Roderick's mother let it go, and she fell into the house behind the woman, into an abrupt darkness that sent her pupils widening to let in whatever light might be scrounged up. She stood still for a second, gaining her bearings. A cavalcade of scents swept through her, burnt toast and the mustiness of old things and the latent sourness of an old house that baked in summertime and was a meat locker in winter. The leavings of those extremes had been stored up in its many decades.

"Come on," Roderick's mother said, "we'll sit in the kitchen."

Jane followed her forward, into a lighter room, one with walls of faded yellow and a high-low oven set from the 1970s, when such things were made to last, and a stove of similar vintage, once white and now gone to a grimy gray, the plug-in heating coils rising above its summit.

"Sit down," the woman said, and Jane let herself into a blue Naugahyde chair and set her hands atop the round table with the chipped edges that showed where the vinyl finish met particle board.

"Roderick's outside. Want me to get him?"

Jane shook her head. "Let's you and me talk first." Opposite her, Roderick's mother tumbled into her own chair, and she grasped the lapels of her robe and sealed them up, giving her ample breasts a snug home.

"So talk," she said.

A flash of something in the window over the sink caught Jane's attention, and she sat up a bit, craning her neck, and looked out. Along the fence near the house, Roderick had ducked into a ramshackle structure, one constructed of two-by-fours and plywood that had gone gray and weatherbeaten.

"What's he doing?"

"Pigeons," his mother said. "The boy raises pigeons."

"Pigeons?"

"Heaven help me," she said. "We got twenty-six mouths to feed around here. Roderick's, mine, and the twenty-four birds he got out there."

"Pigeons," Jane said again, and she pushed herself up for a better look. Roderick was out of the coop now, wielding the spray attachment of a long, green hose, washing down feed bins. "Well, isn't that something?"

"Mrs. Sperling?"

"Huh?"

"You didn't come here to talk about pigeons," the woman said.

"No." Jane folded herself back into the chair and offered the woman a tight-lipped smile.

"Well, what do you want?"

Jane swallowed and tried to cue up the words she had arranged in her head on the drive over. "Well," she said, "the thing is, this isn't an official visit. I assume the letter was about the fight Roderick got into and the fallout, I guess, from that."

The woman scoffed. "Fallout. Bullshit, more like it."

"So, anyway, Miss—" Jane, flustered, managed to retrieve the coming fumble. "I'm sorry, what should—"

"Name's Wanda."

"Wanda," Jane repeated.

"Go on."

Jane nodded. "Right. So, I just wanted to come by and see how he was doing."

"You did?"

"Yes."

"I see." The dubiousness of the words and the distrust on the face Jane stared into told her that Wanda didn't see, and what's more, she wasn't quite ready to accept that Jane was there at all, and it stood to reason that she didn't quite know how it had come to this, a strange white woman sitting in her kitchen on a Saturday morning.

Jane set her satchel on the table. "I brought him some things. Some of the assignments he was working on." She pulled the papers from the satchel and stacked them on the table, then put the satchel under her chair.

"You did?"

"Yes."

"Why?"

A stumper, that question.

"I thought he might want to keep up," Jane stammered out.

"You did?"

"Sure."

"OK."

Through the window opposite her, Jane watched a dozen or so birds take to the sky as Roderick ushered them from the coop with long, dramatic waves of his arms.

Wanda grumbled, an effective attention-getter. Jane rejoined the moment.

"Are you going to enroll him somewhere else?" Jane asked, drawing an annoyed glance. "None of my business, of course."

"Well, I guess I'll have to, won't I?"

Jane let it pass, knowing a rhetorical question when she heard one. For the first time since she had resolved to get involved in this way—even if the involvement turned out to be nothing more than pushing paper across the table to Roderick's mother and leaving the disposition of it to chance—she wondered whether she had fully thought through what she might find in the sublayers of this young man's life. He was bathed and clothed and fed, true enough, and obviously allowed to dabble in at least one hobby, but what else was tucked here into his day-to-day life beyond the school bells? She thought of David's admonition when she had told him what she intended to do. "Don't do it," he'd said. "You can't save him. You can't. You'll just get tangled up in something that'll be heartbreaking." Jane had thought it too cynical by half and too assumptive of her intentions by the other half. Now, she wondered whether he might have been right, whether her time and attention belonged somewhere else, somewhere less futile, somewhere she could disburse her contributions more precisely.

"I'm sorry," Wanda said, the first notes of softness from her. "It ain't you I'm angry at. I know who you are. Roderick told me you pulled him off that boy. He said you're a nice lady."

"That's nice of him to say. I don't think he knows me that well."

"Well," Wanda said, "you made some kind of impression on him. He doesn't have much to say about anybody up at that school. The boy lives inside himself. Like his daddy in that way. A little too much, I'd say, but I can't do anything about that."

Jane clasped her hands on the table and leaned in with commensurate gravity. "What are you going to do, Wanda?"

Roderick's mother sighed and adjusted her robe again and pinched the corners of her eyes and drew her thumb and index finger together, a meeting at the bridge of her nose.

"I'm thinking Watauga Middle," she said, and Jane nodded, for she, too, had thought of the same school, an older campus in the suburb just to the west. "Got a brother over there who can tend to getting him to school and getting him back to me come the afternoon. But he's down on the coast on a job till mid-month, so until then, I guess..."

"Homeschool?"

"Yeah."

Jane smiled and pushed the stack across. "I can bring more over the next couple of weeks."

"Would you?"

"Be happy to."

Jane looked out the window again. A few birds milled atop the coop. Roderick was out of view.

"Why you doing this?" Wanda asked. It was plaintive, not suspicious, not accusatory. If anything, it carried a whiff of bafflement.

"Just trying to help."

"But why?"

Jane gave the question due consideration. The honest truth was that the motivation hadn't formed into a clear reason. Instead, it had amalgamated from a few sources, among them Tim's bloodless decree that Roderick had to go so the other several hundred students could advance uninhibited, Rowanda's pleas on Roderick's behalf, and Jane's own interior sense that the playout hadn't been just.

"I think he got a raw deal," she said, and her insides went queasy at the unvarnished declaration.

"At school?"

"Yes," Jane said, in for a penny and for a pound.

"That the official word?"

"No," she said, her unease growing. "That's me talking straight to you, my own assessment."

"I see."

"I'm sorry," Jane said.

"Well, that don't exactly help, but I suppose I appreciate it," Wanda said. "And you're right: raw deal. That kid what done it, that Nelson boy, it's not the first time he's taken aim at Roderick. First time Rod's gone back at him, though."

"This is what I've heard," Jane said.

"I told him to do it," she went on. "Tried it the other way. Took a day off work to go up there and try to get them to get that boy off Rod. They didn't. Things just got worse. So I told him, I said, 'Rod,' I said, 'I don't want my boy throwin' the first punch, but

I'm also not gonna have you just stand there and get your head beat in.'"

"I see."

"He did what he had to do," Wanda said.

"I understand."

"I wish somebody else up there did." Roderick's mother sighed and went silent for a few moments, and Jane sat quietly, too, and let her eyes drift around the place. From outside the back wall came the unmistakable sound of a screen door banging against the house as if thrown open, and through the glass of the bigger door behind it, Jane saw Roderick's face rise up. He came through and stood on the kitchen floor in muddy shoes.

"I saw your car," he said.

"Roderick," his mother began, torqueing herself in her chair to face him, "Mrs. Sperling—"

"Brought my homework. I was listening."

"I thought you—" Jane started.

"Would want to keep up. I heard."

"Roderick," his mother said. "She thinks—"

"I got a bum deal."

"Well, she does."

"So?" he asked.

"Roderick!"

"It's OK," Jane said. "You're mad. I get it."

"Wouldn't you be?"

"I'm sure I would," she said.

"She's trying to help," his mother said.

"No, she's not," he said to her. "She just feels guilty."

Jane saw how the insolence threw his mother off-stride—no small trick, she imagined—and so she made a snap decision to intervene before everything went tumbling further sideways.

"Can you show me your pigeons?" she asked.

"My pigeons?"

"Out back. Show me."

"They're flying," he said. "Nothing to show."

"Rod." The single word came out of his mother in a long syllable, with a jerk of the head and her eyes angling him back toward the door he'd just come through.

He looked to his mother, to Jane, then back to his mother. He reached behind him for the doorknob and pulled it open again, the cold air outside mounting a charge against the warmth inside.

"Well," he said. "Come on, then."

Dear Claire

August 1, 2014

I never hate any word so much as "so," especially when Jim says it, because I both know what's coming and don't have any idea. "So," Jim says, and I brace myself for it, because everything that breaks me down begins with the same two-letter word, the aftermath of which seeds the ground for the four-letter ones I'll be saying.

Today, Jim says, "So...let's talk about when you found out your father was cheating."

I told him that's pretty far afield.

"Of what?"

Of what I've been coming here to do, I told him.

"Which is?"

I knew he was going to say that. So (that word again), I told him that I was there to figure my shit out, and the words just hung out there like laundry drying in the sun, and the weakness of my position was laid bare.

So we talked about it. And, god, Claire, I hope I've already told you these things before you read them here, but I might not, because the topic is so hard, but I've resolved to do this thing of being accountable to us after these sessions. Even though I cried my way through it not an hour ago. Even though I'd rather go into the living room, where you are, and watch whatever it is you're watching.

I leave these sessions with Jim exhausted, always hollowed out, sometimes cried out, almost every one of those instances afterward, in the car and in the parking lot, because if there's one takeaway I have from this crash-landing of a marriage to your father, it's that I'm not going to spend my time crying in front of men anymore (nor should you, Claire, ever). I go home sometimes and I think there's no currency here with Jim, no ongoing reason to come back, and then time and reflection and reading have their way with me, and it brings me into a clearing and I see it. I see the reason I had to sidle up to that horrible room and throw open that door and go into it and start holding those things up to the light after they've spent so long in the darkness. So here's the further thing: I trust him. Goddammit. I do.

I told him it was dumb bad luck, what I discovered about my father, but that was only half right. It was dumb. I don't think bad luck had much to do with it, honestly. I was in an alleyway—there was one a couple of blocks from my house, and Bobby and I could meet up there sometimes, this little notch behind an abandoned house, no one could see us, and...

Oh, Claire, this is so hard. Bobby. Yes. Bobby. After what he'd done to me, I went back willingly, several times. This time. God. I've been so stupid. It scares me for you, how stupid I've been, because... because I'm not special.

It was April. It was rainy. I saw him, your grandfather, come out of the Blankenships' backyard, and I knew. I knew it as surely as I knew anything. Which I told Jim.

Jim wanted to know how I knew.

His questions annoy me. They're piercing and journalistic, delivered without rancor or judgment or preamble. To engage honestly with them, and with him, means to answer as directly as I'm asked, so I told him: "It's the middle of the day. Mom is up in Denver, I think, visiting my aunt. Jocelyn Blankenship's sons are grown, out of the house. Her husband, he was a sportswriter, is out of town, too, I'm pretty sure."

So, Jim asks me, what happened next?

Dad walked right past us, no more than ten feet away from me and Bobby. Didn't see us. Wasn't looking but straight ahead, walking fast. Walking guilty. I'm putting my pants on, whispering to Bobby that I gotta go, and I follow him home.

Dad goes in the front door of our house. I'm maybe a minute, a minute and a half behind. I bang in. He jumps. He's scared. I can see it on him.

And I let him have it.

By now, Jim's leaning forward, and I'm leaning forward to meet him, into the memory. It's weird, Claire. I've left the place where the memories exist in impressionistic snippets, where time and place are clear but the more trivial details have blurred in time's passages, and I'm looking into the memories as if they're a photograph, high-definition. I don't have to pull them from the recesses. They're right there.

I'm saying to Dad, "I know where you were," and he's just looking at me and, he's not even nodding or acknowledging, but he's also not arguing with me. Your father, the poker player, would call that a "tell." So I pressure things up a little. "I know what you were doing," I say, "and I know who you were doing it to."

Jim wants to know what Dad said, and there's no answer, really. He said nothing at first, and then he kind of looked around, all nervous. Like he's trapped. Like a rat. Like a trapped rat.

And then he asked me how long I knew, and it had literally been, like, eight minutes, but I said, "Long enough."

That's when Jim pissed me off. He asked me why I didn't tell him the truth of the discovery.

"Why are you defending him?" I asked. Oh, I was hot. The anger was flashing and churning. "What do you think a guy who does something like that wants with the truth?" I asked Jim. "He wouldn't even know it if he saw it, the truth."

Jim said he wasn't defending anyone or anything. Just asking questions. Yeah, yeah. So he asks what my father said.

And it was the most pathetic thing, Claire. He said he loved my mother and that he loved Mrs. Blankenship, too. I told him he was full of shit.

Jim again: "What if he was being truthful?"

Me: "What if you fucked right off, Jim?"

Jim: "This isn't about me."

Maybe not, OK, but it seemed like he was concocting bullshit defenses for someone else's bullshit. And, anyway, so what if Dad was being truthful? What right did he have to love some other woman when he's married to my mother?

So then Jim does what Jim does. Asks me if I want to talk about rights or human emotions. The fucker.

I could feel myself rocketing into new stratospheres of anger now, but I didn't have a flamethrower, which I'd have liked to use on Jim and his questions, so I just said, "I don't get you."

"It's not me you have to get," he said. Typical.

"No," I said. "Stop doing that. I asked you what right he has to love someone else. So answer the question."

"It's not for me to say. I can't answer for him."

So I told Jim, not for the first time, to go fuck himself. Congratulations. He got a rise out of me. Go home and tell the wife. Banner day for Jim Jennings. Congratulations.

Jim: "You want to get into this? If you want to get into this, I'll get into this."

I told him to bring it. And, Jesus, Claire, he brought it. By the way, you can't read this until you're thirty-eight years old. I've decided.

"I don't know why your dad was fucking the lady down the street," he says. "I don't know why he decided to, why he kept deciding to,

I don't know if he loved her or didn't love her. Which means that I know exactly as much after one hour with you twenty-five or so years after the fact as you do with a quarter-century's head start. Now, isn't that something?"

I had nothing. He had more.

"I do know, after a career of listening to people talk about their innermost feelings, after hearing them lay bare the most painful and intimate things, shameful things, devastating things, things that have followed them like ghosts from childhood to the brink of the afterlife, that someone who has subdivided his heart into genuine, caring love for two people is about the least controversial thing I can think of."

I had something to say now, but he cut me right off.

"You want to talk about morals and commitments or wise choices, well, we can cast this an entirely different way and say, yeah, your dad never should have let it get to that place. You want to say that, I'm all the way there with you, Jane. Your dad should have kept it in his pants. But you didn't say that, did you? You said the whole idea of bifurcated love was bullshit, and I'm simply saying, in observation and in data and in anecdote, that I think you're wrong. And I think you've been wrong for a long, long time, and because you haven't reconciled that, because you're still the teenage girl who followed your father home and confronted him but never, until today, confronted your own feelings—because that's who you are today, right now, you're a scared and angry teenage girl—this thing has been dogging you for most of your life. So how about this: How about we confront it now? Wouldn't you like to grow up, finally?"

I told him no. I told him I was right and didn't have to confront anything.

"It's your choice."

I told him that I didn't want to. That, furthermore, I didn't want to be in that room with him anymore.

"It's your choice."

I told him that I don't think I'm coming back.

"It's your choice."
I told him I've chosen.
"OK."
Oh, Claire. I've fucked up.

Twenty-eight

Jane stood in the backyard with Roderick, her sneakers sinking into the mud, and she listened as he held forth on his hobby. He had twenty-four pigeons in all, including two pairs on the nest, which were working on expanding the flock and sticking to the coop while the others flew overhead or strutted around the yard. He told her about his prized capuchines, with the tufted feathers that rose above their heads. "I had to trade four of my best homing birds, but it was worth it," he said. He told her about the rollers, now in flight against the gray gloom. When he clapped his hands, they tumbled end over end and kept going. He pointed out his fantails, one black, one white, who sat puffed-up against the January cold atop the coop.

"Both boys," he said. "They nest together."

"You have gay pigeons?" Jane asked.

"It's their business, not mine."

Jane laughed. She wanted to ask how one goes about figuring out whether a pigeon is a boy or a girl, then she thought better of it, knowing that neither biology nor anatomy nor animal husbandry was her professional bag. Roderick then went ahead and answered the unasked question. He stepped to the coop and swept up the black fantail, which agitated in his sure grip, ruffled by the intrusion.

"Be cool, Hutch," he said.

"Hutch?"

"Yeah. Other one's Starsky."

Another laugh. *Who is this kid?* Here they were, two decades deep into the twenty-first century, his age barely in the double digits and hers steaming hard toward a half-century, and he was pulling pet names from the pop-culture touchstones of her toddler days.

Roderick put the bird under an arm and tilted its ass end up, and he pressed two fingers into the feathered undercarriage. "Feel here," he said.

"I don't think I want to."

"Come on."

He withdrew his fingers to make room for hers. She settled them in there. Hutch seemed no worse for the violation.

"Feel how those bones come together at a point?" he asked.

"Yeah."

"That's a boy. Want me to grab one of the girls? The bones are separated. I can show you."

"It's OK," Jane said. "I believe you."

"It's really easy to figure out once you know."

"I'm worried about whoever found out in the first place."

"Well, my dad showed me."

He moved away from her now, facing away, feigning chores at the coop even as his flock plied pathways skyward.

"What's his name?" she asked. "Your dad."

"Roderick A. Watson. Best name there is."

"Of course."

"He died two years ago."

"I'm sorry."

"He was diabetic. They're his birds, mostly. Ours, I guess. Mine now."

"It's nice to have this to…" She stopped.

"Honor him?"

"Yeah," she said.

"I guess."

At once, Jane ached on the boy's behalf in a way that was no longer abstract. She felt like she had enough of the puzzle pieces now to fill in the places where they didn't connect, where she didn't have to disturb unsettled ground by asking a bunch of questions. A dead father, a mother who necessarily worked and thus left him isolated, some number of hours alone here, inside himself and his own interests, a hedge against the rest of the world. She wondered if she should tell him that she knew the precise and unyielding pain of permanent loss, only from the protracted distances of age and geography, having first injected that buffer between herself and her folks of her own volition long before losing her mother. She decided against it. She didn't know where that observation might lead and couldn't assess her ability to go into those darkened places with Roderick. She stood, and she made herself ready to listen if he wished to speak.

He turned back to her now. "Mom tell you I'm going to go to Watauga?"

"You know she did. You were listening, remember?"

"She tell you I hate it?"

"You know she didn't."

"Well," he said, "I do."

Jane stepped toward him. He stepped back. She stopped.

"Can you do it, though?" she asked.

"Why should I have to? Noah's the dick, not me."

"But can you?"

Roderick glared at her and said nothing. She tried again. "I thought the 'A' stood for *ain't a thing I can't do.*"

He snorted. "It stands for *all this shit, all the time.*"

"Can you do it?" she asked.

"Yeah."

"Good. I'd be disappointed otherwise. I'd think, well, maybe it stands for *all that talk and no action.*"

"You don't even know," he said.

"You show me. Then I will."

Wanda came out to see Jane to the car. She wore a tan knit shirt, clean and tucked, a nametag hanging off the breast pocket: Texas Health Harris Methodist Hospital. A stare too long brought the explanation forth: "Phlebotomist." A nod drew out the rest: "Overnights. It sucks. It's also a job." Jane heard that, sure enough. *The things we won't do to keep the chains moving.*

Jane waved to Roderick, who hung close to the step-up porch. Their further chitchat filled in more of the picture. He really was stuck for a couple of weeks, at least, while he waited for his Uncle Philo to cut loose from a contracted job on the Texas coast and be in position to pick him up mornings and get him to school, then bring him back around while his mother slept. Later, there would be dinner and homework and bedtime, and in the late night, Wanda would break away again, and Roderick would have to tend to himself come sunup.

"I'll bring some more assignments next weekend," Jane said.

"Can't wait," Roderick replied.

Wanda, clearly amused, said, "He's such a little smartass."

"Smart, for certain," Jane said. She had seen the transcript two days earlier. Roderick's grades weren't anything that would put him in a valedictory position in a few years' time, if he even managed to make it that far, but cast against the odds she now saw in his circumstances, Jane considered them borderline miraculous. She would be satisfied to see Claire, not nearly as touched by the vicissitudes of the world as this kid, pull a solid B average across the line, the way he was doing.

Jane said her goodbyes to Wanda and went around to the driver's side, poured herself in, started the car, and did a three-point turn in the street, orienting herself to go back the way she had come in. Another wave to Roderick, who returned it, and she was gone.

Where Odell Street met the larger thoroughfare at a T, she set her blinker, edged out, saw a clear path, cut the wheels right and accelerated, and as she brought the steering wheel around to level and straighten her direction, she felt a heavy thump under her feet. The left front wheel went wobbly in the speedup, and the car lurched and dove, like a shopping cart with a compromised wheel. Control ripped itself from her hands, and the car veered left into the opposite open lane, climbed the curb, and deposited itself into a bank of mailboxes.

The collision wasn't damaging, at least not to Jane's body. At a still-low speed, she felt no whiplash or a violent churning of her innards. It was a glancing blow that still shocked, one that reverberated precisely because it was unanticipated, not because of whatever kinetic power it happened to unleash. The airbag implanted in the middle of the steering wheel didn't balloon out, as she might have expected were this some madcap comedy rather than a garden-variety Saturday taking an unintended turn toward disappointment.

She unlatched herself and stepped shakily from the car and walked to the front of it on gummy legs, and here the damage was more profound. She heard voices and turned and looked at the men emerging from the houses set back from where she had run aground, and she glanced from them into the blankness of the gray above her, the brushstrokes of black clouds against the canvas, and she imagined her dollars—the dwindling few she had, and the coming ones she had already earmarked for better things—going into that sky in a funnel, like Roderick's birds granted their leave but with far less certainty about whether they would be coming back.

Twenty-nine

Eric nuzzled Jocelyn's shoulder. He sighed and he breathed in deep, and he took it all in—the unbridled scent of her skin, the fragrant room, blocked out and darkened by the blinds drawn against the mordant gray outside, the laundered leavings of the covers they had turned down before climbing in, naked and giddy and frightened.

It had felt like a jailbreak, coming here, with Jane having toted Claire off to a friend's house—*a friend, already!*—and then gone off to her own errands. Claire, always idly twirling the jewel around her neck that had solidified a new bond between them, had come to him with a hug and an "I'll see you tomorrow, grandpa," and Jane, well pleased by that and by the change in tenor in the house, had kissed his cheek and said, "I'll be back in a few hours," and at last he had been left alone and granted a clear field to come here. A knock on the door, entry granted, and a wordless walk down the hall, Jocelyn's fingers in his grip, both knowing innately where this ended and what it would begin.

Now, he took in the terrain of her, the gentle rise of the breast in his immediate view, the valley of her abdomen just beyond, and the rounded ridges of her hips. Beneath the sheet, out of sight, the place where he had lingered before the want-to had become insistent but the physical response couldn't match.

The intervening years had left impressions on them both—wrinkles where there once had been none, intransigent skin tags, joints that spoke openly of their lifelong overuse, muscles that had lost their tension. A balky hamstring had taken him down for good, knotting as he sat on his haunches and lined her up, and he had toppled sideways, clutching at the engaged muscle, howling. She had come to him and helped stretch it out, the galactic pain slowly and surely ebbing, then she had lain back and brought his head to her shoulder. She now threaded fingers through his hair.

"Like riding a bike, my ass," he said, and she laughed, her chest heaving, and he kissed her breast.

"This is nice, though," she said.

"The nicest," he said.

He propped himself up on an elbow and looked at her. She turned to him, languid but present.

"How about dinner tonight?" he asked. "I'll take you out."

"Oooh, nice. Where?"

"Wherever you like."

"How about Niki's?"

"The place on Rufe Snow?" he asked.

"Davis."

"Right," he said. "I remember. Sure, that'd be great."

"Just you and me?" she asked. "Do you want to invite the girls?" It amused him, the way she said "the girls." It pierced him, too, in light of the needed and promised things he had not yet told them.

"Claire's got a sleepover," he said. "I think Jane has a date."

"Wow, a date. She moves faster than you."

"Almost," he said. "So it's you and me. Maybe after, you could give me another crack at this."

"Oh, pish," she said.

He dropped onto her again now, his face pressed to her, tiny kisses on the soft skin of her neck, tasting her, a trailing dotted line of his lips to her shoulder and down her arm to her fingers, which he drew into his mouth one by one, then on to her hips and up again, kissing and inhaling and feeling her with his tongue and his lips and his fingers.

When his phone intruded, blaring and buzzing from the pants he had left wadded at the foot of Jocelyn's bed, he placed a finger against her parting lips and said, "No, leave it." He kept kissing her, on the mouth now, and soon the ringing ended and here came the pinging alert that a voicemail had been deposited, and soon after that, another ping that signaled a text message, and Jocelyn said, "Maybe you better," so he did. He untangled himself from her and tumbled around until he sat naked on the end of her bed, and he bent over and pulled the phone from his front pants pocket and looked at the screen. Jocelyn moved up behind him, a chin on his shoulder.

Where are you?

He dialed her, no reason to sit through the voice message, and she answered and asked again, and he told her he had been away from the phone.

"What's up?" he asked, and she told him of the accident, and he zeroed in with the requisite questions: where and when and what the hell and how bad? "I'll be there in a sec," he said. He closed out the call and began pulling his clothes on.

"What happened?"

"Jane had a wreck."

"Is she OK?"

"She's fine," he said. "Car might be pretty cracked up."

"Want me to come?"

"No," he said. He wriggled into his shirt and buttoned it, and he knelt to kiss her. "I'll call about tonight."

"I'll be waiting."

He stood again, then walked to where his shoes waited. He kicked them into alignment and stepped into them, leaving the laces undone. He smiled at her and did his standing hand check, two hands to the chest (glasses in the breast pocket), two hands to the hips (wallet, keys), and he was good to go.

"I was in love with you, you know," he said.

She swaddled herself into the bed, radiant. "I know."

"It could happen again," he said.

"Maybe it already has."

If there was a silver lining to it all, Eric thought, it's that Jane's car hopped the curb in a way that gave him plenty of clearance to wriggle underneath and see what had gone wrong. It was as he suspected while she was describing the unfolding to him, a thrown tie rod, the kind of thing that can ruin your day quick.

"What's that?" Jane asked when he climbed out and gave her the assessment.

"Well, steering control, basically," he said, shutting down the impulse to give her the clinical assessment. "Guess you know that now."

"Yeah."

Truth was, Eric was inclined to huck a good deal of the blame onto his own shoulders. Had he given more thought to the way her tires were wearing down back at Christmas, it might have occurred to him to stop and think, yeah, maybe the camber is off-kilter. But he didn't and he didn't, and here they were.

"What about the rest of it?" she asked.

"Cracked grille, bent bumper. Might be some damage to the radiator. There's some stuff, sure enough."

"Jesus. How much is this gonna cost me?"

Eric stooped over and rubbed his hands on his canvas pants, mid-thigh to the knees. "Hard to say. A couple hundred for the tie rod. A lot more, maybe, depending on the front-end damage."

"Jesus."

"I'll get her hooked up. Won't know till she's looked at."

As Eric tended to the task, a car carrying two of North Richland Hills' finest rolled up behind, strobes casting silent splashes around. The young men got out and walked the perimeter of the smash-up, whistling.

"How'd this happen?" one asked Jane.

"Tie rod, he says." She nodded toward her father. He'd pushed the car back from the collision site and was preparing it for the tow.

"OK," said the other. "Sit tight, would you?"

The cops split up and went to the doors of the mailbox owners, who came out to chat. Eric put out traffic cones and positioned his truck to draw up the battered sedan. When the officers returned, they asked for Jane's license, registration, and insurance. She went around to the passenger side of the elevated car and fished them from the glovebox, then handed them over.

"Montana, huh?" an officer asked.

"No," she said. "Here. Seventy twenty-five Payte. I just haven't gotten my license changed over yet."

"How long you been here?"

"Like, two weeks."

"Need to get on that."

"Yeah," she said, curt and quick. "I know. It was Christmas. Happy New Year."

He handed back her documents, and the officers cleared out.

"Come on," Eric prompted her.

Jane stood, cross-armed, face tilted skyward.

"Come on," he said again.

She dropped her hands, clapping them against her hips, and she trudged past him to the passenger-side door, opened it, and climbed in. Eric gathered the orange cones and stashed them, crawled into the driver's seat, waited for a clear path, then made a wide U-turn on Smithfield Road and headed south.

The old garage looked the same, Jane thought, right down to the weather-whipped aluminum sign that fronted the place, the one with her father's name as the centerpiece: ERIC'S GARAGE AND PULL-YOUR-PART. The hyphens had always bothered her, even when she was a youngster and her sense of their misplacement was intuitive rather than grounded in diagnostics, much in the same way that extraneous quotation marks did now. "Enter." No "loitering." She'd have to have a laugh about that with David, whenever she felt like laughing again.

"He kept the name," she said.

"Well, Danny bought more than a bunch of tools and hydraulic lifts and scrap cars," her father replied. "He bought a load of goodwill, too."

The driving force of memory, so strong since her arrival, barreled into her again. Happy summer mornings spent here with her dad had dwindled with each passing year, but there was a sweet spot of recall, times when she had come here with him, the lunches her mother had packed for them both—an aluminum lunch pail for him and a My Pretty Pony plastic carrier for her—and she had whiled away the days skipping rope on the hard, smooth ground of the driveway, pulling cold and sweaty bottles of Dr Pepper from the cooler in the office and sneaking them behind the hulking car carcasses in the scrapyard to be gulped down, and sorting out the nuts and bolts from the big coffee cans her dad dumped out for her. Even now, years since she had seen the place, the hints of oil and grease on the wind carried the flavor of pure nostalgia. She had loved her daddy before she hated him, before she pitied him, before she reluctantly tried to forgive him, forever teetering on the precipice of getting to absolution and falling headlong back into enmity.

Danny Axtell came out of the office, waving, and here, too, time had made its mark. He was a few years younger than she, her father's protégé, the only assistant he'd ever had around the place who came and stuck and stayed loyal. When Eric had begun to feel the weight of the years and the work and went looking for an exit, Danny had stepped up with a bank loan and the desire to take over. That time was part of a rolling sea change in Eric's behavior after her mother had died, as his workaholic ways ebbed and he made yearly pilgrimages north to Montana, not for her and Claire so much as to suck down beers and catch fish with Paul. Now, here they were, six years on, and Danny had kept the place off the ice. It had all worked out.

"Well, lookee here," Danny said when she cranked down her window and poked her head out. "The prodigal daughter." He fairly twinkled at the sight of her, which gave her a warm feeling in the face of her rising fear about the car, and she marveled at how the intervening time had made inroads on him. The hair, still largely jet-black, was ceding to threads of gray. The chin wasn't so resolute anymore, folded back into his throat along with another one. A distended tummy stretched his work shirt. He didn't much resemble the eighteen-year-old with whom she'd had a torrid wrestling session in her parents' garage while a Christmas party went on just inside the door. That had been a fun diversion, albeit brief, and ultimately a case of misaligned priorities. Danny had stopped her before the escalation, grabbing her hands and saying, "No, I can't. I don't want to disrespect Mr. Driskell like that," and that had been too bad, because such disrespect had been her primary objective.

"Hi, Danny," she said. "Good to see you."

Eric, out of the truck, came around to the backside and gave her car a pat on the fanny as he passed. "Thrown left tie rod," he said. "Some front-end damage, too. Can you get her going again?"

"Yeah, sure," Danny said.

Jane hopped out. "How much is this going to cost?"

Danny, hands in pockets, went to the front of the car and gave it the once-over. "Ain't gonna charge you for the labor," he said. "I'd say seven hundred. Maybe a grand, twelve-fifty if there's something I'm not seeing. Maybe less. Hard to say."

Jane bit her lip and hoped. Any amount was too much, under the circumstances, but her assume-the-worst thoughts had carried her well beyond those markers.

"How long?" Eric asked.

Danny shrugged. "A week?"

"I can't be without a car for a week," she said.

"We'll get a rental," Eric said.

"Yeah, because I can afford that."

"Well, honey—"

"What about that?" Danny pointed off to one of the two work bays, at a black car—Jane was no expert, but surely it dated to the seventies—dotted with splotches of gray primer. Its back end was jacked up, one tire off, the other wider than her father's torso.

"Is that a Barracuda?" her father asked with reverence.

"Yep." She looked now at Danny. He was beaming with fatherly pride.

"Does she run?" Eric asked.

"She will in an hour or so."

"What about it?" Jane asked.

"You could have it as a loaner," Danny said. "Until your car's done."

"I couldn't drive that."

"Why?" he asked. "It's not a stick."

"That's not what I mean. I—"

"That'd be perfect," Eric said. "Thank you." He looked at Jane, lips pursed and eyes widening, the universal signal that one should be mindful of gratitude and gift horses.

"Thank you, Danny," she said.

Jane sat on an upturned grease bucket and listened as the two of them chatted while getting the car loose from the tow truck and pushed back into the row of vehicles idly waiting their turn in a service bay. She found herself envying their shorthand and their easy way with one another, as if they had just picked up the conversational thread from wherever it had last been dropped.

"How's business been?"

"It goes. Finally broke down, got a diagnostic computer in."

"That's when I knew I was done."

"Had to," Danny said. "Too many late-model cars out there."

"Scam. They've got us convinced we need a new one every two years."

"I know. It's like buying clothes for the season. Nothing lasts."

"Nothing does."

"Sure enough right."

"But you're hanging in?"

"Yeah, sure," Danny said. "No complaints."

"Well, that's good."

"Could use some help. Just me. I guess that's a complaint, huh?"

"No, I hear you. Hardest part."

"Wasn't so bad for you, though."

"Well, not after you came along. Before, though, it was rough."

"Yeah. I was fifteen. Was happy to have the job and didn't want to lose it. Fifteen! Can you believe that? I don't think you could even legally put me on the payroll."

"I didn't. Paid you cash. Don't tell the feds."

"Lips sealed."

When they finished, they shook hands, and Eric told Danny they would be back for the Barracuda that evening. Jane stood and hugged Danny and smelled the hints of axle grease and afternoon beer on him, and he said, "Not more than seven hundred, I'm sure of it," and she thanked him again for the muscle-car loaner, then she and her dad left him to it.

"Always liked him," she said as Eric got the truck oriented north on Smithfield Road and set a course for home.

"True blue. Not many of them."

"Thanks for your help," she said. "Wish I didn't have to keep asking for it."

"Happy to do it." They split a glance and a slight smile between the gap in the bench seat, and he turned his focus back to the road, to the neighborhood coming up fast, to the right turn and then the left that would take them to the house, and he jiggled his fingers on the steering wheel and he cleared the buildup from his throat.

"Home, sweet home," he said.

Teryn...

January 8, 2016

Sorry to be so tardy in responding. It's been a week like a month.

I'm so glad Christmas turned out the way it did for you and Sabrina. Ours was pretty nice, actually, especially under the circumstances. My dad and I put up some ornaments, Claire got a lot of gift cards (all she wants, so that's good), we had a quiet day. It even snowed a little bit.

It's been a struggle, too, things I'll save for when we're together again and can talk. Paul is talking about coming and getting Claire for spring break. He talks about a lot of things, of course, so I'm not counting on it, but if he did, maybe a few days for us to get together would be just the ticket. Maybe meet in Oklahoma City so we're incognito and we can bury the bodies. Figuratively speaking, of course. (Or not!)

Anyway, I'd like that.

Jane

Thirty

Jane offered to deal some hands of rummy, and she and Eric settled in at the dining room table and got to it. Her mind had settled into some peace on the issue of the car. Even seven hundred bucks was going to be a stretch, but at least she had some notion of how she could keep all those spinning financial plates aloft as she tried to find her way to solvency and a place of their own. Now, Jane found herself preoccupied with thoughts of Claire and whether she was having fun today, their first entirely removed from each other in who knows how long. The overnight invitation from Claire's new friend had, perhaps, excited the mother even more than the daughter. It was a rebuttal of what had worried Jane most about the move, the laden questions of how Claire would get along in an altogether different place from where she'd been born, and on this point the girl seemed to be doing fine. *Better than I am, for sure*, Jane thought now.

The draws and the discards continued apace, if a bit idly, and after a time, Eric set down his first hand and declared a winner.

Jane peered across the table at it, then reached over and spread the three cards.

"No, that's not it," she said.

"The hell it's not."

"Ace of clubs, two of clubs," she said. "Three of spades."

"Spades?" He was incredulous.

"Spades," she confirmed.

"Well, goddamn."

She pulled the cards in. "Let's just start over."

"No," he said. "I'm sorry. My attention isn't here. I'm going to sit down."

Jane stacked the cards prettily and transferred the stack to the dogeared box. "You OK?" she asked.

"I'm fine. Just not concentrating very well."

"Been a full day," she said.

"Boy howdy."

"Any thoughts about dinner?" she asked. "Just you and me, no kid. We could shoot the moon." She leaned toward him, as if to deliver a playful nudge, and he gave that a tight smile.

"What?" she asked.

"Nothing. I figured you'd be out tonight."

She laughed. "Yeah, because I'm swimming in social invitations."

"Chuck Brooks would go out with you in an instant."

"Chuck Brooks," she said, "is best left right where he is, at the bottom of our hill."

"OK," he said, getting defensive. "Anyway, *I'm* going out."

"Oh?"

"Yeah."

"A date?"

A beat or two to ponder the galaxies of meaning attached to that particular word, shaped and sharpened by time and place and juncture of life. And then: "Yeah."

"Well, look at you."

"Look at me."

Jane clasped her hands on the table. "What's wrong?"

"Nothing."

"OK."

Eric got up and worked his way around the other end of the table, past her, into the living room, a heavy drop into the recliner. The TV came on next, and he zoomed through the channel guide.

Jane turned in her chair toward him. "Dad?"

"It's Jocelyn Blankenship." He didn't look at her.

"Oh." Jane tightened right up. She could feel the skin stretch taut against her skull.

He stood up, shut the TV down. "You're pissed."

"No," she said, then she reconsidered. "Yes."

"I knew you would be." He tossed his hands in exasperation. "Typical."

"Typical?" She rose, moving on him.

"Yeah, typical."

Jane stopped herself, stood there, tried to keep the roil from busting loose out of her skin. When she felt as though she had a fighting chance at equanimity, she said, "The only thing that's typical is your selfishness." The words came from her in a low tone, amid a preternatural calm that gave her father no launching point for his own return volley. "That's why you're being a little boy about this, sulking around, on the offensive from the get-go. Because you know it. You know it. So don't tell me the problem is with me when we both know it's with you."

"That's not it." His words were meek.

"I mean, Jesus!" Whatever she had done to fortify her anger against unchecked sprawl now threatened to come undone. "Did you go right on fucking her after I caught you? While Mom was sick? While Claire and I have been here in this—" She looked around at all the pileups of past and present within the walls that held them. "—this house?"

He winced. "Stop."

"No," she said. "You opened this up. So now let's do this. I wanted to play cards."

"It's not what you think."

"Bullshit."

"It's not."

He fell back to the chair. She took the one opposite him. They glared at each other, the bile from their split-open years spilling into the empty space between.

"Well?"

"I love her," he said.

"No. Don't start there."

"It's true. And I loved your mother. And I've about had enough of your suggestions that I didn't and don't and—"

"Don't you *begin*," she said, "to tell me what you've had enough of. You opened this up being all petulant and stupid, and now you want to tell me you're in love. Don't make a sympathy play, Dad. You won't get it."

"Dammit, Jane."

"Dammit, Eric."

"It's not what you think." The words came out of him with thunder, and now he was back on his feet, stalking her, and she was on her own just as quickly, making sure he didn't have to search her out, their shared blood setting the same hardheaded course. "I walked away from her because you told me to and I said I would and because—oh, you'll love this—because you were fucking *right*, OK? You were right. I had no business.

"And I came back here and I kept my promises, not that you'd know, because you lit out, and I saw your mom out of this world, and still I sat here. Six years, I've been sitting. And if you hadn't made me take Claire to the goddamn mall, I'd be sitting here still, because that's where I saw Joc for the first time in forever. I decided I wanted to see her, and she wants to see me, and get this: I can. It's my fucking life, not yours."

Jane fell back again, driven by the weight of the words and the timeline that jumbled in her head and the inertia of the notions and the crush of new information. She cupped her forehead with her hand. She rubbed the temples. The aftershocks thrummed on around her, diffused and yet still screaming.

"Why her?" she finally asked, her voice gone quiet. "There must be a thousand lonely women out there. Why her?"

"How should I know?"

She looked up at him, tight red rings around her eyes. He looked blown up, weary, aged five years in five minutes.

"I have a request," she said.

He stared.

"Dad?"

"You have a lot of requests."

"Well, I'm making another one. Claire and I, we're going to be gone soon. That's been the plan right along, and I think you and I both know it's the best thing. The damn car has set me back some, but maybe I can scramble. Middle of next month, if not sooner, we'll be out of here, and then you can do what you want. OK? I can't stop you. I know that. Just don't put this thing in my face while I'm still here, OK? Don't do it."

Eric slugged the padded armrest of the recliner. "I can do what I want."

"You absolutely can." Each word now took on a softness the ones preceding had lacked. "And you can back me into a corner where I have to tell my daughter—your granddaughter—that, 'Hey, you know that woman grandpa is seeing? Well, I hate to bust up that story about the necklace and the light of his life and all that bullshit, but he was getting his pecker wet with her when I was a girl like you.' And then I'll have to tell her how romantic love is an illusion and that her grandpa isn't a bad guy, really, he's just a *man*, doing what men do, and frankly, Dad, I'm not ready to ruin all of that for her just yet."

Eric went agape. "You're horrifying."

She took the recrimination as if it held no power, and in the broadest possible view, that was the case. Her father's assessment of her shrank in the light of truth as she lived it.

"You have no idea," she said. "Can you just give me some time to get out of here?"

"I don't know," he said weakly.

She stood again, the last time, and she headed for the door and a walk in the gathering dusk. "We'll all be back here tomorrow," she said. "Together. Think about it. Enjoy your date."

"Long walk for a cold night," Danny said, after he had upended the invoices and bills scattered across his desk and scared up a set of car keys on a ring with a yellow rubber tab. He tossed them to Jane, and she snagged them like they were a bloop to second base.

"A long walk is good for clarity. Anything I should know about the car?"

Danny stood and crossed his arms across his chest, his massive left hand swallowing his right elbow and the right hand pinned under the left elbow. "Just that it's a bad-ass mutha. It doesn't look like much yet, but it's got more under the hood than most any car you'll put it up against."

"Well, I'm mostly toting me and my daughter to school. No need for power."

"Intimidate them soccer moms in the drop-off line."

She wanted to laugh—it was a good line—but she still harbored nervousness about the optics of hot-rodding it into the faculty parking lot. She wondered, briefly, if there were somewhere else nearby she could stash the car. Oklahoma, maybe. Then another thought came in.

"Were you serious about needing help?" she asked.

Danny sat again, relaxed. "Absolutely. Know somebody?"

"I might. How young is too young?"

Danny reached across his desk, squirted a dollop of hand sanitizer into his left palm, and rubbed his hands together. "How old's your kid?"

"Claire's eleven."

"That's too young."

"I wasn't thinking of her," Jane said. "How about thirteen?"

He wiped his mouth with his hand, then recoiled at the scent of alcohol. "Well, that's still pretty young."

"He's a good kid. Responsible." Jane stopped there. She was vouching for Roderick based on what she had seen earlier in the day. In the preceding week, she had also seen evidence that he could be willful, disruptive, and, whatever the leading circumstances, violent. Probably best not to overpromise on this kid's suitability and have it come back on her later. "Lives nearby, too. He really could use the outlet."

"Oh, that kind of kid."

Jane's back got up. "No."

"Relax," Danny said. "*I'm* that kind of kid."

"OK."

"Is he a hard worker?"

"I think so, yes," she said. "One way to find out."

Danny chuckled. "OK, sure. Send him around. He got a name?"

"Roderick A. Watson."

"A middle initial and everything."

"You'll find out," she said.

"Well, send him around. I can give him some stuff to do, slip him a few bucks. We'll see how it goes."

"Thanks."

"You bet," he said. "Enjoy Barry."

"Barry?"

"Barry the Barracuda," he said. "The car. Bring it back in one piece in a week, and I'll give you the Toyota back."

She waved the keys at him, twirling the ring on her finger, and stepped out of the office and over to where the Barracuda sat. The patchwork paint job outside belied the exquisite work that had been done within—new black leather upholstery, redone headliner, vinyl shined up, fixtures polished, a new-car smell reinstalled on one that was a few years older than she. Jane sank into the driver's seat, and the car swallowed her up in its cavernous body. In an era when the comfort of travel was being eked away by ever smaller seats and compartments, the room within the Barracuda was almost unspeakably luxurious. She found the ignition, slipped in the key, set her foot on the brake, and gave it a turn. Barry rumbled forth a prompt greeting, announcing himself, then settling into a well-tuned purr.

She slipped the shifter from park to drive, and the car nudged forward, brought to heel by her pressure on the brake. She lifted her foot, set it a few inches right onto the accelerator, and she was out of there, wide back tires shooting up gravel, the headlights coming on at her command, any route she would care to choose illuminated. She swung right at Smithfield Road and tore out, away, away, away, and wishing she could take a route longer than just one night.

Thirty-one

"I'm sorry," Eric said. "Not tonight. It's not good, not tonight."

"Why?"

"I just don't feel up to it."

He fell into the depths of Jocelyn's pause on the other end of the line, one long enough for him to cast, rapid-fire, a half-dozen assumptions about what she must have been thinking. None augured in his favor.

"Remember what I said about living in this thing honestly this time?" she asked, at last ending her silence. "This would be the time to take me seriously."

He chewed the inside of his top lip. "I am taking you seriously."

"I need to feel that."

Eric stared straight ahead, into the bright yellow kitchen walls, Margery's last big undertaking before she got sick—"a kitchen like early morning, that's what I want"—and he took measure of the responses that would be coming out of him. Jane had been right—he had tried to cover up the fault lines of his position with too much defensive offense. He had hoped for a fresh fight instead of a rehash of the ancient one. In the errant bargain, he had gotten an empty house and the sense of impending, permanent loneliness. There could be no such miscalculation where Jocelyn was concerned.

"I told Jane," he said.

"And what did she say?"

"She didn't take it well."

That broke Jocelyn a bit; he could tell from the way it landed. "Why?" she asked. "What's her objection?"

"Well, see—"

"What?"

"I'm trying to tell you." A flash of anger, frustration, impatience, deferred reckoning, all quickly squelched. He reset himself and went at it again. "Jane knew about us. You know, before."

"She did?"

"Yeah. That day I came over to tell you—"

"She knew."

"Yeah. Had found out."

He waited. Her breathing whistled through the line. He wished now that he had gone to her, to tell her this thing, his crestfallen face in front of her slowly realizing face. To hold her hand and to talk softly and to say, here, this is the problem, and it's a big one, for sure, but it's not insurmountable. Instead, he had opted for a quick declination of their plans and kicking down the road any necessary talk about unpleasant things. Another bad choice in a series of them, the resulting path leading deeper into distress. *Why am I so stupid sometimes?*

"You did what we said we'd do," she said now. "Back then."

"I did. But I should have told you anyway."

"I didn't ask."

"You shouldn't have had to."

"Oh, Eric," she said. "Oh, what a mess we made. I didn't think it would still be out there. I thought time would have..."

She didn't finish. Still, he held his tongue.

"Eric?"

"She doesn't want me to see you while she's living here." At this, Jocelyn split fully open. He cooed at her, trying to make whole what had been subdivided, impotent in the effort. "I told her she doesn't get a vote."

"Oh, yes, she does."

"No."

"She does."

"Why?"

"Because I am an old woman—"

"No, you're not."

"Old enough to stay out of impossible situations, anyway. I don't need her approval, Eric, but I do not want her scorn. I'd rather just go back to the way things were."

The dread, thick and sticky, spread out within him. He felt lightheaded, undercut, sapped.

"I can't," he said.

"We'll have to."

"It hurts. I want this."

"I know. So do I. We can't have it."

"Things have been said. Feelings have been felt."

"I know."

"They don't reverse."

"I know."

"And I don't want to reverse them," he said.

"I know."

"Well, then?"

"I don't know," she said, and he held the phone as if it were her, a flailing and futile clinging as they sent their breaths into the space words would be unable to occupy, so why say them?

Dear Claire

August 10, 2014

It's been two days, the only two days I've ever been happy you were with your father, and I don't know how I'm going to hold myself together when you're back here in a couple of hours. How I'm going to keep this from you, not because I'm secretive, but because I can't take another day and night of not being entirely here, not being able to believe what has happened, not being able to walk to the kitchen without being brought to my knees.

Like so many other letters I've written you during this thing, I'm sitting here hoping that by the time you read this, whenever that is, it's not a surprise to you. That, somehow, I've willed myself through these difficult subjects with you in a way that doesn't make me seem crazy and doesn't drive you away from me.

I went back to see Jim on Friday. I know I said I never would, but I did. The factors were many and hard to corral, but it came down to a singular idea: I was committed to confronting these things through the dispassionate responses of a learned third party. Jim had done his job. I had not. It was time to show up, humble up, and cinch it up again.

All week, I was back in those texts he gave me, back in the poems, trying to extract meanings between the words and the lines, things I perhaps didn't see the first time. My journal came out again. I asked myself questions: What if Mom knew about Dad and Jocelyn and simply didn't say? What are the capacities of love, and can it be bifurcated? Why have I never felt it, not once, in a romantic way? Is this missing piece inside me or outside me? Does it even matter? Maybe most of the animal kingdom has it right, and we were meant to follow our base instincts toward non-monogamy rather than obeying this bullshit social order and to bow to something our cells have already ruled upon.

I have to say, it was good intellectual stretching but not much else. I didn't end up far from where I'd been on the questions having to do with my mother and father. But maybe I was ready to keep walking with Jim.

But Jim is gone, Claire.

I got to his office building, and the hallway to his door was darkened. I moved slowly toward it, scared, because...Claire, I just had this sense.

A simple piece of white paper was on the door.

It was from Delilah. She said Jim was gone. Said recent months had been difficult because of his condition and he just couldn't fight it anymore. I never asked about his condition. MS, maybe? The tremors. So, what? Suicide? She didn't say in the note. So I'm left to wonder.

I left, only leaving was no good, because there was nowhere to go and no one waiting for me. You were with your dad. You're going to come home from that as you always do, because he spoils you, because he doesn't see you as much, and you're going to be all daddy did this and *daddy let me do that* and *oh we had such fun, and Claire, I don't know if I can take that, but somehow, I'll have to. I'll have to bite my tongue against the urge to tell you, yeah, well, now we have to care about such things as eating well and sleeping enough and getting up and going to school, because I know those words come out bitterly and are no good, no matter how true and justified they may be. And it will be hard, but I will have to try not to hold them against your dad, because in his own way he's trying to make your life a little more normal and a little more pleasant, and a girl should have her father, and I get that, I really do.*

So I didn't go, not immediately. I stayed. In the entry corridor, downstairs, by the door that for all these weeks I've walked in one hour and out the next, a wooden bench sits next to a plastic tree. I sat on the bench and I leaned into the tree and I cried. And I came home and I cried.

I cried for all of it. I've earned that, at least, haven't I?

Thirty-two

The insistent ping of incoming text messages stirred Jane from restless sleep, in a bed not her own, in the grayed-out haze of a room she didn't remember, swaddled in covers that smelled of too many nights without washing and made scratching sounds against her winter-dried heels. The alerts cascaded—the first one, then again to insist that it hadn't yet been read, then the second, then the third, then those reminders. *Ping-ping-Ping-PING-PING.*

David came in, wrapped in a robe and carrying a mug of coffee that exhaled steam into the room. "Someone wants your attention," he said.

Jane pulled the covers to her chin, her nakedness underneath now glaringly obvious to her. "What did we do?"

A jacked-up eyebrow from him. "Think about it."

"Oh, Christ."

"Ah, yes," he said. "The son. But we were talking to the father last night."

"Oh, God."

"That's the one." He pointed at her, smiled, sipped from the cup, swayed his hips, boogie'd down.

"You could be just a little less chipper," she said, fully awake and fully appalled at her fully reckless choices.

"Do you want your phone?" he asked. "I think it's in your pants, over here." He pointed to a chair in the corner, the landing spot for the clothes she had cast off in the settling night. Recall thudded into her now, the text message to him, the impromptu dinner at the low-rent bistro, the margaritas—so many margaritas— at Abuelo's afterward. From there, the details disappeared into something a bit more malformed and uncertain, but she could fill in the likely details with imagination and hypothesis. In any case, what a fiasco.

"Just give me a sec, OK?" She darted eyes at the door, a signal.

"Oh, yeah, sure," he said, backpedaling to the door and closing it after he cleared the transom. Almost as fast, he opened it again, and Jane flashed the covers atop herself like a malfunctioning cartoon tuxedo. "Breakfast? I've got eggs. Bacon. Frosted Lucky Charms."

"Fine," she said. "Whatever. A second, please?"

"Sure. Right. Sorry." He closed the door again.

Jane waited a few beats, long enough to be sure he wouldn't come back to ask whether she preferred orange juice or chocolate milk, and she scurried out of bed. She put her underwear on, bra next, T-shirt pulled over that, sweatshirt adding another layer, pants pulled up over hips and zipped. She found one black ankle sock and pulled it on, but the other eluded her. She bent and balanced on a single foot, and she pulled the sock on. Not seeing the other, she retrieved her phone and dropped into the chair, bringing up the time—*8:08 and oh won't this be fun to explain*— and the messages.

One, two, three, four from Paul, staccato and in misspelled shorthand:

Sprng brk?

U kno dates?

Lemme kno

Ill call C soon

One from Claire:

Can I stay for lunch mom?

The easiest of the bunch she dealt with first: *Sure, sweetie, just call when you're ready.*

From Paul, she requested the grace of a little bit of time while giving him part of what he sought—*busy morning, let me get back to you, but the break is the final week in March*—so she could move on with the mess she had made.

She went to the floor, to her hands and knees, and she lifted the bed covers and peeked under, and there she found the fleeing sock. She rose up, again did the flamingo-like balancing act, and got it in place. She stepped into her laced-up sneakers, surely as she must have stepped out of them, and she knelt and reached behind her left heel to coax the shoe back into place. Briefly, she wondered about how it had all played out, because she had little connective recall. There had been kissing and groping on the couch, and they had ended up here, and somehow she had to come to full and flagrant nudity, something she had withheld from even Paul until they were well into the Montana years. She shook her head, banishing all of that. She must have felt good, loose, free—predictable byproducts of alcohol. She felt none of those things now.

She opened the bedroom door, and here in the main of the sun-slatted apartment, familiarity came to her. To her left, a hallway, to a bathroom and a second bedroom he had offered to her before creeping mutual drunkenness—she now suspected hers more than his—led instead to shenanigans. To her right, the sectional in bachelor glory and the flatscreen TV bigger than her first dorm room. Dead ahead, David Bourque—*D.B., Done Bedded Him, got it*—with a bowl of cereal in front of him and offers of placation headed her way.

"I'm sorry," he said. "Too much too early. Please, sit down."

He rose, beckoned. She moved forward and sat, tentatively.

"It's OK," she said.

He sat again. "You sure?"

"No."

"I didn't plan it," he said. She detected just a whiff of preemptive defensiveness there. She adjusted her headings for turbulence.

"You didn't even know I was going to invite you out," she said.

"Exactly."

"I know." She said it softly, evenly, nonconfrontationally. Lord, was she tired. "I didn't plan it, either."

"I didn't think you did."

"No?"

"Of course not," he said. "I was just going with the flow. Shakespeare said that."

"No, he didn't."

"Albee?"

She giggled despite herself. "Maybe."

He snapped his fingers. "Charlie Rich!"

"That's it."

At this, he began humming the bars of "Behind Closed Doors," the hit known by everyone, even those who didn't know the man who made it famous.

She laughed again. "Let's simmer down." He drew two fingers across his lips and locked them, then tossed the key.

This was the reason, of course, the why behind a simple, innocent text message from the booth at the restaurant—*you had dinner yet?*—and the how behind a willingness, even a desire, to take matters across the street and soak them in tequila. He was fun and funny and smart and the one true friend she had made— and friends didn't come easily, never had—and now she was here with a deed done and the accompanying emotional load to carry out of his place.

She decided, there, that she should shoot it straight with him, as unlikely as that choice might be.

He shot first. "Regrets?"

Well, now.

"No, not exactly," she said. "Maybe. Yes."

"Well."

"You don't know me," she said.

"I do. Kind of. Biblically, I entirely know you."

"There's a lot—" She stopped and reconfigured her thoughts. "It's been a long time. I'll say that. I thought it was going to be a lot longer. There's some stuff, and—Jesus. I just got here. There's school. There's my kid. Jesus. I'm dumb. I'm sorry. I'm not making sense."

"Jane?" He dropped his head low and bobbed it around, matching up his eyes with hers.

"Yeah?"

"Are you saying you don't want me to be your boyfriend?"

"Jesus," she said. "No. I mean, yes. I mean—"

He picked up a wedge of toast, took a bite, set it down, licked the butter from his fingers.

"Because that would be...*awesome*, if you didn't want that."

"What?"

He balled up a napkin and tossed it at her. It bounced off her sweater. "We hung out," he said. "Had fun. That's it. The whole story, right there."

"OK."

"No biggie."

"OK."

"You sound unconvinced."

"No," she said. "I'm not. Relieved."

"Good."

She stood. "I have to go. I'm sorry. I'm not running out. I just— you know, I really have to go. OK?"

"Go," he said, standing and shooing her with his hand.

"OK."

"I mean, you could stick around. Football and pizza."

"I can't."

"OK, then," he said.

At the door, she opened it, then turned herself around, the doorknob in her hands behind her. He was watching her.

"David?"

"Yeah?"

"Thanks," she said. "I really mean it."

"You bet."

Downstairs, the car was where she left it, sitting macho and consumptive next to David's sensible Hyundai. He had laughed, joyfully at first and then for an uncomfortably long stretch, upon seeing her ride the night before. "There is this whole other life, this whole other story going on with you," he had said, walking the perimeter of the Barracuda in the restaurant parking lot and running a finger along its curves. "It's a graphic novel with a kickass title like *Mama Gearjammer.*" And Jane had held her hands aloft in mock surrender, saying, "Can't put anything past you, I guess."

Now, she slipped into the seat of it, turned the ignition and let the engine settle into a throaty growl. She drummed fingers on the steering wheel and said, "You have no idea."

Jane went home, such as home was, having no other place to go and being disinclined to avoid what surely awaited her there. She had tried not to grant her father too much space in her head after leaving him—an intention made easier by the company and the steady intake of alcohol—but she could imagine now, as she drove toward him, where his attitude must have lain. Pissed off, which she could allow him even as she set her jaw and matched it with her own simmering ire, and wondering where the hell she was. She didn't imagine the latter ever went away, even given their respective ages. Put Claire in her shoes and herself in his and roll out the scenarios and she would land with him, assuming the underlying circumstances were the same, too. From the day Claire came blinking into the world, Jane's focus had been on ensuring that the girl would never make the mistakes of the mother. Jane figured she knew the terrain. Yet the mistakes kept coming. What chance did Claire really have?

She snaked the car off Davis Boulevard and into the tangled subdivision. The roar on the automatic downshift drew curious glances from a few old men in the front yards of houses she once knew, long ago occupied by friends she once had, but her own quick glance at those homeowners yielded no echoes from a time bygone. Right turn on Payte and she was on the homeward stretch, and now came the nervousness that had been lapping beneath the surface of everything else. Her best hope lay in détente—some arrangement with her father that would give her clearance to stay just a bit longer, to keep Claire in relative stability, to blunt the chaos. She held hope and despair in equal quantities.

She found him feet up in the recliner, the pregame show blaring at him. Too early for a beer, he gripped a short glass of orange juice, an unnecessary intrusion on his blood sugar and not at all what she cared to get into just yet.

"Some night," he said.

She sat down opposite him. She set her hands in her lap and wrenched them.

"Just a night."

"Whatever you say."

"I didn't—" she started. She reconsidered. Wielded poorly, each word was its own little detonation. "I picked up the car."

"I know. I called Danny."

"I didn't expect to be out all night."

"A whole lot of not expectin', I guess."

"I'm trying here," she said.

"Well, don't let me stop you." He throttled the TV volume. She stood, found the power button on the set, and shut it down.

"You're a real pain in the ass," she said.

"I could say the same about you," he said. "I do, in fact. A lot." He powered the TV up again, and just as fast, she shut it down.

"Leave it just for a minute, OK?" She sat again, lifted her hands to the side of her head, threaded fingers through her hair and combed them through. *I must look a sight.* "I want to try to make peace, OK?"

He stared at her.

"OK?"

"No peace," he said. "I want you out of here."

Jane sputtered, an attempted interruption with nothing to say, and her father reclaimed his time. "I know you can't go right this minute. You're my daughter. I'm not going to throw you and my granddaughter on the street. You can stay until you're able to go, but I'm not going to be here."

"Dad—"

"I've thought it out. I've thought about it all night. This is what's best. I love you, but I can't live with you. Suspect you feel the same."

"What do I tell Claire?"

"The truth. Or bring her around Danny's, and I'll tell her."

"Wait," she said. "Danny?"

"He's got a bunkhouse behind his office. Remember? That little room where I had all those small-engine parts? Bed, hot plate, icebox, TV."

"Dad, you don't—"

"Want to. Gonna help him out a little. I'm bored. And I've got no better way to fill the time."

"So this isn't about Jocelyn?" she asked.

"Nope."

"Really? I don't believe you."

"Believe what you want," he said. He brought the TV up now but kept the volume low. "She doesn't figure into this."

Jane sat back, incredulous. "So we had this big blow-up

yesterday about Jocelyn, and now you're kicking me out, and it's not about her? Right."

"I'm not kicking you out."

"What?"

"I'm saying it's better this way if you go. I'm going to give you the time and the space to get it done."

"That's what 'I want you out of here' means, huh?"

"Jesus, Jane!" He hurled his glass to the floor, shattering it, the shards and the juice within flaring toward her. "Shit."

"Great," she said. She stood again and headed for the utility room.

"I'll get it," he called after her.

"*I'll* get it."

She came back with the broom and a mop, the head of the latter drenched and wrung out. She worked a perimeter around the broken pieces of glass, jabbing them with the broom bristles to herd them into a pile through the splashes of juice.

"I shouldn't have done that," her father said, his legs still aloft, his manner meek.

"And yet."

"I was frustrated. I don't want to fight anymore."

She knelt with the dustpan and guided the detritus into it with short sweeps. "Whatever. You've already won."

"Jane, just listen."

She set down the broom and dustpan and grasped the mop. "I need to get this done."

"It'll wait. Sit. Listen."

She looked at him, through him, arms limp.

"Please," he said.

She sat. The mop handle rested on her knee.

"She called me this morning, first thing. It's over. She's going to Florida for a little while, to stay with her son—"

"Rob?"

"Brent, I think."

"I remember him," Jane said.

"She had a choice," he went on. "She made it. So let's get ourselves out of this tangle and you can make your choices freely and I can make mine, and neither of us will have any say over the other. OK?"

Jane brought her eyes level with his. "You've always had choices. A long time ago, and now."

"Agreed."

"You didn't choose us either time."

"Disagreed."

"Dad—"

"But I'm not getting into that. Not now. It's done. I love you. I know you don't believe me, you think I'm full of shit, but I do. But goddammit, Jane, I don't like you very much right now, and I'm hoping with some time and distance from you, I will."

She stood again. She dipped the mophead to the floor and scrubbed up some of the juice. She carried the mop into the hallway bathroom, her hand below the head of it to catch any fleeing liquid, and she rinsed it and squeezed it out, and she returned for the last of it, mopping the floor clean. She then carried the tools back to the utility room and put them away.

On the pass back through the living room, she said, "I'll be gone ASAP," and she went to the door and her father's faltering words trailed behind but stood no chance of intercepting her.

From the car, on the reverse of the route she had traveled earlier, she placed a call.

"Spring break. Still interested?" she said, without a greeting, when Paul picked up.

"Yeah, of course. I can have her?"

"As long as she doesn't object, which she won't."

"Great."

"Can I ask you a favor in the meantime?"

"Sure, OK," Paul said.

"Can you lend me some money? Just for a few weeks?"

"How much?"

"Two grand?"

"Wow."

"I wouldn't ask, but—"

"I know."

"Can we just pretend I didn't?"

"Sure. Except...you want me to send the money, right?"

"Yeah."

"I understand."

"I appreciate it, Paul."

"How's Claire Bear?"

"She's fine."

"How's your dad?"

"Fine."

"Tell him the fish'll be jumping this summer. He should come up."

"I'll tell him."

"I'll send it first thing in the morning."

"Thanks."

"Bye now."

"Bye, Paul."

The call blinked out. Claire's subsequent text crowded in.

Can I just come home?

Jane whipped into a convenience store parking lot. *Sure, honey. You OK?*

Just want to go home

Jane thumbed back: *I'll be there soon.*

FEBRUARY
(in episodes)

Monday, February 5, 6:53 a.m.

"Claire, come on." Jane grasped the girl's shoulder and shook, harder than the two times previous. Claire, in her own room in their own apartment at last, groaned and flopped and covered her head with a pillow, which Jane grabbed and flung from the bed.

"Get up."

"I don't want to."

"Obviously."

"I hate it."

"No," Jane said, "you don't." She let herself down to the bed, sitting on the edge, and she coaxed her daughter first into lying on her back, then into a sitting position. Still, the tiny mouth pouted.

"Shower. Get dressed," Jane said. "Maybe I'll let you eat."

"Mom!"

"If there's enough time."

At last Claire rose, rumpled and tossed, and she padded one door over to the shared bathroom, and Jane listened for the flow of hot water. At last satisfied that some progress was being made toward their morning destination, she began tidying the bed. The chore was Claire's, and Jane knew she was enabling the girl's stubbornness by stepping in, but practicality had also come to the fore: If Jane didn't step in and do it sometimes, it wouldn't get done consistently. So...onward.

Jane, later in the kitchen, heard the shower go off, and she knew well the notes that would follow.

Claire came stepping out of the bathroom, wrapped in a towel, one last bit of morning grumpiness to be tossed off before she emerged into the day as a fully dressed girl with a semi-balanced mood: "It's too early," she said as she passed back into the bedroom. *Not an especially trenchant observation*, Jane thought.

Jane gathered an apple and a biscuit and sacked them up. She put away the dishes that had dried in the rack. Put salt and pepper shakers back on their shelf. Crumpled the pizza box from the night before, a Sunday night concession to Claire's pleadings and her own lack of mealtime initiative. Into her purse, she slipped an envelope, addressed to Paul and bound for the outgoing box at school and carrying the first installment of her loan repayment. On cue, Claire came out, jeans and sneakers and her favorite U of M pullover, hair combed, face fresh.

"There's my girl," Jane said brightly. "I wondered where she was."

"Whatever."

Jane came to her, handed her the sack and a small plastic bottle of orange juice. "You ready?"

"Do I have any choice?"

"Not really, no."

"Then, yes, I'm ready."

Jane gathered the purse, right hand making an involuntary check for the envelope after the bag was on her shoulder. Claire set down the sack and the juice, wriggled a backpack onto her frame, then picked her breakfast up again. They went out the door onto the landing, then down the stairs, two full flights to the ground level, Jane's recollection of the move not an altogether banished memory, the constant up and down with armfuls of boxes, trying to get their meager belongings into their new space. Not for the first time, she flushed with gratitude that she'd had the foresight to hire movers for the furniture, and that her father had slipped her a couple of hundred dollars in guilt money, thus giving her the ability to pay them. Had it been just her and Claire, the beds and the couch would still be on the sidewalk, two weeks after the move.

"You're late, ladies."

Jane looked up, smiled.

"Hi, Mr. Bourque," Claire said.

"If we are, so are you," Jane said.

He threw his briefcase through the open door of his car, held up his watch, and tapped the face of it twice.

"Just enough time," he said. "See you there."

"See you there," Jane repeated.

Thursday, February 8, 5:07 p.m.

Jane dropped the handwritten, lined papers along their bottom edge, using the tabletop to bring them into alignment, the three hole punches down the side falling into line. That done, she slipped the red plastic paperclip over the top left corner, then set the sheath down. Hands clenched atop the papers.

"Well?" Roderick asked.

"Give me a second."

"OK."

She drew her thumb and forefinger together, starting at the outside edges of her eyes and meeting at the bridge of her nose. She sniffled. She laughed, just a slight rumble of throaty syllables, to cover it. She rubbed her eyes again.

"It's good?" he asked.

"It's extraordinary," she said.

"I know."

She could forgive the conceit. She could forgive much more than that if Roderick could throw a harness around whatever had inspired this essay and use it to write something else, and something else after that, and something else again.

She passed the papers back to him. "You should be proud of that. Your teacher—"

"Mr. Winker," Roderick said.

"Mr. Winker will be proud of that."

"What was your favorite part?" he asked.

Oh, he's going to break me. Jane looked to the ceiling. The air hung heavy of grease and motor oil and the cast-off leavings of working men. She was grateful to Danny for giving them this space every week or so to play tutor and student, grateful to him for giving Roderick a place to go in the school-and-dinner in-between. She was grateful to this kid for laying down the effort amid the odds.

"I liked it all, but I especially liked the end, where you talked to the pigeon but you were really talking to your dad."

"That's my favorite, too."

It's where her wonder lay, how astounding she found it that Roderick could draw out advanced concepts like metaphor and personification, how he could find those things inside him and express them on the outside. It was uncommon and gifted and beautiful. Was the grammar precise? No, and that might get him reduced marks from the likes of David Bourque, but not from her. Whatever its failings on technicalities, the writing more than compensated by being full-hearted, pumping fresh blood through every sentence.

"You have a gift," she said.

"Nah."

"Do you like writing?" she asked.

"It's OK."

"Please keep doing it."

"Maybe."

"Please?"

"OK."

Roderick reached for the essay, tucked it into the backpack at his feet, stood, slung the backpack over one shoulder, and said his goodbyes.

"Do you need a lift?" she asked.

"It's a short walk."

"See you next week?" she asked.

"Sure."

She followed him out. Danny was stepping from an Oldsmobile he had backed out of one of the service bays, another job done. Roderick ambled over, said goodbye, converted Danny's offer of a handshake into a low five, then he left, walking down the gravel road to the street beyond.

"Thanks again for taking him on," Jane said.

"Thanks for suggesting it," Danny said. "Good kid. Good worker. He's made things better."

"I'm glad."

"How's the Toyota?"

"It's great," she said. "Thanks again." The gratitude was real. Danny had brought it in for a hundred bucks less than his lowest estimate. She and Claire had been able to swing some posters on the wall a paycheck earlier than anticipated.

"I still have Barry," he said.

"The Barracuda?"

"Yeah. We could work out a trade if you want."

She laughed. She took a playful, glancing slug at his shoulder. She headed for the car.

"Not on your life," she tossed back at him.

Friday, February 9, 8:17 p.m.

"It's good that Chuck is taking some time for himself," Eric said.

"Uh huh."

"A man needs that. Can't be all work all the time."

"Right," Jane said. "Now, do a woman."

"Huh?"

"Never mind."

"What are you saying?"

"Nothing," Jane said. "I'm sorry. Good for Chuck."

"That's all I'm saying."

"Mmm hmm." Jane flipped idly through the magazine in her lap, *Good Housekeeping*, of a vintage that suggested her mother's hands had held it first. She thought it an oddity. In a few weeks of living again at home—and what a disaster those had been, on the whole—she had taken considerable note of all the ways her father had erased her mother's presence (no doubt to assuage the grief) and yet had maintained little shrines to Margery dotted all around the place. The magazine, tucked conspicuously into a side pocket on the couch, was the latter. Anyway, it had made for a reliable enough distraction while she waited out Claire's babysitting job down the street.

This is what détente looks like, she thought, and upon further reflection, she thought it not a bad state considering the damage that had preceded it. Her father had made his apologies, such as they were, through small kindnesses and soft words and surprise phone calls to Claire, which counted for quite a lot. Jane had made hers through a willingness to revert to a we're-all-fine-here stance, something that gave her clearance to sit in Eric's front room and chat along the surface of things. *Perhaps that's the best we can do.*

"Do you know the lady he's gone out with?"

"Chuck?" Jane asked.

"Yeah."

"Nope."

"He said it was somebody he knew in school. Seems to like her."

"That's nice."

"Could have been you."

"I'm good," Jane said.

Eric pulled the lever on his recliner and kicked out the footrest, falling supine with a contented warble as his feet, clad in holey white gym socks, found the pad. He clicked the TV to life and cued up the channel by memory, and the Mavericks made a fast break across the screen.

"Wish I was out there with him."

"The Mavs?" Jane asked, a smirk stretching across her face, a chuckle at her own joke rising in her diaphragm. "You never had that kind of game."

"Chuck, silly."

"Oh."

"Good for him," Eric said.

"You'd be a bit of a third wheel, wouldn't you?"

"I don't mean that," he said, and he ceded to his own laughter. "I mean, just generally. A man oughtta date. A man who's lost his wife really oughtta date."

"OK," she said, reproach in her voice.

"What?"

"Old topic, played-out topic. Nothing more to say."

"I'm just talking generalities."

"Uh huh."

"I am." His own syllables calcified.

Jane closed the magazine and gave him the entirety of her attention, something she had been avoiding in the service of cordiality. "I had one specific objection to one specific person in one specific place and time," she said. "That objection has been overtaken by events. Knock yourself out."

Eric, drawing his torso up and looking offended, said, "What are you getting so huffy about?"

"You know."

"Let's just forget it," he said.

"Yes, let's."

Eric fell back into full recline, grabbed his beer can from the side table, and regarded the aluminum glumly. Jane made a play of reading the magazine. On the screen, the Mavericks coughed a pass into the front row. Things were sliding sideways all over.

The door banged open and Claire stepped through. The pent-up tension whooshed out behind her.

"Let's go," she said.

"You're done?" Jane asked. "Already?"

"Yeah. Hi, Grandpa. Let's go, Mom."

"Hi, sweetie," Eric said.

"That was quick," Jane said.

Claire agitated. "Eli came home. Mr. Brooks said I could leave after that. So let's go."

Jane tucked the magazine where she had found it, then stood. She clapped her hips with her open palms.

"Well," she said, turning to her father. "Thank you."

"Come by any time," he said.

The ride to the apartment unfolded in silence, save for Jane's punctuating inquiries that got batted back at her. Claire sat in the backseat, her hoodie cinched up around her face, staring.

Jane asked about school. *Fine.* Making friends? *Some.* Zeroing in on a favorite teacher? *Not really.* She was about to queue up another volley when she stopped herself, some combination of frustration and self-awareness allowing her to journey back to Claire's age and remember what her own responses would have been to questions that amounted to only manufactured chitchat. She shut herself down, then upon reconsideration ventured back in.

"Nice to have a job, huh? A little spending money?"

Claire pulled the drawstring tighter, rendering what was left visible of her face pinched and misshapen.

"Can you tell Mr. Brooks I don't want to do that anymore?"

"Why?"

"I don't like it."

"You did like it."

"I don't anymore," Claire said.

"Why?"

"Annabelle's a brat."

"I see."

"I don't like her."

"I see."

"Will you tell him?" Claire loosed the cinch, just a little, and found Jane's face in the mirror.

"If that's what you want." Jane granted herself a quick look. Claire closed herself up again, leaned back, and stared ahead.

"I do."

"Then I will."

"Thank you."

"But I don't understand it."

"Mom!"

"Claire."

The girl folded in on herself, face red, eyes welling.

"Claire, what's wrong?"

"I just want you to do this thing and not bother me about everything. OK?"

"OK. I'm sorry."

Not another word passed on the ride home. Claire got out, went up ahead, climbed the stairs, let herself into the apartment with her key, and was shut in behind her door by the time Jane caught up.

Jane stepped to the closed door, lifted her hand to knock, then thought better of it. Before the move, before Texas, there had been one child whose sweeping changes in temperament could send Jane scurrying for a solution, a salve. Now, daily, she moved through a school full of them. Intervention didn't work as well as firm rules and a willingness to ride out the dramatics.

"Good night, Claire," she said.

Monday, February 12, 4:32 p.m.

Roderick whipped through the squirming humanity at Walmart as if he were born to it, zigging and zagging, creating a ballet with the clunky carts pushed by plodding shoppers. Eric was less than graceful on all counts, moving more slowly than the kid, impeded by a lack of anticipation and a trick knee that had foretold the all-day rain that drenched them as they dashed from the pickup through the sliding glass of the store entrance. Behind Eric, Claire tagged along, her attention pulled elsewhere by every glittery attraction.

"Hold up, kid," Eric called ahead.

"They're over here."

"I know, but slow up." A backward look now at Claire, drawn in by a sweater hung tantalizingly for passing customers. "Come on, sweetie."

"I'm coming."

"Come on," Roderick urged, standing there, one foot firing like a piston.

"We're coming," Eric said.

Like herding cats, he thought. *Who've been snorting cocaine. In a thunderstorm.* Jane had called a day earlier, nighttime, as he was rubbing liniment into his groaning knee, and had said, "I completely forgot, I have a staff meeting after school. Can you pick up Claire?" Could he? Of course he could. Picked her up, brought her to Danny's place, introduced her to the kid, whom she already seemed to know, then got overtaken by the brainstorm that had been brewing awhile.

You know what the problem with kids today is? Actually, as Eric noodled on the question, he began to think the factors too vast, and the kids too numerous, for a simple answer. But he had a notion about what these two particular kids needed: They needed bicycles. For Roderick, it was a practical concern. The poor kid was too much alone, too reliant on his own wits and means in moving around in the world. For Claire, the need was less fundamental but a need just the same. The girl should be out in the sunshine and less inside her own head in her own room. That was obvious.

And so he had pulled the two of them aside, outside Danny's office, and said, "How'd you guys like a couple of bicycles?" and in the responses had been the precursor to now: Roderick, eager, running out ahead, goading them along, and Claire oddly reticent and withdrawn, amenable to the idea but not particularly energized by it. *Well, kid, it can't be turquoises on a string every time out.*

Eric doubled back and took the girl by the hand, gently so as to communicate intent—*you're not in trouble, we've just gotta go, that's all*—and they walked together to where Roderick stood, impatient and contorted, as if he had to pee and had nowhere to do it.

"Lead on, kid," Eric said, and Roderick whipped around and began charging down the linoleum pathway again, every bit as nimble as before.

"I wanted to look at that," Claire said.

"I know. But let's do this first, OK?"

"OK."

"You've got a birthday coming up, don't you?"

"Not, like, until May."

"Well, we'll come back in May and you can get whatever you want."

Up ahead, Roderick was almost out of their sight. Eric squeezed his granddaughter's hand and picked up the pace.

"Anything?" she asked, as her feet adjusted to the hastened rate of speed.

"Within reason, sure."

"I won't forget."

"I know you won't."

Roderick, a good thirty feet away now, stopped and turned. He looked disgusted. "I don't have all day, y'all," he called to them. "Come on."

"We're coming," Eric said.

"Yeah," Claire said. "Chill."

Monday, February 12, 5:13 p.m.

Jane lay her head against David's shoulder, her tousled hair splashing across his chest. His arms rose above them, and his hands engaged his phone with a fast-thumbed review of whatever social media had to say in their coital absence.

"That's how we do that," she said.

He broke himself away from his distraction and kissed her forehead, a first. "We've got a rhythm, that's for sure."

It had all come about wordlessly and perfectly, a stare from him down the table at her as Rosalie had held forth on this new procedure and that new testing initiative, a slightly jacked-up eyebrow from her, a drive over in tandem, he in the lead and she trailing, and only one question—"Your place or mine?" he'd asked in the parking lot—before they got to it. "Yours," she had said, a bit of disappointment behind it that he didn't know the answer, didn't know it would always be the answer, that she could never have him in her shared space with Claire, not even if the chances of discovery stood at nil.

"What time is it?" she asked.

"Quarter after."

She pushed the covers off. "I should check in."

"OK," he said.

She climbed from the bed, found her pants, bent to scoop them from the floor to retrieve her cellphone.

"That ass, though," he said, and she whipped around to him and saw him grinning, devilish and wry, and she couldn't be angry and also couldn't stop the knowledge that she would replay what they had done here, just as she had replayed the other times, and she would reconsider it and reconsider him and then, given another chance to make a different choice, do it all again.

"Stop," she said.

"I'm just saying."

"I'll be back."

"I'll be here," he said.

She went down the hallway identical to her own, into the bathroom of the same dimensions, and sat naked on the toilet in the darkness and called her father. She pressed the cellphone against her ear to plug up the spillover noise.

"Yo."

"Hi, Dad. Everything good?"

"Yeah. At the store. You done?"

"Almost."

"I was thinking of taking them to dinner."

"Them?"

"Claire and that kid."

"Roderick?"

"Yeah."

"OK," she said. "I can come pick her up after."

"I'll bring her by. You be home in an hour or so?"

"Oh, yeah. I'll call you if not."

"Sounds good."

"Thanks, Dad."

"Bye."

Jane closed out the phone and stood, and she reached for the switch, and the white light flickered and flooded in. She faced herself in the mirror and considered the reflection coming back. Her gaze funneled down to the Caesarean scar, a tagalong with the gift of Claire. It had once been a vermillion hashmark against her skin and now was white and firm, a slight rise on her topography. David had kissed her there as she opened herself to him, and she had flushed with something equal parts pleasure and gratitude. After Claire, that part of her had become *here there be dragons* territory to Paul, and she had missed the light touch of lips and tongue and heavy, heated breath.

She turned off the light and returned to David's room. He lay on his back, the bedsheet just below his shoulders, and he looked placidly toward her.

"Everything good?"

"Yeah," she said.

He smiled brightly.

"What?" she asked.

With a sweeping, dramatic flourish, his left arm and hand cast the bedsheet off his body, revealing a full erection.

"What do you think about that, Jane?"

She nodded. "Impressive."

"It just showed up. You got five minutes?"

She went to him. "I've got eight."

Wednesday, February 21, 6:07 p.m.

"You're still in Florida, then?"

"Still."

Eric reached for the beer bottle in the recliner cupholder, and he spun it a half-turn so the spout faced away. This wasn't what he had envisioned when he had at last stacked up the gumption and called her. The frostiness coming back, shooting across the cell towers between them, was enough to wipe out a season's oranges.

"How long?" he asked.

"I don't know. Longer."

"I miss you."

"Eric—"

"I do."

"I know. And you know that I do, too."

"So come home."

He heard her breathing into the line, considering, maybe, or maybe just waiting him out, hoping he would give up. *Good luck with that.* In any case, the silence stretched on.

"Jocelyn?" he prompted.

"Has anything changed?"

"With what?"

"You know with what."

"It doesn't matter anymore. She doesn't get a vote. This is my life."

"And this is mine," she said. "It isn't the vote. It's the attitude. I've explained this."

"Joc."

"No."

"Just like that?"

"You know what the issue is. I've been clear. I haven't wavered."

Damn.

"But—"

"I haven't wavered." Finality in the words.

Double damn.

He spun the bottle again. "OK."

"I'm sorry," she said. "It has to be this."

"It doesn't."

"It does. For me, it does."

"Well, I'm sorry, too."

"Bye, Eric."

He blinked out the phone and set it in the cupholder opposite his beer, then freed the bottle from purgatory. A click and the TV was on. No Mavericks tonight, but the Stars were on the ice, getting their asses handed to them by those bean eaters in Boston. Eric ratcheted down the volume to ambient noise. He'd never much cottoned to this game, coming as it did to the Metroplex so relatively late in his life, long after he'd given his attention and loyalties over to the Cowboys and the Rangers and the Mavericks. Didn't much understand the game, either—in the unlikely event that someone pulled a gun on him and said *your wallet if you can't tell me what icing is*, well, then, he would have to take comfort in the fact that he rarely carried more than a twenty.

None of that, of course, had stopped him from being a bandwagon-jumper nonpareil when the Stars had taken Lord Stanley's cup in '99, and he didn't give a good goddamn whether Hull had been in the crease or not. And it had been great fun when ol' Jonny Ehret had lived a few houses down, a true-blue Buffalonian who'd been jammed into D/FW by his overlords at Frito-Lay and had endured two Super Bowl losses to the Cowboys and the Stanley Cup defeat to the Stars, and if you think Eric Driskell was ever going to let him forget that, then you don't know the man.

Eric tipped the beer to his lips and took in a mouthful, swirling it down. They were all gone, everyone who'd been in the neighborhood to start with, except him and Chuck Brooks and Evaline Roberson, who hid herself away next door in her ceaseless grief. It put Eric in the strange position of being familiar with every crack in the asphalt and unfamiliar with who filled the preponderance of the houses, most of which had turned over occupants three or four times while he had stayed constant. This made Eric think again of Jocelyn, a thought he didn't want to entertain and yet one that stayed with him, his wants be damned. He hoped she wasn't leaving, too. He needed her as a hedge against the erosions of time. He needed her as a reminder of what he was and what he might still be, on a good day.

He needed her. He knew that much. She didn't know he needed her, and he hadn't found a way to tell her, because the words had become, at times, foreign to him, and his tongue had often become heavy in the saying. He thought now that he'd have to change that, somehow.

Friday, February 23, 12:47 p.m.

Jane came through the front entrance thirteen minutes ahead of the bell ending her lunch break, her fingers working surreptitiously behind her to tuck in her shirt. Tim Meyers met her at the intersection by a bank of lockers. Fleeting surprise moved across his expression, settling into calm in the next moment. *Resting principal face*, Jane thought to herself.

"Was just coming to see you," he said.

"Oh?"

"Cutting it a little close, aren't you?"

"Yeah," she said, flushing. "Sorry. Had to grab my dry cleaning. Took longer than I expected."

"No worries. You made it. Wanted to show you this."

He pressed a printout into her hands, which she took with some hesitation.

"What is it?"

"Read it."

She held the paper close and took it in.

Tim:

Good to hear from you. Roderick has adapted wonderfully here. He's popular with the other kids, he's bearing down with his work and easily passing everything. A little bit of the attitude you warned me about, but it's endearing more than anything. We like him. We're glad to have him here.

His English teacher said one of your people over there has been tutoring him and looking after him. He was very complimentary. Said it's making a difference. Thought you should know.

Been too long. Let's get the families together soon.

Ben

"Oh," Jane said.

"So this is you?" Tim asked. "Helping him out?"

"Guilty."

"I figured."

"He's a good kid," she said.

"I know."

"Did I do something wrong?" she asked.

"Why would you think so?"

"I don't know."

"Well," Tim said, "you didn't."

Jane swallowed. She brought her eyes steady on him. She looked beyond him. "OK."

"I know it's a hardship for Roderick to have to go over there," he said. "Hardship here if he stayed. Rock and a hard place, you know?"

"Sure."

"But this is good. We could look at reinstatement."

"Oh, good." Jane let go a heavy, held-in breath.

Tim laughed now. "I don't think I have a choice, not that I'd choose otherwise," he said. "Ro Jerkins brought me a petition signed by half the school."

"She did?"

"Yep."

"What did you do?"

"I signed it," Tim said.

Jane cackled—loud and true, the first one in she didn't know how long—and she slumped back to the lockers and covered her mouth with her hand.

"Mr. Bourque," Tim said, an edge in his voice, and that brought Jane to her own two feet again. Tim tapped his watch. "You're tardy."

David was coming up behind her, from the entry to the gymnasium. His words were breathy, harried. "Sorry," he said. "Dry cleaning."

Jane slumped again. David charged on past at double time and hung a left toward their bank of classrooms.

"You two ought to carpool," Tim said, looking at her in a way that could be neutral or subtly convicting, a true toss-up.

"I'll get to my room," she said.

"OK." Tim stepped closer. It wasn't threatening, just a closing of the distance so the words would be only for them. "You're doing great."

"Thank you."

"Keep doing great."

"I will."

Tim did a full turn and headed back toward the main office, a purposeful stride that gobbled squares of the industrial carpet beneath him. Jane gathered herself and followed the pathway already cleared by her paramour, the three of them forming a real-life math word problem: *If Person A walks east at X miles per hour, Person B walks south at Y miles per hour a minute later, and Person C also walks east at Z miles per hour a minute later, how long until everything is F'd up?*

Tuesday, February 27, 6:19 p.m.

Jane stood on the porch with Chuck Brooks, running interference for Claire, whom she had already summoned twice. She opened the door again. "Claire, Mr. Brooks is waiting," she called into the house.

"Just a second," came the return call.

This is a dodge, Jane decided. She'd told Claire she could quit Chuck, but not until she finished out the commitments she'd already made. That meant one more babysitting job. Claire had argued, then pleaded, then cried, but Jane had stuck to it. A lesson of responsibility, it was, something that would serve her well later.

We keep commitments. That's what we do.

"Sorry," Jane said. "You want to come in?"

Chuck turned, waved a hand at the sedan in the driveway. "Car's running."

"Ah," Jane said. "I can just send her down."

"I'm here."

"Ah."

She opened the door again. "Claire!"

"OK!"

She closed it. "Sorry."

"No worries. Wish I wasn't going to be losing her."

"Me, too," Jane said. "It's the age, right? They don't know what they want."

Eric peered at the tablet screen. "Nothing?"

"Nope," Claire said. "I gotta go."

"Wait a minute. Did you spell it right?"

Claire huffed and spun the screen back toward herself. "B-r-e-n-t B-l-a-n-k-e-n-s-h-i-p," she said.

"Well, that's right."

"He probably has a cellphone," she said.

"Probably."

"That's probably why he's not listed."

Jane's voice, calling her, swept through the house again. "Grandpa, I gotta go," Claire said.

"Just one more thing," he said. "He's a landscaper. Maybe it comes up like that."

Claire's practiced fingers pounded out the new search: *Brent Blankenship Orlando Florida landscaping.*

A new set of results flooded the display. Claire pointed. "Big B's Lawn and Landscaping," she said. "Brent Blankenship, owner."

"Is there an address?"

"Yeah. Says it's Winter Garden."

"That's not right. He lives in Orlando."

"That is Orlando, silly." She tapped a link, and a map filled the screen. She pointed. "See? It's right there."

"Oh," he said. "That must be it, then. Write it down for me, would you?" He pushed a pen and a pad to her.

"I'll send it to your phone," she said.

"No, write it down." He looked at her plaintively. "Where's your necklace."

"I left it at home."

"OK."

"Claire!" came the call again.

"OK!" she shouted back. She scribbled out the details, grabbed the tablet and slipped it under her arm, then bolted.

Jane smiled at Chuck, who made a parabola on the concrete with his loafer.

"Social life has picked up, I guess," she said.

"I guess. Been seeing Karen Laird. Remember her?"

"I think so."

"Glee club."

"Right," Jane said, still not quite sure.

"You should come out with us sometime," Chuck said. "It would be fun."

"It would be awkward."

"Not if you brought someone." He looked at her, a hopeful lift in his expression. "Any prospects?"

"No, not really."

Claire bounded out, backpack hanging loose off her hand. "Ready."

"I'll drive you down," Chuck said.

"It's, like, three houses," Claire said.

"Yeah, but I, like, just got off work and just came by." His imitation of her was playful and gentle in its mocking. Jane smiled and even Claire seemed amused.

"OK, then," Claire said. "Mom, do you want to come?"

"I'll wait here."

"OK."

They headed to the car, and Chuck turned back to Jane. "Should be home by nine," he said. "Everybody's gotta work tomorrow."

Jane nodded. "Have fun. Claire, I'll be here when you're done."

"I know."

Wednesday, February 28, 10:33 p.m.

Jane opened the dishwasher door and pulled the compartments out one at a time, emptying them methodically, stacking the plates first, bowls second, silverware into the drawer, glasses on the cabinet shelves, cooking utensils in another drawer, same order, every time, every couple of days.

Claire was down, asleep, exhausted by another day of school and homework and the terminal velocity of fading girlhood and the fast coming of whatever was next. She had been fussy all damn day—harder to rouse in the morning, stingier than usual with her words on the drive to school, distant on the drive home, generally disagreeable about trivialities once they were in the apartment. A favorite meal, chicken parmigiana, had been wasted on the brooding silence, then ruined by a stupid fight. Jane, looking over at Claire, had asked where the necklace her grandfather gave her was.

"I don't like it."

"You don't like it?"

"Do you understand English?"

"Do you understand how much jeopardy you're in if you say one more thing like that?"

"Fine," Claire had said. "I lost it."

"You lost it?" Jane was incredulous. "Where, when?"

"Well, if I knew that, it wouldn't be lost anymore, would it?"

"That's so irresponsible, Claire. Don't tell your grandfather. He'll go ballistic."

"I wouldn't want that," Claire said, pouting. Again.

Frankly, Jane had been glad to see her finally hole up in her bedroom for the balance of the evening. When she went in to say good night, Claire was already in fitful sleep. Jane had knelt and kissed her forehead.

Now, she went to her knees on the kitchen floor and used a towel to sop up the water that had shaken loose from the emptying of the dishwasher. That done, she rose again, squeezed the towel over the sink, then folded it over lengthwise, once, twice, and hung it from the cabinet hardware below.

Her phone buzzed on the table. She went to it.

All set for March 25

She typed back: *Huh?*

Spring break

Recall poured back in on her. She had forgotten, in the plodding steps from one day to the next, to look ahead at what was coming. What had once seemed distant was now imminent.

Call me, she typed.

When Paul rang through, she scooped up the phone so as not to disturb Claire and half-whispered, "What does 'all set' mean?"

"Hi, Jane," Paul said with exaggerated cheer. "How have you been? What's new? Got laryngitis?"

Jane carried the phone outside to the landing. "Claire is asleep," she said, her tone normal now if also agitated. "It's a small apartment. What does 'all set' mean?"

"I'm flying down to pick her up," he said. "How is Claire Bear?"

"I thought you were going to drive."

"Two days' drive down," he said. "Two days back. Two days back to Texas. Two days back home for me. Goodbye, vacation. Flying is better."

"Ah."

"How is she?"

Jane dropped one of the heavy sighs she had been keeping in reserve, needful as they were. "Brilliant. Confounding. Moody. Pick a day, spin the wheel."

"I hear you," he said, which might or might not have been true. She rather doubted he understood her, in any case.

"She's doing fine," Jane said. "OK, give me the details."

"I can email you."

"I'll remember."

"OK," he said, and he rattled it off: He would arrive Friday evening, had a room booked at the Holiday Inn out by the airport, she would bring Claire to him, they would fly back to Montana the next morning, and he would fly her back again the following Saturday. Jane did her twisted mnemonics with the details: *It'll be hell without her, H is for hell, H is also for Holiday Inn, got it. It'll be so fucking good to have her back, F is for fucking, F is also for Frontier Airlines from Denver midafternoon on Saturday, got it.*

"So you'll bring her to the hotel?" he asked, as if the answer would be anything other than what she had already agreed to.

"Of course. Just ping me when you're there."

"Will do."

"She'll be so happy to see you."

"I miss her."

"I know you do," Jane said.

"OK."

"OK," she said. "Bye."

Jane closed out the phone, then leaned into the railing, looking the twenty or so feet down to the brown grass and the sidewalk below. Even now, at the end of February, some green shoots were trying to muscle through the sod. The corner was turning on March, and there would be more, and she welcomed the eventual arrival. Fused as her senses were to memory, she could breathe deep, even now, and almost smell the dainty delicacy of the off-pink rosebush that would renew itself each spring in front of her childhood house, an annual splash of color she found herself longing to see again. It had been some winter, full of transformation and stasis, those two things in dynamic tension, and even as Jane's spirits sank with the confirmation of what was coming, she tried to rally herself around the progress that had been made, however scant it sometimes felt. The big problems were still the big problems, but now, sometimes, she didn't feel as though she were fighting them off only to unleash bigger ones.

The phone buzzed. *Come on, Paul, enough.* She looked at the screen.

Want to come over?

David.

She plugged in an answer. *You know I can't.*

I know. Worth a shot.

She typed again. *What are you doing?*

Playing Fortnite. It's rad. You know Kellen Summers? I think he's in this one.

No wonder you're the popular one, she wrote back.

That's me.

See you tomorrow. Lunch.

Yeah, baby!

Dear Claire

September 22, 2014

These letters were Jim's idea, but they are now my privilege and my responsibility. We're going to keep going. The whole point is that you'll read them someday—a long time from now, I hope—when they might provide some clarity for you about me.

I'm going to tell you about when I left your father the first time. Or tried to.

The seeming impossibility of it all didn't sit on my chest, leaving me breathless, when I was cleaning the house from top to bottom, vacuuming carpets and washing baseboards and crawling atop the toilet to get at the grime on the vanity above and scrubbing windows and leaving fresh daisies in a vase on the kitchen table, as if clean glass and cut flowers might mitigate my absence.

It didn't hector me on the drive to the bank, where I withdrew about $1,600—half of the stake your father and I had built together—and asked for it in small bills that I mingled with the *stash I alone had been putting away for months. It didn't whisper in my ear as I then drove up the hill, to the modest little airport sitting over the gritty little city that I had never really asked for but had received just the same.*

No, impossibility had ridden shotgun in silence. It was only as I stood facing the counters, the agent looking at me expectantly, beckoning me to come forth, that the rapid-fire series of "and then what" started hitting my head like rubber pellets squeezed off from a plastic gun.

They had tickets to sell. I wanted one, I thought. I could step forward and hand over some of my stack. Still plenty of time to move through security and climb aboard the two o'clock flight to Denver and, eventually, the six o'clock to D/FW.

And then what?

Well, I figured I could rent a car to get from the airport to Grandma and Grandpa's house, but soon, I knew, I would need one that didn't come with a running daily tab, so the rest of the money didn't leave my hands with the wind. But my dad could get me one, easy peasy, and if he couldn't or wouldn't, my mother would lend me hers at the low, low cost of answering her ever-present questions. I could swing that deal, if it came to that. I was certain of it.

And then what, I stood there wondering, and then what.

Well, a job, certainly, and a long-term place to stay. Those two factors were linked in my mind. Have to get one to sustain the other, and fast. My old bedroom would be available for a bit, maybe even longer than I could stand to be in it, but this, really, was the point of the stack, to be mobile and to be unencumbered. The smallest apartment in the sketchiest development would be fine until I could do better. As for the job, those prospects were both bafflingly uncertain and vibrantly possible. Old farmland was coughing up strip malls at an astonishing pace, the last I'd been in North Richland Hills, and I figured I could work retail if nothing else. I would find something.

And then what?

Well, divorce, right? Eventually, it would come to that. Your father, who wasn't yet your father, would come home from another land-acquisition trip—his absences the irritant I'd allowed to carry my idea this far. He would come home and I would be gone, and he would eventually call for me. And I would tell him, look, the car is in the long-term lot, unlocked and with the keys under the floormat on the driver's side, and you can do what you want with it, because I always hated that car anyway, and I've come to hate you, too, and I don't want to hate you, so I'm here now, and that's that.

I figured he might cajole me, wait me out, call my folks and tell them, look, she just needs some time and I'm happy to give it to her, but maybe you could say something, OK? Let her know she's making a mistake? And they might even do that for him, I knew, might come to me and sit me down and say, honey, everybody struggles sometimes, every marriage is hard sometimes, but you're in this one now and you've got to work this out somehow. But they won't be able to make me, and he won't be able to make me, either, and eventually it will come down to the inevitable: Let's bust this one up so something useful can be built in its place.

And then what?

Well, that was the great gaping unknown, wasn't it? Everything else had an outline, at least. Beyond the bust-up of a marriage, though, lay blackness and the intimidation of a blank slate. And before I got to the airport, that open field of opportunity had called to me, beckoned, insisted, pushed. Now, as I stood there, impossibility had moved in, presenting to me all that I didn't want to consider. My age—not so terribly advanced, but far enough along that some of the decisions I'd made seemed daunting to even try to unwind. The degree I had finished but wasn't using to full effect. The skills I hadn't accumulated. The child I thought, maybe, I wanted to have and feared, maybe, I was growing too old to consider. (I've been wrong about many things, Claire, but never so spectacularly wrong as I was about that. You have blessed me in every way. Please know that, whenever you're reading this.)

I thought about the prospects that were fleeing me. The half of what was mine that I would be walking away from. The home and the steady income and the patina of future security, and all of that traded for what? Something that seemed like gold an hour earlier and looked like a bag of nothing there in that airport.

They asked me again if I wanted a ticket.

I looked up.

They stared at me.

I looked down. On top of it all, I needed new shoes.

I turned and left, and I felt in my pocket for the keys, because I would need them after all, and then I remembered where they had been left, and the whole thing felt silly now, a ridiculous dream rather than an empowering run toward freedom.

The sliding glass door pulled back and let me out, and I walked. Everything was a critical mass, inseparable in its parts, tangled as it all was. But I could unwind that day. I could put what was mine and your father's back from where I had taken it. I could take what was mine alone and hole up at the Best Western for a few days, a little escape, and I could wait until he came back, came down these stairs and out these doors and onward to the place lived. And I could be there for his arrival and I could smile when he told me how nice the place looked, and I could reset and I could try again. I could tell him what I want, what I really need, and I could say it in as many ways as necessary for him to understand.

I could do that, until such time as I could find it within myself to do something else.

I never had the guts until you came along, until you started to grow up, until I could project everything out for the both of us, not just for myself.

I'm such a coward, Claire, but I'm trying not to be.

MARCH

Thirty-three

If Jane allowed herself to look past the venue—the hotel bar, nearly eleven at night—and the company and the bygone years that contaminated all coming time where Paul was concerned, she might have found the circumstance charming, even promising. Here, across the booth from her, sat a man with whom she had been intimate, who smelled of Drakkar Noir then and now and surely forever, a handsome enough and charming enough man, one with a new mustache she rather liked, who leaned toward her and met her eyes with his as she spoke, truly hearing her or at least making a good show of pretending. On her right side was the reason not to be swayed by the rest: Claire, slumped against her, eyes closed, asleep.

"You should take her up," Jane said.

"She's fine. She sure crashed hard."

"All that spaghetti, I shouldn't wonder," Jane said, and she smiled, so as not to give offense where none was intended. She appreciated the meal, appreciated the invitation to join them and to stretch out a few final hours with Claire before she had to let go for a week. She still wasn't sure how she was going to swing from one side of that absence to the other. Her own trip loomed, a few days with Teryn, and while she looked forward to the chance to get together, the plans she had made were mostly a way of patching over the part of her that would be missing.

"So work is going good, then?" he asked, and Jane nodded. It really was, for the most part. Rosalie's intrusions had pretty much stopped, the feedback from Tim—not much, but enough—was encouraging, she felt empowered enough to say her piece in staff meetings, and she had learned to make her own assessments of her coworkers without too much interfering input from David, whose ideas about—well, pretty much everyone and everything— didn't always align with hers.

"I'll get the last of the money to you soon," she said, the mental math spreading out in her head as she said the words, one more paycheck and she'd make it good.

He waved her off. "No hurry."

"Thanks," she said.

"I meant it, you know," he said now. "You could come with us."

"Right," she said, and though she didn't mean it to be harshly dismissive, she watched him deflate in front of her. Softer now, she said, "Did you see Claire's face when you said that? Uh-uh."

"I was looking at you when I said that."

"Paul."

"I was."

And there it was, what she had told him all those months and miles ago as they stood in the living room, severed emotionally if not yet legally. *You'll miss us. It'll kill you when you realize you miss us.* She remembered wanting him to miss them, even though she was determined not to miss him, even though she had built the whole divorce on not loving him, ever. *How's that for fucked up?* she thought. Here he was, the realization in full, and his reaction was predictable enough: the meek tossing of a line back toward the life they'd had before, as if all the elements of it that had blown apart could be reeled in and reassembled. What did he suppose would happen if she got on that plane with the two of them? Did he think she would go back to their house—his house—and back to their bed? That they would all wake up Sunday morning in midtown Billings and have pancakes, the way they did in his memories that no doubt didn't account for all the mornings it was just her and Claire and cold cereal? Could his remembrance of their life together possibly be congruent with hers? If so, he wouldn't be working this dead end of an angle.

"I have things to do here," she said.

"I know."

"It's Claire's time. She wants you to herself."

"I know."

"OK, then. I should go," Jane said.

"Us, too."

Jane nudged her girl into consciousness. "Come on, sweetie."

Claire roused and scrambled out of the booth. Jane followed her out. "I'm tired," Claire said, yawning.

Paul stood and took Claire's hand. "Come on."

Jane broke it up with one last hug for the girl, then Paul came in for his, which she wasn't inclined to grant. She let herself in for half of one, her body turned to his so he could get only an arm around her. She patted his shoulder and she pulled back, scooped up her purse from the floor, patted Claire on the cheek, then turned and left.

The crushing force of night and solitude didn't intrude fully on Jane until she was back in the apartment, sitting in bed in a darkened room, wearing a nightshirt and socks and cotton panties, the bedcovers draped atop her feet, the flat ceiling of her room a magnet for her attention. Claire's liveliness was gone, ensconced in a queen bed a few miles away, bound for the sky in just a few hours. Claire's new bicycle, little used and leaning against a living-room wall, had been the first thing Jane saw upon her return, and it was enough to break loose the tears she had been holding back. She was cried out now but no less bereft, and when she knew that the clock was getting the better of her plans for the coming morning, she texted her regrets to Teryn: *Something has come up. Can't drive up till Sunday. OK?*

Her friend took it seemingly well: *Awww. Whatever you need, doll. See you then.*

David's 1:30 a.m. coital summons, also by text, had been less easily fended off.

Your kitchen light is on.

Yeah?

Come over. Let's... He strung together a few heart emojis.

Can't.

Sure you can. It's easy. I'm a building away.

Can't.

Why?

Just can't. Have to sleep.

But you're not asleep.

But I should be.

But you're not.

We're going in circles.

So let's go another way.

Can't.

You sure?

Yes.

OK. See you when you get back?

Yes.

OK. Night.

Good night.

Jane silenced the phone and put it bedside. She twirled her legs from beneath the covers, feet on the floor, and she stood and blinked into the darkness of the room, letting her pupils widen. Oriented, she went to the door, opened it, the illumination pouring in from the kitchen like the yellow blade from a lighthouse hitting open water. She walked over, found the switch, threw it off, and the dark, no longer hiding in the corners, tumbled in.

Come five a.m., she gave up on sleep and swaddled herself in a pair of MSU Billings sweatpants with a frayed drawstring, a hoodie from Walmart, and a ballcap to pen up her ropy hair.

The car's new tires, insisted upon by Eric and grudgingly purchased (with a price-break assist from Danny), gripped the streets gone wet from a light sprinkle. A new day was caught in between. The streetlamps flickered, keeping faith with the night even as the sun muscled up in the east. It was a yawning Saturday, slow to move, amber light from early-to-rise businesses lighting up corners, traffic in peripatetic trickles, the rest of the world still in bed behind doors closed tight. She envied those who had found and kept sleep. She felt like cold garbage.

The dashboard clock read 5:35. Two hours to takeoff. They would be at the airport now, Claire no doubt petulant if she were awake, more likely asleep on her father's shoulder. Jane had a feeling the clock would be a continual focus for this next week, to the detriment of all else, unless she could stage some sort of intervention against herself now. She resolved to try.

As if on autopilot, the Toyota pushed on, ever closer to Payte Lane and her father's house, a place where she had no pressing business but just the knowledge that he would be awake and padding around. It wasn't his way to linger in bed when useful hours were afoot. There would be plenty of sedentary time later, when beer hour settled in for the balance of the night.

She found the house stilled and unlit, blinds closed tight. Next door, Evaline Roberson, heavy-chested in her morning robe, knelt shakily for the *Star-Telegram* at the edge of her yard, the sallow, white skin tightening on her bare legs in the effort.

"He's not there, hon," Evaline called to Jane.

"No?"

"Left maybe an hour ago."

"Huh."

"Good to see you, dear."

Jane waved as Evaline turned away. "Good to see you."

Jane let herself into the house. Sure enough, it was buttoned up. The scent of hours-old coffee hung in the air. She moved from room to room. Kitchen clean, nothing in the sink. Bed made. The room she and Claire had made their own rearranged back into a catch-all.

"Must have gone fishing," she said to no one. A Saturday, alone, Eric and his rod-and-reel and tackle box on the banks of Grapevine Lake was one man's view of heaven.

She found some scratch paper and left a note on the table:

Dad...

Claire's on her way. I'm headed north to see my Kansas friend for a few days. Think I told you about that. Take care of yourself. Call if you need anything.

J

When sleep finally took Jane down—after the drive home, after she fended off another approach from David in the parking lot, after the fried egg, after the check-in with the online flight tracker to ensure Claire was on her way—it was indomitable. She slept through noon and midday and twilight and dusk, her head under her pillow. Claire's pinging alert that she was there, and gosh, it had changed so much, and oh how she had missed it, didn't intrude, nor did David's *is everything cool?* or Teryn's *hope you're OK* or anything else. Jane didn't wake till she was good and ready, and even then, only Claire got a response, a line of hearts and a *call me in a day or so.*

After that, Jane carried herself into the shower, got the water as hot as she could, and she climbed in. The steam found her nose and her pores and opened her up. She doused her shower sponge with soap and she scrubbed herself, starting at her toes and the chipped and peeling red polish, up to her ankles and her calves and her knees and her thighs, her undercarriage and her midriff and her breasts and her pits, her neck and her shoulders and behind her ears, and she arched her back and dipped her head under the stream, and she came out of it clean.

Thirty-four

Near as Eric could recollect, he hadn't rented a car for the better part of a decade, not since the San Francisco trip Margery had insisted on, the one place on this verdant earth she'd wanted to see, a grimy, crummy, dirty place by Eric's remembrance. But Margery had loved it, left her heart there, in fact, so his input wasn't necessary. Whatever his opinion of the city by the bay, he'd managed the swinging of the rental and even the driving of it just fine back then. Not so now, in the Orlando airport, where he'd been rebuffed by not one, not two, but three major agencies for want of a frequent-renter's membership and/or a reservation.

Finally, as if he had pity coming, they scared him up a Ford Fiesta at a cut-rate joint, turd brown, reeking of cigarettes, and now he peered low over the steering wheel, knees seemingly lodged in his own gut, and he tried to reconcile the foreign place outside his windows with the markings on the AAA TripTik, a narrow assemblage of paper maps he could flip through as he made his way to her.

That, too, had been an ordeal, the phone call to AAA and the request of the maps, another instance in a growing pile of them that Eric just wasn't made for the times he persisted in living through. "Well, you can get our app," said the fellow who'd answered his call. "It's easier." To which Eric had been perfectly responsive at first—"Well, I don't want your app, whatever that is"—and then increasingly shrill, ending with, "Forty-five goddamn years I've been paying annual dues, and I can't get a goddamn map out of you. What the fuck?" A terse hang-up and his TripTik two days later, in the mail. That. *That* the fuck.

Anyway, he was here now, wherever and whatever here happened to be. He thought again of San Francisco, how closed-in and stampeded and gross he found it, and he detected nothing of that here. What he saw now of Orlando, as he shot west on the toll road—instant regret that he'd said no to the rental agency kid who asked if he wanted a toll pass—and took in his surroundings was, if anything, the inverse, a place intractably spread out, with twenty-seven some-odd miles he would have to traverse from airport garage to a door he was now entirely cowed to imagine knocking on. But, he figured, you buy the ticket, you answer the cattle call onto a jet, you go from Dallas to Chicago to Orlando with a sizable layover in the middle, you munch the peanuts, and you take the ride.

No dinginess here, either, just buildings that looked almost too perfect, as if you could push them over and see their Hollywood-style flat façades fall to the street. Palm trees hugging corners and lining boulevards. Pissed-down rain mixing with the humidity that had nearly choked him upon his first step out of doors, and Eric Driskell was not a man unfamiliar with humidity, living his life where and how he did. But this was something different, something strangling, something he feared would leave his lungs wet long after he lit out for drier territories.

He wondered how her boy, Brent, could have come to live here. He wondered how she could possibly even consider it.

He wondered if there was anything he could say to sway her, to bring her back to the neighborhood she was a part of, to bring her back nearer his yearning, his tireless ache at her absence now that he'd been granted a second taste of what he'd longed for all those years.

He fingered the TripTik again, tracing the remaining route. Claire's handwriting on a scrap of lined notebook paper, giving him the address, lay beside it. Five hundred and fifty-five Timbercreek Drive North. It was a lot to put on that little girl, asking her to find his heart all these miles away.

He thought he'd seen Claire that morning, in the airport terminal, but it was a sea of humanity that was swallowing them, and she—whoever she was—had been moving opposite from his heading, on the heels of someone Eric couldn't see. In any case, he hadn't followed *I think it might be...* to any clarification. He knew the girl was Montana-bound soon, maybe that very day, but that was her business and not his. In the early throes of morning, he wasn't even sure he would get on the plane. He wasn't sure he had the gumption or the stamina.

But, as it turned out, he'd had enough of both. As to whether Claire had gotten the address right—he'd taken it all on faith that she had done so—the answer would soon come clear. There lay his last turnoff, up ahead, beckoning in the dying light.

The opener—after Eric had parked, after he had whistled appreciatively at what Brent Blankenship (or someone) had built for himself on the edge of Lake Apopka, after he'd stood nervously on the stoop and waggled his fingers before finally knocking—came out relentlessly banal when finally he had a chance to speak.

There stood bald Brent Blankenship, salt-and-pepper chin beard, staring back inquisitively at Eric from behind the opened front door and the glass of the screen door.

"Your mother home?"

A blink and a deeper stare from Brent.

"It's me. Eric Driskell."

Brent betrayed nothing, a winning poker face formed by circumstance more than practice, Eric reckoned.

"Eric Driskell," Brent repeated.

"Oh my god" came from somewhere behind him. Eric stood tippytoe and looked for a clear view beyond Brent's shoulder, then rocked back on his heels.

"I know," Eric said. "What the hell, right? Maybe just let me in?"

Brent pushed out the screen door, and Eric stood back to let it clear, then stepped forward into an entryway of Spanish tile, a path plotted to the big room beyond and the floor-to-ceiling windows that surely beheld the lake. Once Eric's eyes adjusted to the light, he had to acknowledge that this grown-up, so far largely wordless child he'd once known had done quite well for himself.

"You're wondering what I'm doing here," Eric tossed over his shoulder.

"For starters."

"I'm wondering the same," Jocelyn said, on her feet and rigid, the first person in Eric's sight as he entered the main area of the house, but not the only one. Beyond her, in a kitchen fit for a restaurant, he confronted the staring eyes of those who could only be Mrs. Brent Blankenship and their darling children, a boy and a girl perhaps fourteen and twelve, not that Eric would have any way of knowing, the pegging of children's ages being a game at which he was never very skilled.

Eric stopped short of her, her twitchy attenuation a clear signal that he should keep his distance. "I—" he started.

"This is so inappropriate, Eric," she said.

That did it. That got his dander agitated. He'd left that morning imagining all sorts of possible reactions to his appearance here, not all of them graceful or appreciative, but he'd seen his way clear to such audacity because, Christ, love ought to carry some damn weight in the equation. He was tired, he was sore, he was cranky, he didn't like airliners or alligators or palm fronds, and he wasn't quite prepared to accept being labeled an asshole. Not yet. Not before he'd said his piece.

"Would you like to me leave now, or do you suppose we could sit and talk first?" he asked, mostly directing it at her, but it was Brent who picked up the slack.

"Sit down," he said, showing Eric to the central loveseat in the room. Brent and Jocelyn took the other two that were angled at his at forty-five degrees. The observers in the kitchen cleared out wordlessly.

"So?" Jocelyn said.

"So," Eric said, "I love you."

"You—" Brent rubbed his face, a massive hand moving from erstwhile hairline to chin. He looked at his mother. "Huh?"

"I love her," Eric said, exasperated.

"Eric," Jocelyn said, "I haven't said anything about that yet."

Her son now had his fill of being flabbergasted and was proceeding directly to disbelief, by the looks of him.

"Oh," Eric said. "Oh. Shit."

"What?" Brent said.

"Oh, shit," Eric said.

As it turned out, many things had gone unsaid between mother and son, the kind of things best teased out over deeper conversations in gentler environments, and the kind of things Eric stumbled through like a pratfall-prone comedy king. Their assignations, recent and vintage. The hiding of it from Margery and Ed. Eric's determination that he wouldn't, and they shouldn't, deny themselves again, not now, not after this wait, not after this unlikely reunion.

It was the latter declarations that at last brought Jocelyn's face out of her own palm, though nothing much could be done for her son, who was stuck in reconciling 1990 while his mother and this strange Romeo from another time worked through the now.

"This could have been said on the phone," Jocelyn said. "Should have been said on the phone."

"You might remember that I tried, several times," Eric said, and at this, she brought her steepled fingertips to her mouth and murmured "yes" into them.

"You two," Brent said, eyes on him and then her and then back again on him, narrowed and hostile. "When Dad was…Are you fucking serious? The two of you?"

"Brent, yes," she said.

"I can't believe—"

"You can. If you think about it, you can."

At once, Eric felt as if he should leave them be, a hell of a swing from his willingness toward—his *insistence on*—crashing in on them unannounced. The little truth bombs he'd unwittingly seeded were going off now, and Brent was having to confront the dissolution of the veneer of domestic harmony he'd coated over the truth of his parents' relationship, and Eric felt profound discomfort at being party to the unearthing.

It's not as if he didn't know the broad strokes of it. How, exactly, he and Jocelyn had found their way to each other had dissolved like sugar in this passage of time, but surely some piece of it had been a sharing of their respective lack of fulfillment, some connection that sparked only between them and not back at home with their spouses. But once they had embarked, the ground rules had held. *It's between us. We walk away if others get hurt. We do not unburden our frustrations with the other here, in the space that is ours alone.*

"I should go," Eric said.

"Damn right, you should," Brent said now, his face a tortured twist of distaste and hard-baked pain.

"Brent, no, it's out, let's—" Jocelyn started.

"No."

"I'll go," Eric said. "I'm sorry, I'll go."

"—talk about this, we need to," she said.

"No," Brent said again.

"I'll go," Eric said again.

"Then get your ass out of that chair and do it," Brent said, rising his own ass end up and lurching forward.

Eric stood and skirted right, away from Jocelyn's son and toward her, around the back of her chair, a loop for the door, her hand on his elbow as he went by, a fleeting touch, her son collapsing back to sitting, Eric's squeaky shoes on polished tile, the door breached, the glass door slamming behind him, the footfalls on concrete, that shaky tin can of a rental car responding to his summons after he finally found the key, and Orlando to the south, waiting to gobble him up again.

Thirty-five

When Jane at last decided to just get on with it, get in the car and go, put miles between herself and the mournful loneliness of a place without Claire in it, she made quick work of things. T-shirts and underwear and socks and one change of shoes, a simple pair of flats, along with a commensurate count of jeans. Teryn's insistences had led them to a reservation at a mini-Vegas wannabe just over the Oklahoma line, not as far away from home as Jane would have preferred but perfectly suited for what her friend had in mind.

Teryn wanted drinks and rock shows and the possibility of ill-gotten nookie, perhaps not in that order, and while Jane was less interested in all three—and particularly the last, having had enough of that with *D.B., deep-balling, David Bourque, got it* all of a sudden—she was almost joyous at the thought of a few days with her bestie. On that note, her hopes rested on Teryn's merits and also with the prospect of pushing off the missing of her daughter just a little bit, rather like a boxer resting against the ropes. Sure, the blows would still come, but let them land glancingly while the sustaining air is swallowed and the time is ridden out.

On her meandering way to the freeway headed north, Jane fended off two men, one in her head and one in her phone. She briefly gave consideration to going by the house once more and making sure her father had made it back safely from wherever he'd wandered. The dashboard clock—11:11, a fortuitous number if you're into those things—suggested that she had better not, as did her assessment of her meager emotional reserves. While things with her father had been better since the breach—and sometimes almost good—she dared not flirt with the possibility of upsetting his apple cart at this hour and with these plans. He'd be around in a few days when she came back. It would keep.

D.B., denied boyfriend, David Bourque, got it was a different, heartsick story, one for which she was quickly losing her patience. He sent a text upon her leaving the apartment, *where you going?*, which she didn't entertain until she was well away, thumbing a reply at a stoplight: *On with my life.*

His answers came in a succession, a slow dribbling at first, then increasingly aggressive as he absorbed the burn and unloaded his bruised feelings.

I was just asking
That was uncalled for
Oh, what, you're breaking up with me?
WE WEREN'T GOING OUT, JANE
I just thought we could have some fun
Like we've been having
Or have you forgotten?
I like you, Jane
I really like you
Why won't you answer me?
JANE?
Fine, don't answer
Whatever

This is so immature, Jane
We could have at least talked about this

She let them collect, glancing at each new one as it came in, then back to the road. It was entirely predictable, this turn, and entirely her fault, she figured. It never should have happened with him, she could see now, and even if she were inclined to chalk the first time up to too much booze and not enough discretion, there should never have been a second time. Or a twenty-third, or whatever they were up to now with stolen lunch periods and Claire's absences for sleepovers and after-school activities and whenever else they could jam it in, no euphemism intended.

She hadn't known a man yet who could stand down if he thought he could have it, who would be willing to let her be a sexual being as a secondary or tertiary characteristic if he could make it primary, who would willingly grant her space without having to be aggressively moved out of it. Claire was gone and spring break was here and David Bourque had been moved, against his will, to the periphery, and that's where Jane intended to keep him. She would deal with the particular problem of proximity—his classroom next door, his apartment, visible from theirs, and his car, sharing a parking lot with hers—at some later date. If he couldn't handle being simply a colleague, a status to which they would mutually profess when the implications of their physicality occasionally became too onerous and he'd talk her into acceptance, then let him be the one to move. She was done with that.

She reached into the passenger seat, grabbed the phone, and turned it over so she couldn't see the filling screen. She set both hands on the wheel and rolled her shoulders, locked her elbows, then released the tension. The ceaseless in-between development north of her hometown, running nearly all the way to the state line, twinkled at her in whites and yellows and reds and neon pastels. She ached, feeling anew the unwanted leaving of Claire, and she hoped that eagerness and distraction might come swiftly and fill in the gutters.

Traffic thinned it as she moved ever northward. Denton ahead, then Gainesville, then the Red River, then the rest.

Let's go, she thought.

It didn't take Jane long, just seventy-four miles to churn through in the dark of night, and within an hour and a half, she stood in the unnatural brightness of the hotel lobby, no clock to tell anyone the time, for time is irrelevant in casino life. She slung her duffel high on her shoulder, and she explained, again, that she was there merely to check in and shag a keycard. Nothing else.

"Yes, ma'am, but your party has already checked in," the lobby clerk, twenty-one if a day, "Alec" on the nametag, *A is for asshole, A is for acne, Alec still has acne, got it*, told her again.

"The other member of my party, yes," she said. Again.

"Oh, you arrived separately?"

"That's what I'm saying," Jane said.

"Oh, so you just need a keycard."

"That's also what I'm saying."

"May I see a picture ID?"

Jane produced it and squelched her desire to inquire sincerely whether Alec knew how to read, having seen no other proof-positive evidence that a brain was keeping him going.

He handed back the license and a keycard sheathed in a neat little folder. She tucked the license into her wallet, then placed that in her purse. She brought up the homescreen on her phone for a quick look at the time—1:03 a.m.—and saw David's messages stacked and queued, looking like a cross-cut view of a Michener novel. Maybe later, she figured, she'd see if he had anything to say that was worth a response, which she rather doubted. Failing that, maybe she'd have to block him. She'd need Claire's help for that, but not her subsequent questions. Probably a bad idea, on second thought.

On the fourteenth floor, she left the elevator and its only two other occupants, a sloppily drunk and overly amorous young couple who'd ridden with her from the lobby, their migrating hands and loud whispers and faithful declarations causing Jane to wonder if she'd ever been so all over the place with a boy and whether Claire ever would be, the latter thought a ponderable that clicked her blood pressure up several notches. Off the elevator, she started left, then reoriented herself to the schematic of where the rooms lay, and she U-turned and walked the other direction, casting glances to determine which side of the hallway held the odd numbers and which the evens.

A guy, late forties, perhaps, approached from the other direction, barrel chest and bloated midsection, arms hardened and tanned and hairless, someone who clearly had some experience with imposing his physical will on blunt objects. He toddled forward on legs cartoonishly short and skinny for the load they were carrying, and as their paths came together, he fixed Jane with a stare that sent her own eyes scurrying and her legs swinging forward at time and a half.

She found the door she wanted, held the key up to the number and verified the match, then slipped it into the mechanism, got the unlocking she hoped to hear, and pushed into the room. "Surprise!" began to fall from her tongue until she got an eyeful, the naked backside of a man, his ample ass fully hung out, on his knees, his haunches drawn up, Teryn's Rubenesque calves—God, Jane hoped it was Teryn down there underneath this guy—lazing off his shoulders.

"Oh, God," Teryn said, clearly talking to her paramour or her deity.

"Oh, God," Jane said.

"Oh, God, Jane," Teryn said, breaths bracketing the words. "Just a...few...minutes."

Jane dropped her duffel in a heap and backed up to the door, nearly impaling herself on the handle, then fumbling for a hold of it and the proper turn, at last letting herself back into the hallway. The door closed with an aggressive self-latching. Jane kept backing up, until her spine found the opposite wall. Finally, she let herself breathe, a quick gulp of air. She still couldn't quite believe it, but now, her blood freshly oxygenated, she at least knew she wasn't dreaming. Nightmaring, maybe, but definitely in her present dimension.

"Jane? Jane Driskell?"

She threw her attentions hard right. There, gawking at her, stood Mr. Barrel Chest and Bloated Gut, his face a blend of wonder and disbelief, the particular hanging open of his mouth giving her an accessible reminder of the past.

"It is you," he said, not waiting for confirmation of her own recognition. "Man, I thought so."

"Bobby Drury," she said. "Of all the gin joints in all the towns in all the world."

"You want to have a beer with me?" he said, the pointer fingers turned on himself and the upward lilt of the last word telling her he was unfamiliar with the reference.

Jane considered the door in front of her and what was, or had been, going on there on the other side. She looked at the boy she'd once known, now a man she wasn't sure she should reengage. The very definition of a dilemma, this. Two alternatives, equally distasteful.

"Bobby Drury," she said, *BD, bad day, broken down, got it.*

"Jane Driskell," he said.

She looked at him, staring, not quite believing it was him, and as all the memories flooded in and she heard an exchange with Jim playing in her head—"I could handle Bobby Drury," she once told him, and Jim's rejoinder had been, "I don't believe you've even come close to handling Bobby Drury"—she shoved all of that down and said, "Sure, OK. Let's have a beer."

Thirty-six

Eric stared into the unrelenting darkness at the lit-up numbers on the hotel-provided alarm clock, which came back at him in gauzy red. He'd stared through eleven peeled-off minutes on this round of sleeplessness. It was now 2:24 in the morning, Eastern daylight time, and he had come to a conclusion that fairly stunned him with its profundity: *You don't know how long a minute is until you watch each second of it burn, nor do you know how short a year is until twenty-five of them evaporate while you're doing other things.*

This was a pickle, indeed, being here, being unwelcome, having nothing to do and nowhere to do it for another whole day and seven hours until he could fly home again. He supposed he could wake up—a hell of an audacious thought, that sleep might actually come in the scant hours before daylight—and go back to the airport and beg his way onto an earlier flight, or at least try. But what if they said *no, sorry, bub, no open seats for you*? He didn't know anyone here—no one who would have him, anyway—and he was a little old to go to a theme park, put on mouse ears, and ride roller coasters.

He figured he could come back here to this scrubby Comfort Inn, re-up for another interminably uncomfortable night, and finally go home, ashamed and scarred but with no one the wiser that he had undertaken this fool's errand.

He turned himself over and considered the wall, somewhere out there in the dark. His thoughts bounced from Jocelyn to Margery, with just the lightest of touches on Jane in between. *We should have brought her here when she was a girl, maybe.* But if that had been essential, Margery would have said so, her read on the pulse of their daughter's attitudes and desires always more reliable than his. He wondered what Margery would say to what he was doing now. The distance between her being in imminent jeopardy from what killed her and her being gone was so short, just a few days, really, that they hadn't had much chance to discuss the big questions that lay beyond. Would he love again? Should he love again? Would she want him to, if she could plot out the future she would not be a part of?

In the end, it was of little consequence. He had loved again, and he had done so while she still drew breath, and with Margery's being gone it wasn't a notion he was even willing to entertain until these recent weeks, when old love became new again. Now, he could think of nothing more and could aspire to nothing less, and he figured Margery—on to other frontiers in stardust—didn't need to have a vote.

His phone buzzed from the nightstand, bringing forth another full flop in bed so he could retrieve it. He flipped it open and engaged the speakerphone.

"Joc?"

"Eric?"

"Jocelyn."

"I worried it was too late. I mean, clearly it is, but I just—never mind. I'm babbling."

"You think I can possibly sleep?"

"Don't," she said. "Don't do that."

"What? What am I doing?"

"I can't stop thinking about you."

"Same," he said.

"I can't believe you did this."

"Same," he said.

"You caused some trouble for me here."

"It wasn't intentional."

"I know it wasn't," she said.

"I don't want to lose you," he said.

"I don't want that, either."

Eric propped himself up in bed, two sturdy pillows pushed behind his back, and he flipped on the table light. The white brightness came on like a headache. He closed his eyes. *What's the problem, then,* he wondered. *I don't want to lose you, you don't want to lose me, so what's with all the losses?*

"How is Brent?" he asked softly. It was his lone regret about the whole episode—well, that and its ultimate lack of success in achieving any of his objectives. Jane could tell him all she wanted about his deficiencies as a father, as someone who could assess and understand another person's hurts, but her saying it didn't make it so. He'd seen the pain written across that man's face upon the truth being told about his parents, and Eric ached to be able to take that back and let him find out in another, more humane, more gradual way.

"Shocked," she said. "I think that's fair."

"I shouldn't wonder."

"But he gets it."

"He does?"

"Yeah," she said. "We had a long talk, probably long overdue. There are things he knew about Ed and me and things he looked away from, not wanting to know. You understand?"

"Sure. I know about those things." *Jane,* he noted ruefully, *never looked away, though.*

"A little more information between the lines tends to clarify matters," Jocelyn said. "So that's what we talked about tonight."

"I see," he said.

"And what I'll have to talk about with Rob when I see him. When I come home."

Eric's eyes opened.

"You're coming home?"

"Yes," she said.

"When?"

"Soon."

"And us? Can there be an us when you get there?"

"Yes," she said.

"Oh, Joc."

"I know. I can't deny it. I wouldn't even want to."

"Oh, Joc."

He wanted to spring from the bed, cartoon-style, and high-five the in-room microwave. He wanted to run in circles, then do handsprings down the hallway. He wanted to kiss a baby and buy a beer for everyone. He stayed where he was. He listened to the rapid beat of his filling heart.

"How's Jane?" Jocelyn asked, and his ebullience ebbed, if only a smidge. Jane, he knew, was a subject still bound up in hostilities and remembrances hard to shake. Jane could still make the going difficult, even if they were determined to move forward against whatever her objections might be.

"Jane is on spring break, somewhere in Oklahoma, I believe."

"That's not what I mean," she said.

"I know."

"I'm in this with you," she said. "For as far as it goes, for as long as it goes. I've decided. My word, my bond. I love you."

"I love you," he said.

"But I want to work toward resolution with her, and that's on you, at first. Or if not resolution, at least ground where we can all stand without conflict. It's not too much to ask."

"It's not," he said.

"And I'm talking to myself as much as I am to you. I still need to bring Rob into this, although frankly, he's easier than his brother. More contemplative, and also more likely to hold things close."

"I remember," he said. "Can I see you?"

She sighed, and that was his answer. "Not good. Not here. I'll be home soon, I promise."

"I will be there, too."

"Good night, sweetest boy," she said.

"Good night, my love."

The call dropped out, the night dropped back in, and at last slumber found Eric's settled head and his calmed heart and ushered him into deepest rest, the murmurs of her name carrying him into the hard break of day and beyond.

Thirty-seven

Now that Jane got a look at him in the peculiar light of the emptied-out casino bar, she could see that Bobby Drury's absorption of encroaching time made him nearly a ringer for his old man, Darrell Drury, someone Jane hadn't thought of in nearly three decades and now couldn't fail to see, in her head and in the seat next to her. Drunken Darrell Drury, a shaper of men, or one man, only not in any way the world wanted or needed. Darrell Drury, down inside a bottle most of the time, leaving Brenda to do the work and keep their malformed household one step ahead of ruin. Darrell Drury, who backed down like a scalded dog the one time her father had lit out after him for haranguing Bobby in the front yard, for shrinking the little boy before the neighborhood's eyes. Eric Driskell didn't much care for Bobby, even as a runt—he'd made that clear many times—but he had a sense of justice that the likes of Darrell Drury violated with his mere existence.

Darrell Drury, dead since 1991, felled by a final, fatal assault on his own liver. Darrell Drury, sitting next to her now, from all appearances. She wondered if Bobby's hard tilt toward his father meant that she was likewise shadowing her mother through the decades. When she allowed herself a deep stare into the mirror, she couldn't see it, but it also occurred to her that maybe she didn't know what she was looking for and wouldn't recognize it anyway. She guessed Bobby Drury couldn't see what was plain to her now, but then, he'd never been the reflective sort. She hated him. She also pitied him. She wanted to run, to end this bad idea now before it got worse. She also wanted to stay and see if he'd changed, no matter how thoroughly she doubted that was possible.

They clinked beer bottles upon their delivery by a bartender much more interested in shutting down than in catering to late arrivals. To get ahead of Bobby, Jane asked him first to condense a lapsed quarter-century so she didn't have to explain how she'd ended up a stone's throw from where she'd started.

He was only too happy to do some bragging.

"Moved out to Argyle," he said. "Bought me a cement-pouring business after my boss wanted to retire. Big Deal Concrete. Bobby Drury. B.D. Get it?"

"I get it," she said. "Clever."

"It stands for other things, too."

"Not as I recall," she said.

"Huh?"

"Nothing. Go on."

"I got some big commercial accounts and government accounts," he said, snapping back into his own aggrandizement. "Interstate 35? They'll never finish that. Cash cow, right there. I cleared a half-mil last year, after payroll and taxes and whatnot. Got me an eight-bedroom house. Three garages."

"Impressive. Came here to blow some of it, I guess?"

"Blow off some steam, more like it. Wife left. Four marriages, kaput." His frothy tone dissipated considerably with the revelation, and his face screwed up in something bordering on pain. His sausage fingers worked at relieving his longneck of its label. "Can't figure out why it keeps happening."

"It's a mystery," she said.

"Gosh, Jane, you're looking good," he said now, his bowling-ball body at once crowding into her space. She wriggled in her high-top seat, moving it backward a few crucial millimeters.

"Yeah, but the lighting in here sucks," she said.

Jane was spared the need for more evasive action by the appearance of Teryn, who stood at the entryway to the bar, looking simultaneously ruffled and satisfied. She gave a peck on the lips to the man Jane guessed to be tonight's entertainment— she hadn't had the pleasure of a face-to-face meeting—and sent him on his way, then strode toward them.

"We're closing up," the bartender said upon seeing her.

"Relax. I'm just sitting."

She reached them, smiling, considering Bobby, and got herself into the seat at the right hand of Jane, with Bobby across from them.

"Well," Teryn said. "Well, well. Lookee here."

"All finished?" Jane asked.

"For now."

Jane pointed to Bobby, then to Teryn, then back again.

"Bobby Drury, Teryn. Teryn, Bobby Drury." And then she waited, but not for long.

"*The* Bobby Drury?" Teryn asked.

He reached a hand across the distance. "Karen?"

"Teryn." She folded arms across herself, declining the handshake.

"Sorry, ma'am. I didn't hear it right." He withdrew the offer, looking at his rejected hand as if it might be defective.

"So you're Bobby Drury, then."

"He's Bobby Drury," Jane said. This, she was certain, would be memorable, one way or another. She recalled a long lunch back in Billings, the two of them just getting close at the temp job, and a deep talk about Bobby Drury and other regrettable assignations. They'd dished up their hurts and fast-bonded their nascent friendship. Jane knew Teryn would remember that, too.

"I'm Bobby Drury," he said, a slight, unknowing smile tugging at him. "Sure enough."

"You must have missed the sign," Teryn said.

"Sign, ma'am?"

"Outside the bar."

"I didn't see a sign."

"No Assholes," she said. "You can't miss it."

"Huh?" Bobby looked to Jane for help, or a clue, or something, but she had her head down and her face in her phone, futilely attempting to focus on four new messages from *D.B., opposite of B.D. and yet the other side of the coin, David Bourque, got it.* Reading those was vastly preferable to her now than getting in Teryn's way or coming to Bobby's defense.

"You're an asshole," Teryn said. "You shouldn't be here."

Jane peeked up. Bobby looked entirely cowed, entirely trampled by a rush he couldn't have seen coming. She wondered how many of the four former Mrs. Drurys had felt similarly when it was Bobby playing the aggressor. All of them, she guessed. When she caught him looking toward her again, her attention dove back into her phone.

"Ma'am," Bobby said, "do we—"

"—know each other?" Teryn finished.

"Yeah."

"Not personally, no. Thank God."

"Then why—"

"—am I busting your balls?"

"Yeah."

"You raped my friend." At this, she nodded left toward Jane.

"I did no such thing."

"You did."

"Jane?" He looked at her, helpless. Jane stared back, straining to keep her face blank, her insides a jumble. "That never happened, did it, Jane?"

"Oh, it happened," Teryn said.

Jane couldn't imagine, in Bobby Drury's whole pathetic life, that he'd ever found himself in this kind of threesome, one woman bearing down on him, relentless, the other impassively watching it happen. He looked scared and alone and trapped, and Jane almost—*almost*—felt a twinge of sympathy for him, but it quickly subsided from the rush and from a flaring of Bobby's basic bad nature.

Like a crackling finger of lightning shooting across the sky, his right hand came across the table and plucked the phone away from Jane, then spiked it on the marble floor like a football, the glass and the phone innards shattering and spraying a debris field toward the bar.

"How about that?" Bobby said.

"Get out of here!" the bartender yelled, scattering them. "Get out of here now!"

"Big tough man," Teryn said to the back of Bobby's head as they exited. Jane tugged at her shirt, a silent plea for knowing when enough is enough, but Teryn pulled herself free and strode after him.

"Fuck you," Bobby said, tossing it over his shoulder.

"Not even on your birthday, hoss."

"Come on," Jane said to Teryn, quickening her pace to catch them.

Bobby stomped out through the casino, the seats at its slot machines dribbled with only the hardiest late-nighters. Teryn and Jane diverted for the elevators.

"Holy shit," Jane said. "I knew you'd say something, but holy shit."

They tumbled into the elevator, leaning on each other, laughing, hugging, laughing louder.

"Oh my god," Teryn said. "I think I'm gonna pee."

"You should, after the balling you just got. Basic hygiene."

"Oh, Jesus! Don't make me laugh, or I'll really do it."

"Although," Jane said, "I guess nobody got fucked harder tonight than Bobby Drury did."

Teryn sputtered at that, a spit take without the requisite beverage. The doors closed on them, and Teryn punched the button for the fourteenth floor and knocked her knees together and squeezed her crotch.

"Seriously, don't make me laugh," she said. "Come on, doll. We've got a mini-fridge full of wine."

Jane awoke just before eight a.m. and considered it a minor miracle, given the hour to which they had carried on, nearly three a.m., before Teryn first said "I think I'm gonna pass out" and subsequently did, right on the floor of their suite. Jane now drew herself up in the bed, still clothed, her hair a matted mess on one side, her throat froggy from chatter and laughter. The wine they'd consumed—so much wine, in such cute, tiny bottles— now hung like a paste on her tongue, as if she had spun it back into grapes in the night.

She felt alive and spent, simultaneously. She felt grubby. She bopped her hand around on the blanket for her phone, until she remembered that Bobby had ended its life in an empty bar. In succession, she felt naked without it, then panicked that Claire might be futilely trying to reach her, then grateful that David no longer could. She decided, on the whole, that it was a blessing to be out of reach. Teryn would lend her own cellphone for a call to Claire, and the rest could wait until she could get a burner. Thank God for the insurance upsell the last time she re-upped her plan.

She emerged from the bed, stepping over Teryn's hilariously pretzeled body on the floor, and leaned over the duffel bag she'd abruptly dropped in her haste to leave. She withdrew a Smithfield Middle School T-shirt, fresh underwear and socks, and her favorite red capris. These, she toted into the bathroom along with her toothbrush and a tube of Crest. She and Teryn hadn't exactly made plans, short of their both being somewhere else and unbound for a couple of days, but whatever it would be— shopping, gambling, working out (not terribly likely, but still, an option)—suited Jane just fine.

She stripped down, turned on the shower spray, climbed in, and commenced washing one day off so another could attach itself to her. She thought of Claire and what she might be doing. It was an hour earlier in Montana, but if Jane knew Paul—and oh, she did—he'd be up and banging around and making sure anyone else in the house was up, too. She wondered if he'd ever done anything about that drafty den, caught between a floor-to-ceiling slider and the under-insulated garage. Had he put up a better window treatment or maybe a partition at the door from the garage, the way she'd asked him to do a thousand times? She rather doubted it. She wondered if he'd kept Claire's room for her. Many of her belongings had made the move into the apartment with them when the breach came, then subsequently to Texas, but not all of them. It was important that Claire feel at ease there— not at home, for home was another place now, but comfortable— and now, shampoo in her eyes, Jane felt a powerful compulsion to leave the shower and get on the phone and make sure Paul had everything just so because it's important.

And then it came to her. No phone. No call. No talking to Paul without rousing Teryn, and good thing all the way around. *You'll look like a crazy lady if you call now, about that. She's with her father and she's fine, and you know she's fine, and that's what's eating at you, anyway.*

Jane slumped against the glass wall of the shower and slipped down, down, until her ass found the tile floor and her legs straddled the drain, and she let the spray keep flooding her and she tried to muffle the cries coming up, at last a loser to what she had tried so hard to keep battened down and now could not control.

Thirty-eight

Eric looked up at the man who'd come to him, the traffic on the street in front of him a whoosh and the rest of it pulled back and distant, as if he could reach out, straining, and not touch any of it.

"No, he didn't give me a name," the man said into the phone Eric had handed him, in a daze. "He hasn't said anything."

Eric formed his mouth around the words he wanted, even moved it as if to create them, but nothing came.

"No, he handed me his phone."

Eric remembered this now. He remembered other things, too. That which had pulled back from him—the street and the sidewalk and the little Spanish-style houses across the way—moved in again.

"I called the last number that called him."

He'd woken up happy. That, Eric remembered. Happy and bouncy and ready to go home. Packed his bag, made his bed—yeah, they had people for that, but habits don't just get suspended, especially when they're rooted in the life you'd give just about anything to recapture, if only for a morning. Margery, at the foot of the bed, the top sheet flown high and fluttering down, *here, help me make the bed.* There came times when he crawled to that room without her, beer-drunk, barely getting there, but always, always, every day, he woke up and made the bed. God, how he ached for her sometimes. If she knew what he was on to now—she had to know, somewhere out there as a burst of the energy that escaped her dying cells—she approved, he was sure of it. He'd awoken with two women on his mind, the one not coming back except in recollect, and the one headed his way. He'd awoken and he'd showered and he'd eaten breakfast and he'd decided, like that, to go to where she would be headed soon, to be there and to gather her up and to love her until the day was done.

He remembered all of that. He didn't remember much of this.

"He hasn't said a word. He's fine, I think. No, wait, he scraped his arm, looks like, when he went down. That's when I saw him."

Eric lifted his left elbow first, examining himself. Nothing. Next, the right. The elbow, bloody. He drew his left index finger across the wound, held the finger to his lips, tasted it. Sure enough, blood. *What the hell? Doesn't hurt any.*

"Yeah, sure." The man—youngish, Eric thought, at least relative to the heap on the sidewalk, with khaki trousers and an untucked black T-shirt—held the phone out to him. "She wants to talk to you."

Eric nodded, accepted the phone, held it to his ear, again made formless words.

"I don't think he can speak," the man said, crouching, his face near Eric's and near the phone. He said it loudly. Eric wiped the spittle that got cast on his face.

"Eric?"

Jocelyn.

"Eric?"

Jocelyn.

"Where are you?"

I don't know. Where are you? I'm headed there.

"Eric?"

Jocelyn.

"Eric, give the phone back to him."

Eric held the phone up. The man took it from him.

"Yes, ma'am?"

More came into clarity now. Where he was, yes, the neighborhood with the busy street bisecting it, the tidy houses, the little trees, so puny compared with those back home, the beating sun, coming up, *it's morning still*, the sky brilliantly blue, the gawkers on foot, on the other sidewalk, staring at him. He waved, and a little girl over there smiled and waved back.

"Yes, hi, sir. Name's Jordan. Yes. OK, you familiar with Lake Sawyer? Right. Yeah. Anyway..."

Eric examined the elbow again. He again ran a finger through the blood, now crusting. He again tasted it. It hurt now, whatever he'd done to himself. *Does anybody have a bandage*, he wondered. *Can you maybe stop staring and get me a bandage?* He opened his mouth. Something—an *ummmph*, a nothing—came forth.

"I'll wait here with him, you bet." The man who called himself Jordan flipped the phone closed. He reached down, offering it to Eric, who took it and looked at it quizzically, as if it might answer what he could not. The man sat down, cross-legged, next to him, and turned Eric's way so they could see each other.

"They're coming," he said.

Eric nodded.

"Won't be long."

Eric opened his mouth, then closed it.

"You OK, boss?"

Eric nodded again.

"You went down, man."

Eric shrugged.

"They're worried. I told them not to, you seem pretty with it, except the talking, but, you know..."

Eric nodded.

"Won't be long now."

More of it came together the longer Eric sat there on the concrete, the more he looked at this kind man who'd come to him. He hadn't been able to read the TripTiks in reverse, and at some point—he was pretty sure he was below the freeway he should have taken, hopelessly turned around—he left the main roadway and entered a tangle of houses, knotted up off the main drag. He'd found a corner to stop the empty tuna can of a car and scrutinize things. He'd seen people, walkers, out for the kind of day that surely made this place worth the other tolls of living here, the swampiness and the reptilian hazards and the rest. He'd unbuckled, gotten out, stood up, walked a bit, a question on his lips, never asked or answered.

"I fell," Eric said.

"Yeah, boss. You sure did."

He'd fallen before. He knew that. He remembered.

"I hurt myself," Eric said, jutting the elbow toward Jordan.

"I know. They're coming."

"Good."

"What's your name, boss?"

"My name is Eric. Your name is Jordan."

"That's right."

Eric craned his neck upward, squinting into the sun, watching the clouds on a drift across the expanse. It had all started with such promise, such joy. He could still taste the Comfort Inn omelet he'd wolfed down. He could use some more orange juice. He felt parched, suddenly.

"Nice day," Eric said.

"Yeah, nice day."

"Thanks for stopping."

"You bet, boss."

Nobody had stopped the last time Eric fell, and he hadn't allowed himself to consider in that moment just how lucky he'd been that there was no damage. Alone, he'd been, in the garage, the rolling door to it wide open after he'd toted the groceries in, his fallen heap landing on the heavy shag carpet fronting the door to the kitchen, not the hard, smooth concrete just feet away. He'd gone down and then come back up quickly, and he'd not allowed himself to consider the serendipity of it all. He'd probably just gotten his feet tangled. That happens sometimes. No harm, though. The worst of it had been the porterhouses he'd left behind at Kroger. That had been the stupid part.

Now, though, was something else. He was grateful for Jordan. It was a beautiful day, and he'd been lucky, and he would have to tell her. Jane, yes, but Jocelyn, too. Just as soon as she arrived. He'd have to tell her. About the one in the garage. Not the others. Those were nothing, and just a few of them, and just clumsiness. But he would tell her about that one, and he would tell her about the times when he was increasingly tongue-heavy or even unable to summon the words. She should know. But he wouldn't tell her about the other falls. Not yet.

The one in the garage, for sure. He would. He'd tell her.

Jocelyn and Brent insisted on taking him to same-day care after they arrived. He told them it was silly, that he was fine, that he'd just been a little shocked by the tumble is all, that he and Jordan had been having a perfectly lovely chat.

"Haven't we, Jordan?"

His good Samaritan, after handshakes and deflected thanks, had started edging away, making like he had somewhere to be, which he probably did.

"If it was me, boss, I'd go," Jordan said. "Just to be sure."

"Sure," Eric said. "Fine."

So it was settled. Brent led them back to his house, Jocelyn following in Eric's rental, Eric in the passenger seat, tossing up a minor fuss. "You're not on the rental agreement for this vehicle," he said, all official-like and smug, trying to needle her.

She eyeballed him sideways. "I won't tell if you don't."

"Fine. I can drive, you know."

"I know."

"And yet…"

"And yet," she said. "We're being safe."

"It's silly."

"How many times has this happened?" She followed the question with a hard stare, then put her eyes back on the bumper of her son's car.

"Gotten lost in Orlando?" he asked. "Just this once."

"Eric."

"Twice," he said. "Today and a while back."

"And you didn't say anything?"

"I tripped. What was I supposed to say?"

"You didn't trip today," she said.

"No," he said. "I didn't."

"You need to call Jane."

"And what?"

"And tell her. Let her know."

"She's on vacation," he said. "She doesn't even know I'm here. What, I'm supposed to say, hey, I'm in Florida, something happened, but I don't know what and—"

"—and I'm down here wooing Jocelyn Blankenship, of whom you so aggressively disapprove."

"Joc, don't."

She pushed on, avoiding him.

"Joc."

"This is a mess, Eric."

"We'll go to the doctor," he said. "Then we'll call."

They left the rental in Brent's driveway, then carpooled the short distance to a strip-mall same-day care, Jocelyn and her son up front, Eric in the backseat like the little boy he was being made to feel. Having found Jocelyn impervious to his protestations, Eric went to work on her son. "I'm fine, I feel fine, everything's fine," he said. "Don't you think so?"

"We'll let the doctor decide," Brent said.

"You, too?"

"Hey, that's the rule. You fall down on the street like a busted-ass old man, you go to the doctor."

"Brent," Jocelyn said.

"Just shut up for a bit, huh, Mr. Driskell?" Brent said.

"Oh, that's much better," Jocelyn said.

In the backseat, Eric steamed.

"The scrape aside, you look fine. Blood pressure is normal. No sign of a concussion. Basic cognition is good. And you say you feel fine?"

"I feel fine," Eric told the doctor. "Everything's fine."

"Everything may or may not be fine."

The doctor was impossibly young by Eric's figuring, as if the national physician shortage had prompted the enlistment of twelve-year-olds. Give them a smock and a stethoscope and send them into the breach. He and Jocelyn—Brent had stayed in the waiting room—leaned in and got the straight dope. The confusion was concerning. The falling down, also concerning. The inability to talk for a while, super concerning. The past incident, perhaps concerning. If there were others, perhaps more concerning.

"That's it," Eric said. "Just that one. And today."

So the doctor laid it out: Same-day care wasn't neurology, and Eric wasn't having any of that anyway, so far from home, so the best advice under the circumstances was to go back to Texas and follow up posthaste.

"He can fly?" Jocelyn asked.

"Sure," the doctor said. "I can't see any reason why not."

"OK, then," she said.

"I'm fine," Eric said.

"You probably are," the doctor said. "Better to be sure, though."

Eric lay on his back, awake, in the too-short twin bed of one of the Blankenship grandchildren, in a room hastily cleared out for his one-night stay. A thin Orlando Magic blanket, black with a starburst of blue and silver, was insufficient. He missed the Comfort Inn. He missed home.

He missed Jocelyn, two doors down the hall, here in the wing of the house reserved for dear mothers and grandmothers and damnable interlopers.

She'd been great, handling most everything, including the disposition of his rental car (they'd drop it off in the morning) and the side-by-side seats on the Delta flight back to D/FW. She'd parried her son's complaints that her visit had been ruined by all this mess—"Oh, pish. I was going to leave this week anyway!"— and Eric had held his tongue against the undercurrents of enmity that rippled his way. He wasn't sure when the Blankenship kid had become such a whiner. He'd rather liked Brent, or at least preferred him to the other, the more bookish, less outgoing one. He and Ed had whiled away a not insignificant number of summer nights, tossing Brent a football. The kid sure had gone soft in his advancing age.

Eric, in turn, had handled Jane, to a conclusion that was simultaneously a relief and unsatisfying. She hadn't answered, not once in several calls, and Eric had left a couple of voicemails, the first a paper-over job and the second more forthcoming, in response to Jocelyn's insistence. Jane was off having fun, he told her. Leave her to it.

"I'm fine," Eric said now to the darkness.

He kicked the kid's blanket off his lower extremities and wriggled himself out of bed, into a standing position. He navigated the darkened room on his bare feet, taking one Lego brick to right arch, a startling pain, the objection to which he smothered in his voice box. That wouldn't do, a scream. It would ruin everything.

Now he was in the hall, goose-stepping. He was at her door. He was inside. In just a few short steps, he was beside her, kneeling. He let the scant light flood his pupils, and he found the shape of her, and he set a hand on her cheek, and she roused.

"Eric!"

"Do you love me?"

"You shouldn't be here."

"Do you *love* me?" He stroked her cheek and tucked her hair behind her ear.

She softened. "You know I do."

He lifted the sheet and the thin knit blanket with it, and she slid right, toward the wall, and he joined her. She nestled in, her head on his chest, a tuft of hair under his nose, tickling him. He breathed her in, and he nuzzled her, and he held on.

Thirty-nine

The first time Jane called Claire, on Teryn's phone, she got only a glancing bit of the girl's attention, wound up as she was in the presence of her best friends, Lea Kendrick and Wendy Connerly, who'd piled into the house for pizza and movies the first night and were now hanging around again.

It was a heartache to hear it—both the excited pitch of Claire's voice for the fifteen or so seconds she was willing to talk and the presence of the girls. Jane hadn't seen much of them in that final, stressed-to-the-breaking-point stretch with Paul, nor at all once she and Claire had moved to their bare-bones South Side apartment. She knew now what she hadn't allowed herself to think then. Claire had been escaping to her friends' houses amid the rupture as a release from the pressure cooker at home. What Jane had wanted, that their home be the one where Claire's friends always visited, the better to watch them all grow together, had instead become what nobody wanted, a mausoleum for a marriage.

And now Paul—*Paul*—had put it all back together.

"Let me speak to your father," Jane said once it was clear that Claire had let loose all she was going to divulge.

What tumbled out from there was only moderately more revelatory. Paul had cleared his schedule for an entire week, and whatever Claire wanted, within reason, was the plan. Pizza and movies, skiing in Red Lodge, dinners at her favorite places—Ciao Mambo and its zeppolis—and anything else they could jam into a week together.

"Angling for father of the year, I guess," Jane said, to instant regret.

"Just father. That's what I am, you know."

"I know."

Jane spun off to safer ground. The mishap with her phone, minus the details that looked worse and worse in hindsight. Her intention to buy a burner to get her through until she got home. The necessity of winding down Claire's indulgences as the week progressed so she didn't come back as some sleepless creature who could subsist only on pepperoni, Coke, and Chick-o-Sticks.

"I'm on it," Paul said.

"You are?"

"I am. You don't think I can handle this?"

"I'm sure you're capable," she said. "That was never really a question."

"Well, thanks for that."

"Give her the phone back," Jane said. "We have no proof she can live without it. Tell her I'll call again later, please."

"I'll tell her."

Jane gave herself a flat F, no grading curve, for her ability to be fair with her daughter and her ex-husband. When it came to hanging out with Teryn, she was able to bump that score moderately.

They shopped. More specifically, Jane browsed and Teryn shopped, scoring a pair of oversized sunglasses with sparkly frames at the boutique, primping and strutting and ducklipping in front of the mirror before finally pronouncing them a must-have.

They gambled. Here, their fortunes diverged. Teryn favored the slots and steadily handed over the contents of her purse, with just enough payout pulls to keep her dangling on the hook. Jane played slowly, nickels only, having only a few of them to rub together. At the blackjack tables, where she at last coaxed Teryn, Jane played more confidently. A long-ago lesson from her father—not just blackjack but also her very own laminated probability grid, a guide to what to play depending on her own hand and the dealer's—had seared itself into her memory, and at the quiet table they found, only the two of them and a friendly casino employee, Jane had steadily built her stack. Teryn, by contrast, played erratically and inattentively, more taken by the free drinks than the game. The drinks were pretty good, Jane had to concede. Come late afternoon, Teryn was sinking into her Bloody Marys.

"There's enough here to buy dinner," Jane said, sweeping her hand across her pile of casino chips. "A good one."

"Good. Let's go," Teryn said. "I'm starving."

They went all-out at the steakhouse, with tequila-lime shrimp skewers to start, a couple of bleu cheese wedge salads, the Roquefort filet for Teryn after she asked, for the third time, if Jane really meant it when she said "have whatever you want." And Jane really had meant it, although she dialed her own entrée down to the Cajun chicken pasta, and good thing, she thought, as the bill ran ever higher. *Say hello to a week's worth of quick-boil ramen noodles when you get home.* She found herself drawn again and again to how she'd rather be where Claire was, even if that meant being twelve hundred miles north. She wished that she could have another crack at Paul's invitation, that she, too, could be spending this week on someone else's dime. In the next beat, she knew where that would have led, to pressure from Paul to consider putting the family back together again, a plea rooted in *look how beautifully it's gone this week.*

Never mind that the week would have been an illusion, that they both had plenty of real-world evidence that it just wouldn't work. Problem was, all that might not be enough against the gravity of a rewind. Work in Texas was...OK, actually, most of the time, and sometimes even fulfilling. The David Bourque situation was a hot mess. Relations with her father were a powder keg, sometimes inert, sometimes shooting the works. Roderick A. Watson could be a Nobel laureate or a high school dropout. Maybe both. A mixed bag, at best. Resetting to Montana might prove too tempting, were she in Montana to be tempted, were she seeing Claire's exuberance at being back there. Suddenly, she was grateful that there was no decision to be made.

"What's wrong, doll?" Teryn asked.

"Just thinking."

"I'm just thinking, too," Teryn said. "Just thinking it's time for another drink." She cast about, finding their server three tables away, and snapped for him. "Garçon!"

"Don't do that," Jane scolded.

"I'm just having fun," Teryn said, as the server came around. "Another Bloody, and another in a half-hour. Then we'll reassess." The server nodded, then whisked off to satisfy the request.

"Save some for the others," Jane said, faintly, under the din.

"What's that?"

"Nothing."

Teryn, it had been apparent for some time now, was drunk—uproariously, stupidly, indiscriminately, irretrievably drunk. And though there was something enviable about her abandonment of all inhibition, Jane couldn't help but notice how their differing viewpoints were brought into sharp relief in this environment. She still adored Teryn, of course, but she couldn't relate to her anymore, the way she could back in Billings. Jane had waited until Claire was gone, under the supervision of a purportedly responsible parent, before she'd cut herself loose. Teryn's daughter, Sabrina, was back home in Wichita, staying with a friend for the week, her own spring break another week hence. Jane had talked ceaselessly of Claire, she thought, almost to her own annoyance. Teryn had said nothing about Sabrina, but maybe that's how it goes with a teenager rather than a preteen.

More than all that, their differences were laid bare (literally, in Teryn's case) by the central role of fucking in their ambitions. For Teryn, it was the prize of the week, bumping uglies with any man who passed her admittedly low bar for attraction and who would, in turn, find her worth the effort. For Jane, amid the *don't bother, D.B., David Bourque, got it* crash-and-burn, there was serious contemplation of never, ever, ever having sex again, at least not with a man. They'd discussed their positions on the subject just that morning, when Teryn had flatly said the latter part of all evenings here would be dedicated to manhunts, that she'd either shack up with them or even get another room, to keep Jane out of it.

"I can take a walk," Jane had said. "Just no more bare asses in my face. Once was enough."

There had been more to say, including the unlikely delivery of "you sure you want to be that risky" and "God, I hope you're insisting on condoms"—as if Jane were a paragon of wisdom on either of those points—before Teryn's flat declaration of "my husband didn't touch me the final year of our marriage, so I'm getting laid" made everything moot.

The server came around with Teryn's Bloody Mary, and she made a subsequent show of eating the veggies and other accoutrements—a skewer of peeled shrimp, oh my god!—before she swam through the alcohol again. "Nom, nom, nom," she said.

Jane almost hated to do it. Jane also sensed nothing else to do.

"I should go home," she said.

Teryn's mouth fell open, a half-munched olive laid out for all to see. "What? You just got here."

"It's no good, though. My mind is somewhere else."

"Doll, come on."

"I'm not having fun."

"Is it me?"

"No," Jane said. *Yes. Partly. Sort of.* "The thing is, I've just left too much undone, and it's not getting done while I'm here. I thought I could just let it go for a few days, have some fun, and—"

"I thought you were. I thought we were."

"—and pick it up when I get home. But I can't. I should go. I'm inhibiting you."

"You're not," Teryn said, and in her friend's face, she saw *well, yeah, you are.* Wishful thinking, perhaps. Jane would give just about anything to be absolved of the responsibility of making a choice here, stay or go, two equally unappealing prospects with two uncertain outcomes. Ride shotgun on a few more nights of Teryn's samba through *coitus indulgus* or go south to the considerable messes there?

"I should go," Jane said again.

"OK," Teryn said, "but tomorrow, OK? Let's just hang out, you and me. No boys, I promise."

"It's not about the boys."

"I promise."

"OK," Jane said.

"Movies and wine and popcorn, doll. You and me," Teryn said.

"You and me. After we eat."

"And after my Bloody. That guy promised he'd bring it."

"After that," Jane said.

She set her attention back on her meal, using her fork to send a piece of chicken slaloming through the ribbon noodles and the congealing alfredo sauce, gone almost gray in the subdued lighting and the prolonged exposure to air. It was good, though, she had to concede. She just wasn't very hungry.

Late in the morning, Jane awoke, her right shoulder twisted underneath her, sore and numb when she released her weight from it. Teryn lay next to her in bed, her face turned Jane's way, hair swirled up and fallen over, a line of drool running from her open mouth to the pillow.

It had been some late night, and morning had come too early despite the hour. A stop at the hotel convenience store had yielded more wine than anyone needed, and Teryn's beckonings had finally broken Jane down, eventually making their cavalcade of chick flicks forgettable and unnecessary and buried under shit-talking about the exes and unloading of grievances. Teryn had a job she loved and a future that was uncertain, boxed in as she was by coworkers eyeing the same promotions. Jane had a job she needed and had no assurance she'd have beyond May. Sabrina had a father who was mostly gone, the Christmastime surprise now faded into the past. Claire had a father who...*That's enough*, Jane thought when the subject emerged. *Here there be peril in talking further.*

Jane left the bed, careful not to jostle her friend, and she quietly gathered up her strewn things and repatriated them to her duffel bag. She considered, then rejected, the possibility of a shower. That would wake Teryn and, perhaps, invite a different goodbye from the perfect one they'd had, two buddies eventually moving on from the painful subjects and laughing and carrying on and remembering how and why they'd found friendship in the first place. Jane could live on that awhile. She'd have to.

She rode the elevator downstairs, smelling her own stink, telling herself it would just be a couple of hours until she could stand in her own shower and emerge clean. One stop, a Walmart for that burner phone she needed, and she'd be on her way.

As she passed the front desk, she threw the attendants a grim smile, then pushed on, through the sliding glass, under the canopy, into the brightness beyond.

It took a bit of reconciling and guesswork to remember where she'd left her car, but she found it, and the walking around did her some good. She was moving better, breathing easier, not feeling as grimy. She'd see if that lasted.

She popped the hatch and threw her bag in, then closed it up.

Next to her, a big pickup truck—*one of those all-penis, no-brains rigs*, she thought—hogged up her clearance and the space on the other side. She moved herself to the back of it, saw the Texas license plate, inched her gaze up and took in the stenciling:

BIG DEAL CONCRETE
ARGYLE, TEXAS
IF YOU WANT THE BEST, CALL THE BEST

Above that, on the back window of the cab, she spotted a bumper sticker, black with white lettering, a big red "68" in a circle: YOU DO ME, I'LL OWE YOU ONE.

"Charming," she said aloud. Then, as if startled by her own voice, she looked around and found herself as the only audience.

Jane backed herself into the gap between her car and the driver's-side door of the pickup, withdrew her keychain from her front pocket and slipped it back to her waiting right hand, and she made a quarter-turn and used the biggest key to gouge the door up but good, then smiled sweetly, walked back around to her own door, got in, fired up the Toyota, backed out, and was gone at last, and gone for good.

Forty

Eric had to hand it to air travel: It's an amazing thing, once you've endured the ticket counter and the check-in and the TSA mauling and the waiting at the gate, hoping everything follows the schedule, and have actually gotten your seat and the plane has pushed back and gone. An amazing thing, only then, for you're flying at five hundred miles per hour, up above the birds and everything, and if you're traveling east to west, you can almost make the clock stop.

He and Jocelyn emerged into the white light of a Texas morning, their hands clasped, their hearts bound, his letting hers set the pace. He was chastened; he'd pestered her back in Orlando, told her to stop fussing over him, then he'd acted like he'd lost his bearings in the terminal gift shop, pursed lips and blinking, and she'd told him never to do that again if he wanted her around. He was also happy and grateful and still a little gobsmacked by it all, for here she was, with him. He'd waited a long time for it, and he couldn't help wondering, beneath the hijinks and the irritation and the red-ass he was giving her, whether he had much more time to offer her.

God, I hope so.

They U-turned once they were outside, in the sun, the seemingly simple matter of transportation home a bafflement after they realized they'd come out of an altogether different terminal from the one he'd gone into three days earlier and she'd ridden a taxicab to much earlier than that. Back inside they went, to study the terminal grid and figure out the best way of getting from here to there. A train, from all appearances, so down they went to meet it.

He held her hand tightly through the crowd so they didn't lose touch, and as they waited for their stop, he kissed her knuckles intermittently, lingering there, his nose taking in the measure of her fragrance, besotted. He caught a boy—*maybe Roderick's age,* he thought, *maybe younger*—staring them down, crinkling his face at the flagrant display of affection. He lowered Jocelyn's hand and looked at the boy and said, "She's my girlfriend," and at that the boy's mother became aware and clutched him to her, as if reinforcing her duty to keep her son well clear of strange old men in airports.

"Eric," Jocelyn scolded him, only there was a laugh threaded through it, and he said, "Well, you are," and he went back to work on her hand, and how could she argue with that? She could not.

They found his tow truck easily, a snap, really, the location in the parking lot an easy memory for him, the kind that he figured disproved any possibility that his mind was fleeing from him. He'd just gotten confused in Orlando, and in the garage that one day, and in the mall with Claire when she'd insisted on tromping all over the damn place. But he was fine, totally fine, a case he made to Jocelyn as he insisted that he could manage the drive home, burying her tepid objections in bravado ("I'm still a man, Joc") and benevolent sexism ("You think you could even handle this truck?").

And he was fine, totally fine, and he proved it to her by driving out of the airport, by stopping at the tollbooth, by paying the obscene parking cost, by wondering aloud—to a kiosk—whether it might accept the donation of a kidney instead, which made her laugh.

And he proved it by driving all the way back to Jocelyn's house, not a single mistake in the whole route, not even on the infernal mixmaster, which he hated, its comings and goings knotted up like extension cords. And he proved it by carrying his bag and hers, much bigger and much heavier, packed for a much longer stay, into her house. And he proved it by saying, "Yes, honey, I will call her again" when prompted to reach out to Jane, and by doing it, and by leaving another message.

And he let her take him to the bedroom and help him shed his traveling clothes and put on his pajamas—a ratty old T-shirt and a pair of sweatpants, really, but perfectly useful stand-ins until, she said, she could buy him something better—and he crawled into bed when she asked him to.

"You're tired, and you didn't get much sleep," she said, and she giggled at that, and he so loved the sound of her when she was happy, and he knew what she meant. Back in Orlando, there'd been minor wrestling, then a hasty retreat to the tiny twin bed so they weren't found out. He'd slept terribly, fitfully, anxiously, wanting her again and again.

And she left, just to the adjacent bathroom to slip into her robe, to brush her teeth, to dab off some makeup, and when she came back, he blinked twice at her and tried to say the words, and he couldn't form them or force them out. He could only sit there, gaping at her, as his eyes leaked out and the tears stained his cheeks.

Forty-one

The Toyota had just nosed across the line, having come off the wide, sweeping bridge spanning the mostly dry Red River, a porn shop for truckers dead ahead in Jane's view, *welcome to Texas*, when the call patched through to Claire's cellphone.

"Mom, we're on our way to Red Lodge Mountain," the girl chirped, no hello, just right into it.

"That's great. How are you?"

"Dad bought me a new snowboard."

"That's great. How are you?"

"He says he couldn't stand living in Texas without mountains."

Not quite true, Jane thought, but no skiing anyway, and besides, "Claire, how are you?"

"Fine. I want to live here."

Jane went lightheaded, her senses coming apart, rather like she imagined a dead-on punch to the jaw would feel like. She hadn't had the pleasure until now.

"But you don't."

"But I want to," Claire said.

Jane steered to the shoulder of the interstate, not a gradual easing but an abrupt, jagged leaving of the asphalt for the dirt beyond, a honk trailing her and fading off into the distance.

"Give the phone to your father."

"Mom—"

"Give it to him."

The feedback of a phone being passed from hand to hand, the crunching of tires on roadway somewhere in the background of it, music—goddamn banal *music*—layered in there, too. Jane gripped and regripped the wheel, her arms aching, sweat on her brow, a rumba in her heartbeat, and she waited for the voice that finally came.

"Jane, I—"

"Are you driving? Pull over and give me your full attention, Paul."

"Jane—"

"Pull over."

More noise, more jostling, the radio off—apparently—and the sound of spinning wheels stilled, and he was back again.

"Jane, I didn't want it to come out like this."

"Get out of the car. I don't want her hearing this."

"Jane, it's frigging ten degrees."

"Get out of the fucking car, Paul."

She listened to the wind rustling through the microphone of the phone on the other end. It was Claire's iPhone in the pink protective case with the sparklies they'd glued onto it together— *was Paul going to glue sparklies and hug her when her emotions went splaying out sideways and hold the line against her whims, was he just going to step up now and do all of that?* Jane's heart took a dive into the deepest part of her.

She drew in a breath and held it, and froth churned in her mouth, and it tasted of battery acid or what she believed battery acid must taste like, and she sniffed the air for the scent of her own fear. She wouldn't be able to curse at him again. She'd had one chance and she'd taken it, and if she wanted his engagement up there in windy Montana, she could not speak to him that way again.

"I didn't want it to come out this way, Jane."

"And yet," she said.

"I'm sorry."

"What are you going to do, Paul? Are you just going to become the custodian now? Do you think you can just buy her pizza and snowboards and have that be the job?"

"Jane—"

"Do you figure it's possession and nine-tenths of the law and all that? You've got her now and she's yours? She's mine." She snarled the last two words like a feral dog.

"She's ours," he said, the first fortifying of his voice, and she felt herself crumbling.

"She's mine to raise," she said, and she formed a fist with her free hand as she said it, folding the hand up tight until her fingers hurt and releasing the clench, then engaging it again. "You made that decision a long time ago."

"I'm not taking her," he said. "I'm saying we need to talk about what she wants and be open to how we might approach that."

"When have you ever listened to what she wants?"

"I'm listening now," he said. "She cries herself to sleep at night, Jane, when she realizes another day up here is gone. She cries and I hold her and I tell her it's going to be OK and—"

"Congratulations on your five days as an attentive father, Paul," she said. "It's yeoman's work you're doing."

The wind went on whistling through their connection.

"I'm not doing this now," he said flatly. "It's cold, it's windy, and we're on our way somewhere. I'm turning off this phone and not giving it to her until we're back. We'll be back tonight, Jane. Call tonight and let's talk about this."

"Don't you—"

The wind stopped.

Time, too, if only for a moment. And then it all rushed in on her again, where she'd been and what she'd lost and what she'd found and what she might lose again. In a breath, she thought it impossible for Paul to rise to this. He was always gone, always on some job, never in a position where he had to put someone else first. And in the next breath, she realized he could. He could take the job with the land office in town, keep regular hours, be home morning and night. How many times had she asked him, pleaded with him, pointed at that job and said it's right there for you, so take it? How many times had she implored him, stay here with us, your family? How many times hadn't he done so?

He could do it now. He could take Claire, if she wanted to be taken. This wasn't some little kid, some abstract decision to be hashed out in the unassailable wisdom of a family court judge. If Claire wanted this, she could have it, just on her say-so.

Jane put the shifter in park, having only now realized that it had been engaged in drive straight along, her heavy foot on the brake the only thing keeping the car from tearing out through the strip of grassland paralleling the interstate, through that barbed wire fence beyond, out across that pasture and straight into that endless horizon. She thought, for just a moment, that she should do so and spare herself what appeared to be coming.

She set the parking brake. She let herself out into the standstill air of a springtime swelter. She looked to the cloudless sky that had risen over her. She screamed.

APRIL

Dear Claire

April 11, 2016

It's a Monday without you here, which will be followed by a Tuesday and a Wednesday and a Thursday and a Friday and a weekend, and I will get through them, from all appearances. I know I should be grateful for that, but mostly I'm just shocked, for I never thought I could and I don't really understand how I'm managing to do it even now. I don't want you to ever feel what I feel now, but someday, perhaps, you'll read this and you'll be a mother, too, and you'll imagine being alone in an apartment like this, or a house, or whatever, while your heart is four states away, and you'll know.

Do not feel guilty. Do not ever, ever, ever feel guilty. You had a choice in this, and you made it, and by virtue of your father and I bringing you into this world, we owed you the right to your choices when you came of age to make them, just as we owed you every possible thing we could do for you until your life was fully your own to direct. That's where we are now, and why I'm doing this impossible thing, and why I miss you so. Oh, Claire, how I miss you.

I will have told you all of this on the phone—I'm trying not to call too much, but it's hard, same as everything is hard—but for posterity's sake, when you're older and trying to piece together what happened when, your grandfather has gone into what is known as memory care. It turned out to be lucky that he had his episode in Orlando—oh, I will tell you much more about that someday— because the doctors here fixated on possible answers much more quickly. They thought initially he had something call aphasia—it's an inability to get your words together, and we've both seen some of that, right?—but they're thinking now it's some form of dementia. Still tests to do, results to assess, all of that. Whatever it is has gotten progressively worse, in a really fast, downhill way. He can't drive anymore. He "disappears," often without warning. He's there and he's talking and it's the same him he's always been (for better and for worse—you have the letters), and then he's gone. As if he's been erased right from under your nose.

I'm grateful to him for having pretty much everything lined up— the good insurance he's retained, the paperwork right where I can find it, etc. That's your grandmother's influence on him, no doubt. She could always see beyond the present moment. Better than he can, anyway. Better than I can, too. (I mean, clearly. I never saw this coming, Claire, your being gone from here. Was I not listening? Was there something you said that I should have picked up on? I'm so sorry if I missed anything important and you decided to leave.) Anyway, your grandfather has made everything easier by being ready for this, even if he didn't know it was coming. He needs care I can't give him, he needs it now, and he needs to be able to pay for it without liquidating everything he ever built up in his whole life.

He wants me to move back to the house. Tells me you and I should be living there now that he can't, and it breaks my heart, because I haven't told him about you yet. I can't bear to, and what's more, he doesn't need the worry. I don't know how long I can hold out; even the busiest girl should make time to see her grandfather.

It's sort of a race between his realizing he hasn't seen you and his being unable to realize anything, ever again. (God, it sounds so crude and awful when I put it that way, but if I can't speak freely to Future Claire, to whom can I speak freely? No one.)

I'm thinking I should sell the house. Not right away. It would be an unnecessary flexing of the power of attorney I have and a fight with him that I don't want. I wish we could never fight again, but the old fault lines are still there, all the things we never resolved remain unresolved, and so we clash. Even now. When I just want to love him to the beyond. But maybe soon, I can sell the house, and I can buy another, one not so laden with bad memories. Maybe you'll move back and you can live with me there. Or maybe you'll just come visit. I don't want to be possessive. Come see me, Claire. Maybe in May, when we're both done with school, we'll take a vacation, just you and me, if it all works out. That would be nice. It kills me to have let you go, like I'm not fighting hard enough for you, but I'm trying to trust you and I'm trying to honor the things that I need to get through now. It's so hard. I wish I understood it all.

I wonder when you'll see this, Claire. I wonder how old you'll be, where you'll be living, what you'll be doing, what will engage you and make you feel alive. I wonder if I'll be alive. I wonder if we will have settled the things that are obviously between us now, that we'll be past the ways I've obviously failed you.

God, Claire, I hope so.

Forty-two

Jane pushed the stack of papers back across to Roderick.

"It's good," she said.

"That's it?" He looked at her, grabbed the papers brusquely, stood them on end, used Danny's office tabletop to straighten them, then set them flat on the table under both hands. "Did you read it?"

"Of course I read it." She pinched the corners of her eyes with her thumb and middle finger. "You were right here. We just did this, Roderick."

"What's the sailor's name?" Roderick jutted his jaw toward her, defiance and hurt all in one pose. She had seen this before.

Jane held out her hand. "Can I see that?"

He picked the papers up and clutched them tight to his chest. "Nope."

"It wasn't even about the sailor," she said. "The sailor was, like, a bit part."

"No, but he's in there. And you just read it, right? 'We just did this, Roderick,'" he said now, mocking her. "So what's his name?"

"I didn't make a point of remembering his name."

"You didn't read it."

"I did, too." She again squeezed her eye sockets. It was the last thing she needed, a bunch of guff from a kid who'd read *Treasure Island*—at her behest, no less—and fancied himself a short-story author here because it was Wednesday. "This is good" about covered it. It was good. It wasn't the best thing she'd ever read by someone Roderick's age, and it wasn't even the best thing he'd ever written, so why all the agita about her brief assessment?

And in the next beat, shame swept in on her. He was right. She hadn't read it, not attentively. And surely she could have said something about his inventiveness in moving a story clearly inspired by a nineteenth-century book into a space-age environment, where a so-called sailor—whatever his name was—had never even seen a drop of sea water, out there in the intergalactic beyond.

The fact was, she couldn't recall anything of note from the whole afternoon, the last of her classes after the noontime call from Jocelyn Blankenship and another round-and-round about her father, to the same positions they were always claiming, separated by a gulf of bad blood. God, how she despised that woman. God, how she needed just one thing—*one*—to back off and let her breathe. Like Roderick. Roderick needed to let this one go.

She again held out her hand, plaintively. "Can I please have it? I'll read it again."

"Again? You didn't read it the first time, lady."

"Jesus, Roderick."

He stood, quaking, on the verge of tears, she thought, and he tore the papers in half. "Jesus yourself."

"Don't!" It came out of her as a yelp, as she dove into the table, then fell back again into her chair.

He made a quarter-turn with the ripped papers and tore them again, and again after that, and again until the accumulated stack became too thick for his adolescent fingers. These pieces, he rifled like he would a baseball, across the distance, into her face. His creation settled like confetti into her hair, in her lap, down the front of her shirt.

"You're wasting my time, you're a stupid bitch, and I hate you," he yelled at her, and he grabbed his backpack and tore out of there, the slammed door bouncing off the frame and coming to rest ajar.

Jane sat there, staring after him, the stilled air in Danny's office—her father's office before that—no longer the hints of axle grease and oil but of crackled and burned-out electricity, a disaster that had left everything standing and yet, she feared, nothing was the same as it had been before.

She put her hands on the table, dropped her head atop them, and she wept.

She went home after that, Danny's brief admonition lingering in her head, words that were surely wise about whether Roderick meant it (he didn't, Danny swore) or whether she should try again next week (she should, Danny said) and Roderick's progress as a do-whatever-needs-doing helper at a garage and body shop ("Smart kid—he sees it once, and he remembers it always"). She would see how she felt about next week when next week arrived; she didn't trust herself now to decide anything, and the days had a way of moving at half-speed. A week from now was a long way away, longer than she had ever imagined it could be.

It wasn't just Roderick on her mind. It was everything she was letting slip, knowing she was doing it, ultimately powerless against the slippage or insufficiently motivated to arrest it. Several weeks now without Claire, her bedroom emptied save for the things she had festooned to the wall, her bed last made by her and perhaps never again, and her remaining clothes shipped north at her request. Jane would come out of her own bedroom early each morning, past that confounded bicycle Claire never really wanted, and it would be the same trigger, again and again, and Jane wasn't hiding it well.

The day before, it had been Rosalie, asking after the attendance charts, pitching inquisitiveness about the staff meeting listlessness, and Jane had fended her off with assurances that she would be on top of it henceforth. Surely, Rosalie knew what was up, that only one Sperling girl had come back from spring break. Melinda Brogan knew for sure, teaching Claire's grade, and had lingered at Jane's door at the end of the first day, getting the story in brief, telling Jane she was there if she needed to talk. *Appreciate it*, Jane had thought, *but no*. And there were the lunches, thirteen of them so far, all taken in her room, the better to isolate and to keep closed off from well-meaning interlopers.

Speak of the devil...

David stood at her door, on the landing in the deepening dusk, hands on the railing as he looked down at her as she parked. She couldn't miss him or evade him. She shut down the car, got out, closed the door, locked up, toted herself and her stuff up the stairs, sheer trudgery, heading up to a meeting that was going to happen sooner or later, so why not now?

"I come in peace," he said, holding both hands up as he stepped back and gave her room.

"I'm not at war," she said. She hugged her satchel and leaned into the door as she slipped the key into the lockset.

"Jane, I know."

"Well, come in, then."

Inside the door, she flipped on the light, and the brightness overtook them, on its heels the rancid scent of garbage she should have run down to the bin yesterday. Breakfast plates, and dinner from the night before, littered the kitchen table. She set her things on the breakfast bar and began gathering everything up.

"Sit down," she said, spotting him hanging back by the door. "You're making me nervous."

"I don't want to do that." He skirted her and headed for the couch.

While he sat and looked around as if he were new to the

place—and he was, essentially, all of their erstwhile carrying on having happened in his apartment—she herded cups and spoons and forks and knives and other dishware to the sink, which she plugged and filled with water and soap, the better to start them toward cleanliness. She cinched up the bag in the kitchen garbage, choking off the smell until she could hustle it downstairs to the parking lot.

"So," she said.

"So," he said. "Where's Claire Bear?"

"I'd prefer you didn't call her that."

"Sorry."

She crossed in front, headed to the single chair that sat diagonal from him, where she usually planted herself while Claire bounced around the couch in her manic energy, a sheer vision of amusement and a loss she never saw coming. *It had been hubris not to see it*, she reminded herself again. She poured herself in and looked at David.

"Where is she?" he asked again.

"Montana. What's your interest?"

"Come on," he said. "I still live here. I still see you come and go. I mean, you can tune me out, Jane, but you can't make me go blind. I'm asking a perfectly natural question."

She propped an elbow on her knee and set her eyes into the swale between her thumb and forefinger and waited for the unwanted moment—the torrent always lurking, the snap between bearing up and breaking down—to pass, then she looked up again.

"She's in Montana, with her father. What she wanted." She pursed her lips.

"I'm sorry," he said.

"Thank you."

"I didn't know."

"I know," she said.

"I won't ask if you're all right—"

"Thank you," she said. "I'm not."

"Of course you're not."

They sat in silence for a while, not uncomfortable, to Jane's surprise, and actually welcome in its way. Beyond the strictures of her job—no way to avoid other humans there—she hadn't been around people much, and she found herself grateful for the gesture from David. She looked at him, and he responded with a tight-lipped smile, the kind that conveys *I see you but don't really know what to say*, which she figured was about right for the situation there in her room and in her larger life.

"I don't want to be trite," he said.

"That would be a first, you being trite," she said, and that made him laugh, which made her laugh, which she appreciated more than she thought she could say.

"If there's anything I can do," he started. "Really—"

"I appreciate you," she said. "But there's really not, short of making her magically appear."

"I'm afraid I lack that skill."

"As do I," she said. "Regrettably."

He stood, then ran his hands down the front of his jeans, tidying himself. "I should go."

She stood, too, and walked him to the door. "Thank you," she said once he was on the landing.

"No problem." He stopped, reset himself, turned back to her. "Can I just ask—"

"It was me, David," she said. "I hate to put it that way, because it's so—"

"Trite?" he said.

"Yes."

"I understand."

"No, listen." She hung onto the door, gathering herself again. "I just can't, and that's on me and my situation, and I handled it badly—that's what I do, I handle things badly—and now, the situation is—it's just—"

"I get it."

"—so much more untenable," she said. "It's not just her. It's a mess with my dad and—"

"I'm sorry. I understand."

"You do?"

"I do," he said. "Or, I should say, I can. I can try to understand."

"Thank you. I didn't want to hurt you."

"You did," he said. "But I'll live."

"I'm sorry."

He offered her an extended hand. "Friends and colleagues?" She gripped his hand and gave it a vigorous shake.

"Friends and colleagues," she said.

"Besides," he said, "now I can make my move on Rosalie, who's been my true intended all along. I figure all I need is some Polident and a tanker of Metamucil." He bounded down the stairs, two at a time, taking the last stretch with a flying leap onto the grass, where he turned in pirouette, curtsied and bowed, then waved up to Jane, who waved back crazily and heard her giggles in her own voice, and wasn't that just something? She wasn't sure they were in there anymore.

Forty-three

Jane nosed her car into the space and set the shifter to park and pulled up the handbrake by rote. No chance that this particular bucket of bolts was headed anywhere on a flat patch of asphalt, but the car had been bought in Montana, a more treacherous place for such considerations, and habits had been developed. She took a deep breath into her diaphragm and let it out slowly, a whistling whoosh, then pulled in another, held it longer, then let it go, too.

It had a been a bad day, and by obligation she'd now taken a turn into something unknown—perhaps even worse, perhaps better, but certainly a mystery she didn't need or want. Her father awaited her inside the building just a few strides away, expecting her or no longer aware of her, and such were the circumstances that she never wanted to disappoint him again if she could find some alternative to it. She wondered what she would get. He'd been cheerful the day before, at least at first, before the vanishing act came. She'd been telling him the latest update from Danny, and assiduously avoiding the topic of Claire, and she saw it as it happened, the blankness moving across his face like a silent storm, leaving him to simply look at her, blinking, the way a confused and wordless child might. Two days before, he'd been petulant and bellicose. The day before that, weepy. No predictability at all, just whatever came up on each day's spin of the wheel of misfortune. What really grated on her was how little anyone seemed to be able to tell him, or her, about what was really going on inside his condition. Was he aware when he went missing, or were the threads of the real Eric Driskell—the man who loved beer and the Dallas Mavericks and hated pomp and disingenuity—buried so deep now that there could be no hope of pulling them out again?

And how had it all come on so fast, accelerating now to a certain end? In all the testing and questioning at the beginning, as they tried to zero in on what was happening, doctors asked whether he had been unusually prone to emotional swings or outbursts, and Jane had laughed, because the answer was so simple: *only his whole life*. But, yeah, he'd been inconsistent and shrill and heartbroken and weird. Hadn't they all?

Jane knew, anecdotally, that the balance was shifting, that he was increasingly gone and thus edging ever closer to his final exit. But nobody could put an expectation or a number on anything. "We're keeping him comfortable," they said, again and again, and even that was a lie. Sometimes, he was inconsolable.

Jane left the car. Her flats made clacking sounds on the asphalt. The temperatures had turned warmer of late, a welcome development. On the horizon, she watched the gathering of swirling, angry splotches of gray. A gullywasher coming, good for the agriculture and bad for the weed-choked irrigation ditches, and especially bad for Jane if it came dragging lightning. No Claire to hold onto. Jane knew it was silly to be fearful, but she was commensurately thankful for her daughter's bravery in the face of a storm. God, how she missed her.

"Jane?"

The invocation of her name, from a voice she recognized, whirled Jane around.

"God, Jocelyn, really? This is creepy."

The older woman worked her hands as if she were trying to remove a stain. "He called me, Jane."

"He called you?"

"He did. He asked me to come."

"And you came."

Jocelyn nodded, eyes averting Jane's.

Jane had to give her credit for gall, at least. A phone call from Eric—no less a lucid phone call (*where did he get the phone?*)—was a credible breaching of the boundaries Jane had erected and plainly communicated to her father's paramour. *You are not on the approved visitor list. You are not to contact him. Thank you for bringing him home from Florida—and what kind of vile temptress are you, luring him out there?—but now kindly disappear and leave this family crisis to his family.*

"What did you tell him?" Jane asked.

"I told him I've been giving him some space while they sort out his condition."

"Good," Jane said. *That's what I told him, too.*

"Jane, I love him." Jocelyn looked up now, timidly resolute against what she wouldn't be able to hold off. "He loves me."

Jane shook her head. "I'm not going to say you don't feel something for him. Maybe you do. Maybe you did back then, too. But he doesn't love you, Jocelyn. He probably doesn't know it's Friday. Go home."

She turned away from Jocelyn and headed for the door.

Eric lay adrift inside his own vessel, a relief to Jane given the circumstances, and she instantly felt guilty for feeling that way. She just didn't want to have to confront him about the phone and the call—*and seriously, who helped him with that?*—and certainly didn't want to have to answer his questions about Jocelyn if he somehow remembered what he'd done a day earlier. When Jane came into his room, he smiled at her, but she didn't see any flicker of recognition in it. You smile at strangers on the bus, too, when you don't have anything better to do.

She sat beside him and took his right hand, and she caressed the knuckles between her thumb and her forefinger, lingering there against the rough skin, and here was another way her father had gone suddenly, irreparably frail. It had been mere weeks since he'd lain on his back, hitching up her disabled Toyota with those meaty hands that could manage just about any physical task, and now here he lay, helpless as a newborn. It had all come on with jarring swiftness, taking him away not in increments but in swaths. The occasional doctor's consultation she received couldn't account for the ravenous gobbling of his abilities, his mind, his time, his life. "The way it goes sometimes," that had been a particularly unhelpful bit of deflection. At other times, more was forthcoming—"perhaps it's been happening for a while and he just hasn't said anything," which would at least be in the neighborhood of Eric Driskell's tendencies—but the sum was this: She was losing him, and the things she hoped they someday might arbitrate and set right would be passed on to her to settle in whatever way she could without him.

"I'm sorry," she told him. "I'm trying to understand."

He heard the words, at least, even if the question of whether he understood them was likely to hang out there, unmet. He turned his head toward her, again with that innocent smile, and he attempted a murmuring that produced no sound, just a bubble of saliva between his lips that gently deflated and popped.

"Claire is with Paul."

Eric closed his eyes.

"It's just you and me."

She let go of his hand, stood up, leaned over him, brought the sheet up and tucked it beneath his chin. She sat down again and dropped her head.

"I don't know what happened," she said now. "I thought we were making something of life here. It was getting better, anyway. I thought so. But I was wrong. I guess I never should have left."

She looked up. Eric stared at her.

"But then I'd miss this, wouldn't I?" she said.

He blinked twice, then moved his mouth again, another try. "She'll be back," he said, his voice creaky and scratchy from underuse, and he grimaced under the strain. "You're her mom."

Jane arrested the breakage in her own voice before it could spill into the uncontrollable places. "Well, hey there."

"Hey," he said, then he closed his eyes again, and she sat silently with him, and within minutes, he was asleep, those snores that could rattle windows and saw through drywall heading up toward the ceiling like a dissonant song.

When Jane arrived at the apartment, she parked the car and, her senses on edge, almost immediately saw the figure in the dark, lingering near the stairs. Shorter than David, who'd blessedly stuck to his pledge to leave her be. Wider, too. Jane considered her options. The apartment complex had purported security, but she'd never seen it. A 911 call struck her as too much of a solution, given the dearth of information about who and what. She gave glancing consideration to driving away, but dinner was up there, unmade, and she wasn't in a mood to forgo that.

She opened her door, and that drew attention, at least, but only of whoever was waiting there. She climbed out, put her arms on the roof, and set her right foot in the door jamb so she could drop into the seat again quickly if the situation sent her that way.

"Can I help you?"

"Mrs. Sperling?"

A woman's voice, an instant relaxing of the guard, then tension again because Jane was a woman, too.

"Can I help you?" Jane pitched again.

The woman came forward, into the light, and Jane recognized her.

"Mrs. Watson?"

"Yes."

Jane closed the car door and went to her, and the Watson woman, seeing her coming, lowered herself to the curb and settled in. For the briefest of moments, Jane wanted to ask how she knew where to come, then she abandoned the impulse. One, didn't matter. Two, Roderick knew, having come over the day her father bought the kids the bicycles. A long way away, that day, in efficacy if not in spins of the orb.

"What are you—" Jane stopped the thought and reconsidered it. "Aren't you supposed to be at work?" *That wasn't any better*, she thought. She stood now near the woman, off to the side, looking down at her.

"I took the night off. It's important."

"Did something happen to Roderick?"

"Yes." The woman cupped her hands to her eyes and drooped perilously low and caught herself but kept the water shut off.

Jane joined her on the curb. "What?" Her mind and her imagination headed for the most unspeakable outcomes, the most jarring and irreparable harms, the worries she'd had since David had called him the smartest kid in school, with no suggestion that anybody much cared about that distinction. "What happened?"

Roderick's mother gathered herself. She sniffled and snorted and wiped her nose with her sleeve.

"I know you kicked him out. I know you're done with him," she said.

"I didn't kick—"

"I told him you should be done, the things he said to you," she said. "I told him that for sure. I told him he can't talk that way to anybody, let alone a teacher, let alone you. Not after what you've done for him."

"Wanda, what hap—"

"He's been expelled. Again."

"Oh, no."

"Fighting. Again."

"Oh, no," Jane said again. It was, all told, less severe than she had feared, simply because Roderick was presumably still a living boy. The other implications quickly took up the same space in her mind. "He was doing so well."

"I don't know what to do."

"I'm so sorry."

"I'll lose him now for sure," she said. "School, that was the last thing keeping him. He liked it. He likes you. I'm sorry he's so bad at showing it."

"I didn't kick him out," Jane said. "I was just—I was just taking a break from him. I don't know that I can do him any good right now. I've—" She dug around for the words that were simple enough in the rote recitation: *I've lost my daughter. I'm losing my dad. I'm losing my mind.* Nothing useful came.

"Things are really hard right now," Jane settled on. "Too hard to be called a stupid bitch on top of it all."

"Roderick told me."

"He did?"

Roderick's mom nodded. "He's awfully sorry. So am I."

"Well, thank you for that. He knows I'm not stupid." She smiled, hoping that would lighten things.

"I should go." Roderick's mom scrambled onto her feet, surprisingly nimble for the girth she carried.

"Why did you come here?" Jane asked, standing to meet her.

"I don't remember."

"Wanda, please."

That broke the woman open again. "I'm sorry," she said. "I've no right to ask. But will you help him?"

"Look, I—"

"Will you please, please help him? I'll pay anything, some way,

I'll pay it. That other principal said the same thing yours did, said he's a good kid, maybe they'd consider reinstating him if—"

"But two expulsions, one semester," Jane said. "One semester, two expulsions." It didn't sound good, whatever the order.

"I know."

In her head, Jane spun through her calendar for an opening she couldn't see but knew she would create just the same. She wondered if the defiant young man who promised to make her cry—and had succeeded, she grimly noted—would be at peace with getting her tears for free, without preamble. She couldn't see the breakages coming these days.

"Give me a few days to get myself arranged," Jane said, and in Roderick's mother's bursting glee, she swallowed Jane's hands with her own and shook them vigorously.

"Thank you, thank you."

"Tell him I'll meet him Tuesday afternoon at Danny's. Other days, he might have to go wherever I'm going."

"Fine, fine."

"Hospitals and things. You sure?"

"He told me about your dad. I'm sorry. He'll be fine. I'll make sure of it."

"OK, then," Jane said. "I'll find out where he is in his classes, and we'll keep him on pace. But listen. Listen. I can't handle it if he fights me or calls me names. I can't. I'll feel awful, but I'll have to stop. OK? Will you tell him that?"

"He knows."

"But will you tell him?"

"Yes, ma'am, I surely will," Roderick's mother said.

They shook hands properly, and Jane stood on the wet grass below her stairs and watched the woman leave, and once she and her car were on the go, Jane fell back into her patch of troubles, now either added to or receiving a dose of unexpected grace. She couldn't know which and didn't rightly care. "It must be a test," she said, to no one. "It must be."

Forty-four

In the years that followed, Jane would tell people—new arrivals in her life, friends she couldn't have known she would gather, coworkers who, at long last, lived on the inside of her circle and not the periphery, loved ones she couldn't have expected—that the call had rearranged everything, and what a surprise, too, because it all had been rearranged enough, again and again.

It came at 5:57 p.m. on a Tuesday. She noted the time because the phone began to twitch there on Danny's office table, lighting up, the digits clear to Jane and Roderick as they began digging in on his stack of work, and the 406 area code that registered neither with her nor the phone itself drew her further attention.

"I really should take this," she said, standing up, heart already revving, waviness in her legs. *Who calls on a Montana number other than a Montanan, and one I don't know? It cannot be good.* Already, her assumptions were oriented to the depths. Claire, in trouble. Paul, incapable. Her world, in tatters and spiraling fast.

She went out the door, into the dusty repair yard, the phone at her ear. "Claire?"

"No." A man's voice.

"Who's this?" she asked.

"Is this Jane?"

"Who is this?"

"Bert Daly. Do you know who I am?"

"No."

"I'm—"

"Yes!" she said, recognition coming a beat late, like the pause put in by a television censor.

"You do."

"Bert Daly, mister—former mister—to Teryn."

"Yes," he said. "Listen, you must be—"

"—wondering why you're on my phone?"

"Yes, and how—"

"—you got my number?"

"That's correct," he said.

She leaned against the aluminum wall of the small hut holding Danny's office, her father's office before that, oxidized into rust by the years and the elements. She looked across Smithfield Road, there in the distance, to the houses she'd known her whole life. Dusk was coming fast, bathing them in amber.

"I was wondering that, yes," she said. "And now, frankly, I'm worried."

"Teryn is OK," he said.

"Thank God."

"Will be OK. I'd say she's far from OK at the moment. Look, Miss—"

"Jane."

"Jane," he repeated. "Look, I've messed this all up. It's thirty-one hours from Accra to Wichita and I'm fried and—look, can I just start again?"

"I wish you would."

Roderick banged out the door, startling Jane, and he held his hands out and whipped his head in a half-turn. *What gives?* Jane held up her left hand, the palm squared up with him, and gave him a sideways glance that said, wordlessly, *in a second*, a response that apparently satisfied him. Back in he went.

"Teryn had a car crash," Bert said now.

"Oh, no."

"She was drunk."

"Oh, no."

"She has a few days to heal up, then it's into a rehab program."

"Heal up?"

"Some cracked ribs. Nose smashed the steering wheel. Lacerated spleen, which is probably the trickiest of it, addiction aside. Pretty minor, considering. Pretty minor for who she hit, too, so..."

"Sabrina," Jane said. "How is Sabrina?"

"Sabrina is fine. Shaken. I guess you could say we all were. Are. She's been alone—at the hospital, mostly, but alone. I got here as fast as—"

"Of course you did," Jane said. *Ghana to Kansas. Jesus. Stuck on a plane, waiting. How could anyone stand it?*

"So here's the thing, and the reason for the call," he started, and Jane could have scripted the rest, but she let him slide through every word of it, mumbles to keep him going, as he laid out the plight. "Rehab is a necessity, just on the face of it. But now there are legal considerations and the need of time and giving her the best chance to emerge whole. You see? And Sabrina has a month or so left of school, and I have the finish of a planting season sixty-two hundred miles away, and we have this problem."

"We?" Jane said, to her instant regret.

"The Daly we," he said. "You may hang up if you wish. It's certainly not your problem."

"I'm sorry. Go on."

"We have this problem: Teryn needs time, Sabrina needs

tending to, I need to close up my affairs in Ghana so I can get back here where I'm needed. Can you help? I feel foolish for asking. Teryn said I should. She insisted, in fact."

"Can I take Sabrina?"

"Yes," he said. "Yes, that's what we had in mind. Her teachers will work with her on the distance. She has her assignments. But she needs a bed and food and—"

"Supervision," Jane said.

"That's correct."

"She can't go to Ghana?"

"She can. But passports, inoculations..."

"I see," Jane said. And she really did see, every element of it. Why Teryn had him call. Why she thought it would be an easy fit. She could hear Teryn's voice in her head, what she would have said if she hadn't had to send her ex-husband on this errand, entirely sensible and entirely out of bounds: *Well, you have room now.* The mere edging in of that thought made Jane angry, an emotional state where she knew she too often camped out these days, and she had to arrest her tongue from flopping out what Teryn, and Bert, might be missing in this request of theirs. Her father. Roderick, who was now at the door again, looking at her searchingly. Her job that she might not have much longer from the recent appearance of things. The scatterings of lives both here and thirteen hundred miles northward.

"I can pay you, of course," he said.

"I'm not a service," she said.

"No, of course not," he said. "I didn't mean it like—"

"I know what you meant." She steamed. She relented. She sighed. She started again. "Of course. Of course I'll do it. Why wouldn't I do it? Of course I will. Teryn needs this."

"I need this," Bert said. "Sabrina needs this."

"You, I don't know," Jane said now. *The truth hurts.* "But I'll do it for Sabrina. For Teryn."

"I understand."

"OK," she said. "How are we going to do this?"

The sorting out was surprisingly straightforward: Bert said he would stay in Wichita until the weekend, make sure Teryn got safely transferred from the hospital to the rehab center, help Sabrina pack up, then fly her down to D/FW International, from which he could make an easier journey back to Africa. Jane thanked him particularly for that last part, not relishing—or having time for—an eleven-hour round trip to Wichita amid the other smoldering crises.

That done, she and Roderick bunkered in again, apologies offered for the interruption of their time together. She had requested, and received, an accounting from each of his teachers of what he would have cover, alone, for the remainder of the school year. He had used his time alone in the office to divide the stack into piles by subject matter: books, instruction sheets, assignments. Atop the English stack sat a sealed, blank envelope.

"What's this?" she asked.

"It's for you," Roderick said.

She plucked it with her fingers. "What is it?"

He shrugged.

She slipped a nail into the corner flap of the seal, where the adhesive didn't reach, and she sliced the top open and removed the sheet of paper inside. It was folded in half, then again. She unfurled it. Jotted handwriting in blue ink stared back at her.

"What's it say?" Roderick asked. "Winker was all mysterious and stuff."

"Just a sec."

Ms. Sperling, if there's anything—anything—you need with Roderick, just call. I don't expect to hear from you, because it seems you've given him everything he needs, at least in this subject. I hate to lose him, and I suspect he's being scapegoated for something that's not entirely his fault or for something that at least has a reasonable explanation. But he's a funny kid. He doesn't have anything to say about that, so here we are. Thanks for doing this for him. He's worth it.—Gene Winker

She folded the note again, slipped it into the breached envelope, then stuck that in her purse, at her feet.

"What's it say?" Roderick asked again.

"He likes you," she said. "Is he a good teacher?"

"He's OK. For a teacher."

She laughed, and Roderick seemed well pleased with himself for getting to her.

"Do you want to talk about what happened?" she asked him, quick and to the point so she didn't second-guess herself and so, perhaps, he would rise to the invitation.

"Not really," he said. "I mean, I did what they said. But the kid had it coming, like the other one did. Nobody wants to hear that."

"Your Mr. Winker seems to think the same thing."

"He's not as dumb as he looks," Roderick said, looking to her for another laugh she didn't intend to give him.

"He believes in you," she said.

"He should," Roderick said. "I'm great."

She now granted him another chuckle, something smaller and less committal than before, his needs—and her intentions—lying beyond the mirth.

"OK, now," she said, "let's bear down. We're going to do this, right?"

Roderick, his pencil already set into the task, looked up and said, "What did I just say?"

Jane came home in darkness, no interloper at the foot of the stairs, no David on the landing, calling down to her. Just silence and the dropped blackness, pierced in places by the dusted streetlamps beaming down. She liked that the nights still leaned toward chilly, though that would be changing soon, she knew. She wondered how their first summer in Texas would go, and she found herself desperately clinging to the plural possessive pronoun, knowing that Claire would be back, at least for a matter of weeks. Longer, Jane hoped, hope being all she had—that Claire was just working through a phase of missing the place she was born to, that Eric would proceed gently to his own destination, that she would find out soon enough what she would be doing come fall. More of the same, she hoped. That word again.

She carried herself upstairs to her door, then let herself in, and the only companion she had these days, loneliness, bit into her like the wind. The day to day had become a game of distraction in Claire's absence—*if I can just keep myself busy at school, with Dad, with Roderick, then I can hold what's missing at bay*—but home, where she should be most comfortable, had become a trap that held only her and what she most feared. Being alone. It would be funny if it weren't so crushing. How much had she pined for it, especially in those early years with Paul, before Claire? It had a quality of gold, endlessly yearned for, precipitously scarce, and now that she had as much of it as she could imagine holding, she found it worthless. Fool's gold, and she was the fool.

She set her things on the table. Down the hall she went to Claire's bedroom, preserved. She turned on the light. Bieber on the wall, festooned there in various degrees of poutiness, optimized for bursting little girls' hearts. Jane liked it, liked the tactile nature of it, a closing of the distance between her and her daughter. Where Jane had clipped Ralph Macchio and Tom Cruise from glossy magazines, Claire had used her inkjet printer to push out Bieber and that other guy and the other one whose names Jane always forgot. The printer and its capabilities were still on her desk, waiting for Claire. The stars of her pre-teen galaxy were all waiting on her.

Jane turned off the light. She was caught between backing out, as she usually did, and staying, as she didn't think she could. Finally, she went to the twin bed, eased onto it, her backside down on the blanket pulled taut and tucked under the corners. She lay her head onto the pillow stack, gone cold from Claire's absence. She turned her head to the right and nestled her nose in and smelled her gone girl. She closed her eyes, and she tried to get her fingers around the hope slipping away from her.

Forty-five

Jane waited until Saturday, when she and Claire had a scheduled call, before revealing the change that was coming. It's easier that way, she bargained with herself, easier to just tell her what's what, hear her complaints—and, oh, how Jane hoped she would have them, for those would be necessary indicators that some part of the girl remained with her in the apartment—and deal with those before preparing the room that had once been hers, and might yet be again, for someone else. Then, Sunday, the meetup at the airport and the launch toward whatever awaited this cobbled-together arrangement.

It was the idea of the room revamping that punched Jane in the gut after she had already agreed to it. She'd come home for four consecutive nights now, after her sessions with Roderick, and she had folded herself into Claire's bed and slept till morning. It was getting to where the bed and the room smelled more of her than of her daughter, perhaps a necessary passageway to its next occupant.

Not for the first time, she found herself grateful that things with Roderick, for the better part of a week, anyway, had not added to the burden but instead had been a leavening in almost every way. He attacked his work, even the subjects that didn't hold his interest the way literature did, and he set a pace that would have him well ahead of where he needed to be by the end of May. She could sign off on his advancement to the eighth grade, whether in a brick-and-mortar school or in Danny's shack reeking of grease, and he could keep going, somehow. Even Tim had suggested that Roderick's future held some brightness, if also a perilously thin margin of error from the viewpoint of the school district.

He had come to her Thursday, told her what he knew, told her to keep on with it, and he'd said he would seriously consider reinstatement were there no more incidents. "Noah Nelson will be at the high school," he had said, "and I've not heard a peep from anyone else who has a problem with Roderick. Even at Watauga, they tell me they'd love to have him back. Kid just needs to know when to walk away from a fight."

"Or," Jane had said, "other kids need to know to leave him alone."

"Fair enough," Tim had said.

What he hadn't said, what nobody had addressed in any concrete way, was Jane's own future beyond the task of filling in for the departed Mrs. Andersen for the remainder of the school year, a stretch growing ever short. It was the way it wasn't being discussed that most unnerved Jane when she was given to pessimism, which was most of the time. Rosalie's manner of communication mostly resided in correctitude. Tim's was more personable but also more shrouded in administrative wrapping. David steadfastly kept his distance. He also didn't know he would soon be enlisted to help with Roderick's speech instruction.

Oh, well, she thought. *Finish strong and leave it to the fates.*

Jane placed the call at two p.m. sharp, one p.m. Mountain, right on the tumbling numbers from one-fifty-nine. She used the video call feature on her smartphone, something she had steadfastly resisted amid David's sex-driven overtures and now found indispensable in her communications with Claire. She needed to see her girl's face, her skin, her eyes, the curve of her mouth to even begin to trust that she was OK.

Claire picked up the call, but she was distant from the drop, as she tended to be, as if this were just another obligation and not the most desperately important thing Jane would do all week. Just once, Jane thought, she would like a little enthusiasm to come back her way. Just once.

"How's school?" Jane started.

"Fine."

"How are your friends?"

"Fine."

"How is your dad?"

"I'm fine," Paul chimed in from somewhere nearby.

"Fine," Claire said.

"Do you want to come back here? You can." Jane knew it was manipulative, putting Claire on the spot, and every call, she came at her daughter with some variation on the same question. She told Paul she would—it was only fair—when Claire trenched in and said she wanted to stay. "She doesn't know everything she needs to know yet, and you can't help her with all of that the way I can," she had told her ex in the late-night phone call when the two of them settled on the arrangement. "I'm going to fight for her."

"I, like, miss you and stuff, Mom, but no," Claire said now, another crushing answer.

Paul made a sad-trombone sound, and Jane wanted blood. She closed her eyes, forgetting she was on camera, then opened them again and tried to silently flush the anger.

"Would you like to hear how I'm doing? How Grandpa is doing?"

"Sure."

Jane laid it out there, larding up her report with as many names and places as she could, anything that might ping Claire's interest. She said how Mr. Bourque had asked after her—he had, once or twice, always careful with Jane's feelings—and how Roderick was plowing through his work like a champ, their having covered Roderick's latest run-in with authority the previous week. She told Claire that her grandfather was fading steadily but still had the occasional good day, when he was lucid and almost the man they both knew, and that she saw no reason he wouldn't be around come late May. She did not tell her how she had fended off his Jocelyn question with lies—she did not want Claire to even know there was a Jocelyn or a question—and had threatened the memory care staff with holy retribution if anybody ever gave him a phone again. She told Claire that Danny's candy jar was brimming now that she wasn't there to receive his handouts of Peppermint Patties whenever he saw her.

She then got to it.

"One other thing," Jane said. "Do you remember Sabrina?"

"At school?" Claire asked.

"My friend Teryn, her daughter."

"Oh, yeah. I liked her."

"She's coming to live here for a few weeks," Jane said.

That penetrated Claire's disaffection and satisfied Jane in a way she knew it probably shouldn't.

"Why?"

"Yeah, why?" Paul said, off-camera.

"Claire," Jane said, "do you suppose you could go and sit somewhere I don't have to have a conversation with both of you?"

Claire spiraled her eyes, a too-common reaction that had the benefit, for Claire, of drawing a too-hot reaction from her mother whenever she did it.

"Whatever," Claire said.

"I'll go," Paul said. "Stay there."

"Would you, Paul?" Jane asked with dripping insincerity. "That would be great."

She waited a few beats for his departure, then started in again, gravely.

"Sabrina's mother is sick," she said.

"What's wrong with her?"

"She's sick."

"Is she going to die?"

"Honey, no. But she needs help, and Sabrina needs a place to stay and—"

"Couldn't she, like, stay with family?"

"It's complicated, Claire."

"Why does she have to stay in my room?"

"Because we help the people who need our help."

"Is she going to be there when I come visit?"

"I don't know," Jane said, cringing at the last word of the query, knowing the point of view it carried.

"Am I going to have to sleep on the *couch*?"

"Honey, it's going to be fine."

"This sucks."

"It can't suck that hard from four states away, Claire."

The picture on Jane's phone flickered out, the modern version of a hangup. At once, she found it crushing and exhilarating in a way she knew was probably inappropriate. It shouldn't have been a fight, and she shouldn't have been mocking at the end, but the squabble had unearthed something of value.

Claire cared about her life in Texas. She could be territorial about her room. She might yet choose to assert herself, right here. Jane's thoughts flickered to Jim, and she grinned at the sideways movements he would sometimes make to get into her thoughts. Jim, possessed of seemingly endless patience, a quality forever scant in her own reserves, would tell her that sometimes you have to be quiet, sometimes you must be still, and when you're silent and still, sometimes the answers come.

In the absence of anything else, she told herself now that she was willing to try.

She stood from the couch, walked down the hall into Claire's room, and began remaking it for another girl.

April 16, 2016

Guess what I found under your mattress.

A clue?

Very funny, Claire. Want to try again?

I don't know.

I found a leather string with a knot on one end. It was snapped in two. Know anything about that?

No.

It's missing a pendant, though.

Claire?

What?

What happened to the pendant?

I don't know what you're talking about. It was your stupid idea to mess with my room.

And it was your idea to tell me that you lost the necklace Grandpa gave you when apparently you didn't. Do you want to tell me now what happened to it?

No.

You don't want to tell me?

I don't know what happened to the stupid necklace.

You clearly know something. What, the leather piece just fell off your neck, snapped on its own, and crawled up inside your fitted sheet? That's the story you're going to go with?

I don't need a story.

No, you really do. But it needs to be a lot better.

It's your stupid apartment and your stupid bed. The story is whatever you want it to be.

All I want is the truth.

Claire.

Leave me alone.

Tell me the truth.

Claire.

LEAVE ME ALONE

Tell me what happened and I'll leave you alone. That's the deal.

I got mad at Grandpa. I got mad and snapped the necklace and threw the pendant out the window of the car.

That's the truth?

THAT'S WHAT HAPPENED

When did this happen?

I got mad at Grandpa like a million times.

But this one time. When did it happen?

I forgot. I felt bad about it later and I saved the strap. That's the truth.

OK.

IT'S THE TRUTH

OK, Claire, I believe you. Why didn't you just tell me?

Because you'd get mad LIKE YOU ALWAYS DO.

I'm not mad. I was confused. I was worried. I'm not mad.

YOU HAVE RUINED MY DAY

Claire.

THIS IS WHY I LEFT AND CAME TO LIVE WITH DAD BECAUSE YOU'RE AWFUL

Claire, please.
I HATE YOU

Jane turned off the phone and shoved it across the table, stung and shocked into silence. She didn't want to be tempted to try again with texting a placation and just continue digging the hole she was in. She slipped a finger under the leather piece and lifted it slightly, making it dance. She had almost missed it, just a tiny section peeking out of the fitted corner of the sheet. Had she not seen that, she wouldn't have extracted it before wadding up the sheet and adding it to the laundry. It would have been days, then, and a washing, and maybe the strap would have disappeared into a sock or a pair of underwear or a towel, gone again, no one the wiser for a long while. Another easy lie for Claire at that point. *I don't know how it ended up in the linen closet.* Who could have challenged her?

But this was obvious concealment. Why?

Jane reconsidered the text exchange. The last of it seared her memory; she wouldn't have to consult the transcript. Claire had been caught in a lie, not for the first time. Her pride burned. Understandable. She was lashing out. Also understandable, but the force of it like a punch to the nose, or what Jane imagined a punch in the nose to be. Sudden and painful and flabbergasting. Under pressure, Claire had coughed up the truth, also not a first, but Jane couldn't recall a blowout that would have prompted such a violent outburst. The worst conflagration between grandfather and granddaughter had been the impetus for presenting the necklace in the first place; she couldn't recall any clash between them that even rivaled it, but she also knew she had been something less than attentive when things were flaring between her and David. Another manifestation of that mistake.

Tomorrow, Jane thought. *Tomorrow, I'll apologize. If she doesn't apologize first, and I hope—God, I hope—she does.*

Tomorrow, Sabrina comes.

Tomorrow, everything changes. Again.

<h1 style="text-align:center"><u>Forty-six</u></h1>

Jane stood on the baggage-claim side of the doors through which travelers emerged from the main terminal. She scanned faces and pairs and looked for the girl she knew walking with the man she didn't. She had received the message she wanted that morning—*I don't hate you Mom I love you*—and had responded in kind and had spent the balance of the hours before lunch finishing up the house, mopping floors and cleaning the kitchen and making the whole place welcome, or at least antiseptic. The place smelled now like it had the day she and Claire arrived, before their belongings came up and made it familiar.

She hadn't been able to eat, having fallen headlong into an attempt at empathy for Sabrina. The arrangement was perfectly sensible and perfectly screwed up, all at the same time. How awful she must feel about this separation from her mother, seeing her father fly off, having to bunk in with a woman she barely knows. Now, at the baggage claim, Jane still found herself mired in those thoughts. Was Sabrina only now coming to the truth about Teryn's peril, or had she known all along? *For that matter,* Jane asked herself, *how come you never said anything? You had to know. Coward.*

Finally, she spotted Sabrina—same strawberry-blonde hair in the same style as she'd worn it in December, freckles like a starburst across her nose and upper cheeks, yet looking older than before because she was older, like Claire was older, and how much of Claire was she missing now, a daily drain of their time together, spent apart...

Jane caught herself before she took a tumble into all of that. She waved. She smiled gamely. Sabrina waved. Jane walked toward her, and him. He was tall and thin and neat, wearing a suit, an expensive one, a standout in the scrum of T-shirts and flip-flops and the grimy smell of packed-in travelers.

She reached them. She opened her arms for a hug, and Sabrina stepped into it. She held the girl tightly and whispered "I'm glad you're here" in her ear. She released her, then extended a hand to her father.

"Hi. I'm Jane."

"You're not what I expected," Jane said as she and Bert stood on the periphery, watching Sabrina as she lingered by the carousel, waiting for her suitcases. As soon as the words worked themselves out of her, Jane wanted them back. Too prosaic. The kind of thing she would subsequently have to define for him. Not good.

"What did you expect?" he asked.

Jane shook her head. "I don't know. You know Teryn and I became friends amid our divorces, right?"

"Teryn mentioned that, yes."

"So it won't surprise you that what I know comes from—" She fumbled the words, then gathered them in. "A certain point of view."

"Ah," he said. "You expected horns, maybe? A barbed tail?"

"I'm just saying, I had a name and a particular situation and—"

"Bert," he said, and he offered his own handshake, which she accepted. Funny. He was funny. "So maybe you expected an oblong yellow head with a tuft of black hair? Unibrow?"

Jane snorted a giggle. "OK, that was good," she said. "Can I just back out of this line of conversation now?"

"Sure," he said. "No problem."

They reoriented themselves to Sabrina, who soon fished one suitcase off the carousel and turned to them, holding up a single finger. One more. Bert focused on her, ready to help.

"Think of how uncomfortable this would be for you if I used my full name," he said, side-mouthing.

"Norbert," she said, pulling a tidbit from a remembered email from Teryn.

"Yeah," he said. "Family name. Damn uncreative Irish-German farmers. Most of the kids in my hometown had Norwegian ancestry. What I wouldn't have given to be named Jhalmer instead. Sven. Ingomar. All vast improvements."

Jane snorted again.

"I think, at its peak, there were nine people who had the name," he went on. "Me, my dad, and his dad are three of them."

A third snort. "Stop it," she said.

Sabrina pulled the second suitcase off the carousel, and Bert went to help her, his long, graceful strides carrying him through the gathered travelers. Jane shook out the laugh that had collected in her throat, then followed in his wake.

Sabrina didn't say much on the drive to the apartment. She had cried a bit upon her father's leaving them to catch a train to his terminal, but mostly she had been brave about the whole thing. Bert had held her, cradled her head, kissed her hair, all of it tender and unrehearsed. Jane, standing deferentially aside, had trouble reconciling what she saw with what she had heard when she and Teryn were thick as man-disdaining thieves, trading stories of marital woe like little boys swap baseball cards, the two of them lost in their conspiratorial gaggles during lunch breaks. She couldn't say that she now doubted Teryn, exactly—her friend's sincerity, and her own, at the time was nigh unimpeachable—but she did wonder if nuance had gone missing, for both of them, amid the onrushing pain. Was there someone who looked at Paul now and wondered what kind of irredeemable shrew she must be, leaving him there in Montana, alone?

She shook her head to clear the notion. No comparing the two situations. She knew that.

"It's so big," Sabrina said as the Toyota cleared the mixmaster, sling-shotting off the ramp to the final stretch home. The Mid-Cities of first Euless, then Bedford, then Hurst, and finally North Richland Hills hung off both sides of the freeway, all strip malls and chain restaurants and banks and schools and housing developments that stretched to the thinnest horizon in all directions. As a girl, a teenager, Jane had known all the routes, the invisible boundary lines between the shapeless cities, but she mostly found it all a puzzlement now. Too much had moved in during the interregnum between disappearance and reappearance, and her world had grown smaller in the bargain.

"Are you hungry?" she asked. Sabrina shook her head.

"Do you want to see or do anything?"

Another declination. "Just want to see where I'm going to be living," Sabrina said, the words flat and even and still calibrated for heartbreak.

"I'm sorry," Jane said.

"I know. You're being awfully kind. I appreciate it."

"Your mother, she'd do it for me."

"I know."

"It's going to be OK," Jane said.

Softly now, almost imperceptibly, Sabrina said, "I know."

Jane admired the plan, such as it was, that Bert had formulated to hold together their fallen-apart family. When he finally got to Accra, he would be six hours ahead of them, at the end of his daily obligations after lunch was had here—Jane wanted to be careful not to crowd Sabrina, but she had already decided she would make a break for the apartment at lunchtime—and he could hop on a video call with his daughter. To Jane, he had simply said, "Text any time, call any time, ask anything." It hadn't been a dump-and-run, the very thing Jane had feared when she agreed to take Sabrina in, and for that she was grateful.

She came off the freeway maze onto Davis Boulevard, the main thoroughfare of her youth, and they subsequently shot through the older part of town with the more readily accessible memories. No matter how old she got, she figured she'd look at the Whataburger on the corner with Harwood Road and remember December 1990, a rainy night, a date she had badly wanted with Darren Ogletree, where they ate after seeing *Misery* at North Hills Mall. He had held her hand. She had thrilled. Monday, at school, he had held it again in the hallway, and she had rocketed into the stratosphere until she saw the erection pressing against his Dockers, until she saw that others saw it, too, and she had written him a note for delivery between periods, flushed with embarrassment: *I don't feel the click with you.* Stupid. Mean. Unforgiving. He wrote novels now, good ones, and lived in New Hampshire, and every time she got a sideways glance at him on social media—not often, as she purposely avoided those realms—it came with a pang. She felt silly for the feeling, which now reignited, that she might have loved him had she not scuttled the chance. She never got there, with him or anyone else. She never would, she suspected.

She almost told Sabrina the story—the erection judiciously excised from it—but aborted when the words were wet on her tongue. Instead, she silently prodded the Toyota along to Mid-Cities Boulevard—Watauga Road, in her day—and turned right. She would not burden this girl with her own past, only the immediate future. The public library was behind the apartment complex. A good coffee shop was, too. Both were agreeable places for Sabrina to unwind and study while Jane was blocks away, shepherding seventh-graders to their onward destinations. This could be home, for a handful of weeks anyway. Together, they could make it so.

"Almost there," she said to her surrogate daughter, even as her wishes trickled to her own northern bright.

April 18, 2016

Is the jetlag bad?

I don't mind flying. The six-hour time difference, seven back home, that's the killer. There's no way to absorb it immediately. Takes a day or two. Maybe three.

You still call Montana home?

Why wouldn't I? I have a house there.

Where?

Billings.

No, I mean where in Billings?

Heights. Off Hawthorne.

Ugh.

I know. But close to the airport. It's a consideration.

My husband—ex-husband—and I lived in the Heights early on. I don't know. Felt like a different city. Plus, all the good restaurants were elsewhere. Not that we could afford them.

What happened there?

With my husband?

Yeah.

A little early to be sharing that, isn't it? And by a little early, I mean write me again in 2021.

I'm just making conversation, asking a simple question. You know a lot about my marriage.

Anything you want to dispute?

Not a thing. I'm certain Teryn very accurately told you what the problems were from her perspective.

You were never home.

"Never" is hyperbole. But accurate, largely.

You're in Accra now.

Yes. Yes, I am.

So, point goes to Teryn.

I'm not disputing that.

You're no fun.

You're just on the wrong subject. I'm lots of fun.

OK, then, tell me what you're fun at.

Tell me what happened with your husband.

You first.

Why?

I asked first.

No, you didn't. I did.

Fine. I never loved him.

Wow.

What?

I mean, I asked you a question and you answered me. I'm impressed. Most people would back into an answer like that.

I'm not most people.

No. No, you are not.

Shall I elucidate?

Only if your elucidations are copious.

I doubt he loved me, either. But it's of little consequence. I didn't love him. And once I had absorbed the full import of that—what it meant to not love him, what I had asked him to be despite my not loving him—I could not remain married to him any longer. I ached to lose the marriage—the security of being married, but not him so much—but I couldn't have it.

I'm sorry.

It's not your fault.

But I'm still sorry.

Thank you. OK, your turn: What are you fun at?

Do you have a pencil handy?

No, I'm going to memorize it.

It's a list.

A short one, I bet.

A bet you'd lose. OK, here goes: I'm fun in a bookshop. I can and will read anything you put in front of me, from the owner's manual on a 1974 Gremlin to a history of colonial rule in Africa to a rom-com featuring two divorcees, a cat named Rainey, and a leading man named Tyrone. I'm fun at a ballgame—I will let you keep score, if you wish, but only if you let me buy the beer—and I'm totally fun at a concert, no matter the band. I'm fun with a dice game and on a playground, and I'm so much fun with a bowl of popcorn and a Jimmy Stewart movie on TCM, you can't even believe it. To name just a few things.

Wow.

Yeah.

What kind of a starter would you put on a '74 Gremlin there, chief?

A 3.8L.

Get out of here.

No.

How did you know that? (I Googled it, BTW.)

I had a '74 Gremlin, Jane.

Wow.

Yeah.

That's amazing. My father would like you.

Oh?

He's into cars and ballgames, too.

Yeah, but I'm not really into cars. I was a farm kid. Grew up on the Hi-Line. You had to learn to fix stuff. I had a Gremlin. Not very sensible or reliable. It had to be fixed a lot.

You don't seem like a farm kid. Nice suit you were wearing Sunday, chief.

Why do you call me that? Chief?

Better than "asshole."

Wow.

Not that you are. I'm just saying.

OK, thanks for clarifying.

My pleasure.

I mean, I can be. I suppose anyone can be.

Thanks for warning me.

Not a warning. Just...self-awareness, I guess. Can you be an asshole sometimes, Jane?

Aren't we supposed to be talking about your daughter?

We did. Now we're talking about this.

We should go back to her, though.

OK, how's she doing?

Well, it's been only two days, but pretty good.

I know. You already told me.

I did, didn't I?

It's OK. You don't owe me a daily conversation, about Sabrina or anything else.

Good. That's a bill I'd let lapse.

But it's been fun nonetheless.

It has been, yes.

Good night, Jane.

Good night, Not Very Fun Guy.

Forty-seven

Come Thursday, all of Jane's obligations met in a Gordian Knot that she gathered up in her car and took to the memory care center. In the passenger seat sat Sabrina, to whom she had promised a dinner out that had been delayed by Rosalie's collaring Jane after school, to go over end-of-semester testing and lesson plans. Behind her, in the back, sat Roderick, drumming feet on the back of Jane's bucket seat. He had squawked something fierce when they had collected him at Danny's, saying he had work to do today and they could punt the lesson plan a day. Jane's retort: "Nope. Schoolwork comes first. Even Danny says so." Into the car Roderick went, reluctantly.

On the short drive over, Jane laid out the plan. See her father, work quietly on homework, then everyone would go to dinner somewhere nice. She worried a bit about the financing of that. The food bill for her and Claire alone sometimes frayed the bank account on top of all the other draws from it, but Bert would be sending money soon, and besides, Claire hadn't been there in a few weeks to chug through milk by the gallon and cereal by the case, the remembrance of which might have sent Jane spiraling if not for the load, actual and metaphorical, she was toting. For that, for distraction, for duty, she gave silent thanks.

At the memory care center, she said hello to the front desk staff, same as always, told Sabrina she was welcome to come up if she wanted, but if she was skittish at all about medical facilities and old people she didn't know, there was a waiting area downstairs.

"I'll come," Sabrina said.

"I'll stay," Roderick said.

"Oh, no, you won't," Jane said, and she laughed when she saw the way he was grinning at her, the imp.

On the second floor, three doors down, they found Danny standing beside Eric's bed. The men were shaking hands, it seemed, and Danny disengaged and went into his pocket.

"Can't go anywhere in this town without running into riff-raff," Danny said, his words jumbling like a train derailment.

"What was that?" Jane asked.

"What?"

"What did he give you?" She looked now at her father, his eyes open, propped up, lucid from the looks of things. "Hi, Dad."

"Hi, gang," Eric said. Sure enough. Lucid. Fixating on Sabrina, he said, "Do I know you?"

"Never mind that just now," Jane said. "Danny?"

"It's my phone."

"Your phone." Jane imagined she must be changing color, like Yosemite Sam after Bugs Bunny tells him to *shaddap.* "Who'd he call?"

"Jane," Eric said.

"Who'd you call?"

"You know who I called."

"Yes," she said. "And now I know who your source is for the phone calls. I can't believe this."

"Jane," Eric said.

"You," she interrupted him. "Shut up."

"Jane," Danny said.

"And you," she said, cutting him off, too. "You come with me." She cast a finger across Roderick and Sabrina. "You two wait right here."

She grabbed Danny by the wrist, not gently like she had that one night long ago, and she tugged him toward the door. They were on the scrubbed-down linoleum in the hallway, redolent of pine, when she heard Roderick say, "Jeez, old man. What'd you do?"

It was a question she wouldn't have to ask. She continued pulling Danny toward the elevator, and he continued to comply, work boots scruffing the shine, like the scolded child she considered him to be.

By the time they reached the parking lot, the tears had come for her, driven by shame and humiliation as much as anger. An eight-second elevator ride had been interminable. She couldn't look at Danny, one of her people, virtually part of the family, for fear of what she might say, things she would never be able to pull back again once they swam through the air between them.

After she had walked him to his pickup—bright orange; she wondered how she had possibly missed it on the way in—she no longer had ugliness in her lungs for him, only a need to explain and to be heard.

"I can't have it, Danny," she said. "He's fading away. We're his family. I don't want to keep you from him, but if you do that again, I will."

"I won't do it again."

"How many times?" she asked.

"Three or four."

Jesus.

"Or?" she prompted.

"Four. Today was four."

"I'm so disappointed," she said. She fell back and leaned against the bed of the pickup. She planted her face in her hands. He came to her.

"I'm sorry, OK? He asked, and I—I guess I just didn't want to say no. Didn't know why I should."

"If you knew this woman—"

"Jocelyn?" Danny said. "I know about her. Have for a long time."

Jane looked up. "You knew?"

Danny looked at her as if he had stepped in it again, as if he realized what it all meant now. "I mean, yeah. He was my boss. You know?"

"No, I don't."

"He confided in me."

"Lucky you."

"Jane." He reached for her. She yanked herself away.

"He didn't confide in us," she said. "He ever tell you how I found out? It wasn't a confessional, I'll tell you that."

"No." Danny pursed his lips. "I just knew it ended and he didn't talk about it. Shit, Jane. I'm sorry."

"You should be."

She turned from him, dipped her head, and wept again. He lingered.

"Can I say something?" he asked.

"What?"

"When he calls, she tells him she can't come see him, that he needs family around now. He cries, Jane. He cries, and he tells her he loves her, and she tells him she loves him, and he gets himself together, and he hangs up. Not so much crying today, before you came, which was good. He was in a good mood today."

She turned to him. "He doesn't know what love is, Danny. He doesn't know where *he* is, half the time."

"Maybe. He knows both of those things when he talks to her."

She clenched her lips and shook her head. "Just don't give him a phone, OK?"

"Yeah, OK."

"I'm sorry I was mean."

"I'm sorry, too."

She left him there, to climb into his truck and leave. She had business yet. A bathroom in which to splash water on her face and towel it dry, a moment to consider the tack she wanted to take with ears in the cornfield and eyes in the potato patch, as her grandfather was given to say. The rest of a day and a night to get through, one that had gone from distracting to enraging to absolute shit, without boundaries to keep one from spilling into the other, and with the persistent missing of Claire a thrum beneath it all. She might wonder how it all went from so good to so bad so quickly, but she couldn't, because by her reckoning it had never been all that good in the first place.

Upstairs, she found her father asleep and the kids playing a board game—*Sorry*, appropriate—that Roderick had found in the lounge. Eric's head was thrown back, his chin tracing the ceiling, that adenoidal snore she knew well blaring out, white noise in the room.

"He just went out," Sabrina said. "A couple of minutes after you left."

"Yeah," Roderick said. "It was weird. He went all quiet and shit."

"Roderick."

"Like he was here and then gone," he finished.

"Vanishing," Jane said. "That's what I call it. Well, listen, let's go. Roderick, I'm sorry. Can we double up tomorrow? This didn't go quite the way I had planned."

"The 'A' stands for *all good*."

"What's this?" Sabrina asked.

"It's a long story," Jane said.

She knelt and kissed her father's head, thankful for the things they wouldn't have to say, hopeful that they wouldn't have to circle back to them. Then she waved toward the door, and the three of them filed out.

She took the kids to Niki's, an Italian place she and Claire had visited regularly and Claire liked, the memory of that a stinger in an early evening that had gently taken a promising redirection. Sabrina and Roderick, despite the gap in their ages, seemed to genuinely like each other, the way Claire and Roderick liked each other, and Jane saw possibilities in that. One kid she had to keep on the straight and narrow to an indeterminate best chance of getting back into the public school flow. The other she had to keep healthy until her parents could step in again. She thought now maybe each could be an ally in the other's upkeep. *That would be a nice turn given all the wrong ones*, she thought.

After the food arrived—lasagna for Roderick, spaghetti and meatballs for Sabrina, linguine and clams for her—Jane snapped a few sneaky photos and sent them winging out to Sabrina's dad. About the only thing that had gone to plan these few days of the arrangement had been Jane's determination to come home at lunch, a time that paralleled Bert's video calls. Jane had grown fond of his punctuality and dedication, not really hearing the conversations he and Sabrina had but nonetheless bearing witness. The early-morning hours seemed to be the hardest for Sabrina, when Jane was scurrying around, attention scattered, the cold reality of where her guest was living and why lying evident between them. The midday calls brought forth a different girl.

At once, Roderick slumped left in the booth, creasing Sabrina's space. She laughed and gave him a check with her shoulder, and he snapped back against her.

"Roderick, what's—" Jane started.

"Shhhh."

"What?"

This time, Sabrina let him hold his position against her, which left her wedged against the back of the booth, bewildered.

"Talon just came in."

"Who?"

Lower, under his breath, he said, "Talon."

Jane mimicked his low tone. "Who's Talon?"

"The kid I fought."

He let himself off Sabrina, sitting in his own space but dropping his head low, as if evading detection.

"Where?" Jane asked, oscillating her head.

"Don't look," Roderick said, almost in a hiss.

Jane looked at him, nonplussed.

"I want to go," he said.

"What?"

"We're eating," Sabrina said.

"I want to go," he said again.

"OK," Jane said, "OK. Just a sec, OK? Let's get this boxed up and paid for and we'll all—"

"I'll wait outside," Roderick said.

"What?"

"Let me out," he said to Sabrina, who slid from her spot to oblige him.

"It'll be just a sec—" Jane started.

"I'll wait outside."

When Jane and Sabrina came out to the car, Roderick was gone. Jane walked through the parking lot, scanning the side streets, trying to draw a bead on him. They hadn't taken long, three minutes tops, but that would be enough time for a boy of reasonable speed and resourcefulness to slip into the suburban grid in the advancing dark and piece together any number of routes to where he'd be headed. Jane knew she couldn't let it go. Neither his age nor the distance—a good three miles, easy— would let her leave it to faith that he would get home safely.

She and Sabrina piled into the car and set out. Their boxes of food rode in the backseat, sumptuously filling the air.

"Well, this is exciting," Sabrina said.

"It's something," Jane said.

She first plied Davis Boulevard, moving north, alternating her eyes between the left side of the thoroughfare and the asphalt itself, telling Sabrina to watch on the right. When that yielded nothing, she turned left on North Richland Boulevard and cut across to another arterial, attempting to triangulate his possible routes. At Holiday Lane, she turned left, on a slinky stretch that would lead her, eventually, to the high school where she had waited out her childhood, yearning to leave and never come back again. *How'd that work out, Jane?*

They spotted him coming off the greenbelt that paralleled Holiday, an undeveloped stretch jammed between housing tracts and the creek. He stepped out of the high grass and onto the concrete bunting of the curb, and the headlights from Jane's car alighted on him there, casting a shadow behind him. Had he emerged just a few seconds later, he would have been behind them and, perhaps, impossible to find.

Jane wheeled the car to the opposite curb and stopped it. She brought the window down.

"Roderick, get in the car."

He goose-stepped over, ashamed. She unlocked the doors. He climbed into the back.

"Where's my dinner?" he asked.

"Where's your head?" Jane sent back at him.

"We were, like, right there," Sabrina said.

"I didn't want to wait."

"Why?" Jane asked.

"I didn't want any trouble. Talon and his folks were in there, and they're all mad and stuff. You know, trying to stay on everybody's good side."

"Right."

"It's like I always say," Roderick said. "The 'A' is for *all you need is discretion.*"

"Discretion?" Sabrina said. "What kind of seventh-grader are you?"

"The best," Roderick said. "The best kind."

"Grab your dinner, hotshot," Jane said. "I'm taking you home."

Back at Danny's garage, Jane helped Roderick gather his things and stuff his backpack, the boxed lasagna riding on top, then said goodbye as he sliced into the night on his bicycle. After he was gone, she gave Sabrina the dime tour, dusty childhood memories of adoring her father, before she didn't, before she did again.

"I practically grew up here," she said, sweeping an arm about the place. She considered that, then laughed. "I guess, in a way, you pretty much saw everywhere I grew up tonight. Sorry about that."

"It was weird and fun," Sabrina said, shrugging. "I like weird fun things."

"It's home," Jane said.

"I want out of Kansas so bad," Sabrina said. "When I graduate, I'm gone."

Jane smiled, thinking again of her youthful aspirations and the chases that ensued. "I said the same thing. And did for a while. It pulls you back, somehow. Sometimes."

April 21, 2016

You said I could ask you anything.

You can.

OK: Why did you abandon your daughter?

I didn't abandon my daughter.

Come on. You know what I know. Don't be evasive.

I'm going to answer the question.

Good.

But you're going to have to reframe it because I disagree with the premise.

You're going to split hairs?

It's not a hair. It's a whole head. Ask me what you want to ask me without using the word "abandon" and I will answer you.

You promise?

I'm waiting.

OK: Why have you been so absent from your daughter's life?

Was that so hard? :)

Dammit, why?

Sorry. I'm being glib.

I just hate emojis. Don't be cagey.

I won't be: Because my work was somewhere else, and because amid a divorce I wanted to be just about anywhere else, and because I was stupid and thought there would always be time to catch up on the things I was pausing to get divorced. The questions are yours to ask, but let me tell you this: If I could revisit the ten questions I most regret my answers to, in my whole life, the preponderance of them would have to do with what I did or didn't do a few years ago. OK? I was an exemplar of what not to do when your life is falling down around you, and the only solace I can take from it is that I know this, so if ever my life is crumbling again, I'll make better choices.

Wow.

How's that?

That's an acceptable answer.

I'm so glad.

You pass.

Thank you.

Can I ask you something else?

Sure.

Tell me about where you grew up.

You lived in Montana.

Yeah, the city. Such as it was.

Not much to tell. Barely a dot on the map.

Still...

Have you ever been to Opheim?

I've been very few places in Montana, considering how long we lived there. If I went anywhere, it was usually south, headed here. And not even that, very often.

Opheim isn't really a destination. It's way up there. Almost Saskatchewan.

I bet Paul has been.

Oh?

Land man.

Ah. Yeah. Probably. There's not much to Opheim, but if growing wheat is your thing, it's a pretty good place to be. My dad grew wheat. His dad grew wheat. I didn't want to grow wheat.

What do you grow?

Here in Ghana? Cassavas, yams, pineapples. Other stuff.

How in the world did you get into that?

Well, I went to Montana State and studied ag because, you know, farm kid.

That's where you met Teryn, right?

Yep. Football game. She sat the next row down from me. She was loud.

LOL

Then I got my master's at the University of Minnesota and needed a job. Teryn and I were married, living in this tiny off-campus apartment. The USDA had a recruiter on campus one day. I applied.

So what's your job, exactly?

I'm like an agricultural attaché. I help developing and maturing countries use their resources better, get better crop yields, that sort of thing. Look for opportunities for partnerships.

You're a U.S. governmental official, though?

Yeah. News flash: The U.S. doesn't grow one hundred percent of its own food supply. It's in our best interest that places like Ghana grow well and grow efficiently.

Smarty-pants.

Guilty.

Hard on a marriage, though, I guess, a job like that.

Hard on a family. When it was just me and Teryn, it was great. We got moved around a lot. Europe. Asia. The tropics. After Sabrina was born, we settled back in Billings. But I was gone a lot, obviously. Fissures set in.

Fissures, huh?

You know, the whole smarty-pants thing.

I would have liked to see some of those places.

I highly recommend it. Expands your world, though it has a way of making the place you live in seem a little smaller.

Montana always felt that way to me.

Understandable.

North Texas feels too big sometimes.

How so?

Jane set her phone down. Every nightly text conversation with Bert had edged up against the personal, simply on account of whom they both knew and loved and the girl now in Jane's charge. This one, if she wasn't careful, could tip into the extremely personal, and from there into who knows where. She found herself giddy to think so and scared to find out. These exchanges, kept in their cellular box, had asserted themselves as the best part of her day, but only for a week or so. What would she do with something bigger and more unmanageable?

She plunged in.

It's the effects of time. I left, and it kept growing.

You thought it wouldn't?

I didn't think at all. I left when I was able to—by the way, your daughter is making the same noises about Wichita—and I put it all in the rearview. Bucolic early childhood, fond memories of my girlfriends, less-fond memories of some boys I knew, the whole of it. I left, and I didn't care if I ever saw it again. That's the vanity of a young woman. I'm not a young woman anymore.

How old? I'm just curious.

43

You're young yet, says the 46-year-old.

That's funny.

Please, go on.

I'm not sure where I was headed. I moved back here in December—for a job, of all things, and for an absence of purpose in

Billings—and I've come to find out that it didn't really care if I ever saw it again, either. You know?

I understand.

I don't mean to knock Billings, by the way. But this is home. I realize now it always was, but I don't know it anymore, either, so that's what I mean, I guess, when I say it seems too big.

You don't have to apologize to me on Billings' behalf.

No?

No. I moved to Billings—we moved, I guess I should say—because it was familiar and offered some ease of movement to the places we went. Easy enough to get to Opheim when my folks were still alive. Teryn's folks were right there. Are, I should say. That I'm still there is inertia, mostly.

Again, Jane set the phone down. It was past midnight. She thought she should go. She thought he would go. She picked it up again.

My dad is dying.

Oh, I'm so sorry.

Frontotemporal dementia, they say. Advanced, and devouring him before our eyes. They say he's probably had it awhile. We missed the signs. We weren't here to see them is more like it.

It's robbery. It's the theft of a person and everything inside.

That's it. That's exactly it.

My mom had Alzheimer's. It was a long, slow fade. It's not my place to say, Jane, but you may find, in the end, that you're happier for the quicker exit. Respectfully.

Maybe. What about your dad?

Seven years dead when she left. Heart attack, keeled over in the barn. Forget what I said about faster being better. It's terrible, either which way.

My mom's been gone almost that long.

I'm sorry. It's tough, whatever the circumstance. I feel like I might have overloaded your plate.

It's fine. It's just a wait now. A wait, and hope for an easy journey, if he has to go.

Mom, in that final year, she had weeks and weeks at a time where she was just gone, but every now and again, I'd get a call, out of the blue, and she'd be lucid the way I once knew her to be—she was a schoolteacher, like you—and she would bend my ear endlessly about how much she missed Dad, how she'd do just about anything for one more chance to hold his hand or smooch him on the lips.

That's really sweet.

Yeah, it is, but it's also completely counter to the life they had together. It baffled me and my brothers how they ever paired off in the first place. It was almost like they won each other in a drawing, only there was no trading for a different partner or just cashing in for something useful, like a tank of gas. Most years, I was certain they hated each other. In the years when I wasn't sure it was hate, it was massive uninterest. They just didn't compute at all.

Wow.

Yeah. So I'd tell her, "Mom, look, you don't miss him. You just miss something you can't have back." Like I was so smart and I could just tell her what she did or didn't want.

What did she say?

She told me there were things I didn't understand about love. Which is obviously true.

I say again: Wow.

Yeah.

How many brothers do you have?

Two. One older, one younger. Leon, then me, then Oscar.

They smarty-pants like you?

Ha. In their own way, I guess. Leon's the wheat farmer, like Dad and Grandpa. He knows more about ag than I do but doesn't have the book learning. I'm grateful, though. He stayed home, and that allowed me to roam. I owe him big.

Oscar is an engineer at 3M. Smartest guy in any room, who says the dumbest things. Totally reactionary in his politics and in his comportment. His life is a trail of failed relationships and battered friendships. Somehow, he keeps a job—probably because they don't let him out of the lab.

What about you?

There is only me. And Claire. We've been raising each other.

How so?

Oh, it's late. Tomorrow? I can dig in on that expansive topic tomorrow.

Sure. I'm sorry for keeping you up.

You haven't. It's been wonderful. Good night, Bert.

Good night, Jane.

Forty-eight

Jane went deep on sleep for a few hours, until patches of coming daylight began to punch up from the east, glancing through her bedroom window. She brought herself up, and the fogginess fell from her, and she was again in the moment of her last consciousness. She had told Bert things she had told only one person, Jim, and in ways she hadn't even put them to him. More than that, he had told her things he didn't have to impart, about what he called his failures as a husband and a father, a level of self-reflection she had never seen from a man. She remembered dropping into slumber thinking she might regret her own words come daylight and hoping that he wouldn't regret his. Now, in the fuzzy morning, she regretted nothing. She wished only that they could have kept going.

She sat up in bed and checked the time on her phone, 5:07 a.m. She had a notion, but she wasn't sure she had the time. She brought up her email, and the messages populated. Amid the mailing lists she had signed up for in piques and never again read and the ceaseless junk mail inspired by long-ago purchases of footwear and faulty home appliances, one message stood out.

Hi, Jane...

I don't know what to do with this except to just put it out there: It feels like a rubicon was crossed tonight, but we—the you-and-me we—have this problem. I think had you been in my town or I had been in yours, I would have asked you out a few hours ago. No, strike that. I'm certain of it. Here, I would have taken you out for a marvelous Ghanaian stew, thick and hearty and layered with seasonings. In Billings, maybe Village Inn pizza (please, please tell me you liked it). Where you are? Your pick. I would have asked you out, and I would have been nervous, and I would have tried my best not to show it, and I would have listened to anything you wished to say.

But we have this problem: I can't ask you out for five weeks.

You will notice I don't mention other problems, because I don't think there are any other problems, but amid these circumstances, amid the friendship you've had since I was nothing but an abstraction to you, you might not share that opinion. Teryn is your friend, and maybe you're feeling sneaky about all of this. So I feel I must be fair and present you with a no-judgment, no-wrong-answer choice: If you can wait five weeks and want to continue as we have until then, as it's all we have right now, I will "see" you in our text box tonight. If you can't, or think we shouldn't, or have any other objection at all, we can fall back to occasional check-ins about Sabrina and leave it at that.

There is no wrong answer. There is only yes, let's go on, or no, let's not.

I know my answer, were the question put to me. But I'm putting it to you, and I will respect your response, whatever it may be.

Bert

Jane drew her legs down off the bed, then found the floor

with her feet. She stood, and she felt lightheaded, and she felt extraordinary, a feeling that had not blown through her in she didn't know how long. She padded down the hallway in her underwear and a T-shirt, rapped on Sabrina's door, heard the mumble, made her apologies, then finally asked if the girl would mind fixing her own breakfast.

A mumbled "no problem" came in response, the answer that sent Jane back to her room. She picked up the phone, with Bert's question still hanging there in the pixels and her answer in kind moving toward her fingertips.

Yes, let's go on.

She went to the house on Payte Lane for the first time in weeks. She was pleased to see the lawn freshly cut, after she had just engaged the weekly service for however she long would need it, a tenure as yet undetermined and in the hands of higher powers. After she parked in the sloped driveway and emerged, she saw Evaline Roberson wobbling across her yard next door, headed toward the daily *Star-Telegram* and wearing that same old housecoat.

"Hi, Mrs. Roberson." Jane waved behind the greeting.

"Hi, dear. How's your father?"

"Hanging in."

"That's good," Evaline said. "That's real good. Best he can do. You, too." She leaned and creaked and almost fell over but grabbed the paper in one strong hand and lurched herself back to almost erect.

"It's good seeing you," Jane said.

"You, too, dear."

Inside the house, Jane sniffed the air and divined its strange mustiness, a combination of what she had always found there but also splashed by extended absence, something the house had never seen under the auspices of the Driskell family. Atmospheric dust had filtered down and settled, noticeably so. She would have to add a housekeeper, or perhaps just face inevitability and sell.

Or, alternatively, face practicality and move in, a prospect she still couldn't see despite its undeniable graces of cheap living and more than enough room for whoever might land there. The thought alone, of Claire and of her gaping absence, lacerated her heart.

She wandered the rooms, looking for something she didn't think she could find. A hint, an answer. Endorsement. Every lesson that would be imparted by an elder had come and gone. For better or worse, and often for both, she had the tools her father and mother could give her. And here she was, in deficit. She had squandered them, one by one by one.

She checked her watch. It was 6:01 a.m., and she had eighty-nine minutes on a stretch. Less than that if Rosalie had a mind to be overly officious today.

She got on with the getting on.

Jane lingered in the driveway two blocks over, her fingers defying her, gripping the steering wheel. Here, near the precincts where she had skulked with Bobby Drury and gathered ill-gotten and ill-advised carnal knowledge on top of that which had been imposed on her, the past remained suspended in the present. Finally, she coaxed herself out. "Do it. Just do it."

She left the car. She jogged up the sidewalk that unfurled like a snake to the door. She leaned on the doorbell before she could decide to hit reverse on everything. When she heard nothing from the other side, she leaned on it again.

The door opened.

"Jane."

"Jocelyn."

"What do you want?"

"I want you to come with me," Jane said. She took note that Jocelyn was already dressed, which presented a small bit of gratitude against the churning of her guts. "In my car."

"I don't think I want that."

"What, you think today is when I make you disappear?" Jane

asked, saltiness hanging on her breath. "I could have done that a long time ago."

"No," Jocelyn said, "I definitely I don't want that."

"OK," Jane said. "How about you follow me in your car? Probably better that way anyway."

"Where?"

"Just follow me."

Jane led Jocelyn from the parking lot into the memory care center, walking at a pace the older woman struggled to match. At the front desk, she told Allison, the receptionist, the deal. "This is Jocelyn Blankenship. Please put her on the approved visitation list for my dad, would you?"

Allison asked for Jocelyn's ID, checked the name, then told her to keep it handy whenever she visited, just in case anybody asked. Jocelyn, who had sniffled on the walk from the parking lot, burst into full-on crying, and Jane said, "Easy now. He needs to see you happy."

"I am happy," she said.

Jane walked her to the elevator. "It's the second floor, Room 205," she said. "They'll bring him breakfast soon." She pressed the up button. They waited.

"Thank you," Jocelyn said, a sentiment Jane expected but didn't want to hear. She'd woken up with an unwelcome but unshakable notion. She needed to do this, her feelings about Jocelyn be damned, and she needed to do it not just for him but also for herself. And once she had decided, the heaviness of the burden had come off. It had been the damnedest thing.

"Evening is my time," Jane said. "Please respect that. The rest of the day is yours. Please come see him. He needs it." Her own voice cracked, betraying the ice she'd been packing around the prospect of Jocelyn for so long. "He needs you."

The ping came. The doors opened. Jocelyn stepped in, chose her floor, adjusted herself, then smiled at Jane.

"Jocelyn?"

"Yes?"

"You're welcome."

The doors closed, and Jocelyn was gone.

April 30, 2016

You seem so certain.

Do I? I'm not. I'm hopeful.

I am hopeful, too.

That's a good thing. That's the best thing.

But what if it's not what we're imagining it to be?

That would be a disappointment, for sure. But what if it's even better?

MAY

May 8, 2016

Dear Claire,

Happy birthday! It's Sunday here—where you are, too; that's silly!—and I'm getting this done so it's out with the mail first thing and, I hope, in your hands on your big day, your 12th birthday.

Oh, Claire, how I wish I could be there for it. How I wish I could see you. Touch your face. Kiss your cheek. But I will be on your phone. You will be in my head and my heart.

We miss you so much. Your grandpa, he had a really good day yesterday, and he said he loves you and wanted me to be sure to tell you. Roderick says hi. Mr. Bourque, too. They all ask about you, all the time. I tell them you're doing fine, and I sure hope you are.

May 11, 2004, was the best day of my life, and it will forever be the best day of my life. I met you. And I promised you, the first time I saw you, that I would do everything possible to make your life beautiful. I'm trying, Claire. I'm really, really trying.

Forty-nine

Come noontime, Jocelyn set the tray on wheels between her and the edge of the bed, same as always. She leaned across the arm of her chair, feeling the crease in her stomach, and retrieved the canvas bag and its contents. She set it on the tray, then stood and began extracting lunch. A tuna salad sandwich, cut diagonally, Eric's favorite. Gelatin, cherry, in a pull-top cup. Carrot and celery sticks she would eat idly when he did not, which seemed to be the way of things lately. He wasn't eating a lot of the food the staff brought him, either, not anymore.

She sat herself down again, the daily spread between them, and still he slept, just within her reach. The food was an offering, a bid. An invitation, should he be able to make his way to her.

She stared beyond him, to the window with the shade she had pulled back, and into the brightness of midday. Jocelyn endeavored to hold space only for positivity, both for Eric in those moments when lucidity graced him and for herself when the closing of the day would come down with its threats of darkness and despair. She knew it wasn't fair—those times of awareness and handholding and conversation probably amounted to less than a couple of hours in all these days, and the source for more was swiftly running dry—but she also knew fair didn't have much of a place at the table. She thought again of how different it had been with Ed, as cancer ate him from the inside out and she begged the universe to take him when the pain got so that the hospice workers doped him out of meaningful existence. He lingered another week, then quietly receded, and that end, at last, had been a reprieve.

But this, Jocelyn had long since decided, was an injustice. Eric wasn't owed just more time. He was owed what he once had been, and not that long ago. *She* was owed it. That's what Jocelyn had decided. But to whom or what does one appeal? The most pregnant question of all, and an unanswerable one.

"Goddammit," she said, under her breath, she thought, but loud enough to fracture the silence inside the door and the ambient noise beyond it.

"Don't you cuss in here."

She cast eyes to him, astonished.

"Eric."

"Jocelyn," he said. That lopsided grin of his came out. She could have cried.

"What are you doing?"

"Watching you," he said.

"Why didn't you say something?"

"I liked the view."

"Oh, pish."

"Is it summertime?" he asked her.

"Might as well be."

"Let's go swimming."

"Oh, pish," she said again.

Whatever had brought Eric to the surface took him back to the depths as quickly, the blankness moving across his face as she fed him a last bite of sandwich, a genial but unrecognizing smile crossing his lips. Jocelyn dabbed the corners of that smile with a napkin and kissed his forehead, and he rolled toward the sun and more slumber.

These hours with him were a constant renegotiating of her expectations. That first day, after Jane had allowed her in, he had been almost giddy, almost his full-on self, upon seeing her. The fade had come quickly, yes, but he'd been in the vicinity of what he used to be, and they'd held hands and talked excitedly of this unexpected renewal. A day later, as reality edged in again, there had been a short but honest conversation about what was stalking him, the death out there but not yet fully in view, inevitable in a way that wasn't abstract. Each new day, though, brought less of him around. Some days, not even a little bit. She would bring his lunch and stay till midafternoon, when she would tote it home and eat it alone at her little table.

So today, she decided, was a gift. Something precious she could hold and take out on some future day that was not as kind. Something she could tell Rob that night when he called, as he did nearly every day, and inquired sincerely about this unexpected love of her life. She might even tell Brent, who was coming to grudging acceptance in his own way and at his own speed. She had laughed, against her best effort not to, when Brent had asked, "You're not marrying this codger, are you?" Even after the giggles had been smothered, she hadn't been able to beat back the sarcasm. "Oh, yeah, sure we are. We're thinking about having a couple of children, too." She had felt bad only when he'd sulked and said it was an honest question, and besides, he just needed to know if he and Rob and Jane were going to have to fight over things in probate, and then she had laughed all over again.

Jocelyn opened the driver's-side rear door of her sedan and set the canvas bag on the seat. She closed the door, then opened the front door and settled into the compartment. She closed the door.

She started the car. She peeked in the rearview mirror and saw Jane's Toyota swing wide into the parking lot.

Jocelyn set the car into drive and pulled away.

It had been a good day, as these days go.

Fifty

Jane stacked the papers neatly on Danny's desk, then pushed them across to Roderick. He'd done flawless work, no hyperbole. She had looked. It had become a personal challenge to her, to find something she could correct, some lesson she could impart. She could find none. The kid bore down and got it done, with the better part of a month to spare.

"Well," she said, "as far as I'm concerned, you're an eighth-grader. My opinion doesn't carry the weight of the school board, but I will tell anyone who'll listen."

"I guess I better change my name," he said.

"What's that?"

"Roderick Straight-A Watson."

"Nobody could dispute it," she said.

"Did you get me a gift?" he asked.

"A gift?" She gave him an incredulous laugh. "This is the gift, pal. Every day, doing this has been your gift."

"I know."

"But," she said, "it's been a gift for me, too."

"Well, here's another." He wrenched himself in the chair opposite her, digging into his pocket. He brought forth a closed fist, extended it halfway across the table, and opened his fingers. The object clattered against the wood.

Seeing the flash of aqua, Jane reached for it, taking it in her palm. Turquoise. She fingered it with her left thumb and forefinger, turning it over, a revelation of the inscription she expected to see.

"Where did you get this?" she asked.

"Remember that Talon kid?"

"Yeah."

"He had it. That's what the fight was about. I couldn't get it from him the first time, but I don't give up."

"But how—"

"I don't know. But I saw him with it, and he was bragging about the girl he got it from, and—"

"Roderick, why didn't you tell someone?"

"Who'd have believed me?"

This kid, Jane thought. *Maybe we can get him back in school. Maybe we can get him graduated. Maybe there's a time in his life, coming sooner than anyone thinks, when his upbringing here won't matter much against all the achievements he has stacked up against it. But what is any of that if he can't trust?*

"I would have believed you, Roderick."

She sat still for the rest of his story, holding fast against the rage assaulting her head and pushing against the more actionable parts of her. Schoolyard braggadocio about a girl who gives it up easily—*she's twelve as of today, goddammit*—that landed in the wrong set of ears. Claire might have been a myth to a bunch of kids on a playground who didn't know her, but she was real enough to Roderick. So, next, a violent scrape. Suspension and expulsion. Roderick keeping his own counsel. It's why he ran that day from the restaurant. It's why Claire ran all the way back to

Montana. Jane hadn't deduced any of it until the key parts started filling in, then the rest came racing up on her.

"You know how you're always on me to use my words and not my fists?" Roderick asked her.

Jane nodded.

"It worked. I waited for Talon at the school today. I followed him home. I told him that the jewel belongs to a friend of mine and that I didn't care what happened between them, but she needed it back. I asked him to give it to me."

"And he did?"

"Well, I might have told him about the irrevocable consequences of noncompliance." About the last thing Jane wanted to do was smile, but when he said that, she had to. The final four words were the very ones Tim had used when talking about Roderick's prospects for reinstatement and the boundary line he would have to stay behind if he were permitted to come back to school.

"*I* care what happened between them," she said. "How does she even know this kid?"

Roderick shrugged. "I don't know."

Ninety minutes later, Jane held her hand out to Eli Brooks. The leather strap, fetched from the apartment as Jane apologized to Sabrina for running right out on her again, dangled off both sides of her palm, with the jewel holding it down in the middle.

"Do you recognize this?"

"I'm not sure," the boy said.

"I think you are sure," Jane said. "I think you do." The likely answer to her own question—how did Claire even know this boy?—had come to her in the apartment complex parking lot, after she'd chewed on it all the way home and reconsidered every interaction she could remember with Claire. She'd taken the stairs two at a time to get the leather piece, then dashed back out to the car and come here.

"Eli, come on," Chuck said, standing between them, close, like a referee.

"It's Claire's," the boy said.

"And how did it end up with a boy who goes to Watauga Middle?" she asked. Her dead calm—almost serenity—left her puzzled but also grateful. She needed answers now, and she knew that being crazed was no way to get them. There would be time for that soon enough. The monster slept but was also alive.

Chuck looked at his son. "Talon?"

"Yeah," Eli said. "Talon. My friend."

"What did this Talon do to her?"

"Ripped it off her neck. Broke it."

"What, just, 'Hi, Claire,' then he steals her necklace?"

"Come on," Chuck said. "Answer her."

Eli looked down. "He was flirting with her, telling her she's pretty. He asked her if she'd ever been kissed, and she said no. He asked if she wanted to try it. She said yeah. So they, like, kissed, and he reached for her, you know, and she pulled back and—"

"He broke her necklace," Jane said.

"Jesus," Chuck said. "Jane, I had no idea. God, Eli, why didn't you say anything?"

Eli said nothing.

"Jane, I'm—" Chuck began.

"I think I have it now," she said.

She left.

"Claire, I need to tell you something, OK?"

"OK."

"And I'm sorry that I have to tell you today of all days, but just know that I have to, OK?"

"Is Grandpa dead?"

"No. Oh, Claire, no." Jane scolded herself. She should have just come out with it and not let Claire's anxiety fill in the open boxes. She had called Paul on the drive home, to let him know, to ask him to please make sure she could talk with Claire alone. His questions had followed in line with hers—"Who is this kid and what did he do to her?"—and he had agreed that Jane should handle it first. She appreciated that. She should have just plunged in, though.

"What I mean by 'I have to tell you' is that I don't have any questions for you. I want to tell you something, and we can go from there. OK?"

"OK."

Jane gathered a breath, then started spending it.

"Back in February, you babysat Annabelle, but Eli came home early, and you were done. He had another boy with him. You liked that other boy, and he was nice to you and said nice things to you, and he asked you if you wanted to kiss, and you did. And he reached for your breast, and you pulled away. His hand got caught up in your necklace, and it broke. You had the strap, and he had the treasure piece. You came home and you hid the strap. When I asked you a few days later where the necklace was, you said it got lost, and I got mad at you and called you irresponsible. But it didn't get lost, did it? This boy broke it."

Jane stopped, for air and for her flooded mind to work out what had crammed into it even as she emptied herself of the words.

"Talon," Claire said. "That's his name."

"Yes, Talon."

"I'm sorry, Mom," and that broke Jane, who said, "Sorry for what? Claire, *I'm* sorry. That boy should be sorry, and if I ever get my hands on him—"

"Mom, no, please don't do that."

"He should be sorry," Jane said.

"Mom, this will sound stupid, but this is like the worst and best birthday, all mushed together. I've felt so bad about this. I really messed up."

"Claire, no. This is not on you. I'm sorry I didn't figure it out sooner, but it's not on me, either. It's on that boy. Please, don't ever take responsibility in your life for what boys choose with their own brains to do, OK? Promise me?"

"I promise. Mom?"

"Yes?"

"I want to come home."

Jane, who had been sitting on the edge of the bed, stood up in her stocking feet and swayed her hips in celebration.

"Are you sure?" Jane asked.

"I am."

"We'll talk about it soon, OK, you and me and your dad? We'll sort it out. In the meantime, do you think you can finish strong there?"

"I can. I don't like Lea Kendrick anymore, though. She's all stuck up now that she has a boyfriend. But that's not why I want to come home."

"Well, don't write her off yet. People sometimes surprise you in good ways, too."

"Thanks, Mom."

"Happy birthday, Claire. I love you."

"I love you, too."

May 12, 2016

Do we tell each other our "history"?

Those quote marks are carrying a lot of water for that question.

You know what I mean.

I do. Is it important to you?

It seems like the kind of thing you'd want to tell someone if you were feeling feelings, you know?

Are you talking about me or you?

What?

Who's feeling the feelings?

You are. And I am.

That's a good answer.

I'm just saying, there's history. Not all of it pretty. Some quite ugly, in fact.

For me, too. We're in our forties, Jane. A fair assumption that we've done things we wouldn't do now or we've been hurt.

I'm just saying, I'll tell you, if you want to know.

And I'm saying the same to you.

I don't need to know like this.

Nor do I.

I want to tell you when we can be together.

So do I.

I guess I'm thinking about it because I found out Claire has had her first boy experience—a kiss that went pretty badly for her. I'm thinking about how I've spent her life trying to encase her in bubble wrap, to keep the world away from her, and it still found a way in.

I'm sorry. Is she OK?

I think so.

Life tends to do that.

Yeah. It did with me.

I'm sorry for that, too. Here is life. Terrible and beautiful things happen.

I'm ready for the beautiful things.

Me, too.

We're going up to Wichita this weekend to see Teryn. She's graduating from rehab.

Sabrina told me. Good. She'll need the support.

I wonder if I should tell her about the beautiful things.

It's up to you.

What if she doesn't think they're beautiful? What if she thinks I'm breaking the girl code?

Well, I don't know anything about girl codes. But here's the thing about beautiful things: They are impervious to someone else's opinion.

I like you.

I like you right back.

Fifty-one

They sat in a sprawling, misshapen circle in a room the size of a banquet hall, the fifteen graduates of at least twenty-eight days' sobriety. Sitting with them were their supporters, all invited guests, alternately smiling big and somewhat cowed by the environs, who swelled the total number well north of thirty. By alphabetical order of last name, the graduates stood and told their stories for those assembled. Anonymity, the program director said, would come beyond the walls of the treatment center. This, she said, was accountability writ large: You tell your story, you tell what you've learned, and you talk out your strategy for dealing with addiction when life has you in its teeth again.

Teryn Daly went third.

She stood up. She gripped the shoulders of her daughter, on her right, and her best friend. To Jane, she looked better than ever—miraculously so, almost. She was not only lighter but also not bloated by drink. She wasn't slathered and blighted by the makeup she used to cake on. Her eyes were free of what had seemed compulsory glassiness. Jane reached across herself and caressed the hand on her right shoulder.

Teryn remembered her first drink ever, a peach wine cooler in Jimmy Thompson's pickup in the West High parking lot. She told how her father kept so much beer in the garage that she could filch it almost at will. She recalled a free snort of cocaine in college and her profound gratitude that she couldn't afford to buy another try because "I would have sold everything I had, including the virginity I no longer possessed, to feel that way again." Teryn was funny. Teryn was apologetic to her daughter for the things she'd already said and those that were still coming, but, she said, "You heard Sally: That's what we do."

Teryn broke hearts. She talked of days on end without a drink at all, times when "you think you've finally dropped it, like a TV show you loved and just quit watching," only to end up blitzing yourself over a long weekend. She spoke of rampant, freewheeling, unbound sexual encounters, and Jane cringed at the memory of Oklahoma and the larger picture she couldn't, or wouldn't, put together while they were there.

Teryn courted honesty. She said she didn't know about tomorrow. "News flash," she said. "I still like alcohol. I still love alcohol." But today, she said, she had decided that she'd had enough of it.

When Teryn was done, Jane figured there couldn't be a dry eye in the room. She couldn't say for certain. She couldn't see.

Afterward, Jane drove them all back to Teryn's apartment, which she and Sabrina had stocked that morning with food, bottled water, and soda pop. Teryn wouldn't be driving until she sorted out the DUI, with many steps yet to be cleared on the way to that goal. Treatment was done, and sentencing awaited. In the meantime, Teryn said, she would learn to live a different way and be grateful to still have a job and the opportunity to impart temperance to herself.

Sabrina retired to her room and the job of restocking it. She hugged Teryn and kissed her on the cheek, then did the same with Jane. After that, Teryn and Jane took to the couch.

"What's new?" Teryn asked, and Jane had to crack up about that. Pick a number.

"Not much."

"Oh?"

"My dad…"

"I know, doll. I'm sorry."

"There's this other thing," Jane started.

Teryn rotated on the couch, a leg up under her, the ankle lolling idly off the cushion. "Do tell."

"I feel like you're going to be mad."

"I'm not."

"You don't even know it yet," Jane said.

"I'm not," Teryn reiterated.

"But I can't not tell you."

"Tell me," Teryn said.

"I like Bert," Jane said. Direct. That was one way to go about it.

"Bert?" Teryn said. "My Bert? My former Bert? Gosh, how do you say that?"

"Teryn, yes."

"Hmm."

"Are you mad?" Jane asked.

"Mad?" Teryn asked. "No, I'm not mad." She readjusted, changing legs as props. "Bert's likable. I'm surprised, I guess. Has anyone told you he has legs like a stickman? On the plus side, if you get mad at him, you can snap him in two."

"Are you messing with me?"

"No, doll. I'm not."

"I don't care about his legs."

"Well, that's good, because…" Teryn held her thumb and forefinger a millimeter apart, and Jane slapped at her hand, laughing.

"On the bright side," Teryn said, putting her hands parallel and drawing them away from each other, eyebrows arched for hilarity.

"Stop it! Oh, wait, really?"

They laughed and laughed, and Teryn let herself up and into the kitchen for a bottle of water. She came back sipping from it and sat down again.

"I was so scared," Jane said. "Girl code."

"I get it," Teryn said. "I told you, I got over Bert a long time ago, and he got over me. Plus, I have this other thing now."

"I know. You're going to be great."

"Yes, I am."

"Seriously, though," Jane said. "I have to tell you. I think I might love him."

Teryn gripped the neck of her bottle like it was a pullet. "Love, huh? Well, that's something else, isn't it?"

"I've never loved a man. I've told you."

"I know you haven't, doll. And I believe you."

"And it's completely ridiculous," Jane said. "I mean, I've spent twenty-five minutes with him at an airport baggage claim. How could I love him?"

It was the question that tugged most insistently at her, even though she could line up the answers any time she wanted: How he was with his daughter, how he was with her, how she couldn't fluster him no matter how hard she tried—and she did. How he talked about a world that was mostly theoretical to her, because he had seen so much of it and she had seen so little. How he listened to what she said about her own world and didn't see it as hopelessly small, the way she did. How he asked after her dad, every night. He couldn't be real. But he was.

"I don't know, doll," Teryn said. "Love is weird."

"I'm sorry," Jane said.

"Why are you sorry?"

Jane leaned in. "Because I know you care about him."

"Well, yeah, sure, but I don't *love* love him. Not anymore. If you dig a man with skinny legs, who am I to object?"

"I didn't expect you to react this way."

"What did you expect?"

"I don't know. I thought you might hit me. Yell at me. I wouldn't have blamed you."

"Well, I'm full of surprises. Just you watch."

"I know you are," Jane said.

"Besides," Teryn said. "I think he loves you, too. The boy sent me a stack of letters from Africa and told me all about it. He's gone, girl. I'm talking a gone pecan."

May 14, 2016

You wrote her letters and told her?

Um…surprise!

Yes, that's what you are. Continually so.

To be frank, I wrote her letters to encourage her, because she was not allowed phone calls or internet access, and in the course of those letters I might have said a few things.

About me?

And about me. And about us. The presumptive us.

Weren't you taking an awful chance that she'd react badly?

I didn't think so. I've known Teryn a long time, obviously. And in every letter, I emphasized that she and Sabrina and I remain a family—a scattered, severed family, but if you're expansive in the way you define the term, it can't be anything else. When she's in danger, our daughter is in danger, which means I'm in danger. The same follows with all the good things. What's good for her is good for Sabrina is good for me. And the reverse is also true.

That's amazingly progressive.

I don't know about that. It's the only thing that makes sense.

So what are you and I?

We are potential. We have put a down payment on adoration, with an option to buy.

Ooooooh.

We'll know more in two weeks. I'm going to fly to Wichita to see Sabrina and Teryn, then come down to see you.

Claire is coming home. We haven't worked out the timing, but she's coming.

Well, that's wonderful. I look forward to meeting her.

I don't know if it will time out that way.

We'll see.

I don't know if it's a good idea for the two of you to meet right off anyway.

I understand.

Do you?

Of course I do.

Are you sure?

Of course I am.

OK, I believe you.

I'm glad.

I adore you.

Well, don't buy the adoration yet. Give it two weeks.

I adore you, and it seems impossible. How does this work, Bert? I'm living in Texas, you're living in Africa, you used to be married to my best friend. I don't even know what I'm doing next fall. Maybe we shouldn't complicate it right now.

When would be a good time to complicate it, then?

Smarty-pants. I'm just saying, maybe we shouldn't.

Or, maybe, we should be still and see what happens. Fourteen days, Jane. I'll be there Saturday, the 28th. That's enough time for a butterfly to beat its wings and change the course of history.

Fifty-two

Jane looked down from the top row of the aluminum bleachers, remembering an article of faith from her childhood that she once absolutely detested and now figured she'd have to warm up to, if things today went the way she hoped they would.

There are two seasons in Texas: football season and spring football season.

The truism of the second half of that saying was embodied down on the finely lined field by the burly girl wearing practice jersey No. 88. To look at her from a distance, no one could deduce her gender, and that, as it turned out, was precisely as Rowanda Jerkins wanted it. She was a good deal larger than many of the boys on the field with her, as fiercely determined as any of them, and also singularly different. Ro Jerkins had to appeal first to an athletic department, then a school administration, and finally a school board for her opportunity at spring tryouts. She came to the last of those appeals carrying a petition signed by a preponderance of the school, with handwritten letters of recommendation from every teacher she had. The unanimous sentiment: *Let Ro Play.* Posters to that effect festooned the interior school walls. Today, May 19, belonged to her, and the stands brimmed with the people who had made it so. Jane sat in a line with many of Ro's admirers: David Bourque, Principal Meyers, and Roderick.

The day couldn't have broken better for any of them, or for Ro—a late-spring Texas afternoon straight out of central casting, green grass cut just so, chalk lines pristine and precise, a bluebird sky.

Down on the field, Coach Pryor blew a whistle, a signal to the kids to line up in kickoff formation. The white shirts, with Ro in the middle, fanned out across the field behind the ball. The receiving blues awaited the kick in tiers, the front line, the middle line, and the fastest two kids at the back, to receive the ball and advance it.

Another whistle, and Ro moved out in front of her line, her steps choreographed, the strides practiced and perfect, until her right foot found the fat part of the ball and sent it skyward. Jane slipped a hand above her eyes like a visor, followed the ball's end-over-end path up, up, up, then down, down, down into the receiver's waiting hands. As he tucked it away, No. 88 hit him in the chest and stretched him out across the grass.

Jane, and the rest of them, hit their feet and chanted in unison: "RO!"

Coach Pryor, upon finally relenting on the question of Ro Jerkins' entitlement to a tryout, had told her that if she couldn't be a frontline performer on special teams and at least a reliable backup on offense or defense, if not both, then it would be a no-go. It wasn't fair or unfair, he said, just a numbers game. He had a finite supply of regular-season jerseys, and he needed a contribution from everybody who wore one.

The first kick and tackle should have answered the question, by Jane's reasoning and by David Bourque's shrill insistence, yelling from the bleachers at Coach Pryor until Tim shushed him. The field-goal competition settled the matter.

The candidates numbered four to begin. Coach Pryor started them with a twenty-yard attempt, no rush, just a kid and another kid to hold the ball, and the uprights sixty feet away. Ro went first and made her kick. Sam Dano made his, as did Russell Weeks. Bo Johnson's sliced left, far off-target.

Coach Pryor backed the successful kickers up five yards and had them go again. All three kicks sailed between the bars.

At thirty yards out, Russell Weeks missed.

At thirty-five, so did Sam Dano.

Ro made her kicks at forty and forty-five yards before shanking a fifty-yarder.

It didn't matter.

The position belonged to her.

The onlookers scattered after Coach Pryor's bullhorn announcement of who had a spot on the team come autumn and who would have to try again in the fall. Ro's name predictably drew the loudest cheer, and Roderick climbed on the top deck of the stands and did the robot dance, to everyone's amusement, and especially that of Principal Meyers. "You'll do that only at sanctioned school events next fall, right, Mr. Watson?" Roderick caught the meaning immediately and said, "I promise."

Tim then leaned over to Jane. "I'll have some more news soon. I know you've been waiting."

"I have," she said.

"We'll talk next week. I don't mean to be mysterious. It's just not official. But it will be. If you've got an expiring lease or something, renew. Please."

"I will."

She checked her watch. If form held, Bert would be up in four hours or so. She would be waiting. There were things to say now, at last.

At Jane's request, David agreed to get Roderick back home while she made her final appointment of the day. She parked in the usual spot. Swept in the front door. Tossed a greeting at Allison, who would be shifting out soon.

"Mrs. Blankenship left a few minutes ago," Allison said to Jane as she clattered down the hall the elevator. *Good*, Jane thought. *Good timing.*

Upstairs, she found her father serenely asleep, the line of his mouth a wobble like the rarest moment of Charlie Brown's cartoon contentment. Jane could smell Jocelyn's dainty perfume on the air, as usual. She had come to like it, actually, and if her father had some ancillary benefit of aromatherapy, all the better. She checked the flowers that Jocelyn brought on the regular, the blooms still hardy on the latest bouquet.

She sat down in a roller chair and pulled it up alongside him.

"We had a good day, Dad. Maybe the best day. I wish you could have been with us."

She took his hand and held it.

"So much is changing. So much has changed. You helped me come back here, where I belong. I'm grateful. I miss you. I never thought I did or would, but there you go. It's always a surprise with you."

She rose, her attention pulled away from him. She wandered around the end of the bed, to the other side. A newly framed picture rose along with the others she had brought in, faces with names that he could try to hold before they forever ran through him like water.

She leaned in, peering closer.

Recognition of her father and her mother flickered before she saw herself tucked between them. Her dad relaxed back on a poolside lounge chair, his hair black and wet and brushed back by hand, his torso bare and tanned above his swim trunks. Little Jane folded into him, with his right arm pulling her in. Her mother, her long hair under a swim cap, wearing fashionable black sunglasses, leaned into him from the other side. It was obviously the Blankenships' backyard, obviously no later than 1980 or '81—Jane hadn't yet started showing the curves that came early in her development—and for the life of her she couldn't remember it. But it was them, no doubt about it. Eric and Margery and Jane Driskell. Maybe Ed Blankenship behind the camera. Maybe Jocelyn herself.

They sure looked happy.

Maybe they had been.

May 19, 2016

So you're almost done there.

Yep. Final paperwork. Close up the office. My effects are somewhere in the North Atlantic by now, I imagine.

And you leave for Kansas on Monday?

Correct.

And here next Saturday?

Also correct.

I'm staying in Texas, Bert.

Of course you are. That's where I'll be looking for you.

I mean staying *staying.*

I know what you mean.

I wish I could consider something else, but I can't. This is where I belong.

Of course it is.

I'm sorry.

Why are you apologizing?

I know you wanted to hear something else.

I'm fine. Really. I am.

I'm glad. I'm not. Not about this part of it, anyway.

Well, remember what I told you: Be still. Wait. You must be willing to accept the elegant solution, even if it's not the one you thought or hoped it would be.

OK. Where's your next assignment?

I'm still waiting to hear. Gonna take the summer off.

Maybe I'll come visit, wherever it is.

Maybe. That would be really nice, if you did.

So I'll see you Saturday, then?

Maybe I'll see you first, Jane.

Fifty-three

A week and a day brought the end of the semester, the end of the school year, the start of another summer, another wait, and, finally, the next spin. The tests were all taken and graded, and Jane had pushed every student she had on to the next stage— even the ones whom, in the drudges of February and March, she feared she might have to hold back. What public education looked like, to her mind, depended on where you got an eyeful of it. In her classroom, it presented at the cellular level—a teacher, diligent if also sometimes overwhelmed, and discrete students of varying backgrounds and talents and motivations, all trying to find a common cause and push toward it. Pull back a little bit, though, and the works begin looking more like a machine driven by cogs or spokes, and a misfiring part could put the operation in jeopardy.

For months, Jane had felt like that misaligned piece of the whole. Today, though, she was rejuvenated by a little axle grease in the form of trust.

Tim Meyers slipped into her classroom against the outward flow of kids after last bell, turning himself sideways to find a seam in the current.

"You're coming down to the auditorium?" he asked.

"Wouldn't miss it."

"Good. It's done, Jane. I have your contract for next year in my office. Swing by afterward, and we'll make it official. If I could do it, I'd give you a lifetime deal."

She threw her arms around him, hugging his neck, then pulled back, as if the inappropriate venue for such displays had only just occurred to her.

"Sorry," she said.

"All good. See you down there?"

She nodded.

The mood in the auditorium revealed itself as a vocabulary word: ebullient.

Several hundred kids, the shackles of daily schoolwork thrown off, rollicking, chants and shouts and excitable chatter rising to the ceiling in a roar. Tim took to the lectern and shushed them, that blend of friendliness and authority that Jane often marveled at, the way it was effortless and yet inaccessible to so much of the faculty, herself included. She had admired him since they were kids, but this, she decided, was something else: an ideal meeting of a man and a job.

He went through perfunctory remarks, thanking everybody for a successful year, commending their patience at waiting out one last thing before their headlong dives into the summer that waited outside the walls.

One by one, the department heads—the teachers and coaches—presented the faculty awards to the best students in the various study areas, by grade level. The standouts in language arts and mathematics and science and yearbook staff and choir and the rest strode across the stage, getting certificates and high fives from Tim. Ro Jerkins received a standing ovation when Coach Pryor called her out for the athletics awards, saying, "Only one kid in this whole school is the leading scorer on the girls basketball team and the kicker on the football team." Ro cried, something Jane thought she'd never see.

The last bit of pomp, Tim said, concerned an award voted on not by teachers but by students. Jane, sitting next to David in the front row, grabbed his hand and shook it, this being the most predictable outcome ever.

"So without further ado," Tim said, "let's give it up for the Smithfield Middle School teacher of the year for 2016, Jane Sperling."

Next to Jane, David sprung to his feet, leading the ovation. He held out a hand, and she rose onto wobbly legs. He led her to the stairs on the side of the stage, and she went up, then across to Tim, who said, "Let's try that hug again, OK?" She obliged him. She didn't think she could possibly be more surprised, until she turned to face the cheering kids and saw Claire and Paul standing in the back row, clapping.

She looked down at David, her mouth hanging open. He held a closed fist to his right ear and mouthed "I called her."

Of course he did. Of course he would. And, of course, Jane hadn't seen any of it coming until it was all upon her. It didn't all have to be chaos. Some of it could be delight. She waved to her girl and blew her a kiss, then walked down into the next hug she had coming.

May 28, 2016 (just before midnight)

That was really nice.

Yes. Yes, it was.

I'm glad we did it, even though I know I'll miss it. I'll miss you.

This isn't the end, Jane.

I know. We have a few days more.

And other days to come.

I know.

Jane?

Yeah.

This is cute and all, but I'm right next to you. Put down the phone.

Jane giggled, then set the phone on the nightstand. She rolled to her right, into his embrace. Her bare feet stretched out, finding his legs, every bit as skinny as Teryn said they were, and the rest of him, every bit as loved as she knew he would be.

She nestled into him, grateful for their day together, grateful to

Paul and Claire for having their own adventure down in Austin and San Antonio, and grateful for nothing more than Claire's settling in again at home in a few days. It was time she yearned for, separated from her now by time she didn't want to wish away. Life and its paradoxes.

"What do you want to do tomorrow?" she asked.

He stroked her hair, tucking it behind her ear.

"Sleep in," he said. "Breakfast. Go do something spectacular or pedestrian. It doesn't matter, as long as you're there."

She kissed his chest.

"Take you on a date," he said now. "See if you're interested."

"You don't have to audition."

"I know," he said. "But if I'm going to be living in Texas, I'd better get this right."

She pushed herself up, astonished. She looked down at him. He grinned.

"Got my next assignment. What are the odds?"

JUNE

Fifty-four

The Sperling girls were like collapsing dominoes held up only by the solid frame of Bert. Claire, rounding into earliest womanhood and fifteen pounds heavier than she'd been just six months earlier, leaned heavily into Jane, who bowed at the waist under the imposition and leaned into Bert, who held the line.

Across the hole in the earth and the mahogany casket perched above it, Jane could look in a straight line into Jocelyn's sorrowful eyes, but she made a strenuous effort of not doing so. The chasm in that in-between space was not just practicality but also a metaphor. For everything that had been forgiven—more than Jane had ever thought possible, as the grudging respect she accorded Jocelyn overtook her bit by bit—there were a dozen things, in the ever-present past, that wouldn't be forgotten. The closeness they would never have was irretrievably trapped in the difference between those eras.

At Jane's side, Claire wept ceaselessly, the finality of it all having finally penetrated a heart that hadn't yet dealt with real loss. Jane gripped the girl and held her close, and as if an involuntary reaction, Bert tightened his hold on Jane's shoulders.

The words, such as they were, had been of comfort, if not particularly tailored to Eric's particular mien or talents. The Driskells were not churchgoing folk, never had been, making them something of an anomaly in their neighborhood. Tim Meyers had called in a favor from an old student, now a Baptist minister, and the right Rev. Kevin Blakeney had risen to the occasion with a rote recitation of homilies intended to soothe the living. That had been the job, and it had been met.

Jane allowed herself a peek now at Jocelyn, who locked in with her ever briefly, a slight upward lilt of her mouth in acknowledgment. Jane felt her face move in the direction of a smile in return, but she couldn't know if she had succeeded, and she looked away. Jocelyn had given her the same look three days earlier, when Jane had called from memory care and told her to come. "He's leaving," she had said, a most perplexing idiom for what was really happening. He was being torn away, entirely too early and entirely for good.

The downward movement of the coffin's platform began with a mechanical protest, a sharp noise that punctured the silence. Inch by inch, the coffin dropped toward the bottom of the hole. Claire's weeping gained momentum. Bert's grip drew tighter. Jane watched as the deep brown of the coffin lid yielded to the darkness below.

When it was done, the Blankenship boys, having bracketed their mother, stepped to the fore, took shovels in hand, and tossed in blades of dirt, a ceremonial benediction. In sequence, Claire peeled off, then Jane, then Bert, headed to the car waiting for them in the parking lot beyond, hands of friends and colleagues and loved ones—Danny, David, Roderick and his mother, Rosalie, Teryn, Sabrina—reaching out, comfort in the offing. Grim smiles formed, and condolences were rendered, and still the three of them walked in the direction of the sun.

At the house—Eric's house, Eric and Margery's house before that, Eric and Margery and Jane's house for a while long, long ago, someone else's house soon enough—Jane found herself gloriously, and surprisingly, thankful that she had decided to host a reception. It had, of course, been less a decision and more of a granting of perhaps the last wish Eric was able to give words to, on the last day marked more by alertness than recession. "Celebrate me," he had said, and Jane had nodded and replied, "Yes, of course," a promise made in the moment being easier to send forth than the actual planning of an event once real and unfettered grief had moved into the spaces he no longer occupied. Jane had been astonished by the full-on assault of it, after assuming she would, in a sense, be relieved that her father was no longer burdened. She was not relieved. She was still feeling cheated, fighting an anger she couldn't put in any coherent sentence.

But the reception was the release that dulled the edges for her. It wasn't big—maybe fifteen people, maybe only a dozen—but it was joyous, a handful of people who knew and liked and loved Eric, and a smaller handful who knew and liked and loved Jane and Claire. Grocery store fried chicken and potato salad and a sheet cake and cases of beer and soft drinks bound the loose congregation, which rippled along with every story and memory shared. Jocelyn and her sons had begged off, thankful for the invitation but inclined to bunker in alone, and that had been a relief, Jane decided. The burden of carrying on and remembering Eric had been split between his daughter and the woman he loved, and Jane sensed now that each would make her way without the other.

Jane drifted through the room, a glance thrown to and caught by Claire, who sat between Aunt Glenda and Uncle Jon and received the attention they heaped on her. Jane touched elbows and slid sideways against the stream, and she found the north star of Bert, who was locked in conversation with Danny. She moved on, toward the kitchen, until at last the crowd dissipated into a whirr of white noise.

Teryn stood at the sink, her hands on the counter and her elbows rigid. Her shoulders rose and fell and rose again.

"Teryn?"

Her friend spun, and eyes and nose and flushed features confirmed it.

"Teryn," Jane said, "what's wrong?"

"Oh, doll. Nothing."

"What's wrong?"

"I'm sorry. I'm just emotional."

Jane went to her, locked her thumb and middle finger around Teryn's left wrist, and pulled her out of the kitchen, through the utility room, and into the dank garage, which had gone smothering and swampy in the heat of the day.

"What's wrong?" Jane asked.

"I'm stupid."

"You're not."

"I've done stupid things."

"Yeah?" Jane said. "We should form a club."

Teryn retreated, tiny steps, until her back was against Eric's workbench. For just a flutter, Jane was distracted by the swelling grief that he would never again turn a screwdriver here, never again need a muffler bracket, that she would, in some time and way, have to liquidate the earthly remnants of him. She shook off the incoming wave and focused again on her friend.

"Honestly?" Teryn asked.

"Honestly."

"I'm jealous," Teryn said, and the penning-in collapsed and she put her face in her hands and wept. "I'm jealous of you and Bert and what you've found together."

Jane's mouth opened, a guttural sound escaping.

Teryn looked up. "And I know that's just stupid and unfair and childish, but I am, Jane. I didn't realize it until today, seeing him there with you, supporting you, that he's heading down here to be with you. To *live* with you."

"Teryn—"

Teryn held up a hand. "Let me finish."

"OK."

"You're going to say something sensible. I'm not being sensible right now. I am unreachable by your sensibility. I'm goddamn hurt and goddamn despairing, and it's my goddamn fault. So don't say it, OK?"

"OK," Jane said again.

"I wish you hadn't seen me. I'd have climbed on top of it. I'd have been OK."

"Don't hide from me," Jane said. "You're right. I was going to say something sensible. But I won't."

"Please don't," Teryn said. "Not right now, OK, doll?"

"OK."

"And please know that I hate myself for saying this when your dad just died. I'm such an asshole."

"You're not," Jane said.

"It's not you I'm mad at. You know that, right?"

"Of course," Jane said.

"Well, maybe a little. Maybe Bert, too. Just a little."

"Just a little," Jane repeated.

"I'm entitled, right?"

"Yes."

"Thank you for that."

Jane nodded.

"We'll talk tomorrow, OK?" Teryn said.

"OK."

"Thanks, doll. I think Sabrina and I should go."

"I understand."

"There's nothing wrong with me that a night in a hotel, some pizza delivery, and a dumb movie won't cure."

Jane stepped to her. "Can I give you a hug?"

"I wish you would."

JULY

Fifty-five

Jane stood on the balcony of the downtown condominium she had picked out and Bert had agreed to buy, despite his having seen only photographs and a shaky cellphone video. Two stories, three bedrooms and two bathrooms, a full garage below her feet. Enough space for today and all coming tomorrows, whatever they might hold. In these past few weeks, she had taken to stacking her hopes like building blocks.

"When will they be here?" Claire asked, next to Jane, her chin on the railing.

"Any minute now."

Bert's words from the night before, from Teryn's place in Wichita, where he was picking up Sabrina, stuck in her ears. "It'll be my place, and your place will be yours, and eventually, I hope, we'll find our place. I'm going to give you room, Jane. But I'm moving toward you."

His sentiments had been what she had found him to be, at his core. Considerate. Wise. Not rushing in. Not shying away. That second day together, back in May, after he told her he'd asked to come out of the field, to lead a county office for the USDA in Fort Worth, she had run away from him, distant and fearful, and he'd let her go, let her dash to her car and drive away for a few hours, let her calm her nerves about so many things before she'd come back with the questions on her head.

She'd asked them, one at a time, while he cooked a meal of banku for her, its fragrances swirling the air: *What if it doesn't work? What if I'm not ready? What if you're not ready? I just got my daughter back and there are so many Talons in the world, and what if she needs me now more than you do? What if I need her now more than I need you?*

He hadn't flinched. He hadn't backed up. He had, simply, fed her and answered her and held her and reassured her and quietly gone to Montana and packed up the contents of a life and prepared to move again.

She thought of all the phone calls of the past month or so, the video kind abetted by Claire and the other kind, too, just voice to voice, and his steadiness from so far away. Eric's passing, not at all unexpected, still had come on relentlessly, taking away Jane's breath and threatening her faith. Thirty hours before he left, Jane had brought in some old VCR tapes she had found and a player that blessedly still worked, and she and Claire had watched the years-ago replay with Eric, while he mostly slept, but he'd awakened to see Margery flitting across the screen, an Easter morning in the '80s, and he'd said hello to her and drifted off again. A capital-letter Good Day, that was, then he was gone the next.

Then Bert had come, just for a couple of days, and after that, another goodbye to Jane in an airport. Raw feelings had been patched up. That fractured family Bert had talked about, his with Teryn and Sabrina, had grown by two. Jane and Claire were in, attached by threads to the rest. They would all lope along somehow, five disparate humans and one extant love affair, into the seasons of life and the advancing of years and whatever those might bring. The last time Jane had seen Bert, he'd kissed her and promised to be back soon. Soon had come slowly, but here it was, crossing into view.

At the mouth of the cul-de-sac, the moving truck made a wide swing left, then straightened out, its nose pointed toward them.

"There they are," Jane said. "Let's go down."

Claire was already ahead of her, through the sliding glass door and bounding toward the landing, her young legs gobbling the stairs two at a time. Jane gulped a breath, then followed her. At the bottom, she heard Bert's voice on the other side of the open front door—"Hello there, Claire"—and it was like a gentle retort that had come again to meet her doubts and fears. Not to blot them out, but also not to let them have the final word.

He stepped inside the door. Jane walked straight into him. Straight home.

Acknowledgments

Somewhere in the guts of my desktop computer, this novel exists in Word document form, and the metadata reveals an interesting fact: I started working on this story on June 1, 2015. As I write these words, it's early 2025, so this is easily my longest-gestating novel. Here's hoping it's a healthy baby!

This is my first set-in-Texas novel, and I suspect it won't be the last. As titular Jane Sperling tells another character fairly late in the proceedings, home pulls at you. I set *Jane, Divided* not just in my hometown but also, in large part, directly in the neighborhood where I grew up. What I found there may come as a surprise to those who shared that enclave with me (for instance, the streets now have alleyways), and to those folks I say this: Remember, it's fiction. For that matter, also fiction of a kind are our memories of growing up there, no matter how vivid they seem. The lens that sees in reverse is attached to an unreliable camera, and nostalgia can be a tricky thing if you use it to relitigate the past. I've tried not to do that here, whether through Jane or anyone else. They're the players. I gave them a stage. And that stage has alleyways. Let's move on.

Gratitude goes out to Margo Turley, Naomi DeMarinis, Sue Vigesaa, Richard Ford, Kristina Ford, Corby Skinner, Bruce Ferber, Scott McMillion, Jim Thomsen, Amanda Riley, Todd Keisling, Julie Schultz, Craig Huisenga, Jessica Powell, Kathi Fitzgerald, Courtney Shultz, Angela Renfro, Monica Thomas, Judith Arnold, Milana Marsenich, Gwen Florio, Malcolm Brooks, Allen Morris Jones, Mary Finnegan Ryan (RIP), and others I'm surely forgetting. Some read this thing. At least one contributed something without possibly realizing it. Others listened to my incessant talking about it. Still others are my touchstones for sanity in a business that doesn't grant a lot of it. That's particularly true of Nalini Akolekar, my agent. Thank you, thank you.

My parents gave me a corner of Texas to call home. It's been a progressive gift. I ran away from it in my youth, but as I suggested at the top, it calls to me across the miles and the years gone by, and its blessings have multiplied in my advancing age. I was granted memories in that place, and those are the essential building blocks of what I do. I'm a lucky boy.

Finally, thanks to Elisa Lorello, my best friend. Still. Forever.

Craig Lancaster
Billings, Montana
Spring 2025

About the author

Casey Page

Craig Lancaster is the author of eleven novels, a collection of short stories, and two produced, full-length plays. His work has twice been honored by the High Plains Book Awards (*And It Will Be a Beautiful Life*, fiction, 2022; and *600 Hours of Edward*, first book, 2010), has won an Independent Publishers Book Awards gold medal (*The Art of Departure*), and has received assorted regional, national, and international recognition.

A former sports journalist and pipeline inspection specialist, he now works as an analyst/content specialist for a research firm in financial services, serves as the design editor for *Montana Quarterly* magazine, and takes on freelance editing and design work as his schedule and his willingness allow.

He lives in Billings, Montana, with his longhair miniature dachshund, Fretless.

Check out more of his work at www.craig-lancaster.com.